OUTNUMBERED

Chardonnais let go of the warrior's arm, and the Crow fell. The little trapper jumped over the body and latched his hands around the throat of the Indian with the bloody knife. The Crow responded by kicking him in the knee.

"*Merde*," Chardonnais cursed again as he lost his grip on the Crow.

The third warrior who had attacked him now pounced on his back, knocking him forward. He landed hard on his chest, and his face smacked the snow-covered ground. Chardonnais thrust upward with arms and legs, lifting the Crow, who quickly clamped a forearm around his throat. Chardonnais still managed to get to his feet, and he grabbed the forearm and strained to break its grip.

The second warrior charged, knife blade leading the way. Still trying to get loose from the arm on his throat, Chardonnais braced himself to be stabbed, tightening his stomach muscles, knowing all the while that it would not keep him alive.

Look for these books in the
MOUNTAIN COUNTRY series

SOUTHWEST THUNDER

and coming soon

MOUNTAIN THUNDER

Available from HarperPaperbacks

WINTER
THUNDER

JOHN LEGG

HarperPaperbacks
A Division of HarperCollinsPublishers

This is a work of fiction. The characters, incidents, and dialogues are products of the author's imagination and are not to be construed as real. Any resemblance to actual events or persons, living or dead, is entirely coincidental.

HarperPaperbacks   *A Division of* HarperCollins*Publishers*
10 East 53rd Street, New York, N.Y. 10022

Cover illustration by W.A. Dodge

First printing: February 1994

Printed in the United States of America

HarperPaperbacks and colophon are trademarks of HarperCollins*Publishers*

❖ 10 9 8 7 6 5 4 3 2 1

For you, Mom :
Once again,
all I can say is,
thanks for everything.
I love you.

1

St. Charles, Missouri
Mid-July, 1833

LUCIEN CHARDONNAIS PUT ON the unaccustomed pants of fine wool and then sat down to pull on a pair of fancy city-made boots. He stood again, picking up a ruffled silk shirt. As he began pulling the garment on he caught his reflection in the mirror. He stopped with his shirt partway on and turned to face his reflection. He was not sure he liked what he was seeing.

His looks per se weren't the problem. He was a reasonably handsome man, and he knew that. Indeed, he was even a little vain.

Chardonnais was almost five-foot-seven and somewhat bowlegged. Thick, black hair covered his swarthy face virtually from eyebrows to past his chin. The tangle continued down to his chest and covered that, too, except on the long, jagged scar running from just under the left nipple down the left side and curving in toward the navel. The hair on his head was long, too, and curled slightly just below the level of the shoulders. His eyes were dark, glittering coals that were expressive in joy or in menace, and he had a short, squat nose that had been broken on several occasions.

What had caught his attention in the mirror was the scar. He had gotten it almost six years ago now, but in many ways it seemed like only yesterday.

He and his two partners—Ezra Early and Abe Rawlins—had been in the Uncompahgre country, trapping a little stream on the western side of the San Juan Mountains. This was the third year that the three men had been on their own. Before, they had been employees of General Ashley's company. Chardonnais and Early had gone west with Ashley's brigade in 1822; Rawlins had joined up the next year. During the first rendezvous, the three had bought themselves out of Ashley's contract and had become free trappers.

In those three years the friends had devised a system for trapping and keeping camp that worked for them. The three men rotated the jobs each day so that none was stuck with too onerous a task for too long.

One of the three was always in camp. He would tend the fires and the horses and help the women— this was the second year the three had Indian wives— gather firewood, cure beaver plews, and take care of other such camp work. The other two men would work the trap lines. One would wade in the stream. He would check the traps, with luck haul out a drowned beaver, toss it to his partner on the riverbank, and reset the trap. The man on the riverbank would quickly skin the beaver: slitting the skin on the belly and the four legs and then carefully peeling off the whole hide. Unless it was starving times, the carcass was tossed away, though on occasion the tail was served. Roasted up, it was quite a delicacy.

Since the skinning was rather easy, the man on this detail was also given charge of keeping a close watch out for Indians. One could never tell when some sneaky red critters would up and attack or run off the horses or something. That job was not too demanding either, though it raised a man's tension considerably.

The one in the camp had to be mighty alert, too, since Indians would be prone to head for a camp because that's where the horses and women were, if the trappers had women. It was also where the food and supplies, including lead and powder, were kept.

Chardonnais had the camp duty that day. He was kneeling over the fire as he made lead balls for his rifle and pistols when suddenly something didn't seem right. He froze, testing the air with his senses. He finally realized what it was—the birds were quiet.

He rose and began turning, at the same time pulling one of his two flintlock pistols. An Arapaho was almost on him and swung his tomahawk. The warrior missed, and Chardonnais blew a hole in the man's belly.

"*Sacre bleu*," he muttered when he saw the six other warriors. Two had gone straight for the horses; two more had grabbed the women—Early's wife, Falling Leaf; and one of Chardonnais's women, Yellow Feather—and the last two were heading for him.

"*Merde*," Chardonnais snarled. He grabbed his other pistol and fired, hitting a warrior, but not killing him. As the trapper tried to get his knife or tomahawk out, the other Arapaho was on him.

The warrior's knife opened a large gaping slash in his chest and abdomen. By then, though, Chardonnais had gotten out his own butcher knife and shoved it hilt-deep in the Arapaho's innards.

Chardonnais was losing strength rapidly as he shoved the dead warrior away from him. He wobbled and saw the camp as if through a piece of gauze. He managed to get his rifle from where he had laid it on the ground when he had started working. He had trouble getting back up straight, but finally did. He aimed as best he could with his rapidly dwindling strength and fired. As he went down he thought he had managed to shoot one of the two Arapahos stealing the horses, but he could not be sure.

Then he fell. He was conscious but unable to move, with the blood draining quickly from him. And there was little he could do but resist weakly when an Arapaho warrior came over, knife in hand. The Indian grabbed the trapper's pitch-black, wavy hair in one hand and moved the knife toward his head.

Then there was the roar of a gun, and the Arapaho fell atop Chardonnais, brain matter leaking out of a large hole in the warrior's head. It dripped on Chardonnais's face, but he was barely aware of it. He thought he was going to suffocate, since he did not have the strength to move the corpse off him.

There was more gunfire, a few war whoops, and then a shouted, "Waugh! Reckon we showed them critters."

Chardonnais felt a little better as he heard his good friend Ezra Early speaking those words.

Abe Rawlins walked over to where the warrior was lying on Chardonnais. He was a little nervous, thinking that perhaps the French-Canadian trapper was dead.

Rawlins grabbed the back of the Arapaho's greasy buckskin shirt and lifted the burly man. A look at Chardonnais's ghastly wound gave him pause. "Ezra!" he called. "*Pronto.*"

Early, still trying to make sure that all the Arapahos were dead or gone, did not like being interrupted. But something in Rawlins's voice made him spin and trot over. He knelt at Chardonnais's side and peeled back his shirt.

Rawlins was on the wounded man's other side. "Goddamn if it ain't just like this here little French fart to lay here takin' a goddamn *siesta* whilst we're runnin' off them red devils. Lazy ass son of a bitch. That's what ye are, goddamn ye."

"I am make de wolf bait of, eh," Chardonnais said in a faraway voice. "It's good I go under wit' my two *bons amis* at my side."

"Eat shit, froggie," Early snapped. "You ain't goin' under if this chil's got anything to say about it. Abe, fetch up our medical sack and a couple of them new plews. Once you've done that, you can finish makin' sure those 'rapahos're gone." Early couldn't remember exactly how he had become the small group's physician, but whenever anyone needed doctoring, he was called upon. He hoped he was never seriously wounded; he'd be in the hands of a couple of incompetents, he had sometimes thought with a grin.

Rawlins nodded and moved off. He was back in moments with the requested items, as well as a canteen of water, a jug of whiskey, and a few strips of buckskin. "Thought ye might need them other things," he announced before heading off again.

Early nodded absentmindedly. He eased Chardonnais up a little and poured some whiskey into him before easing him back down. Early ripped the wounded man's calico shirt wide open. "Damn, boy, you really know how to do it, don't you?" he muttered.

Early got out a curved needle and some long pieces of sinew. He splashed some whiskey on them as well as on his hands. "This here's gonna take some doin's, Lucien," he said as he pulled some sinew through the eyehole of the needle. "You've been cut from tit to meatbag, no doubt about it."

Chardonnais nodded weakly. "Maybe you should not waste your time, eh?" he said.

"It's my goddamn time to waste, so shut your flappin' hole." He jammed a stick between Chardonnais's teeth. "You're one lucky chil', Lucien. That red devil's blade didn't cut nothin' important."

"Too high for dat," Chardonnais mumbled around the stick.

"Jesus, can't you stop thinkin' with your pecker even when you're on death's door?" Early asked rhetorically as he dabbed at Chardonnais's wound with a piece of the man's shirt. "All right, ol' hoss, here we go," he said as he hunched over his friend, needle ready.

Chardonnais braced himself, and lay stiff as a board as Early poked the needle through one piece of skin, tugged the jerking piece of sinew through to the knot on the end, and then went through the procedure with the skin on the other side of the gash.

Early did not look up when Rawlins returned and said, "They're gone. We sent them critters packin' but good." He knelt next to Chardonnais and offered his hand to his wounded comrade. "Squeeze, my friend," he said, "if you're of a need to."

Chardonnais nodded and squeezed hard. Rawlins seemed nonplussed by it all.

"The women all right?" Early asked as he worked on another stitch.

Rawlins chuckled a little. "They're just fine. I expect there's a couple 'rapahos who're countin' their blessin's. Fallin' Leaf like to geld one of them critters. I expect at that point he told his *compañero* that it was time to skedaddle."

Early nodded, paying most of his attention to his work. It took him the better part of half an hour to get the wound stitched up, and another ten minutes to finish off the job. He made up a poultice of yucca root and slathered that all over Chardonnais's wounds. Then he lay a beaver plew, fur side down, on the wound. With Rawlins's help, he finally wrapped some buckskin strips around the patient's chest and back.

"Here," Early said, "take some of this."

"I don't want none of dat laudanum. *Mais non!*"

"You either take it or I'll have Abe sit on you and pour it down."

"*Merde,*" Chardonnais mumbled, but he took two sips of laudanum from the bottle.

Then Early and Rawlins carried him to his lodge and set him on the bed of buffalo robes.

"Rest now, boy," Early said. "You'll be good as new in no time."

"Shit, I will. I am gone under for sure, and we bot' know dat."

"You go under now, you little shit, and it'll be all your own goddamn fault."

In less than two weeks, Chardonnais was making some trips outside, helped by Yellow Feather, and within a week of that, Early and Rawlins could hear him making love with one—or maybe both—his wives.

"Jesus, Lucien," Early said the next morning, "can't you ever give it a rest?"

"*Mais non!*" Chardonnais said with a wide grin. "You two are just jealous dat I am *le grand homme.*"

"Big man, my ass," Rawlins snorted. "Only goddamn reason you've got to hump some unlucky lass every two goddamn minutes is your pecker's so small you can't find it."

They all laughed. In the five years Chardonnais

had been in the Rocky Mountains, his prodigious appetite for women had become legendary. It was spoken of around campfires from Taos to the Milk River.

It was several more weeks before Chardonnais was recovered enough to allow them to move on. And another month or so before he was the Chardonnais of old.

2

CHARDONNAIS BEGAN BUTTONING the fancy shirt, wondering just what he had gotten himself into this time. He was, by nature, an impetuous man, given to quick changes of mood without any real reason behind it. More than once his rashness had brought him close to death. Somehow, though, his two partners always seemed to save him from himself.

"What de 'ell am I doing 'ere?" he muttered aloud.

The previous summer, Ezra Early had had to rush back to the family farm in Indiana to see his ailing father. When he had gotten back and talked about it during the winter, Chardonnais decided that he missed his family and would like to see everyone again.

As the three men had made their way down toward Taos as they did every year, he suddenly decided that he would go to see his family. He bid farewell to his partners and rode off in the company of a few other men who were heading for roughly the same destination.

Lucien Chardonnais was the youngest of the six children of Marcel and Yvette Chardonnais. Like all his siblings, he was born in a small town near Lake Superior.

9

When he was eight or nine, though, his father moved the family to St. Charles, Missouri. It was a town that had many French-speaking residents, and the Chardonnaises fit in well.

Lucien had not been back since coming west eleven years ago. His father and mother were, by now, elderly, and he might not have the opportunity to see them again.

His family hadn't known him when he rode up. They had sent away a boy of seventeen, and he had come back a strong, tough, fierce man.

The way he was dressed didn't help them recognize him, though he had stayed true to his roots in that he had as much color and flash about his clothing as he could. He wore a bright red calico shirt—dirty but still red. His buckskin pants had been beaded, bangled, and decorated. His moccasins were fixed in a bold pattern of blue, green, and white beads. Some of the fanciness of his pants and moccasins was marred because both were blackened by grease and smoke. A wide red sash circled his waist. Two big pistols were stuck through the sash, as was a colorful sheath encasing a large knife. A small patch knife dangled by a thong around his neck, as did a large, heart-shaped ornament of silver. He casually carried a large-bore flintlock rifle. On his head was a vivid green knitted wool cap, the top of which flopped to the side.

He was stopped at the doorway of his parents' house by his mother, who didn't recognize him.

"*Mais, Maman. C'est ton fils Lucien.* But, Mama. It's your son Lucien."

The woman looked at him skeptically.

"*J'ai cinq soeurs et frères.* I have five sisters and brothers."

The woman still looked disbelieving.

Chardonnais nodded. He set his rifle against the building and rolled his left shirtsleeve up. Then he held out his arm. Despite the dirt and grease, the crescent-shaped birthmark was plainly visible.

"*Mon fils!* My son!" the woman shouted. "*Entre, vite!* Come in, quickly!"

After a couple of days Chardonnais was rather sorry that he had returned. Not that there was anything wrong exactly, but he was used to the high solitude of the Shining Mountains. He was used to the ways of his two partners. He was not used to having so many people in so small a place, as happened when his brothers and sisters, with their spouses and children, visited him at his parents' place. He found he missed the easy camaraderie of Early and Rawlins, and their frequently filthy banter.

Even seeing his childhood friend Michel LeBeau did not pick him up any. LeBeau simply was no substitute for Ezra Early and Abe Rawlins.

Then he met Mademoiselle Marie Bouchard. She was perhaps five feet tall and might have weighed ninety pounds, if that. The skin of her face was sparkling, set off even more by the rosy red of her perfect lips. She looked as if she had been sculpted out of a soft, though firm material. Everything about her made Chardonnais catch his breath: her small, perfect nose; her delicate ears; the slim waist and the considerable rise of her breasts; her graceful neck.

He was not smitten with her. Smitten was an inadequate word by a long shot. He felt more as if he had drowned in the endless depths of her beauty.

Chardonnais met this vision of perfect loveliness in her father's house. François Bouchard was a merchant and fairly well-to-do. When he heard that Chardonnais—a man who made his living in the far mountains and whom he had known somewhat when Chardonnais was younger—was visiting, he asked him to call.

Chardonnais had taken a seat across a small, hand-built table from Bouchard. "What can I do for you, monsieur?" he asked in English.

"I'm interested in de Rocky Mountain fur trade," Bouchard said. He spoke in English, proud that he had learned the language of his adopted country. He thought such a thing was only right, and as he was now an American citizen, he would use English as much as possible.

"What about it?"

"I'd like to get involved in it—from a merchant's standpoint."

"I don' t'ink I can help you, monsieur. I am but a poor free trapper, who makes his money t'rough catching beavair and selling de plews to de highest bidder."

"Exactly," Bouchard shouted. "I want to be de highest bidder."

"Den you will either have to go to de mountains and bid at de rendezvous, or you can go to St. Louis and make a bid when de suppliers return wit' de plews."

"To whom do you sell your beavair pelts?"

"Usually to de Bent-Saint Vrain Company. Dey are ol' friends in de mountains."

"And where are dey locate?"

"Taos."

"Eh?"

"San Fernando de Taos. A city in de Mexican lands."

"But why dere?" Bouchard asked sharply. He did not like giving any business to foreigners, as he would see it, even if the Bent-Saint Vrain Company was owned by Americans.

"Many of de suppliers at rendezvous, dey try to steal. Dey charge prices so high dat you can sell a whole wintair's catch and not have de money for a good spree and still outfit for de next season."

"Why not come back here and sell dem?" Bouchard saw this as a possible way to break into the fur trade.

"Too far to go. Too crowded wit' people. It takes too much time. And," he added with a grin, "dere is no place to have a real spree."

"I suppose de last is true, but do you really need a drunken debauch that sucks you dry financially?"

"*Oui*," Chardonnais said seriously.

"But why?" Bouchard was puzzled.

"You spend seven mont' of de year standing in freezing water up to your ass almost, fighting Indians and grizzly bears, sometimes starving, facing cold a man who lives here has nevair encountered—you do all dem t'ings, and you will see why we like a spree come de summer."

"But wouldn't it be more prudent to save at least a little portion of it?" Bouchard asked. "Surely a man who works so hard for his money wouldn't want to spend it all on a summer festival of liquor, fighting, and fornicating, no?"

"Dat is de best t'ing about all dis," Chardonnais said with a laugh. He sobered. "I have put away a little," he confessed. "But not so much." He grinned a little. "Dem Indian women, dey want much foofaraw and such. All dat costs money."

"I would t'ink so," Bouchard said flatly. "Well, all dat aside," he continued after a moment's thought, "can you introduce me to de men who can help me enter dat business?"

Chardonnais shrugged. "If dere are any in St.

Louis, maybe yes, maybe no. I know most of dem; I have worked with many of dem, too. But whether dey would want more competition for de fur dollars . . ." He shrugged with outspread hands.

Just then a young woman walked into the room, and Chardonnais's mouth went dry and his palms got moist. He was beginning to think he had gone under and was in heaven.

The young woman—she was about sixteen, Chardonnais estimated—stopped behind Bouchard's chair and squeezed his shoulders. "Would you and your guest like something to drink, Papa?" she asked. She had no accent at all.

For a few seconds, Chardonnais had figured the young woman was Bouchard's wife. It would not be all that odd for an older—middle-aged—man to take such a young wife. But he was much relieved to find out she was Bouchard's daughter.

"A bit of brandy for me," Bouchard said, patting one of her hands on his shoulder. "Monsieur Chardonnais?"

"Brandy sounds good to dis chil', too."

The young woman looked at him strangely for a moment, then nodded and left.

"My daughter, Marie," Bouchard said, nodding to the doorway the woman had just used.

"*Mais non!*" Chardonnais said. "Little Marie?" He held a hand about three feet from the floor.

Bouchard laughed. "You've been gone a long time, Lucien. She was but four den. Now she is of marrying age." He sighed. "And dat is a trying time for a father."

Chardonnais nodded in agreement, though he had no notion whether it were true or not.

Marie returned with a tray on which sat two half-full brandy snifters. She approached Chardonnais first and allowed him to take a glass. Then she brought the other to her father before walking out again.

"Before we make a toast, I have somet'ing to ask of you, monsieur," Chardonnais said.

Bouchard nodded, mystified.

"I would like your permission to court Marie," Chardonnais said bluntly.

"She has a beau," Bouchard cautioned.

"Is she serious about him?"

"Who can know de mind of a woman, eh?" Bouchard said with a shrug.

"Dat does not sound like she is serious about him. So, may I become another beau for Marie?"

"I have no objections. But I t'ink we should ask Marie, no?"

Chardonnais shrugged and nodded.

Bouchard called for his daughter. She came in the room with a question on her face. "Monsieur Chardonnais would like to court you. Would you object to dat?"

Marie thought about it a few moments. She did have one man calling on her regularly, but she was not sure she liked him enough to have only him as a beau. Of course, Michel LeBeau was more handsome than Lucien Chardonnais. The latter was missing two teeth from the one side of his mouth; his hands were oversized and covered with calluses, and he was poorly dressed. Still, he was an adventurer, if what she had heard about him was true. He was a man who had treated with the wild red Indians, had lived dangerously, and come back alive to talk about it. There was something to be said about such a man. Finally she decided that having Chardonnais court her would not be all bad. It might make LeBeau more attentive to her. Besides, she could always end the arrangement if Chardonnais turned out to be a poor suitor.

"That'd be nice, Papa." She smiled at Chardonnais and left, the hem of her light blue silk dress swishing a little as she walked.

"To successful enterprises," Bouchard said with a grin, raising his glass.

Chardonnais smiled, raised the glass, and then drank. He knew that Bouchard figured this was a sure way into the fur trade. Chardonnais didn't mind him thinking that, although he might be disappointed when he realized that Chardonnais could be of little help to him.

3

IT WASN'T UNTIL TWO MORE weeks had gone by that Chardonnais found out that his competition for Marie's fair hand was his childhood friend Michel LeBeau. That bothered him for a little while, but then he shrugged it off. He and LeBeau were men now, not boys playing on the bank of the Missouri River. They could compete fairly for Marie's affections without hating each other. At least Chardonnais felt he could do so. There was one way to find out if LeBeau could also do so.

He and LeBeau met in a saloon one evening. Over cups of rum, Chardonnais said, "I didn't know you were courting Marie Bouchard until just de other day. If I had known, I would not have asked to court her myself. But now dat I have come to know her a little in de past few weeks, I find I am unable to stop courting her."

"She is somet'ing special, eh?" LeBeau said flatly. He wasn't sure how he felt about all this.

"*Mais oui!*" Chardonnais agreed. "What I t'ought is dat we can court her both, but still remain friends, eh?

If she picks you over me, den I will go away, back to de mountains."

"And if she picks you?"

"Den you will give us your blessing."

"I don't know, Lucien. *Merde.* I've been calling on her for more dan a year now, and I t'ought she'd consent soon to marry me. Now dis."

"She didn't say she was close to doing dat," Chardonnais said quietly. "When her papa ask if she mind I come to call on her, she say dat will be fine by her. She showed no hesitation. Are you sure you're as close to her as you t'ink?"

"Yes, dammit," LeBeau snapped. He polished off the rest of his rum and stood. "I must t'ink about dis," he said. "We can meet here in two days, eh?"

"Oui."

LeBeau was bitter when he came into the saloon two days later. He had spoken to Marie and learned that she was not nearly as fond of him as he had thought. That angered him, but it also saddened him. He suspected that some of her love for him had been transferred to Chardonnais, and he thought that if the other man had never come along, Marie would have consented to marry him soon. He was determined to duel Chardonnais for Marie's affections. But he decided that he would wait at least a little longer. For some reason, he felt the time was not right. He grudgingly admitted—only to himself, to be sure—that he hoped Chardonnais would do something to turn Marie's affections off Chardonnais and back onto himself. If that happened, there would be no need for a duel.

He sat across the table from Chardonnais and explained some of what he had been thinking. He did not mention the duel, hoping to spring it on him sometime later. "So," he concluded, "it's up to Marie who she chooses, eh?"

"I t'ink dat is only right."

"You mind if I ask you somet'ing?"

Chardonnais shrugged. "Depends on what you ask."

"You humped any Indian women?" he asked flatly.

"Why do you want to know dat?" Chardonnais countered.

"Just curious."

"I t'ink you're full of shit," Chardonnais said harshly. "I t'ink you ask me dat so maybe I answer yes, and den you can run to Marie and tell her she shouldn't want dis beast who humps wit' de Indians, eh?"

LeBeau's eyes blazed hotly in hurt and intimidation. He wondered how Chardonnais could see into the ruse so easily. He nodded, turned, and began walking toward the door. Two rivermen, big burly men of French extraction, stopped LeBeau and asked him for money. The rivermen were drunk, or so it seemed from where Chardonnais was sitting.

Chardonnais watched for a moment, not wanting to get involved. But LeBeau was still a friend, despite their rivalry over Marie Bouchard. Plus, Chardonnais was basically a fair man, and to win Marie's heart because his rival was literally beaten out of the competition did not suit his nature. He rose and strolled over to the confrontation.

"*Excusez-moi, messieurs,*" he said politely, "but you are bothering my great friend."

"Piss off, little man," one of the boatmen said in French.

"Such manners," Chardonnais said with a note of sarcastic disappointment.

One of the two rivermen turned his full attention to Chardonnais. "You want your ass stomped, stay where you are. When me and Pierre finish with that piece of shit"—he jerked a thumb in LeBeau's direction—"we'll take care of you," he said, still speaking in French.

"Then you better get some help, you stupid shits," Chardonnais responded in kind.

"I've had about enough from you, goddammit," the man said as he launched a ham-sized fist at Chardonnais's head.

Chardonnais took two fast steps backward. The man's punch missed, and its power made him spin halfway around. Chardonnais jumped into the breach and slammed three powerful punches to the man's kidneys. The man groaned and sank to his knees.

But Chardonnais could not worry about him now. The man named Pierre had charged and smashed into his side. Both men crashed onto a table, which creaked but did not break. It did fall over, though, sending Chardonnais and Pierre to the floor. Chardonnais had managed to get turned enough to land mostly atop Pierre. He bounced off the riverman, but that did not matter since Pierre had taken the brunt of the fall.

Chardonnais scrambled up, just in time to have the other riverman slam his locked fists into the back of his head. Chardonnais went stumbling unwillingly forward, hit the edge of a table, and fell. Seeing the two rivermen coming at him again, he slipped to the other side of the table and flipped it over. All it did was slow the two men a little. It was just enough time to get to his feet and slide his big butcher knife out of the hard leather sheath. He had, since returning to St. Charles, been leaving his pistols at home, but he carried the knife with him wherever he went.

"You're going to need more than that," Pierre laughed.

"Maybe, maybe not. Why don't you come see?" Chardonnais challenged.

The two charged around the table. Trying to ignore the knot of pain in his head, Chardonnais spun to his left, took two steps, then dropped almost to the floor in a squat. He threw his arms around Pierre's legs, then pushed up, flipping Pierre over his shoulder. Pierre crashed into his friend and both fell.

As the two rivermen tried to untangle themselves Chardonnais walked calmly up. He grabbed one's hair and pulled the head back. "You stupid bastards should know better than to pick a fight if you're so goddamn clumsy."

Pierre tried to punch Chardonnais in the knee. Chardonnais skipped out of the way, letting the other man's hair go. The two rivermen got to their feet. Anger clotted on their faces. "Just who the hell're you anyway?" one asked.

"I am Lucien Chardonnais, a free trapper," Chardonnais said proudly in English. He flicked his knife and it stuck, quivering, in a tabletop. "I am de meanest, ass-kicking son of a bitch you two lumps of pig shit will ever meet. I spit at danger. I eat live mountain lions for breakfast, and I am made angry by you two ass wipes." He paused. "So, come, try what you want. But don' be surprise when I make wolf bait out of you."

Pierre looked at his companion. "You ever see anyone this crazy, Louis?" he asked in French.

Louis shook his head. "Never."

"Are you two going to start kissing each other next?" Chardonnais asked sarcastically, still using English. "De next t'ing I know, you'll be humping on de floor."

"Bastard," Pierre snarled. He charged, startling even his friend, with his own knife in hand. Chardonnais was ready for him, though. He caught Pierre's knife arm. As Pierre's momentum carried him along, Chardonnais twisted the arm and spun sideways.

To keep his arm from being broken, Pierre had to go down to the floor. As he did so, Chardonnais grabbed his knife from the table and plunged it into Pierre's heart through the back. Just to make sure, he pulled out the blade and stabbed Pierre again, all the while keeping an eye on Louis.

The riverman was still stunned. He and his friend Pierre had never been taken in a fight. Never even had much trouble in one. And here this bandy-legged man had knocked them both around and finally killed Pierre. Louis was almost at a loss for what to do.

"Well?" Chardonnais said cockily. "What will it be, eh? You going to stand dere and make funny eyes at me? Or will you take your friend away? Or do you still want to tear me apart, eh?"

"*Fils de garce!*" Louis bellowed. He jerked out the flintlock pistol he carried in his belt and began to pull back the hammer.

Chardonnais flipped his bloody knife in the air a foot or so high, and caught it by the hilt when it came down. He pulled it back and then threw it. The blade sank into Louis's flesh where the shoulder and chest meet.

Louis dropped the pistol, and he pulled out Chardonnais's knife with his left hand. "I can still use dis," he warned.

Chardonnais figured he had had about enough of this big slob. He grabbed a wood chair and clobbered him with it. Louis went down, dropping the knife.

Chardonnais began beating him with the chair.

LeBeau shouted for someone to stop Chardonnais, but the rest of the saloon's patrons were not desirous of getting anywhere near Chardonnais. At least not anytime soon.

Chardonnais finally stopped beating Louis when the riverman was a bloody blob. Breathing hard, he dropped the chair and picked up his knife. He wiped the blade clean on Louis's shirt and then slid it away. He looked at LeBeau and grinned a little. "*Allons-y.*"

The fight had pushed any idea of a duel with Chardonnais out of LeBeau's mind. But it had spawned another idea. Just after he and Chardonnais parted company a few blocks from the saloon, he headed for the nearest constable's office.

Soon after, several constables rapped on the door of the Chardonnais house and asked that Lucien be brought out.

"What for?" his mother asked.

"He's wanted in the death of two men at a saloon, ma'am," the constable in charge said.

"Don't worry about it, *Maman*," Chardonnais said, stepping to the door. "This'll be cleared up soon."

He went peacefully with the constables, even handing over his knife without argument, and was locked in the jail. Then the bartender and whatever witnesses could be found were brought in. All of them said the same thing, that the two rivermen had started things.

After several hours the constables shrugged, handed Chardonnais back his knife, and let him go. Chardonnais never did find out that it was his "friend" Michel LeBeau who had brought the charges that had sent him to jail, even if only briefly.

Chardonnais's mother looked terribly disappointed when her son returned home, and he explained what had happened. She could not be comforted, knowing as she did now that her youngest son was a murderer.

"It's not like that, *Maman*," he told her in French. "Those two would've killed Michel. Or me."

His mother was not crying, but he could see the hurt deep in her eyes. "Those two men weren't the first you've killed, were they?" she asked.

"No," he responded flatly.

His mother was inconsolable, at least for a few days; then she seemed to take it less harshly. He helped his own cause by keeping away from saloons and spending more time with Mademoiselle Marie Bouchard, both of which pleased his mother considerably.

What his brothers and sisters thought of all this was not really voiced, and he would not have cared even if it were. He got along with his siblings well enough, though none of them was very close to him.

Of more importance to him was how Marie and her father looked at him after the incident.

Unknown to Chardonnais, LeBeau had tried to turn Marie against him by painting him as a murderer and savage. She almost believed him, until she learned through her father that Chardonnais had saved LeBeau's dignity, if not his life. That turned her more against LeBeau, and she began rebuffing some of his requests to spend time with her.

Bouchard himself, once he learned the facts, was not at all unpleased. He'd much rather have a man like Chardonnais—a man who could defend himself, his family, and his friends—as a son-in-law than a seemingly spineless man like Michel LeBeau.

4

CHARDONNAIS AND MARIE WERE in the sitting room of the Bouchard house. Chardonnais was edgy as a caged wildcat. He had been thinking of this moment since he had first seen Marie. Now that he thought the time was here, he found himself uncertain, and that was an odd feeling for a cocky man like Lucien Chardonnais to have.

Finally he quit fidgeting and went to the plush overstuffed chair in which Marie was sitting. She seemed composed, serene. He knelt next to the chair and took one of her small hands in one of his oversized paws.

"I know we haven't known each other long, Marie," he said quietly. Now that his plan was in action, he felt his confidence building. "But in dat short time, I've come to love you more dan anyt'ing. And I'd be pleased and proud if you were to become my wife."

"Are you asking me to marry you?" Marie asked, not surprised.

"*Oui.*"

"You must ask Papa."

"I know dat. But I didn't want to go to him until I knew you'd accept me. If you don' want me, I won't bother your papa."

"I accept. . . ." Marie said.

Chardonnais's heart jumped, and he felt he was the happiest man on earth.

Until she added, "With some conditions."

"Such as?" he asked warily.

"One, you must give up your western adventures."

"I t'ink I can do dat," Chardonnais answered without thought.

"You must find proper employment. Papa can help you with that, I would think."

"*Oui.* More?"

"You must stay out of saloons and other low establishments, and you must stop fighting and carousing."

"Dose are tough t'ings to do," Chardonnais admitted. "But for you, *ma chère*, I will do dem."

"*Bien,*" Marie said with a bright smile. "*Très bien.*" She lowered her eyes coquettishly. "I will enjoy being your wife, Monsieur Chardonnais," she added.

Chardonnais was walking on air again, though he tried to temper his happiness with the thought that he must still approach François Bouchard to ask to marry his daughter. He left the Bouchard house soon after, still feeling terrific. All his thoughts were on the future.

That night, Chardonnais ate supper at the Bouchard home. Afterward he and Bouchard went into the den, where they got cigars and brandy. Once they were seated, Bouchard looked at Chardonnais and smiled a little. "I have heard dat you have somet'ing to speak with me about. Is that right?"

"*Oui.*" Chardonnais paused only a moment. "I would like to have your daughter's hand in marriage."

"I see," Bouchard said noncommittally. "And have you discussed dis with her?"

"*Oui.* She say she is happy to be my wife — if you approve of course," Chardonnais said diplomatically.

"I expect my son-in-law to have a good job, not one that has him traipsing all over de place, treating with Indians and such."

Chardonnais nodded. "Marie says maybe you can help wit' dat."

"I suppose I can." Bouchard paused, looking at the glowing tip of his cigar for a moment. "And I want my son-in-law to be a peaceful citizen, not a man who gets into public brawls."

"I was t'inking just de other day dat I am getting too old for such doin's. It's time dis ol' chil' settled down and made a family."

"Just de words I like to hear," Bouchard said, beaming. He had thought up until a month ago that LeBeau would be his son-in-law, and he had not been displeased with the notion. Now he was glad such a thing would not happen. LeBeau had shown himself to be a man of questionable habits and weak character. Chardonnais might be a little wild, he figured, but having a lot of spirit was not bad in and of itself. If the man could learn to control himself and to change his habits a little, he would probably be an excellent son-in-law.

"Den you say yes?" Chardonnais asked, wanting to make sure there was no misunderstanding.

"*Oui,*" Bouchard said firmly. "And when will dis historic event take place?"

"I would t'ink soon," Chardonnais said. "Now dat I have made up my mind to do dis, I want to get it done."

"A little eager for the marriage bed, aren't you?" Bouchard asked with just a touch of rebuke.

"Dat is true a little. But more is de fact dat de

mountains, dey have a pull on a man. It's not an easy t'ing to deny, dat pull. If I am marry, den I can fight de pull of de mountains."

Bouchard nodded. It made sense in a strange sort of way. And he certainly had no qualms about marrying his daughter off soon. His only problem was that people might think she had been forced into the situation. Here, in heavily Catholic St. Charles, that could be a very serious matter. He expressed this to Chardonnais.

"I understand," Chardonnais responded. "I'd have de same concerns if it was my daughter." He paused, thinking. "What if we talk to de parish priest, Père Duchesne? I will tell him—it is de truth—dat Marie and me we did notting wrong. Dere might be some people talk about it, but when our first anniversary comes, and we have no children yet, den dey will stop their talk. You'll see."

Bouchard nodded. "All right, Lucien. If Père Duchesne says it is all right, we will have de marriage in one mont' from today."

"Dat suits this chil' just fine."

The four of them—Bouchard; Marie; her mother, Bernadette; and Chardonnais—saw Father Duchesne later that week. It took little to convince Father Duchesne that the younger couple were serious about each other and that their relationship had been pure. He would begin the Reading of the Banns on Sunday, allowing the wedding ceremonies on the appointed day.

Chardonnais got to see a lot less of Marie after that. She was always having dress fittings or some such nonsense. He began to feel like a cheap piece of agate in a bucket of pearls. He didn't even see LeBeau anymore. He had wanted to explain to his friend that there had been nothing against him in Chardonnais's courting of Marie Bouchard. But his friend seemed to have vanished.

About the only person with whom he felt even a little comfortable was his brother Jacques, who was only about two years his elder. Jacques was married and had three children already. He owned a small tobacco shop, which kept him busy. But he always managed to find a few minutes to talk with Lucien when the younger brother came along.

When Lucien had gone to get a suit for the wedding, Jacques accompanied him as encouragement. Lucien was appreciative.

Finally, almost in exasperation, Chardonnais asked Bouchard for a talk. His future father-in-law readily agreed. They met in Bouchard's den after supper one night.

"I am to believe dat you will give me a job when I am married to your daughter, no?"

"Yes."

"Doing what?"

"I haven't quite decided yet. Why do you ask?"

"Can you put me to work now?"

"I suppose. Why?"

"I have notting to do wit' myself. Marie, she's always busy wit' preparing for de wedding. You're busy wit' work. My brothers, dey all have t'ings to do." He smiled regretfully. "I'm not a man who likes to sit doing notting. I'd rather work, even at somet'ing I don' like, dan to sit doing notting."

About the only thing he had been doing was visiting brothels around town. His prodigious sexual appetite was easy to indulge in the Rockies, but here he was forced to visit the bordellos. He planned to continue doing so after his marriage. Certainly a virgin like

Marie Bouchard could not be expected to handle such an appetite. He also expected that Marie would look the other way—as all good women did—when he made these excursions.

Being alone so much also allowed him to think too much. When he was in a questioning phase, he could see all sorts of horrible aspects about the most common, everyday things. He needed some kind of work to keep his body—and his mind—active enough so that he didn't build up any more troubles in his mind.

"I don't see why we couldn't put you to work now," Bouchard said. "I just assumed you'd not want to work till after de wedding."

"I don't need dat much time to get ready," Chardonnais said with a grin. "I have my suit. Dat is all I need, I t'ink."

"I suppose it would be." Bouchard laughed. "All right, come see me tomorrow morning at de office."

Chardonnais showed up and was ushered into Bouchard's personal office. Bouchard ran a profitable shipping and trading business, and he had no real idea of what he was going to do with Chardonnais. For now, he put him to work directing men loading and unloading wagons at the company's small warehouse a few blocks from the office.

Right from the start, the other men gave him a hard time. Mostly it was muttered comments about the boss's soon-to-be son-in-law and such. Chardonnais, who had a volatile temper, actually managed to keep it contained.

After work, though, he waited at the opening of an alley the men used to go to their favorite saloon. Six of them came at once and stopped when they saw Chardonnais planted squarely in the alley in front of them.

"Go home, dammit," Wilber Grimshaw, one of the workers, said bravely. "We saw enough of you at work. Now we're on our own time."

"*Oui*. I am, too. And I want to discuss your manners wit' you all."

"Get out of the goddamn way, froggie," Sam Witherspoon added. He was a big man, the biggest of the lot, and had had his share of barroom brawls. He almost always came out the victor in them. He was not afraid of Chardonnais, even if the stories about him were true.

"Not until you listen to what I have to say."

"You wanna know what I think about what you gotta say, bub?" Witherspoon said sarcastically. "This's what I think of what you gotta say." He unbuttoned his fly, took his penis out, and urinated on the ground.

Some of the piss splashed on Chardonnais's moccasins. Chardonnais stood without moving until Witherspoon had put himself away. Then he lambasted Witherspoon a solid shot in the face. The man fell like he had been poleaxed.

The other men were dumbfounded. No one had ever knocked Sam Witherspoon almost to unconsciousness before. Not with one punch.

"You know what I t'ink of your smart-ass remarks, do you?" Chardonnais asked rhetorically. "I will show you what I t'ink of dem." He stood there and unbuttoned his fly. He pulled himself out and pissed all over the prostrate, though conscious, Sam Witherspoon.

When he had his pants done up again, Chardonnais said, "De first one who makes de smart remark to dis chil' again will get de same. Or worse," he warned. "*Bon soir.*" He turned and walked away.

5

THE WEEKS UNTIL THE wedding dragged for Chardonnais, though he was working every day. His job didn't consist of much actual work, and he was almost as bored now as he had been before.

The only interesting note about the job was that Sam Witherspoon had not shown up the day after Chardonnais had coldcocked him. The others did, and went about their jobs without much fuss. They kept wary eyes on Chardonnais for half a day, then decided that he was not one to cause trouble, though if some-one else did, he would surely finish it. They began to relax as the day passed.

Witherspoon appeared the next day, trying to pre-tend nothing had happened, but not disguising his hate much. None of that bothered Chardonnais, who smirked at him at every opportunity.

Witherspoon was making a strong effort to get his coworkers to band together to make some mischief with the French-Canadian, but they weren't buying it. Once, Chardonnais left the area and went inside the ware-house. He stood close to one wall so he could hear.

"I'm tellin' ya, boys, all we gotta do is back him up against a wall, then I'll whale the livin' tar out of the French-speakin' little bastard. What say, boys?"

There was a long, ragged sigh before Charlie Fenster said, "No, Sam. You brought that on yourself the other day. We were all ridin' Mr. Chardonnais pretty hard, and for no goddamn good reason that I can think of."

"Whatcha mean no reason?" Witherspoon asked. "He's a goddamn frog, plus he's the boss's ass-kissin' son-in-law. That's enough for me."

"Well, it's not enough for me," Fenster said. "Nor, I expect, for the other boys. It's plain as day he don't like bein' here no more'n you and I do. But he's got his job to do, same as we do."

"Shit on that. I don't let *nobody* piss on me and get away with it."

Fenster shrugged. "Then it's you got the problem. If you're so goddamn tough, you take him on by yourself."

"By sweet Jesus, I might just do that," Witherspoon snarled.

"Fine," Fenster responded. "But leave us out of it."

That night Chardonnais surreptitiously followed the men to the saloon they frequented. He waited outside for ten or fifteen minutes, giving Witherspoon and the others time to get settled in. Then he pushed through the doors of the place.

The interior was about what he had expected—a foul den full of stench, decay, and scum. All the talking stopped when Chardonnais entered, and most of the men began whispering excitedly to each other. Witherspoon seemed oblivious.

Chardonnais marched up and grabbed Witherspoon's greasy, lice-laden hair and jerked his head back. Suddenly his knife was against Witherspoon's throat. "I hear you say you are going to whip de shit out of me? When're you going to do dis, eh? When I'm a hundred years old?"

"I'll do it now," Witherspoon croaked, trying not to have his Adam's apple bounce up and down too much, scraping the knife blade. "You put that goddamn pigsticker away and I'll wipe the floor with you, you festering little bag of shit."

"Ah," Chardonnais said with a grim smile, "so he is a big man wit' all his friends around to help him, eh?"

"He ain't no friend of mine," Fenster said. The others in the saloon seemed to agree with that.

"You'll all keep out of it?" Chardonnais asked.

The men chorused in the affirmative.

"Well den, *lèche-cul*—ass licker," Chardonnais said calmly, "perhaps we should start de shivaree, eh?"

"Anytime you're ready, froggie."

Sam Witherspoon did not know just how close he came to death in that moment. The other men who could see Chardonnais's face knew that he had to use all his self-control to keep himself from sliding the knife blade across Witherspoon's throat. Instead, he moved it carefully away and then slid it into the sheath. "*Allons-y.*"

"What the hell's that mean?" Witherspoon asked as he got up and turned to face his enemy.

"It means," Chardonnais said with a smirk, "dat you move like an old lady—a sagging-tit old squaw— and dat you need to get your fat ass moving."

"You peckerwood," Witherspoon snarled. He swung at Chardonnais.

Chardonnais danced out of the way. "Is dat de best you can do?" he asked lightly. Then he found out that Witherspoon did have at least one friend in the saloon.

He had not expected it, had thought himself invincible, until someone grabbed his arms from behind. The cockiness faded fast.

"That's good, Paulie," Witherspoon snapped. "Good. Now I'll show this scum-suckin' piece of French shit to mess with Sam Witherspoon!" He stepped up and punched Chardonnais in the face as hard as he could.

Now it was Witherspoon's turn for surprise. The punch had not seemed to affect Chardonnais at all. Witherspoon did not let that stop him, however. He began raining punches on the Frenchman's face, stomach, and chest.

Chardonnais bore it for a few minutes, until he could work some steam up. Suddenly he shoved back as hard as he could. His short, strong legs drove Paulie Ryan back, until he slammed into the wall. His grip eased and Chardonnais broke free. Witherspoon was heading for him again, so he grabbed Ryan's arm and swung the man around. Witherspoon charged right into his friend, and both fell.

Chardonnais stood, breathing heavily, warily watching the crowd for a few minutes. No one else seemed ready to take him on. Witherspoon and Ryan were still trying to get untangled and stand. Chardonnais walked up and kicked Ryan in the face. Then he grabbed Witherspoon's hair and pulled him to his feet. Halfway up, he kicked him in the stomach, and then released him.

Sam Witherspoon sagged, grunted, and then vomited all over himself.

Being careful not to get any of the vomit on him, Chardonnais picked Witherspoon up until he was almost on his feet. Holding the nape of his neck in a powerful right hand, he smashed Witherspoon's face into the wall. He did it three more times before letting Witherspoon fall again.

Chardonnais knelt at Witherspoon's side and rolled him onto his back. Before he could say anything, he spun his head around, his senses having told him that danger was imminent. But Charlie Fenster and his friends had grabbed Ryan and pinned him on his back to a table.

"You just stay outta this, Paulie Ryan," Fenster said. "Sam's had such treatment comin' to him for Lord knows how long."

Chardonnais nodded at Fenster. Then he turned back to Witherspoon. The man's face was a bloody, broken mess, but he was still conscious. "You no longer work for de Bouchard Company. You understand dat?"

Witherspoon nodded weakly.

"*Bon.* Since you have just quit de company, dere is no need for you to show up. Any pay due you will be brought to your place. Got dat?"

Again Witherspoon nodded weakly.

"*Adieu,*" Chardonnais said, rising. "My t'anks for helping, Mr. Fenster," he said.

"It was nothin'."

Chardonnais slid a gold coin out of a pocket. "Maybe so. But you and your friends dere have a drink on me." He handed Fenster the coin and walked out into the growing darkness.

He never saw Witherspoon again. He told Bouchard that Witherspoon had quit but that he hadn't given a reason.

Bouchard looked quizzically at Chardonnais. "What happened to your face?" he asked.

Chardonnais knew his face was bright with purplish-yellow bruises and that he was a fright. But all he said was, "I had a run-in wit' a mule yesterday."

"This have anything to do with Monsieur Wither-spoon's sudden desire to seek employment else-where?"

"You don't want to know dat."

"Yes, I do."

Chardonnais grinned. "No, you don't. If you did, you might have to do somet'ing you don't like, eh? Workers're easy enough to come by. He won't be missed."

Bouchard sat there staring at Chardonnais for a few moments. Then he nodded. What Chardonnais had said was true. Not that it made any difference now. He knew damn well from Chardonnais's response that he had had a run-in with Witherspoon. Suddenly he grinned. "He look worse dan you?" he asked.

Chardonnais laughed. "*Mais oui.*"

Bouchard nodded. He sent Witherspoon's pay home with Fenster later that day and put the whole thing from his mind.

Chardonnais's acceptance at work increased con-siderably then, and he tried a little harder to fit in. But within him was a growing tension that he did not understand. At times he thought it was because of where he worked. He had been a free trapper for a long time now, not answerable to any man but himself. But now to hire on and do some mundane job for pid-dling pay, with no sense of danger or adventure, those things ate at him.

At other times the problem was *why* he worked where he worked, but for a slightly different reason. He was the boss's son-in-law. Or soon-to-be son-in-law. It was the only reason Bouchard had hired him. Chardonnais was sure he couldn't have gotten a job with Bouchard's company if he hadn't been in love with Marie.

There, however, was an important ingredient in the stew that Chardonnais's life had become. He was in love with Marie Bouchard. Deeply in love. It was the only reason he would take such demeaning work at such an insulting salary. He'd just as soon starve or freeze to death in the mountains than do such work.

He wondered what there was about his situation he could change. There was precious little, he discovered. He didn't think he could stop loving Marie. He could, he supposed, look for other employment. But there was little he knew how to do—or wanted to do. About all he knew was reading sign, finding beaver, surviving in a harsh, treacherous land of tall, rugged mountains, tumbling, deadly rivers, savage animals, and hostile Indians. None of that was good enough to get him employment here in the city.

He could guide freight wagons on the Santa Fe Trail or something similar. He could do that work, but it would keep him away from Marie for much of the year. That being the case, he figured he'd be better off just going back to the mountains to trap, which he preferred anyway.

Seeing the joy on Marie's face—on those now infrequent times when he was actually in her company—helped keep his temper in check. He could not give up in the face of that delicate assault.

So he kept going to work at Bouchard's warehouse every morning, no matter how difficult it might be. To relieve some of the tension, though, he spent more time in saloons—and in brothels. In the former, he tried to keep out of fights. In the latter, he tried hard not to compare the women with the Indian women with whom he had been acquainted in his eleven years in the mountains.

One afternoon, as he was sitting in a saloon trying to douse some of the fires of discontent with rum, it hit him that he had an Indian wife out in the mountains. He had been through a succession of them since he had had Yellow Feather and her sister, Slow Elk. With his reputation for sexual excess, he was soon known throughout the Ute bands, and it had become harder to find a woman. But he had found Looks Again two years ago, and they had been reasonably happy together since. Of course, his annual trips into Taos helped, since she was shed of him for the summer.

Chardonnais had not thought of Looks Again since he had seen Marie for the first time. Now that he had, he realized that he missed her more than he was willing to admit.

Sitting there in the saloon, he suddenly laughed. This was, he figured, just one of his frequent bouts of melancholy. Be that as it may, there was something tremendously appealing about Looks Again and an Indian woman's way of treating a man.

Then thoughts of beautiful Marie—she of the delicate features and soft, pleasing perfume—overcame him. With a grin for the future that lay before him, he headed home.

6

IT WAS THE MORNING OF his wedding, and Chardonnais was beginning to have doubts—serious doubts—about it all. That huge scar marring his torso was more than just a scar. It was a diary of his past. It was not the only scar he had, not by a long shot. A man didn't spend ten, eleven years in the harsh environment of the Rocky Mountains and not pick up battle scars. Each scar on his body had its own story to tell.

Chardonnais touched the one high up on his chest, on the left side. He had taken an arrow that time, against some Crows that were hellbent on stealing horses from the three partners. That had been—what—seven, maybe eight years ago, he thought. The dates were beginning to blend together. He had saved Early's life that time, taking an arrow in the shoulder that would have pierced his friend's heart. Nothing much but a simple thank-you was needed, or made. It was always that way. The three knew each other so well, had been together so long, that everything became almost rote to them. Each had saved the other dozens of times. It was the way they were. No thank-you had to be made or great protestations of undying gratitude. They simply did as best they could at helping themselves—and their partners—survive.

Suddenly he realized that that was the thing he missed most being back east here. Marie's love, Bouchard's benevolence, his parents' care, his siblings' consideration, none of it amounted to anything when compared with the brotherhood and unqualified bond he had with Ezra Early and Abe Rawlins. The three men were as different as the night from the day, yet all of a same mind on some things.

The loss of their friendship would be the worst pain—maybe the only one—brought by his marriage to Marie Bouchard. He might never see the two partners again. And if he did, their relationship would change drastically. He would be the odd man out.

Chardonnais sat on the edge of the bed and pulled out his small clay pipe. He filled the small bowl and tamped the tobacco down with a hard, grimy thumb. He used the candle to light it, and he sat and puffed while he thought.

Can I really give all that up? he wondered. Then he thought, *But what am I giving up? And what am I gaining in all this?*

He tried to look at it dispassionately, which for him was nigh onto impossible. He was passionate about everything in life, good and bad. He could love with as much energy and passion as he could hate. Still, he wanted to look at his life calmly and rationally.

Let's see now, he mused, clouds of smoke ringing his head as he puffed furiously. He would lose a wife, Looks Again. She was a good woman, well practiced in what she needed to be. On the other hand, Marie Bouchard knew the arts of civilized women as well as her Ute counterpart knew the mountain arts. Marie was the kind of woman almost guaranteed to help a man advance in society. Trouble was, so was Looks Again. It all depended on what society one wanted to advance in. François Bouchard was a pillar of his society, but Strong Bear was as well respected in the Uncompahgre country as Bouchard was here in St. Charles.

Then there was the matter of friends. Chardonnais had two friends out in the mountains who had risked their lives to save his and would do so again without thought. He had no one even close to that in St. Charles. It was possible, he figured, that if he spent ten years or so here, he might make alliances as strong as the one he had with Early and Rawlins. But even if he did, it would be different. There was something about sharing danger, of comforting each other in times of serious trouble, of facing starving times together that made not just a strong bond, but a powerful and special one. He knew he could never find that in any civilized place.

Which was another problem. He wasn't at all sure he wanted to live in "civilization." It was, as he had told Bouchard earlier, too crowded, too full of hustle and bustle. He was a man who, despite his fiery nature and fun-loving soul, often preferred the solemnity of the mountains, or at least the easygoing life in Taos and other Spanish towns. St. Charles, or even St. Louis, had nothing to compare with Taos. Not the food, not the openness of the women, not the festivals. Nothing.

Chardonnais was in a real quandary now. As he toted it up the benefits of being up in the mountains far outweighed the benefits of living here in St. Charles. If it were not for Marie, there would be no contest. But Marie certainly was a powerful incentive to stay here, get married, and raise a brood of children.

A rap on the door broke his concentration, which he figured was all for the better right at the moment. "*Entrez,*" he said.

His brother Jacques entered and grinned. "Only an hour and a half," he said. "You'd better hurry." He suddenly asked, "Everything all right, Lucien?"

Chardonnais nodded. "I suppose." He couldn't help but think what Early or Rawlins would say to him on such an occasion. They would rib him unmercifully and lewdly, and he would give back as good as he got. But here, with his own brother, all he got was, "Only and hour and a half. You better hurry, *mon frère.*"

"You certainly don't seem all right," Jacques said, coming farther into the room. "Something I can help with?" he asked, concerned.

"No," Chardonnais said quietly. He was having another dose of melancholy and knew it would pass sooner or later of its own accord.

"You having second t'oughts?" Jacques asked with a knowing smile. "I did when I was getting married."

Chardonnais nodded. "*Oui.* Second t'oughts." How mundane a phrase, he thought.

"Just wait until you get to de church and see your beautiful Marie. Your doubts'll be gone in a second."

"I hope so," Chardonnais said insincerely.

"Dere's more to dis dan second t'oughts, no?"

Chardonnais nodded. "*Oui.*"

"Would you like to talk about it? I'll listen."

"I don't know as if you'd be able to help me anyway, Jacques."

"No harm in trying den, is dere?"

"I suppose not." He sighed and placed his pipe on the table near the bed. It had gone out anyway, and he didn't feel like lighting it again. "I t'ink I am giving up too much to marry Marie and stay here," he said flatly.

"Mais non!" Jacques said, shocked.

"Mais oui," Chardonnais insisted. "I have friends out dere who are . . ." He couldn't really explain it. "Dey are special somehow. Closer to me dan you and all de others."

"Dat's reasonable. You've been with dose men a long time. You'll build friendships here."

"I'm not sure I want to," Chardonnais said sourly.

"Don' say such t'ings," Jacques said, almost horrified.

Chardonnais shrugged. "I should not have brought dis up," he said flatly.

"Dat's what brothers are for, eh."

"And friends."

"What does dat mean?" Jacques asked, seeming a little angry.

"Because friends—good friends like I have in de mountains—dey would try to help me instead of sitting dere and acting superior and saying notting dat I don't already know."

"I'm dat bad?"

"Oui. It's no reflection on you, Jacques. You are saying what you t'ink I want to hear. Or what you t'ink I should hear. I have been away so long dat everyt'ing here is strange to me now. I was wrong to even come back."

"Mais non!" Jacques calmed down a little. "You can tell me what is troubling you, Lucien. I'll listen and try to advise well, not just tell you what I t'ink you should do."

Chardonnais looked at Jacques. It had been a long, long time since he had counted on anyone but himself—and his two partners. But he was not a man to hide anything either. He shrugged and swiftly explained his thoughts and feelings.

When Lucien had finished, Jacques exclaimed, "Mon Dieu. You have made a jumble of dis."

"*Oui*," Chardonnais acknowledged. "De question now is what I should do about all dis."

"You want me to tell you what I t'ink you should do?"

"*Oui*. It is why I say all dese t'ings to you."

"God help me," Jacques said, "because dere will be hell to pay from many folks, but I t'ink you should pack your t'ings and get yourself back to de mountains wit' your Indian woman and your two *bons amis*."

Chardonnais looked at his brother in shock and surprise. He had never expected Jacques to say such a thing. Maybe to postpone the marriage a little or something, but not that. "Is dat what you really t'ink?"

"*Oui*. Do you t'ink I'd lie?"

Chardonnais laughed hollowly. "Who knows?"

Silence grew and spread, until Jacques couldn't stand it any longer. "Did you get dat from de Indians?" he asked, pointing to the huge scar on his brother's chest.

Chardonnais nodded. "Goddamn Arapaho he was. I t'ought I was gone under—dead—dat time. But my friend Ezra, he patch me up good as new."

Jacques laughed a little. "Not quite good as new," he said, "but at least you're alive."

"*Oui*. And all because of Ezra and Abe. If dey hadn't come back so soon and run dem damn red devils off, I would've been made wolf bait of *vite!*"

Jacques laughed, too, and felt a sort of relief. He had been tiptoeing around his brother, thinking him some sort of savage. But he realized that Lucien wasn't all that different than when he had left. Not deep down, anyway. He looked at his brother in a new light.

"You really belong out dere in dem mountains, *mon frère*," Jacques said. "*Oui*. You don't belong here wit' all dese people and such t'ings."

Chardonnais nodded. He had known it all along but had not wanted to admit it to himself. "Well, den," he said, "I better get to Marie's house and tell her, eh?"

Jacques shook his head and got a conspiratorial look in his eyes. "*Mais non!* You must just go. Flee. If you go talk to her now, you'll change your mind and stay here. Den you'll be miserable de rest of your life."

Chardonnais nodded. "And if I leave now, people will say I ran away."

"So? None of dese people will ever see you out dere, and if you spend another ten or eleven years out dere before you come back here again, most everyone will have forgotten about it."

"You're *très fou,* very crazy," Chardonnais said.

"Perhaps," Jacques said. "But you had better get moving, eh? Before dey all come looking for you. I will stall dem if I can."

Chardonnais nodded again and held out his hand. He and his brother shook hands. "*Merci, mon frère,*" Lucien said. "*Merci bien.*"

"*De rien.*" Jacques felt very odd. Here he was, the older of the two, and yet he thought himself somehow childlike around Lucien. It was, however, a good feeling to have been able to help his brother.

Lucien turned and was already tossing his meager belongings in a buckskin sack.

"I'll go out and try to head off trouble, Lucien," Jacques said. "So I t'ink dis is de last time we see each other, eh?"

Lucien stopped and looked at his brother. He nodded. When Jacques left, Lucien went back to his frantic packing. He noticed on the mantel clock that the wedding was supposed to begin in less than forty-five minutes. He stepped up his pace.

Twenty minutes later he was in his buckskins and was carrying his bag of belongings toward the livery stable. And ten minutes beyond that, he was galloping out of St. Charles. He stopped once and looked back, knowing he had made the right decision.

Still, he would miss Marie something awful. Then he smiled a little. She would have Michel LeBeau to pour out her sorrows to.

7

CHARDONNAIS FOLLOWED THE Missouri from St. Charles, moving quickly. He wanted to get away from the city, lest some of Marie's offended relatives come looking for him. If he didn't miss Marie and hate the thought of having hurt her like this, it might've been funny.

He was also in a rush because he wanted to get back out west. It was near the first of September already. Early and Rawlins would've left Taos long ago and would be working their way through the San Juans toward Strong Bear's village. The Utes would be making their fall hunt right about now. There most likely was even some snow high up in the Uncompahgre country.

Chardonnais had a long ride ahead of him, maybe two thousand miles of prairie and mountain country, past a dozen or so hostile Indians tribes, past thousands upon thousands of migrating buffalo, through lands infested with grizzly bears and rattlesnakes.

None of that mattered, though. He was happy to be back on the trail. The only thing that did bother him about it all was the length of time it would take. At times like this, he wished he had the capabilities of a bird. As a hawk, he could sail out to Strong Bear's village in a week, maybe less. But on horseback, it would take several weeks.

By pushing himself, Chardonnais made it to Independence a couple of days after leaving St. Charles. He figured that most, if not all, of the wagon trains heading for Santa Fe had left already, but there was always a chance of hooking on with a late one. He almost wished not, since that would take a mighty long time. He could make a lot better time on his own. But with a wagon train, he would have ample protection.

Another possibility at Independence was in seeing some of the other mountaineers. Four or five experienced mountain men could ride through most of the Indian country pretty much unmolested.

He was in luck, finding three men he knew from the mountains just about ready to leave. They, too, wanted to get to the trapping grounds before it was too late. So, in the company of Jacques Ducharme, a trader Chardonnais had known for some years, and Roscoe Shea and Jed Boatwright, whom he knew only casually, Chardonnais rode out.

The four were experienced travelers, and they rode in silence for the most part. They made their camp the same way. There was no fuss, no trouble. They stopped at a mutually agreeable time. Each men did some of the chores that needed doing. All four had someplace to get to, and each wanted to get to it as quickly as possible, so they were not disposed to sitting around the fire yarning, as they might have at other times.

At the Crossing of the Arkansas, Chardonnais and Boatwright kept following the Arkansas River.

Ducharme and Shea crossed it, taking the Cimarron Cutoff, heading for Santa Fe.

With just the two of them, Chardonnais and Boatwright were a little more loose with their words. They might sit and jaw for half an hour or so before calling it a day. They chatted little while riding.

"You're that crazy Frenchman who rides with Ezra somebody and Abe somebody, ain't you?"

"Crazy?" Chardonnais asked with a smile. He sighed. "You're not de first to say such a t'ing to me. *Oui*. Ezra Early and Abe Rawlins and me have been casting our traps together for some time now."

"Actually, Mr. Chardonnais, all I've heard about you and your two friends is good. Y'all have a hell of a reputation in the mountains."

Chardonnais nodded. "We have worked hard for dat. And you?"

"I come out only a couple, three years ago. With the Company."

"I spit on de Company," Chardonnais said.

"Them critters don't shine with me no more, either," Boatwright said with a chuckle. "That's why I run out on 'em," he added sheepishly.

"A good t'ing you done dere, hoss. You got enough supplies to make de season?"

"Ain't sure. I'm a mite shy on some things. But this ol' chil'll make do."

Chardonnais smiled. He liked the younger man's attitude. He and his two partners often felt the same. "Where're you headed?"

"I'll know when I get there," Boatwright said with another laugh.

"You better get dere soon before winter comes along and takes a big bite out of your ass."

"I've had that happen before, too," Boatwright said

more solemnly. "What were you doin' back east? If you don't mind me askin', of course."

"I had dis crazy notion to visit my family."

"Don't sound like a crazy notion to me."

"It was crazy once I got dere and found I had notting in common wit' dem people. I missed de high mountains."

"It does have a special pull on a man at times, don't it?" Boatwright offered.

Chardonnais nodded.

Several days later the two men spent the night at a rickety little log post at the confluence of Fountain Creek and the Arkansas. The trading post was run by William Bent for the company owned by him, his brother Charles, and Ceran Saint Vrain. Chardonnais knew all three partners in the company.

In the morning, Chardonnais sat with Bill Bent in one room. "Think you can spare some goods, on credit?"

"For you?" Bent asked, surprised. "I thought Ezra and Abe'd have all what you need."

"Dey do. It's for dat ol' hoss rode in here wit' me. He says he lit out owing de Company and is tryin' to make it on his own."

"Hell"—Bent laughed—"if it helps screw the Company, I'm all for it."

"I'll make good on it if he don't."

Bent nodded.

When Chardonnais and Boatwright rode out two hours later, Boatwright had a pack mule loaded with enough supplies to last him the winter, if husbanded some.

"You have any idea of what you want to do, boy?" Chardonnais asked as they rode.

"Not really," Boatwright answered. "Maybe I can

latch on with some old-timers who don't mind havin' a youngster about their camp."

"You can t'row in wit' me and my friends," Chardonnais said flatly. He wasn't sure his friends would agree to it. He wasn't even sure Boatwright was useful enough to have along. Still, the young man had the makings of a good man in the wilderness.

"I can't ask that," Boatwright protested.

"You didn't ask. I asked you."

"I'd be honored, Mr. Chardonnais."

"De first t'ing you have to do is stop all dis calling me Mr. Chardonnais. I am Lucien. It's a good name and you should use it, eh."

"Yessir."

"Just one t'ing. If my friends, dey don't want no company, den you'll be on your own."

Boatwright shrugged and nodded. "I'd be no worse off than I am now, I guess. It's a deal."

Chardonnais was pushing both horses and both pack mules now, wanting to catch Rawlins and Early as soon as possible. He and Boatwright began working across the Sangre de Cristos, with snow falling harder, in big, soft wet flakes that piled up quickly.

"I'll be glad when we get across these goddamn Sangre de Cristos," Boatwright complained.

"You won't say dat when we get over dem and den we have to cross de San Juans, which are bigger."

"Oh, shit," Boatwright groaned. "Maybe I should've took a job in Independence instead of comin' out here like a damn fool."

"You knew what you were doing."

"True, but I gotta have somethin' to complain about."

"*Merde,*" Chardonnais muttered.

The worst part of the journey, at least for

Boatwright, was coming through Wolf Creek Pass. To him the land just continued to rise and rise and rise, as if it would never end. Then it tumbled down just as sharply into a gentle valley. That was not the end of the San Juans, however, as they had several more passes to make it through before Chardonnais turned them north roughly along the course of the Animas River.

More than a month after he had ridden out of St. Charles, he came on a Ute camp at a place of hot springs. It was Strong Bear's village, and Ezra Early and Abe Rawlins were there.

"Well, good goddamn Jesus," Rawlins drawled, "would ye look at this. Goddamn little frog fart comes a-wanderin' in here ages after we're supposed to have set out traps. Just moseys in like he ain't got a care in the goddamn world. Christ, I ought shoot the little bastard."

"Don't do that," Early piped up. "It'd be a hell of a waste of good powder and ball."

"*Mes amis!*" Chardonnais exclaimed as he slid off his horse. "It's good to see you, even if you two are crude and stupid."

The three embraced for a moment; then Rawlins asked, "Who's your friend there, froggie?"

"Dis is Monsieur Jed Boatwright. Jed, dese are my two great friends, Ezra Early and Abe Rawlins."

As Boatwright slid off his horse and extended his hand, he took stock of the two men, as they were doing to him. He was a little surprised. He had expected to see two giants or something, even though Chardonnais was a small man.

Both were big men, no doubt, with wide chests and shoulders and slim waists. A wad of tobacco bulged in Early's right cheek. His thick, curly, dark brown hair cascaded out from under a felt hat and down onto the broad shoulders. Except for a little stubble, he was clean shaven. He had faded gray eyes and might have been handsome were it not for his mashed-flat nose and a somewhat distorted left cheekbone.

Early wore a faded shirt of plain osnaburg. His pants were fringed buckskin—dark, smoky, greasy, bloody, filthy buckskin. There was a single tall eagle feather in his high-crowned hat and he wore heavy moccasins. Two big flintlock pistols were stuck in the wide leather belt, each held in place by a thin piece of iron that formed a clip. A powder horn and shooting bag hung over his right shoulder and rested against his left hip. Another buckskin pouch dangled at the other side. He had a tomahawk jammed into his belt at the small of his back, and a large knife in a beaded sheath hung from the belt at his left hip. A rawhide thong around his neck held a heart-shaped piece of leather, through which was stuffed a small clay pipe.

Rawlins was also a big, rangy American with broad shoulders, slim waist, no behind to speak of, and long, powerful legs. His long, dour face bore some resemblance to a sad hound dog's. Under his low-crowned felt hat—which he wore in the field; for a spree in Taos, he wore a sombrero—a thick mane of wheat-colored hair reached to his shoulders. He wore a fat mustache that dropped around his slim lips and hung off the points of his square chin. Otherwise he was clean shaven.

Unlike the others, Rawlins wore boots instead of moccasins and spurs that had huge rowels. The rest of his costume was almost identical to Early's: fringed buckskin pants and cloth shirt. He wore a knife in a plain, hard-leather case hanging on the left side of his wide leather belt, just in front of a pistol. A matching pistol was on the other side and there was a tomahawk in his belt at the small of his back.

Early and Rawlins shook hands with Boatwright. The young man was a lot like the two, only younger. He was fairly tall and lean, but he had a raw, unpolished look about him. His dark brown eyes looked hungry and determined. His short-cropped black hair was shaggy and unkempt—something that did not put off the three mountain men. He was also unshaven, but that was to be expected on the trail. He was poorly clad in buckskin pants that were pocked with holes, boots that were long past their prime, and a linsey-woolsey shirt that had seen better days.

"What's he doin' here?" Rawlins asked bluntly.

"We were riding de trail together. He run out on de Company and needs work. I t'ought maybe he could work wit' us for de wintair." Chardonnais paused. "But I told him he could do so only if you two shits say it was all right."

8

"WHAT THE HELL'S GOT INTO ye, Lucien?" Rawlins asked in mock anger. The two, along with Early, were in Rawlins's lodge. Rawlins's wife—Scatters the Clouds —worked quietly in the background, watching over their four-year-old son, Standing Eagle. The three partners were gathered around the fire debating the addition of Jed Boatwright to their trapping expedition this year.

"What de hell's got into you?" Chardonnais responded, his anger real.

"Jesus goddamn Christ, Lucien," Rawlins went on. "The three of us hosses was always enough, dammit. We don't need no goddamn others." He winked at Early.

"Oh, and so I am in de wrong here, eh?" Chardonnais demanded. "Ah, *oui*. It must be. All de time, I'm de wrong one. It ain't right. *Merde*. It sure ain't." He was working himself into a fine fettle.

"Pipe down, ye goddamn little frog fart, ye," Rawlins said with a chuckle. He was generally amused by Chardonnais's tantrums and wide mood swings.

56

"I won't pipe down, you long-legged sack of buzzard shit," Chardonnais ranted. "Always make de fun of me, try to make my life hell. *Merde!* I don' know why I put up wit' de likes of you."

"Goddamn, Lucien," Early snapped, growing somewhat irritated, "calm down before your eyes pop out." When Chardonnais stopped muttering, though his eyes still steamed, Early asked, "All right, Abe, what's your problem in lettin' Jed ride along with us?"

"Well, now, I never said I had a problem," Rawlins responded in a long drawl. "I never did. All this chil' did was to ask froggie there why he wanted that ol' hoss cuttin' into our doin's. He still ain't answered."

"Well, Lucien? What do you say?" Early said, turning toward the French-Canadian.

Chardonnais shrugged. "He was a good hand on de trail. I t'ink maybe he'll be good at trappin', too, eh. He don' have to cut into how many plews we take. *Mais non.* You ever t'ink . . . No, you don' ever t'ink. Let me say it another way. Did you ever consider de chance he might take more plews dan you, Abe? Is dat what your problem is, eh? You figure dat chil's going to outshine you somet'ing fierce in makin' de beavair come?" Chardonnais grinned insolently.

"Eat shit, you little fart. Ol' Jed out there couldn't wipe the sweat off my balls in makin' beaver shine, you son of a bitch."

"I t'ink I hit de nail on de head," Chardonnais said almost gleefully.

"Bah," Rawlins snapped. "I've took enough of your insults, you little turd. One more and I'm gonna mash your fat ass into a ball and toss you in the river." A small smile tugged ever so slightly at his lips, making the long, drooping mustache wriggle a little.

"Well, den you better do it soon, eh. I got to go see my Looks Again before I have de big problem!" He laughed, rolling back from his buttocks onto his spine. All traces of his anger were gone.

"Good goddamn," Rawlins said with a little grin. "Somebody ought to whack that thing off and give it to somebody knows how to use it."

"Maybe you, eh?" Chardonnais responded as he rocked back up into a sitting position. "You got so small a pecker you can't even hump a flea. Maybe I give you half of mine, eh? Den you'll be t'ree times de man you are now." He was laughing so hard that tears were rolling from his eyes into the tangle of beard and mustache.

"Christ, you're a disgustin' son of a bitch, Frenchie," Rawlins said with a laugh.

Early let the laughter run its course before saying, "We still ain't decided whether we want to bring Boatwright along with us."

"Well, I still ain't certain," Rawlins said. "We don't know much about him."

"We took on Ezra's friend Bart not so long ago," Chardonnais countered.

"True, but Bart didn't come with us into the mountains neither."

"*Oui*," Chardonnais conceded. "But he did not want to. If he did, we would've had to teach him everyt'ing. But Jed, now, he's been in de mountains a couple year. We don' have to teach him notting."

"Nothing?" Rawlins said with a half grin. "You think that young hoss out there knows every goddamn thing he needs to know?"

"*Merde*," Chardonnais muttered, casting his eyes heavenward. Then he looked at Early. "Why do we put up wit' dis fool, eh?"

"He's always good for givin' us a laugh," Early said, chuckling. "And he's easy to make fun of. Hell, face it, Frenchie, ol' hoss there gives us a heap of amusement, and he don't take much care a'tall. No more'n a pet buffler anyway."

"You two assholes're hopeless," Rawlins snapped. But the others could see he was not serious. He sighed. "Despite my bein' so put upon, I'll concede to ye. If you two ol' niggurs don't mind him along, I reckon I can put up with him."

"Den it's up to you, Ezra," Chardonnais said.

"I suppose havin' him along won't put this ol' chil' out none." He paused a moment. "But listen to me, Lucien. You best tell him that if he tries any buffler shit with us, he'll be made wolf bait of directly."

"I'll tell him," Chardonnais said seriously. "And if he turns out to be trouble for us, I'll put him under myself."

Early and Rawlins nodded.

"Speaking of our old friend Bart, how is he?" Chardonnais asked. "You did see him in Taos, didn't you?"

Early shook his head. "Ol' hoss took himself back to New York."

"And left dat pretty young lady of his behind all alone?" Chardonnais asked, eyes wide in surprise.

"Hell, no," Early said with a laugh. "Took her with him. They got married, went on down to Mexico, and got themselves a sailing ship."

"I'll be damned. He coming back?"

"Don Francisco says so. The don said he'll make sure Bart has some work when he gets back. I think he paid for the trip, too, so's Bart can show off his purty young wife to those devils back in New York."

Chardonnais nodded. Then he grinned and stood. "Now, monsieurs," he said grandly, "I have some business to see to!" The laughter of his two friends rang in his ears long after he had left the lodge, heading toward his own.

Looks Again was expecting him, had been since he arrived in camp. She was surprised he had counciled with his two friends before coming to see her, but she knew that as soon as he was done with business, he would come to her. She had watched for him to leave Rawlins's lodge. When he did, she quickly shucked all her clothes and then waited for him, naked, on their buffalo-robe bed.

Chardonnais stormed into his lodge and smiled widely when he saw that Looks Again was waiting for him. Within seconds, he had skinned off his pants, sash, accoutrements, and shirt and was pumping furiously atop her.

Looks Again bore it stoically, knowing that very soon after he was done this time, there would be another time—a long, patient time, one that would meet all her needs.

That he was concerned about her needs was one of the reasons Looks Again loved Lucien Chardonnais. Yes, he could be troublesome with the frequency of his sexual demands, but still, no Ute warrior would be as considerate a lover, let alone as considerate a husband. Looks Again had heard from others about Chardonnais's sexual needs, and how annoying they could be. But she had not found him to be overbearing. She thought that the other Ute women with whom Chardonnais had mated were maybe not women enough for him. Perhaps, she had thought often, they were the cause of the trouble, perhaps always asking for foofaraw and refusing his needs. And she knew that some of those women were offended by his beard and the thick mat of chest hair. Looks Again had been surprised and a little scared when she had first encountered his chest hair, but she found it didn't bother her much.

Chardonnais grunted softly a few times, and then his back bowed as he reached his climax. Finally he sank down on Looks Again's breasts, breathing hard. With a small smile that he could not see, Looks Again stroked his long, thick black hair with slim, dusky fingers. She could feel him shrinking inside her, but that, too, would change soon.

And indeed it did. Within ten minutes, she began wriggling her buttocks a little. Chardonnais pushed up on his hands. "*Ah, ma chère,*" he said with a mischievous grin. "It is time for you now, eh?" He answered his own question. "*Mais oui!*" He bent his head and kissed her hard.

When they finished, Looks Again was sated. With a warm, pleased smile on her lips, she fell asleep entwined in her man's arms.

Chardonnais was aroused again the moment he awoke. Looks Again smiled to herself. She had awakened a little while ago and encouraged his arousal, unbeknownst to him. But she did not help him too much. Not yet. She wanted that full, breathless feeling that comes with being completely fulfilled.

When he came awake, Chardonnais was more than willing to help his woman achieve that goal.

Afterward, both still nude, Chardonnais and Looks Again ate a large, filling breakfast. Then with a big sigh, he kissed Looks Again gently. "I must go, *ma chère,*" he said softly. "Much as dat t'ought displeases me."

He dressed and stepped outside. There was a cool bite in the wind, but it was pleasurable. Much better than the humid heat of St. Charles. And it was much better here than in the overcrowded city. A man should

be in a place like this. There was something unnatural
in living all bunched up together like city dwellers did.
No, this was where he belonged, not in St. Charles.

A momentary sadness overtook him. Marie
Bouchard had been some woman, the loveliest he had
ever seen, white, red, or brown. But he knew now he
would have been miserable there. And, sooner or later,
he would have fled, heading back to these mountains—and maybe to Looks Again.

Looks Again was as special in her own way as
Marie was in hers. She was not as beautiful as Marie, it
was true, but she was quite pleasing to the eye. She
was fiery and full of spirit. Her skin was a shining copper color, and she had full breasts rising proudly over a
firm stomach. Her legs seemed longer than they were
because of her slimness, something not common
among her people.

Other things, too, attracted him to her. Many
were things he could not put a finger on. Perhaps
the way she looked as she bent over the cook fire,
perhaps the sunset in her dark eyes, perhaps the
always lurking smile. He could not say for sure that
he loved her, but if he didn't, it was the next thing to
it. He was happy with her, and wanted to keep her
with him always. She would help him forget Marie
Bouchard.

He smiled at the pleasant thoughts as he walked to
where Jed Boatwright had set his little camp. The
young man was sitting over a small fire waiting for coffee to warm. He had a threadbare blanket around his
thin shoulders.

Boatwright grinned as the French-Canadian
walked up. "Mornin', Mr. Chardonnais," he said, trying
to be chipper. He grimaced a little as the older man
squatted by the fire. "I'd offer you some coffee, Mr.

Chardonnais, but I ain't got but about one cup left in the pot, and that ain't warm yet."

Chardonnais shrugged and nodded. "Tell you what, hoss, let's go on to my lodge. Looks Again's got coffee made, and dere's always a bit of food ready."

Boatwright's eyes lit up. "I don't want to put you out none."

"You won't. Come."

Soon they were sitting at Chardonnais's fire, leaning on willow backrests. Chardonnais sipped a cup of coffee. Boatwright had gotten one cup of coffee and poured it straight down his gullet, then politely asked for more. It was poured, and then he was given a bowl of hot buffalo stew.

Boatwright tasted the latter, and his eyes grew wide. "By the sweet Jesus," he exclaimed. "This is nearabout the best stew I ever tasted."

Looks Again beamed but said nothing. Chardonnais smiled.

When Boatwright had finished that bowl of stew and was working on another, Chardonnais said, "My partners, dey say it's all right you come wit' us."

"Really? Hell, that's great," the young man said truthfully. Indeed, it had even diverted his attention from the stew for a few moments.

"*Oui*. But I tell you dis here and now, monsieur. If you do anyt'ing against me or against my friends, you will be gone beavair right away. You understand dis?"

"I screw up you're gonna plant me in the ground," Boatwright said with a smile.

"*Mais oui*," Chardonnais said, then paused. "Dese men are de best friends a man can have. You do your job and help out when and where you can, dey might become your good friends, too. But I won't hesitate not one minute to kill you if you turn against dem."

Boatwright looked into Chardonnais's dark, commanding eyes and he was not sure if he liked all he saw there. He nodded. "I ain't aimin' to paint my face black against none of ya, Mr. Chardonnais. God's truth."

"Den t'ings're all set." The trapper grinned widely, the humor back in his eyes. "Except for one t'ing."

"What's that?" Boatwright was already attacking another bowl of stew.

"You need a woman."

9

"A WOMAN," BOATWRIGHT SAID, almost to himself. "Damn, that sure as hell'd be nice." Then he sighed deeply. "But I ain't got enough foofaraw for a fling with a woman before we pull out, much as I hate admittin' that."

"I'm not talking about a just-for-one-night woman," Chardonnais said. "You'll need a woman to cook for you and take care of your plews and make your clothes and such t'ings." He laughed. "And to keep you warm in de cold winter nights, eh."

"Hell and tarnation, Lucien, I got no horses to give her pa."

"Dere are ways to get around such a t'ing. Strong Bear and de other chiefs here, dey are good men, and will help us out."

"That's all well and good, Lucien, but I'd not feel comfortable with such a thing. Besides, you and your friends've been more than enough help already. I can do without a woman."

"De problem is dat we can't do without you having a woman."

"What the hell's that mean?" Boatwright asked, confused.

"We don't want you looking at our women during de long winter, eh. You got no woman and de rest of us do, dere might be problems."

"I never looked at it that way before," Boatwright acknowledged. "I know with the Company there was always so many boys that it didn't too often get to be a problem. The ones had Indians wives had their own little camp." He paused, thinking, then nodded. "But I can see how it could cause a heap of trouble with only four of us."

"*Bon.* You see t'ings clearly." He paused. "Now it's time for you to go. I'll see about dis—after I tend to some business." He winked, and Boatwright walked off.

Early in the afternoon Chardonnais presented a shy young Ute woman to Boatwright. "Dis is Blue Rattle," he said. "She's Looks Again's sister and Strong Bear's daughter. She's a good woman."

Boatwright nodded tentatively. He had experience with women, particularly Indian women, but this seemed different somehow. So cold-blooded. And the girl seemed so shy. This would all take some getting used to. He smiled at Blue Rattle, trying to make her a little more comfortable.

She smiled back a little, but kept her eyes downcast. She was uneasy with this. After all, this young man had not given her father any horses; nor had he come around courting her. She had to admit, though, that he was a rather handsome man—for one with skin so pale. He was poorly dressed, however, and that was not a point in his favor. She sighed. She had no choice in the matter, at least not right now. She would see what kind of husband he turned out to be. If he was a poor one, she could always eject him from her lodge. Of course, in a winter camp with just the four white men and their wives, that might be a little troublesome, but she would wait and see. After all, he might not turn out to be too bad a mate.

"You speak any English?" Boatwright asked.

Blue Rattle looked blank.

"I don't speak no Ute," he tried.

"You better use de sign language, eh," Chardonnais encouraged. "Once you get her feet moving in de right direction, things'll be just fine. She has a lodge you two will use. You want her to set it up?"

Boatwright shrugged. "When're we leavin'?"

"Morning, I t'ink. Dis afternoon, me and de others want to use de hot springs here."

"They any good?"

"*Mais oui!* Dey can make you feel like a new man. De Utes've been using dem since time began, I t'ink. And dey are a healthy people."

"Would your friends mind if I was to join you at the hot springs?"

"No. Even if dey did, dere are enough of de springs dat you could keep away from dem."

Boatwright nodded. "Well, if she don't mind, I'd be obliged if Blue Rattle was to put up our"—how strange! he thought—"lodge here."

Chardonnais nodded. "Anyt'ing else?"

"Does she have a horse to tote the lodge and all?"

"*Oui.*" Chardonnais grinned. "You get de best of everyt'ing." He paused. "Well, I got a little business wit' Looks Again. After dat, me and de others're going to de hot springs." He headed off, his walk odd because of his bowed legs. But to any onlooker, he was a man who walked with confidence—almost to the point of arrogance.

He entered the lodge with a big grin on his face.

"Not again?" Looks Again asked with a laugh.

"*Mais oui!*" Chardonnais said with an enthusiasm that was natural to him.

"It's no wonder all those other women got rid of you," Looks Again said in Ute. But she was laughing.

"Ah," Chardonnais said with a shrug, "but now dey miss *le grand homme*. Come, *ma chère*. To de robes we go."

Across the camp a little way, Boatwright sat rather embarrassed as he watched Blue Rattle and some of her friends putting up the lodge that he and his new woman would soon occupy. He felt he ought to be helping somehow, but he knew that was not the Indian way. Not any tribe he had ever met anyway. He figured that if he offered her help, she would be treated as unworthy by her own people.

It did not take all that long, and soon enough he was moving his gear and meager supplies inside. Blue Rattle had disappeared with her friends right after the lodge was put up. Boatwright wondered where she went, but he decided not to worry about it just yet.

Blue Rattle returned soon, leading a horse to which a travois was attached. On the travois were her possessions. She quietly began bringing them into the tipi. On one of her trips Boatwright asked in sign, "Do you want me to help?"

She looked at him in surprise, then smiled and shook her head. With signs she said, "This is woman's work."

Boatwright nodded. Still feeling a little odd, he sat in the lodge, away from Blue Rattle's path. He watched her as she came and went, came and went. He decided he liked what he saw. Blue Rattle was short and slender. Her movements were lithe and graceful. Her face was a little flatter than Boatwright might have asked for had he had his druthers. Her hair was long and loose with a pitch-black sheen to it. Her voice was soft and melodious. Her buckskin dress was decorated with small tin cones, beads, and bits of shells, and was fringed along the hem and the yoke.

All in all, Boatwright figured, he had gotten the far better of this deal. He just hoped his new wife wouldn't hold that against him too much.

Before Blue Rattle had finished her chores, Chardonnais strolled up and called Boatwright. "Come, *mon ami,*" the ebullient French-Canadian shouted.

The two headed for the hot springs a hundred yards or so toward the east. Early and Rawlins were already there, as were a number of Utes, both men and women.

Without embarrassment, Chardonnais shucked his clothes and eased himself into one of the hot springs. "Ah, *très bon,*" he said with a delighted sigh. "*Très bon.*"

With a shrug, an embarrassed Jed Boatwright followed suit. "Hey, goddamn, this does feel good," he said with a little laugh.

"Now maybe you'll believe me when I tell you t'ings, eh," Chardonnais said with a chuckle.

"Well, just 'cause it feels good don't mean it does a body good."

"Dat might be true, but it does help. De Utes and mountaineers often have rheumatism and such. Dese waters take dose troubles away for a while."

"I might even believe that," Boatwright said with a laugh. "I'd heard some men from the Company say that, but I never had a chance to use these waters before."

Boatwright was feeling mighty jaunty when he climbed out of the waters and into his clothes. With

Chardonnais, he headed back toward the Ute camp. He self-consciously entered his lodge, not quite knowing what to expect.

Blue Rattle was there with two of her friends, who got up quickly and left. Blue Rattle sat there, not quite sure what she was supposed to be doing.

Boatwright had found himself quite aroused by the warmth of and the languor induced by the hot springs, and he wanted nothing more right at the moment than to toss Blue Rattle down and climb into her. But as uncouth as he might be, he was still too much of a gentleman to do something like that.

Seeing some pots on the fire, he pointed and instead asked in signs, "Food?" He felt like an idiot.

Blue Rattle nodded. "Are you hungry?"

"Yes. Very." He smiled, trying to make her more at ease, which, he hoped, would in turn make him more comfortable, too.

"Sit," Blue Rattle said as she stood. She got a horn bowl and with a horn ladle dipped some thick buffalo stew into the bowl, which she handed him. "Coffee?"

"Please." Boatwright found it mighty hard to talk in sign language with a bowl of stew in his hand, and he decided then and there that if this relationship was going to go anywhere, he was going to have to learn Ute, or Blue Rattle was going to have to learn some English. Both would be best, he figured after a moment's thought.

Using a horn spoon, he dug into the stew and promptly burned his mouth and tongue. He bellowed and spit the mouthful of food out, frantically waving his hand near his mouth.

Blue Rattle was horrified for a moment, thinking that her cooking was so bad that even a usually ravenous mountain man couldn't eat it. Then she realized what had happened. She giggled just a little. Then a little more.

"This ain't funny," Boatwright snapped.

Blue Rattle was laughing for real now, hiding her sweet laughter behind a small, slim hand.

Boatwright got caught up in it, and he forgot his anger. He started laughing, then said, "Well, I guess it is after all."

When he stopped laughing, he slurped up a more cautious mouthful of stew. He smiled. "It's very good," he said in English. When Blue Rattle looked blankly at him, he put the bowl down and signed, "It's very good," while saying it in English. He figured if one of them was going to have to learn another language, the learning might as well start now. He repeated it in English several times.

Blue Rattle said it, tentatively and heavily accented, but understandably.

Boatwright smiled warmly at her. When he finished eating, he lit a pipe and puffed away while sipping at a tin mug of coffee. Darkness had fallen and it would be time for sleep soon. He was still uncertain of how to approach Blue Rattle about it.

Blue Rattle relieved him of that duty. When she saw that Boatwright's pipe had gone out, she rose and took his hands and tugged him toward the robes. He did not resist, and before he knew it, he and Blue Rattle were naked and lying on the soft furs.

Boatwright lost most of his nervousness as he ran his hands over Blue Rattle's lean form. What little remained after that went away with an explosive, shuddering blast that shook him to the core.

"Damn, woman," he muttered breathlessly some time later. "God, that was good."

Blue Rattle could not understand his words, but

she understood the feelings. She was basking in a warm, rosy glow that she would never have thought could be instilled in her by a white man.

Just to be sure that it wasn't some kind of mistake, though, she encouraged Boatwright to make another attempt before too much time had passed. And when she went to sleep soon after, it was with the comforting feeling that she had not been wrong. She was also beginning to think that this forced marriage might not be all that bad after all.

For his part, Boatwright knew for certain now that he had gotten the better of this arranged marriage. He couldn't feel too bad about it, though, since he was determined to do as well by Blue Rattle as he could.

10

THEY MADE ONE HELL OF A procession moving out of the camp near the hot springs. They moved on down a narrow trail, one worn deep into the mountains by the passage of millions of feet and hooves. Because of the slimness of the trail, they rode in single file.

Ezra Early led off, eyes alert, senses wary. He was followed by his wife, Falling Leaf, and then their three-year-old daughter, Straight Calf, in a travois. Rawlins's woman, Scatters the Clouds, followed with their son Standing Eagle. The precocious four-year-old rode his own pony. Following the boy was Blue Rattle. Then came Looks Again, riding proudly. Behind her was the cavvyard of pack mules and extra horses, loosely herded by Chardonnais and Boatwright. Then came Rawlins. It wasn't so much that he really preferred to be a bit away from everyone else as that next to Early, he had the best senses. It seemed as if the two of them could almost smell danger coming.

They headed northwest, roughly following the Uncompahgre River, aiming for the Colorado River several long days' ride away. The day was cool, with a

light though biting wind blowing into their faces, hint-
ing of the wicked winter lying in wait for them.

The first night they simply made a quick camp.
The next night they made their camp near where Cow
Creek entered the Uncompahgre, and settled in for a
while to trap. They trapped the Uncompahgre and Cow
Creek, working wherever they found heavy beaver
sign. This area had pretty well been trapped out over
the past ten years or so, but the four men figured they
could bring in a few early prime plews.

They continued that pattern as they went along,
stopping for however many days it took them to trap
out a stream or pond.

"Good goddamn," Boatwright marveled one night
three weeks after they had left the hot springs, "you
boys can make beaver come with the best of 'em."

"Hell, did you ever doubt it, eh?" Chardonnais said,
tossing another bone out into the darkness. Two coyotes snarled and snapped at each other trying to get
the bone.

"Well," Boatwright said, scratching his stubbled
chin, "I didn't doubt you too much."

"Den why are you surprise, eh?"

"Because from what I've heard, this area's been
picked clean for years."

"*Oui.*"

"But you—we—are still pullin' out aplenty of
plews."

"What the hell'd you expect?" Early asked face-
tiously. "We're all upstandin', clean-livin', God-fearin'
niggurs. And so the Great Spirit above smiles on us."

"Jesus," Chardonnais snapped, "dat's about de
dumbest t'ing this chil' ever heard."

"Well, hell, Lucien," Rawlins drawled, "it sure as
shit ain't your talents bringin' them goddamn beaver

into our traps. Nor is it your sunny disposition. Hell, any goddamn beaver gets a good look at that ugly, hairy face of yours and he's gonna cache right off. Probably take all his kinfolk with 'im, besides."

"Yep," Early allowed. "Maybe we ought not to let that little fart anywhere near our traps no more. We can't afford lettin' them beavers get a look at him. Hell, it'd like to scare the shit out of them poor beaver just gettin' a whiff of him."

Chuckles began percolating in all the men, and a few stifled giggles came from Early's lodge, where the women and children had gathered while the men sat around a fire in Rawlins's lodge.

"You're just jealous, bot' of you, goddamn," Chardonnais growled in mock anger. "I can made de beaver come better dan either of you. Hah! I can do better dan either of you at anyt'ing."

"You sure as hell can sling the buffler shit better'n I can," Early said with a laugh.

They grew quiet then, thinking their own thoughts. Chardonnais and Early puffed on pipes; Rawlins had made himself a corn-shuck *cigarillo* and was smoking it.

Finally Rawlins filled the gap. "I hope to hell we start bringin' in plews that're primer than what we got us so far."

"They have been purty poor, ain't they?" Early commented.

"Another couple weeks and we'll be following de Colorado. Den we will find prime beavair."

"I hope so, Frenchie," Rawlins said quietly. "I sure as hell hope so."

"Well, now that you've pissed on this doin's," Early said as he rose, "I reckon it's time for this chil' to go close his eyes."

They continued on, moving every few days. They trapped McKenzie Creek, and Horsefly Creek and Spring Creek and any other creek or pond that had beaver. Soon their camps took on an almost comical look as nearly any available branch sprouted willow hoops holding beaver fur.

The women were kept busy with the plews. They did most of the curing, setting up and taking down the camp, making sure there was always firewood, that food was ready at any time, making jerky and pemmican for the swiftly approaching winter.

The men, on the other hand, worked the trap lines, acting as teams. They cared for the horses and mules, loaded and unloaded most of the supplies, hunted regularly, and kept a constantly wary eye out for enemies, of which there could be many, both two-legged and four.

A month and a half after leaving the hot springs, the small group reached the Colorado River.

"Where do we head from here, eh?" Chardonnais tossed out for debate that night.

Early shrugged. If any of the three partners could be called their leader, it was he. He was the most level-headed of them. Chardonnais went from high to low in the blink of an eye. He was passionate about life, about everything he did. Abe Rawlins, on the other hand, was taciturn. He seldom revealed anything about himself, preferring to get through life being laconic—unless he was making fun of Chardonnais and Early, particularly Chardonnais.

"I say we go up de Colorado," Chardonnais said firmly. "Dere are plenty of streams along de way to trap. And maybe we can winter near dose stinking hot springs."

"Up near North Park?" Early offered.

"*Oui.*"

"Along Willer Creek maybe?" Rawlins hinted.

"Dat shines wit' dis chil'," Chardonnais said.

As he had done since hooking on with the three partners, Boatwright kept quiet. He was the youngest, but more important, he was an outsider. As such, he knew his place. It was a little hard for him; like any other man with the gumption, gall, and talent to make his living trapping beaver in the high mountains, he had a healthy streak of arrogance. Still, he had enough sense to know he should keep his mouth shut for at least a while. He also had the sense to realize that if he just sat there and listened, he'd learn a hell of a lot more than he would if he was flapping his gums all the time, trying to get his two cents' worth in.

On the other hand, a well-placed question here and there often greased the wheels of education. Like the time he had so "innocently" asked, "You boys ever been to Pierre's Hole?"

"Well, I'll allow as we have," Early said with a nod.

"*Mais oui!*" Chardonnais added. "Plenty times. One time dere, we had us a tangle-up wit' de goddamn Blackfeets."

"They're bad Injuns, I hear," Boatwright offered, prompting the others again.

"Dose Blackfeets are de worst goddamn critters de good Lord ever put on dis earth. *Sacré bleu!*"

"Ol' frog fart there's right in that, boy," Rawlins said. "But this chil's counted coup on those red devils more'n once. Waugh! But I have. Them critters don't put no fear in me."

"Counted coup on dem, you say?" Chardonnais offered. "Like de time dem Blackfeets catch you and was about to poke you up de ass? Dat time? When me and Ezra, we had to come save your worthless ass. Dat's all me and Ezra ever do is pull your nuts out of de fire."

"At least I got some nuts to be put to the fire, you stump-suckin' little shit ball," Rawlins drawled.

"And dat's only because I give you some of mine dat one time—right after I saved your fat ass from dem Blackfeet buggerers."

Boatwright was considerably surprised at the byplay. Most men did such banter of a time, but with these three it was almost constant—or at least almost constant when they were sitting around without much to do. He knew, though, that this was all right only between the three; no outsiders were asked in. He thought that if he spent another five or six years in the mountains with these three, well, then they might just invite him to be a full partner in the activities. In the meantime, he would keep his own counsel. Except to ask innocuous questions. Like: "Well, what happened to him?"

"Abe was out hunting," Chardonnais said, "when a Blackfeets war party of what . . . six or seven warriors—"

"More like fifty, dammit," Rawlins growled.

"Fifty? Hah! More like two. Anyway, dem red devils caught ol' Abe dere and was having a little fun wit' him when—"

"Havin' some fun, my ass . . ."

"*Mais oui!* Dey was after your ass," Chardonnais said, laughing.

"Don't you go believin' that cow-humpin' little snot," Rawlins said to Boatwright. "This ol' chil' was just havin' hisself a time entertainin' them shit-eatin' peckerwoods. I was flingin' 'em every goddamn which way."

Chardonnais was rocking with laughter. "Den . . .

Den . . ." he gasped. "Den why did you need your pants down around your ankles if you was whipping dem Blackfeets, eh? Can you explain dat to our new friend?"

A smile cracked Rawlins's stiff countenance, then spread. "Because, goddamn you, Frenchie, I was gonna butt-hump those red critters and I was just softenin' 'em up a bit." He was laughing almost as hard as Chardonnais now.

Early had said nothing, but Boatwright could see that he was laughing too hard to say anything.

"You made some spectacle," Chardonnais gasped. "You were roaring and shouting and t'rowing dem Blackfeets around, all de time with your puny little pizzle flapping in de wind. . . ." He had to stop. He couldn't speak and laugh so much at the same time. His sides were hurting.

Finally some semblance of order returned, and the men drew in long drafts of air to settle their innards.

"Well?" Boatwright asked after a considerable silence.

"Well what?" Chardonnais asked.

"What happened, dammit?"

"We made wolf bait out of dem devils."

"All of 'em?"

"*Mais oui!*"

"How'd it get started?"

"Like I said, Abe was out hunting. Since he was alone, he didn't go too far from de camp. We heard him yelling and hollering, and we knew dis was poor bull for sure. Me and Ezra, we jump on our horses and ride like hell."

"They really got his pants down and were . . . were . . . trying . . ." Boatwright's face got very red, and he stammered to a halt.

"His pants was down all right," Early said. "Somehow in the ruckus, his belt come off and his pants fell down. He was some goddamn sight, I'll say to you, boy. Ol' hoss there was a-swingin' in the wind, just like Lucien said. He didn't think it was none too funny at the time, though, much as he'd like you to think he was bein' brave and all."

"I t'ink he was sweet on dem Blackfeets," Chardonnais said conspiratorially. "*Oui*. He t'ink he was going to impress dem wit' his little bug pecker. I don' t'ink he did, though."

"Hell if I didn't, goddammit," Rawlins said with a grin. "They was impressed enough with me that they weren't payin' no mind to you and ol' skunk humper over there," he added, pointing a long index finger at Early. "That's how you two got the upper hand on them red critters."

"Listen to dis load of buffalo shit, eh," Chardonnais said, looking at Early. "I say de next time he gets into trouble wit' de Blackfeets or any other Indians, we should let him handle it all by himself."

"That oughta teach him a goddamn lesson," Early said with a laugh. He paused. "Truth to tell, ol' Abe there had sent two of dem Bug's Boys over the divide already, but he was bein' some hard pressed by those devils. His pants droopin' down like they was had cut into his maneuverability a considerable much. And they wasn't too heedful of me and Lucien stealin' up. I got my two right off. Lucien had himself a wee bit of trouble with a big, unfriendly cuss of a Blackfoot, but soon took him out. Me and him took out another, and Abe got the last one. We raised us some hair that goddamn day."

Rawlins and Chardonnais nodded seriously.

Boatwright said nothing. He was impressed, and knew somehow that the truth had finally come out, despite all the foolishness and name-calling. Jed Boatwright decided he would not like to get in a fight against these men; alongside them against a common enemy, yes, but not as their foe.

He thought about it that night as he lay close to Blue Rattle, wondering just what he had gotten himself into. Then he smiled into the darkness. He had no complaints. These three men had gotten him a fine woman, they knew every beaver stream and pond in the Rockies, or so it seemed to him; he had taken more plews than he ever had before, and in places he had been told were trapped out years ago. No, he had nothing to complain about in having hooked up with Lucien Chardonnais, Ezra Early, and Abe Rawlins. He fell asleep happy.

11

THE SMALL GROUP PUSHED a little harder. Winter was pressing on them now, and the smaller creeks and ponds were beginning to freeze over. Once that happened to the bigger ones, they would have to stop most of their trapping until spring.

They also had to find a place to winter up, and make sure they were comfortable enough. The four men worked in two teams—Early and Rawlins as one; Chardonnais and Boatwright as the other. They would alternate their duties by days. One day, one team would run the trap lines, and then hunt. The next day those two would watch over the camp and take care of any duties there, while the other team went out.

Each day they shot animals for food, hides, and robes. Elk were plentiful and made good jerky and pemmican. Not as good as buffalo maybe, but still plenty good. The elk hides were excellent for clothing, too, and soon elk skins joined all the beaver furs hanging up around the camp, the women keeping busy tanning them. Deer—both whitetail and mule—were also plentiful. And in the mountain meadows, the men fre-

quently found buffalo and would take down as many as
they could reasonably process.

Their camps became a forest of beaver pelts, elk
skins, and buffalo hides. Meat racks, with all sorts of
meat adorning them, were ubiquitous around the
camps. The women were constantly busy. Since they
were all from the same band and had known each
other all their lives, they worked well in concert.

With all the fresh meat, the small group ate well,
since the choicest cuts would go into the cooking pot—
if not eaten raw—first off.

They had become accustomed to being the only
people within miles when Chardonnais whistled out an
alarm one morning. Early and Rawlins, who were down
in the creek not too far off, heard the telltale call of a
night owl. They stopped and looked up.

"Shit," Early said as he splashed toward the shore,
"I hope it ain't no goddamn Blackfoot Lucien's warning
us about."

"We'll know soon enough."

They trotted back toward the camp. When they got
near it, they melted into the brush alongside the small
clearing. Early answered Chardonnais in kind, letting
the French-Canadian know he and Rawlins were all
right and nearby. No one was visible in the camp, and
Early figured that Chardonnais had gotten everyone
into the trees. Rifles primed and ready, they waited.

A few minutes later a voice called out, "Hello, the
camp. Any ol' hosses in there?"

Chardonnais breathed a sigh of relief. He hadn't
been sure of what had tipped him off that someone was
coming. Nor did he worry about it. Someone was coming, he knew that much, and that was all he needed to
know for right now. He had whistled out his alarm and
then, with a determined-looking Boatwright, had qui-

etly shooed all the women and children out of the camp and into the trees and brush. When he heard a white voice, he was relieved.

Still, no one came out of the trees just yet. It might be a white voice, but just because a visitor was white didn't make him a friend.

A tall, reedy white man mounted on a large brown mule edged into the camp. He wore a short blanket capote, the hood of which was down. Buckskinned legs stuck out below the capote. One mittened hand was on the reins, the other on the rifle lying across the front of the saddle. The man hadn't shaved in some time.

Chardonnais grinned and stepped out of the trees. "*Bonjour, mon ami!*" he said, opening his arms wide in greeting.

Early and Rawlins moved out of the trees, too. "*Hola, amigo,*" Early said with a grin. "Come set a spell at the fire."

Chester Hamm nodded and grinned. He was a burly, barrel-chested man, with oversize ears and a nose to match. He was also a man who liked to have himself a spree, and it showed in the light coating of dissipation in his eyes and the latticework of veins on the large snout. "Them doin's shine with this chil'. Soon's I get my boys." He turned and rode off.

Chardonnais turned back and called, "It is all right now. Come."

Looks Again, Falling Leaf, Scatters the Clouds, and Blue Rattle edged warily out into the open, the two children crowded up behind them.

Moments later Hamm and five other men rode into the camp, along with seven Indian women, five half-breed children, and eight mules laden with supplies and plews. They all dismounted, tied their horses, and moved toward the one big fire outside in the camp.

"Who's this here chil'?" Hamm asked, pointing at Boatwright, just before he pulled out his tin cup and poured himself some coffee.

"Name's Jed Boatwright," Boatwright said with a firm nod.

"You hirin' on new folks, Ez?" Hamm asked.

Early shrugged. "He just sort of fell in with Lucien. He's showed himself to be a steady hand, so me'n Abe got no complaints."

Hamm nodded. "You know all my boys, don't ye?"

"It's been a time," Rawlins said. "Mayhap ye best introduce 'em again."

Hamm nodded. "I'm Chester Hamm," he said. Then he announced the others, pointing to each as he named him: Francis Murtaugh was red-faced, hard-eyed, and square of jaw; Wes Webster was a tall, thin, jovial man; Maurice LeClair was the opposite of Lucien Chardonnais, being tall and almost elegant looking; Auggie Burkhardt was a man of medium height and quite stout; and Emilio Morales was a broodingly suave man with eyes that darted all over, never seeming to rest.

All the men had filled their cups as they sat or squatted around the fire. The eleven women were busy serving up what food was cooked, and putting much of the day's fresh meat on the fire.

"Where's ol' Fitzsimmons?" Early asked.

"Casey's gone under."

"No," Early said, his disbelief echoed by Rawlins and Chardonnais. "How'd it happen?"

Hamm smiled a little and shook his head. "It was the goddamnedest thing this ol' niggur ever saw, I swear. Jesus." He paused for a sip of coffee, the liquid's heat bringing a steam cloud that hovered around his face. "We was up in the Wind Rivers a couple months ago. A storm caught us out in the open. We tried hustling down that mountain trail, a big-ass ol' cliff on one goddamn side and nothin' but a whole lot of down on the other. The rain wasn't too bad and stopped quick enough, but, Jesus, it was rainin' lightnin' down on us."

"This one of your tales, Chester?" Rawlins asked skeptically.

"By my mother's grave I swear it ain't, Abe." He shook his head again, still unable to believe it. "Wasn't shit we could do but move on ahead. Next thing we hear this great sizzlin' sound. I turn to look back and there's ol' Casey standin' there smokin'. Goddamn if that wasn't some sight. Then he got hit two, three more times by the lightnin'. Just fried that poor bastard. He was dead on his feet, you could see it in his eyes. Then he toppled down into the chasm."

"Jesus," Early breathed.

"Mon Dieu," from Chardonnais. He swiftly made the sign of the cross, something he hadn't done in years.

Rawlins sort of chuckled, and everyone turned to look at him as if he had lost his mind. "Goddamn, what a way to go under," he said, somewhat in awe. "Shit, that'd shine a heap more with this ol' chil' than the way many a feller's gone under."

The others mulled that over for a few moments, and then they all decided Rawlins was right. Being taken by fire from the sky was certainly better than freezing to death, or being mauled to death by a mad griz, or dying slow from a wound gone gangrenous.

"Hell, such a t'ing's cause for celebrating, eh," Chardonnais said. He got up and went to their stores and got a jug. Not to be outdone, Hamm got a jug from his supplies.

When the two men came back, before they could retake their places, Rawlins stood. "Well, I don't know about y'all," he drawled, "but this ol' hoss ain't gonna set out here freezin' his ass off while there's several lodges to hand."

They all trooped into Chardonnais's lodge, since it was the closest. They pulled off their capotes and buffalo or bear coats and tossed them aside, along with their mittens and gloves. Then they all resettled themselves around the fire in the lodge.

Rawlins grabbed the fur-wrapped earthen jug and pulled out the cork. He took a long swallow. "Damn, now that's better."

The women hustled in and out, carting in meat that had been set on the fire outside, and putting it on the fire inside. They also brought more wood in.

The men began eating as they talked, gobbling down large bites of meat. Pound after pound disappeared down their gullets. Every once in a while one would stop for a few minutes and grab a buffalo bone. With his tomahawk, he would whack open the bone and scoop out the thick marrow with a grimy finger. Then he would slather it on a piece of fat or just shove the finger in his mouth and lick off the marrow.

Ten mountain men could do quick destruction to two jugs of Taos Lightning, and more had to be pulled out before long. They soon ran out of fresh meat and began some of the partially dried buffalo and elk. The good food—and the whiskey, of course—helped oil the men's tongues.

One or another of them would start with, "I mind the time . . ." and then he would be off on a tale, expanding his own heroic role to enormous proportions.

Their frolics, though, left them all with pounding heads and sour, churning stomachs. Some of the women did not think it funny, and let their men know it—in the way of loud voices, as much clanging of pots as possible, and getting the children wound up enough so that they bounced around the camp screeching and laughing.

"*Mon Dieu,*" Chardonnais moaned, holding his head. He stumbled out of his lodge to get away from Looks Again. The cold bit deep into him, and he closed his capote. The cold air helped him a little, settling him. He tottered down toward the creek and sat heavily next to Early.

"Jesus goddamn Christ, Lucien," Early moaned, looking bleary-eyed at his friend.

"*Oui,*" Chardonnais agreed. "Why do we do dis?" he wondered aloud.

"Hell if I know, but I'm of a mind to not ever do it again."

"Dat'll be de day," Chardonnais responded less than enthusiastically.

"Tell you what, ol' hoss, we make a pact. Next time one of us gets the stupid goddamn notion of guzzlin' down a year's worth of Lightnin' at one sittin', the other's to shoot him down right then and there." The speech left him winded and with his head pounding more than ever.

"It's a deal," Chardonnais said, knowing that neither one of them meant it.

Sometime later—he wasn't really sure how long it had been—Chardonnais stumbled back to his lodge and crawled into the robes. He felt as if he had just passed through the digestive tract of a diseased buffalo.

Almost as soon as his head hit the robes, Looks Again began talking to herself—loudly.

Chardonnais groaned again and stood up. The maneuver left him dizzy and fighting to keep down whatever was in his stomach. He finally settled himself. "Let me tell you one t'ing, woman," he rasped, each word banging around in his head. "I will miss you very much. *Mais oui*. But if you don' stop this howling, I will put you under. Do you understand me, eh?"

Looks Again was not afraid of Lucien Chardonnais. He had never hurt her, and she thought he never would. Still, he seemed mighty sick, and he just might do as he said. She searched his bloodshot eyes, wanting to know if he were serious. What she saw in there was a deep affection for her, but also a startling amount of pain. *He must be really suffering,* she thought. "Come," she said softly, "lay down."

She sat on the robes and gently tugged Chardonnais down, where he lay with his head in her lap. She gently massaged his throbbing temples. Eventually, the lines of pain began to fade from his hairy, swarthy face, and before long he was asleep.

Looks Again slipped easily out from under him and eased his head down. She rose and stood for a moment looking down at him. She felt a pang of envy. Both Early and Rawlins had children by their Ute wives. But she was still childless. That was strange, she knew, considering Chardonnais's frequency of intercourse. She thought perhaps it was she, but then, she had been using medicine passed down from her grandmother's grandmother's time. Perhaps it was time to stop with the medicine and let things happen as they were meant to be. She smiled then, and turned back to her work.

It took another full day for the men to recover completely. All except for Boatwright. He was fine by the afternoon of the day after the carousing, but he had something going for him that none of the others did any longer—youth. They didn't hold it against him, though. Or at least not too much.

The following day Hamm and his men went out hunting and brought in a heap of fresh meat. "That's for bein' so generous with your own grub with us and our womenfolk and kids and all," Hamm said.

"*Merci*," Chardonnais said.

"We can't go replenishin' your Lightnin', though," Hamm added with a laugh.

Chardonnais grinned back. "Dat's all right, *mon ami*. Dis ol' hoss, he's had enough of dat shit for a time, eh."

"Amen to that, Lucien."

12

HAMM AND HIS MEN STAYED in Chardonnais's camp that night, and were set to leave first thing the next morning. As they were getting ready to pull out Chardonnais approached Hamm.

"What can I do for you, hoss?" Hamm asked.

"I have some business to discuss wit' you."

Hamm shrugged. "Sure. Speak your piece."

"Let's walk down by de stream a little, eh?" Chardonnais suggested.

"Don't make no never mind to me."

They strolled off. Once they were out of hearing range, Chardonnais asked, "You interested in getting rid of Casey's woman?"

Hamm scrunched up his face in thought. "Reckon the idea wouldn't put me out none. Why? You interested in her?"

"*Oui.*"

"But you got a woman."

Chardonnais nodded, then grinned. "But sometimes one woman ain't enough for dis ol' chil', eh."

Hamm laughed. "Ah, yes, now I remember what

91

all them boys around the mountains say about you."
Like many another man, he wondered if there was any
truth at all to the rumors. Looking at Chardonnais now,
he could believe it, but looks were often deceiving.
"What're you fixin' to give for her?"

"A fusee. One of de best."

"What'n hell'm I gonna do with another cheap-
trade rifle?" Hamm inquired.

"You're not her father, and you're not her man,"
Chardonnais said, a little irritation showing.

"I'm the closest thing she's got to either one out
here," Hamm said.

"What're you going to do wit' her?"

"I ain't figured that out yet. But, hell, I don't have
to get rid of her."

"I don' have to have her either. But you sell her to
me—cheap—you'll be getting rid of another mouth to
feed."

"Well, that's sure a fact that this ol' hoss can't
deny. But on the other hand, she's an extra pair of
hands to work on all the plews and such."

Chardonnais nodded. "Dat is true. *Mais oui!* But,"
he added shrewdly, "t'ink about when de wintair
comes. Soon. When de food is short and starving times
come to visit a man. What den, eh? You need another
mouth to feed den?"

"Reckon not." Hamm stopped walking and rubbed
his chin while he thought. "But, hell," he finally said, "I
just can't give her away. Christ, ol' Casey'll be castin'
bad spirits at us from the happy huntin' ground up
above I do that."

Chardonnais nodded. That was a fair assessment.
"All right," he allowed. "Two fusee and an oak wiping
stick."

Hamm mulled that for a few moments, then nod-

ded. "That shines with this chil'. You do know she's got
two kids, don't you?"

"*Mais non!*" Chardonnais said. "I don' want none of
dem."

"You gotta take 'em," Hamm insisted.

"No."

"What'n hell'm I supposed to do with 'em?"

Chardonnais shrugged.

Hamm thought that over for a while, then shook
his head. "No deal, Lucien. You either take the kids
with her or she stays with us. Christ, Lucien, you don't
want I should break up a mother and her kids, do ye?"

"I suppose not." Chardonnais had a momentary
doubt. Then he shrugged. He could not be concerned
over trivialities. "*Oui.* I will take dem."

"Runnin' Deer's all yours." Hamm grinned. "I'll tell
her soon's she and the others finish packin' and such."

Chardonnais nodded. With a small swagger in his
step he headed back to the camp. Looks Again looked
up from her work, wondering about the smug smile on
her man's face.

When she found out, she was less than happy.
Looks Again generally was not one to embarrass
Chardonnais in public, though she thought nothing of
telling him just what was on her mind when they were
in the lodge alone. She managed to keep her temper
in check outside the lodge when Chardonnais
brought Running Deer and the two children—a five-
year-old girl and a two-year-old boy—into the lodge
that morning, but she exploded as soon as the flap
was closed.

"What is she doing here?" Looks Again demanded,
her tone colder than the ice on the puddles down by
the creek.

"She is mine now, too," Chardonnais said, trying to

carry off by bravado what he figured he could not do by bluster or charm.

"I don't want her in my lodge," Looks Again said, spitting on the ground in Running Deer's direction. "And I don't want her children here either."

"Dis is my lodge, too," Chardonnais insisted, growing indignant.

"You want that woman," she said, pointing an accusatory finger at Running Deer, "you can have her make you a lodge to share with her. She's not going to stay in my lodge!"

"But, Looks Again," Chardonnais said, an edge of anger in the words, "I do dis for you as much as for me."

"Oh," Looks Again said haughtily. "Now you speak with two tongues. Your words can't be true."

"*Mais oui!*" Chardonnais insisted soothingly. "You will have help wit' de plews and making meat and all de much other work you have."

Looks Again acknowledged that with a nod. As tired as she had been lately, and with all the things that had to be done, some help wouldn't hurt, she thought. But she was also certain there was more to this than what Chardonnais had told her.

"And," Chardonnais added almost smugly, "I won't have to bother you all de time for going to de robes." He smiled ingratiatingly, figuring for sure that he had won his point.

"So, I'm not enough woman for you in the robes? Is that what you say to me? Are you such a big man you need another woman? Well, hah, that's two women you'll leave unsatisfied!"

"You're not satisfied in de robes?" Chardonnais asked, surprised and hurt.

"No. Never," Looks Again said flatly.

"Merde," Chardonnais muttered, crushed.

"So," Looks Again said triumphantly, "you must choose. That dog of a Shoshone—with her two squalling children. Or me."

"Well, maybe I just choose her, eh?" Chardonnais said stubbornly. "Maybe she is not so cold in de robes that she can't be satisfied."

"Don't try to blame me for your faults."

Chardonnais turned to Running Deer. "Go outside," he ordered, using signs, since he knew next to nothing of her language.

With a shrug, Running Deer took her children, turned, and left. She didn't much care one way or the other. All she wanted now was some shelter from the elements and food. This banty little French-Canadian could hump her, if he wanted. It couldn't be any worse than it had been with Casey Fitzsimmons, and it certainly couldn't be as bad as having to satisfy Chester Hamm and the rest of his men whenever they wanted something a little different.

"I t'ought you would be glad I got you help."

"I am."

"Den what is de trouble?" Chardonnais was confused.

"The trouble is that you want to share the robes with her." Looks Again was still steaming, but trying to be civil.

"But I t'ought that'd please you."

"Why would my sharing you please me?"

Chardonnais was rather flabbergasted. "My demands in de robes aren't too much for you?" he asked, surprised.

"No."

"But all de others . . . ?"

"I'm not one of the others," Looks Again said simply.

"But if I don't satisfy you, even though we go to de robes so often, why—"

"You please me."

"But I . . . You said . . ."

"I know what I said. You aren't the only one who can speak with a serpent's tongue. They were just words."

"Mon Dieu," Chardonnais muttered, shaking his head. "Den you really like what I do in de robes?"

"Yes."

"Show me," he said with a disarming grin.

"What about the Shoshone?"

"I don't know," Chardonnais said seriously. "I can't just turn her and her children out into de wintair." He thought for a little. "What if we keep dem in de lodge here for a while. She can help wit' your work and chores."

"And you'll leave her alone?"

"Oui," Chardonnais vowed.

Looks Again nodded, accepting it. Chardonnais had never lied to her, and she had no reason to believe he was lying now.

"Of course," Chardonnais said slyly, "we don' have to tell de others dat I leave her alone, eh?"

"Maybe. How long will she stay with us?"

Chardonnais shrugged. "I'll get rid of her soon as I can find someone to take her off my hands."

"What about your friends here?"

"Mon Dieu! No, no." Chardonnais was almost in a panic.

Looks Again smiled. "They'd find out your little secret, wouldn't they?" she said. She was teasing Chardonnais, though not maliciously.

"Dat would not be good for either of us," Chardonnais said with a laugh. He was rather relieved. He was not in need of another woman simply to have another woman. Looks Again knew his needs and was ready to meet them, knowing that she, too, would benefit. But when he was miles away from her, in Taos—a town full of earthy, lusty señoritas—well, that was a whole different story.

"No, it wouldn't," Looks Again said solemnly. Then she giggled.

Chardonnais nodded. He turned and opened the lodge's flap and stuck his head out. He beckoned Running Deer with a crooked finger. When she and her two children entered, he said, "Looks Again, I give you dis woman to help wit' de chores."

"I can do what I want with her?"

"*Oui.*" He wondered if Running Deer understood English and how much of this exchange she was getting. Her face betrayed nothing.

"And if I choose to chop off her head?" Looks Again asked, picking up a tomahawk.

"Dat would be messy in de lodge here," Chardonnais said a little nervously. He wasn't sure how serious Looks Again was at the moment.

Looks Again nodded, feigning disappointment. "Do you speak Ute?" she asked in Ute.

Running Deer looked blankly at her.

"Do you speak English?" she asked in that tongue.

Running Deer nodded. "I know some. I speak some."

"Good. Remember, this is my lodge," Looks Again said sternly. "If you don't do what I tell you, I'll toss you and your children out into the ice and snow. You understand?"

"Yes." The meekness in her voice was not reflected in her eyes.

"You and your children'll sleep there." Looks Again pointed to a shabby pile of blankets.

Chardonnais was about to protest, but decided that silence was the better part of valor at this point. He realized he had been an absolute fool. It wasn't bad enough that he tried to bring another wife into the lodge—even if that act was considered to be thoughtful of Looks Again—but he had to bring in a Shoshone. The Utes and Shoshones had been making war since the time of Looks Again's grandmother's grandmother's grandmother. He was certain now that Running Deer would have a hard time here in Looks Again's lodge. Chardonnais just hoped that his wife would soon show her kind nature once she had firmly established who was the boss in this lodge.

Feeling a sudden gloom spread over him, he headed outside. His three friends were sitting around the open fire. The other women in camp were working. Chardonnais squatted down and poured himself some coffee.

"Hey there, ol' froggie, how'd bringin' that new squaw into your lodge go over with Looks Again?" Rawlins asked, trying not very successfully to hide his grin.

"Don' ask me dat," Chardonnais said with a grimace, feeling even more lousy.

"Hell, I'll wager two butcherin' knives that she don't last two days in there before Looks Again pitches her out on her plump little ass," Rawlins said with a laugh.

"I'll take that bet," Early said. "I'll offer up half a bar of lead that it takes three days."

"You're on, *amigo*." Still grinning, Rawlins looked at Boatwright. "You want to get in on this, boy?" he asked.

"Well," Boatwright said slowly, as usual speaking carefully around these men, "I don't know as if I got me anything good enough to wager against them things."

"Hell, it ain't what ye offer, boy," Rawlins growled. "The idea is you wager somethin' that means a little somethin' to ye. But not somethin' ye can't do without."

"Will my ol' one-point blanket do?" Boatwright asked.

"Sure as hell will," Early said agreeably. "What's your guess on all this?"

"I say Looks Again'll keep her around till we make winter camp," Boatwright said confidently.

The others hooted and jeered. "Jesus, boy," Early said, laughing, "you've gone plumb loco. Looks Again ain't ever gonna put up with a Snake livin' in her lodge. You mark my words, boy."

"We'll see," Boatwright said confidently.

Rawlins squinted across the fire at Chardonnais. "Jesus, Frenchie, what the hell ever got into you? Talk about someone goin' loco. Christ, you bring a Snake into your lodge and expect Looks Again to put up with it?"

Chardonnais scowled and shrugged. He had taken boneheaded actions before, but he couldn't recall one quite this bad.

"Well, it's your ass, Lucien," Early said with another grin.

"When the hell're we pullin' out?" Rawlins asked.

"Mornin'," Early responded. "We got a few things need doin' here. Our trap lines've been overlooked some the past couple days. Besides, the women need a little time to get everything ready."

13

CHARDONNAIS, BEING MORE excitable than any of the others, chafed at the slowness with which they were traveling lately. It wasn't so much the frequent stopping to set out their traps for a couple days. That was to be expected. What did bother him was the length of time it was taking to make and break camp. Adding to the problem was the amount of supplies and plews they now had. Twelve mules were laden with pressed beaver pelts or meat and other supplies. They could move at little more than a slow walk.

Looks Again could sense the tension in her man, see it stamped on his hard, weathered face. She let it be for several days, but she felt him growing worse with each passing sun. Knowing his volatile temper and his abrupt mood changes, she began to worry. So one night she decided to see if she could do anything about it. She mostly doubted that she could, knowing his temperament, but she had to try.

Trouble was, she was tired most of the time now. Even with Running Deer helping, her work seemed endless. Indeed, there were times that she thought having the Shoshone around caused more rather than less work. There was always another plew to be scraped or another rack of meat to be put up or taken down, another buffalo robe to be grained, another elk skin to clean of hair. And then there was the lodge to put up and take down, food to cook, firewood to gather. It was endless, and with the cold temperatures and biting wind, Looks Again could feel herself wearing down.

Because of all this, she really was of no mood to baby Chardonnais, but she still knew she had to try. For one thing, if he exploded, it could be very bad for her. Far more important, though, was the simple fact that she loved Lucien Chardonnais. She did not know when it had happened. It had and she accepted it. And because of it, she also wanted to keep his mind from straying to Running Deer.

After they ate their meal that evening, she wandered down to the creek, which was covered with a thin coating of ice. She took her small tomahawk, whacked the ice, which broke easily, and cleaned her face with the frigid water. Then she stuck her hand up her dress to clean herself as best as she could; she did the same up top. By the time she finished, she was freezing. She quickly filled her wood canteen and hurried back to the lodge.

Chardonnais sat cross-legged at the fire, gazing moodily into the flames. He was braiding a rope of horsehair, but seemingly making little real effort at it. Looks Again looked at him, seeing the tightness of the shirt across her man's broad back. She wished she knew of some way to make herself more alluring to him. She felt sad when she could think of none. She sighed at the harshness of her life. She glanced over at Running Deer and smiled malevolently at her and her two children. Just the other day she had been thinking of having a baby. Now might be the time and place to start. With that thought in mind, she headed toward Chardonnais.

Looks Again knelt right behind him and began kneading his tight shoulder muscles. He stiffened a little, as if he did not want her touch, but then quickly gave in to it. He tossed aside his project and put his hands on his knees, elbows out.

A few minutes later Looks Again said, "Come, husband. Let's go to the robes."

"I ain't ready for sleep yet," Chardonnais growled.

"Who said anything about sleep?" Looks Again countered, trying to sound cheerful.

Chardonnais looked up over his left shoulder and smiled a little. "You sure are some at making me feel good, Looks Again," he said quietly.

Looks Again could hear the truth in his words, and a flush of pride ran through her.

"But what about her?" Chardonnais chucked a thumb over his shoulder.

"She can watch, if she wants," Looks Again said maliciously. "Or go outside so she doesn't have to watch a real woman in the robes with her man."

Chardonnais shrugged. They rose as one and headed toward the robes. In moments they were naked and entangled in each other's arms and in the soft, comfortable robes. Looks Again pushed Chardonnais flat on his back and straddled his middle. She smiled lecherously and said, "Maybe if you can't see your pizzle, it won't be so anxious."

"Maybe," he said with a laugh. He was feeling considerably better already.

Looks Again was aware of Running Deer and her two children heading out of the lodge. The three were bundled up against the cold. It was not that the

Shoshone was shy or that she was concerned that her children would see people making love. That was a natural part of life, and it was seldom hidden from the children. But Running Deer would not allow herself to be so insulted.

"I feel sorry for de children," Chardonnais said.

"Me, too," Looks Again said with a touch of sadness. "But they'll be all right. And maybe someday we'll have some of our own to worry about." She had not meant to mention it, and now she felt as if her heart had stopped as she awaited Chardonnais's reaction.

"*Mais oui!*" he said enthusiastically.

Looks Again bent and kissed him, long and deeply, then pushed herself back up. She took his rough hands in hers and placed them on her breasts. Chardonnais needed no encouragement to begin stroking and teasing them.

Looks Again's eyes closed and her back arched as she allowed the warmth of his body to soak into hers. Absentmindedly, she ran her hands—and her stubbed, split fingernails—through the mat of hair on his chest.

Chardonnais moved one hand from a breast and worked it between their bodies, where he could use his fingers to give her pleasure.

Looks Again shuddered a little as delightful tremors rippled up and down from her crotch, splashing her with a soothing, yet exciting warmth. She moaned and began wriggling her buttocks in response to Chardonnais's urgent, insistent fingers.

Then she fell forward onto him, almost spent. She decided then and there that she liked the feel of his soft chest hair against her breasts. She thought for a few moments that she would never leave this position, that she and he would stay this way forever. That would not be so bad, she thought.

Despite her climax, though, Chardonnais's hands and fingers had not stopped, and Looks Again could feel the heat—and the pure simple animal lust—rebuild in her like the sun rising on a summer's day. She pushed herself back up to allow him more room to work his magic.

Chardonnais was happy to accommodate her. He raised his head and pulled her forward by one breast. That brought her close enough that he could tongue one soft, pliant nipple as his hand worked on the other.

As Looks Again felt herself rising to another climax, she pulled her torso back and lifted her middle. With swift certainty, she guided him into her. Both groaned in pleasure.

Release was not long in coming for either of them, and Looks Again once more sank down on Chardonnais, breathing heavily.

As he stroked Looks Again's hair Chardonnais smiled into the night. Looks Again was unlike any woman he had ever met, red or white. She took in stride his raging libido and did not begrudge him his flings with the señoritas in Taos. That he came back to her was all that mattered to her, or so she had told him once. He had believed her.

But there was a lot more to Looks Again than that. She seemed to have some innate sense of how to handle his often swift-changing moods. She knew when to speak and when not to, when to berate him for his foolishness and when to leave him alone.

Chardonnais suddenly thought about Marie Bouchard. He wondered how she was doing. He was annoyed at himself for having run out on her the way he had. Still, he knew that the deed was done and that nothing would ever change it. He wondered now if he had ever really loved Marie. He was certain that he had not. He had been more than smitten, true, and liked her considerably. But he did not love her. Had he stayed and married her, he might've one day come to love her, but somehow, deep down inside, he knew that would not have been the case. He tried to push those thoughts out of his mind.

Looks Again, lying atop her husband, could feel him tightening up. She pushed a little ways up and looked at him, worry creasing her smooth copper brow. "Is there something wrong?" she asked anxiously.

"No, *ma chérie*, no."

"Don't lie."

Chardonnais's eyes widened in surprise, and his temper flared ever so little. Then he smiled. "*Oui.* I was lying." He paused, idly stroking Looks Again's back, then nodded. "Maybe I shouldn't say dis to you, but I will."

Looks Again's worry flared anew.

"When I was gone dis time, I went to de place where I was a boy, way far to de east."

"To where the Cheyennes live?" Looks Again asked innocently.

"Much farther dan dat. While I was dere I met a woman. She was only a little girl when I left dere so long ago. But now she is a woman."

"She is a Pawnee, yes?" Looks Again asked.

Chardonnais laughed a little. "*Mais non!* She is white, like me."

Looks Again pushed her torso up. "You lie to me again," she said angrily. "There are no women among your people."

"But yes, dere are. How do you t'ink I got here? And Ezra and Abe and Jed and all de others?"

"From women like me."

"What makes you t'ink dere are no white women?" he asked.

"I have never seen one."

"I guess you haven't," he said thoughtfully. "But dere are."

"Then why do all men like you come and take women like me?" Looks Again was dumbfounded.

"Dat's hard to explain, Looks Again," Chardonnais said in measured tones. "Most white women—de ones considered good women—don' like to do dis."

"Do what?"

"Fornicate."

"They don't?" Such a thing was almost inconceivable to her.

"No. Dey t'ink dere is somet'ing bad about it. Dat dey will burn for all eternity for doing it except to have babies, but even den dey aren't supposed to like it."

"Those women are crazy," Looks Again said firmly. She could think of nothing better than to have a man who cared about her making love to her. It was pure pleasure. Anyone who could think that was bad had to be touched in the head, she thought.

"*Mais oui!*" Chardonnais said with a laugh. Then he sobered. "But dey are dere. And I met one while I was in de east. Once a little girl, now a full-grown woman."

"What is she like?"

"Pretty of face. She is a bit taller dan you, but not so filled out here." He reached out to bobble her breasts a little. "Or here." He ran his hands along her smooth buttocks.

"And does she think it's bad to couple?"

Chardonnais nodded. "*Oui*, as foolish as it is."

"Why do you tell me this?"

"Because it's right dat you should know, Looks

Again," he said seriously. "I almost stayed dere wit' her."

Looks Again wasn't sure whether to be dismayed, angry, hurt, or all three. "Oh?" she said noncommittally.

"*Oui.* She turned my head. Her looks, and de smell of her perfume, de—"

"Smell of her what?"

"Perfume. Sweet-smellin' water dat you splash on. You remember I brought you some from Taos last year."

Looks Again nodded. "Yes, I remember now. It was good for only once, and even then I had to take less than a whole washing with it."

Chardonnais laughed, making Looks Again's breasts jiggle enticingly over him. "*Oui.* I remember dat. Wit' dat water, you should just sprinkle a little on yourself. A touch here and here, and here maybe," he added, touching the valley between her breasts, the back of her ear, her throat. "Maybe I will bring you some more de next time I go to Taos, eh? Would you like dat?"

Looks Again nodded firmly, though she still thought the idea ridiculous.

"Among my people, a marriage is done by a priest—a shaman of our religion. Dere are certain words dat must be said, promises made, and it is supposed to be forever."

"For all time?"

"*Oui.*" He paused, thinking he had said too much already, that he was a fool for having mentioned it at all. But now that he had come this far, he could not see stopping. "I asked dis young woman to marry me—in front of de priest."

Looks Again suddenly tightened, her muscles growing rigid. Worry and fear and a touch of anger flickered across her face.

"But on de day it was supposed to happen, I sat dere t'inking of being forced to live in dat city forever after. Of not having my friends around. And I t'ought much of not having you. I took off de funny clothes dey want you to wear to a wedding and I run off. Back here."

Looks Again relaxed considerably. "You said no good-bye to this woman?"

Chardonnais shook his head. "*Mais non*. And I feel bad about dat. I should have. But I told my brother what I was doing, and he told her for me."

"I'm glad you came back," Looks Again said simply.

"I am, too," Chardonnais responded truthfully. The confession seemed to relax and invigorate him.

"And you don't want Running Deer?"

The Shoshone had come back an hour after leaving. She and both her children were sleeping.

"No," he said firmly. He smiled. "Now come here, woman. We got other business."

Feeling full of pride, Looks Again was more than happy to comply.

14

"YOU MUST NOT WORRY on the trail, Lucien," Looks Again said sternly to Chardonnais in the morning.

"I'm not worried," Chardonnais protested.

"Yes, you are. You worry that we take too long on the trail. You worry that the women and children and supplies make you crawl along. I can see these things in your eyes, in the way you talk and carry yourself. Don't worry. We'll find a place for winter soon, and you'll have many plews to take back to Taos with you."

"I suppose you're right, *ma chère*. But dat is me. I need to worry about everyt'ing. To tell me not to worry is to tell de grizzly bear to put away de hump on his neck."

Looks Again giggled.

"But I'll try, Looks Again. I'll try."

Chardonnais did relax some, trying to fight his volatile nature. He succeeded to some extent, but not as much as he knew he should. It didn't help that snow fell regularly and the temperatures barely rose above freezing these days.

Looks Again found herself becoming more tolerant

of Running Deer, but she figured that was mainly because of the children. As much as she hated the mother, she liked the children. She could not bear to see them suffer, so she treated Running Deer at least a little better.

At last they pulled into a sheltered valley not far from some hot springs. Strong Bear's village was set up at the far end of the meadow, amid the trees along Willow Creek. There was also an encampment of mountain men farther up the creek.

Early, in the lead, stopped at a likely spot for a camp. He issued some orders to the women and then remounted his horse. He and his three companions trotted across the frosty meadow toward the white men's camp.

"*Hola,* Gilly," Early said as he dismounted. As Early was the nominal leader of his group of free trappers, Gilly McFarland was the leader of his small group.

"Ezra!" McFarland said with a wide smile. He was a big, burly man who seemed perpetually happy. "How's doin's, ol' hoss?"

"Never been better."

Early's men and McFarland's men—Cy Adler, Kurt Schmidt, and Dale Bishop—greeted each other warmly.

"You plannin' to winter here, Gilly?" Early asked.

"Had figured on it. But that's afore those critters showed up." He pointed to Strong Bear's Ute camp. "Me'n the Utes just don't get along at all."

"Where're you fixin' to head?"

"Up toward the Medicine Bows. There's a few places there ain't been too misused over the years."

Early nodded. "You got time for a little visitin'?"

"Hell yes, boy," McFarland said with a hearty laugh. "There's always time for this chil' to set to some doin's. We got us fresh buffler, elk, even some antelope. We'll fill your meatbags but good, boys."

"*Bueno*," Early said. "Let us get our camp settled and then we'll hoist a jug or two."

As Early and his men headed back toward their own camp, Chardonnais said, "I t'ought you said you weren't gonna do dat no more."

"I never said no goddamn such thing," Early answered with a straight face. "I think it was you who said that."

"I wouldn't say somet'ing like dat."

They all laughed as they dismounted. The men took care of the animals while the women set up the camp. It was near dark when the men headed toward McFarland's camp. Of the women and children, only Running Deer and her two youngsters went. As soon as Looks Again, Falling Leaf, Scatters the Clouds, and Blue Rattle had heard that McFarland's men all had Shoshone wives, the three had decided to stay at their own camp. Chardonnais had expected this, as had the others, except Boatwright.

Chardonnais had noticed on an earlier brief visit that while there were four men in McFarland's camp, there were only three women, all Shoshones. He smiled as he rode toward McFarland's in the fading, cold sun.

Soon the men were all sitting in McFarland's large lodge. Meat was roasting and jugs were waiting. Within moments of planting themselves cross-legged or against willow backrests, they were digging into both the meat and the whiskey.

"I heard you give up the mountains, Ez," McFarland said as he gnawed on a buffalo rib.

"Nah. I got a letter last year, in the spring. My pa was doin' poorly, so I headed east. Got there just before he crossed the divide."

"You have my sympathies," McFarland said softly, meaning it.

"Ol' froggie there," Rawlins said, "now he went back just this past spring. Decided he couldn't live another day without seein' his family, which didn't want his high-smellin' carcass around anyway."

"That true?" Bishop asked.

"You know better dan to listen to dat coyote-humping fool," Chardonnais growled. "I did have a hankering to see de old place, though, dat much is true."

"So how was your old pap and mam?" McFarland asked.

"About de same as dey were when I left dere back in twenty-two," Chardonnais said with a sigh. "Only older and more worn."

"See, you little fart," Rawlins chimed in, "ye wasted all that goddamn time and energy when you could've been havin' a spree with the rest of us down in Taos."

"It wasn't all a waste of time," Chardonnais said thoughtfully.

"Eh?" Early questioned. "What the hell's that mean?"

"Notting," Chardonnais grumped, realizing he had said more than he wanted to.

"Don't give me that buffler shit, Frenchie," Rawlins said pointedly. "Ye best tell what ye meant, or there's gonna be a heap of angry critters ready to sit on ye till ye talk."

"*Merde,*" Chardonnais muttered, knowing there was no way out. He figured he could make up a story, but sooner or later the truth would come out, and then they'd all give him a hard time about telling tales.

"Come on, you stumpy little bastard," Rawlins said. "Speak up."

Chardonnais sighed. "Dere was dis woman dere. . . ." he started.

"Jesus goddamn Christ," Rawlins hooted, "can't you keep your pecker in you 'skins even when you're around your sainted mother?"

"Eat shit," Chardonnais said. He was getting angry, and he didn't want that. He speared another hunk of antelope meat on his knife and chewed at it a little before continuing. "Her name is Marie Bouchard, and a prettier woman dan de likes of you'll ever see. *Mais oui!*"

"Shit," Rawlins snorted. "Probably looks like my aunt Matilda—a hunnert years old with no teeth left in her head, bones all contorted up with rheumtiz."

"Or," Early interjected, "more like your aunt Matilda's ailin' cow."

"You two would try de patience of a saint," Chardonnais snapped. He muttered some imprecations at the sky and chewed on a mouthful of antelope. "She was de finest-looking woman maybe I ever see," he went on quietly.

Rawlins bit back a new retort. Something in Chardonnais's voice caught him up.

Early had caught it, too, and waved off any comment the others might be thinking of making.

"And I ask dat girl to marry me."

"Ye up and done what, ye crazy goddamn fool Frenchman?" Rawlins exploded.

"You heard what I say. I ask her to marry me."

Early nodded in sympathy. "And she turned you down? I'm sorry, *amigo*."

Chardonnais shook his head sadly. "No. She say she will have me. Can you believe dat?" He sounded like he didn't believe it himself. "Dis fine lady whose papa is the booshway of a big freighting company. A lady who has dresses of silk and such t'ings, not like de women out here." He stopped, eyes looking off into the past.

"Well, Jesus, Lucien, get on with it," Rawlins snapped. He could not stand suspense of this kind.

Chardonnais brought himself back to the present only with a great effort. "On de day of de wedding, I walk away."

"Goddamn you, Frenchie, you sufferin' sack of shit," Rawlins snarled. "If you was gonna tell us a goddamn tale, why didn't you make it better'n that one. Christ, was that lame."

"It's true," Chardonnais said simply.

Rawlins looked across the fire at his longtime friend. "By Jesus, I think the stumpy little bastard's tellin' true," he said quietly.

"Why?" Early asked. He was as dumbfounded as everyone else. It was just a matter of him finding his voice first.

"I don't know for sure," Chardonnais said with a shrug. "Part was I would miss dese mountains. I even t'ought I'd miss you two shits, but dat can't be true." He shrugged again. "I just didn't feel like I belong dere. I belong out here, living free, breathing clean air. Not back dere in dat city wit' all its smells and closeness. Not even with *ma belle* Marie."

The silence that arose was broken by the snapping of the fire, the swish of the wind, and the soft, quiet voices of the women in another lodge.

"Well, hell," Rawlins finally said, "at least you made one person real happy."

Everyone looked at Rawlins, trying to figure out what he meant. Suddenly Chardonnais laughed, tentatively at first, and then with more conviction. "*Mais oui!*" he said. "Dat Marie, she is much better off wit' me gone away out here. I would've made her miserable had I married her. And dat would not do, eh."

"Jesus, Lucien," Early said, "women're gonna be the death of you yet, you dumb son of a bitch."

"Damn, boy," McFarland said, "you're foolin' in some dangerous waters you get mixed up with a white woman, especially one whose pa's got some dollars banked."

"Hell, he's had trouble with every goddamn kind of woman you can think of," Rawlins said. "Don't matter none if she's white, red, or brown. Christ, he's got him a fine Ute wife, yet he'll hump anything that comes along. As long as it's got tits, he don't give a flying goddamn if it's two-legged or four."

"I've heard some about that chil's predilections," McFarland said with a knowing nod.

"But that ain't the end of it, neither," Early said with a low laugh. "Here he's got that fine Ute wife right along with him, and that dumb bastard goes out and gets him a Snake—with two goddamn squallin' little brats to boot—to come live in his lodge."

"And his Ute wife didn't mind this?" McFarland asked, disbelief in his voice and posture.

"Mind?" Rawlins said with a raucous laugh. "Hell, I'm surprised you boys all the way up here didn't hear her goddamn screechin'. Ol' Lucien there, he just comes slinkin' out of his lodge with his pecker draggin' in the dirt, lookin' like a whipped puppy."

Chardonnais sat stiffly, failing to see any humor in the situation, though everyone else certainly did.

"What's really bad about it," Rawlins continued, "is that Looks Again ain't lettin' him do any humpin' with her, or with that Snake, so we've had to keep a close watch on our horses. A couple of the mares've been keepin' an eye cocked for Frenchie there. Hell, I think I caught him eyein' me up one day we was on the trap lines."

"*Merde!*" Chardonnais spit. "You can't hump de

women as good as I can even in your dreams," he added stiffly.

"Well, shit, froggie, if I wanted a goddamn goat for a partner, I'd go out and get one. I sure as hell don't need a two-legged one rollin' his eyes at me."

Early and Rawlins knew it was time to back off or Chardonnais might explode. With some whiskey in him, and a knot of anger eating at his insides right now, he was like gunpowder sitting too close to a fire. The two indicated to the others that it was time to change the subject.

Chardonnais stewed about it for a while, but the whiskey, the food, and the friendly chat on battles lost and won by his friends served to soothe him a little. Eventually he could see a little—very little—humor in the way he had sometimes lived. He finally sighed, letting the last of the anger go. He leaned over to Dale Bishop on his right and asked, "Dere are four of you, but only t'ree women. Is dat right?"

Bishop nodded. "Yep. My woman drowned a couple months ago crossin' the Green."

"You in de market for a new one, maybe?"

"I might be. Why?"

"I got one Snake wife too many, says my Ute wife."

"She the one came over here with you boys?"

"*Oui*. Her name's Running Deer."

"I ain't got a whole lot I can use to pay for her."

"Make me an offer."

"Two four-point blankets and a knife."

"I take it. And I t'row in de childrens for notting."

Bishop rose. "Might's well make the deal now before we get too full of Lightnin' that none of us can think."

15

THE MEN WENT EASIER ON the whiskey than they had the last time. It was too late in the season and there was too much work to be done for such frolics.

Still, Early and his three friends were not entirely sober when they rode back to their camp. As they unsaddled their horses Boatwright lurched over to Early. "You owe me half a bar of lead," he said, words slurred.

"What'n hell for?" Early asked, a little irritated. All he wanted was to get to bed and sleep off the whiskey.

"Our bet," Boatwright reminded him. "You, too, Abe. You owe me two butcherin' knives."

"What bet?"

"About Runnin' Deer."

Rawlins stood there, leaning against his horse, trying to think. It was hard as hell with all the Taos Lightning running through his veins. But something began to coalesce. "Goddamn, you're right," he mumbled.

"Well, I don't remember no goddamn bet."

"Yes, you do," Rawlins said. He wanted to vomit but was bound and determined not to give in to it. "We

117

bet how long it was gonna be before Lucien shed himself of Runnin' Deer."

"Damn, that's right," Early said. "Now I remember." He didn't seem overjoyed at the remembrance.

"Little bastard might've won," Rawlins said as he began lurching toward his lodge, "but he ain't gettin' paid till tomorrow. Maybe the next day if I feel as bad as I think I'm gonna feel."

Rawlins wasn't all that bad off come morning. Neither were his three companions. The same could not be said of some of the men they had had their spree with. As the four gathered at the fire for their morning coffee, Rawlins said, "Goddamn, maybe I won't have to pay snotface over there after all." He pointed.

Dale Bishop was riding toward their camp. With him were Running Deer and her two children. Following them at a little distance were Gilly McFarland, Cy Adler, and Kurt Schmidt.

Bishop stopped near the fire. "Gimme back my blankets and knife, Frenchie."

"*Excusez-moi?*" Chardonnais asked, surprised.

"You heard me, you shit-eatin' frog."

Chardonnais shoved himself up. "Nobody calls me dat," he said tightly, anger beginning to simmer.

"Hell, them two assholes do," Bishop said, pointing to Rawlins and Early.

"You best watch your mouth, boy," Rawlins drawled, also rising. His face was hard as stone.

"I got no beef with you, Rawlins," Bishop said. "My beef's with the frog there."

"Dat's twice you call me dat name," Chardonnais said, the warning strong in his voice. "If you do it a t'ird time, I'll cut your heart out and shove it up your ass." He paused, waiting to see what Bishop would say or do.

Gilly and his two other men rode up, stopped, and dismounted. They said nothing as they moved to stand next to Early, who also had risen, and Rawlins. The five watched Bishop and Chardonnais.

After a few moments of silence Chardonnais asked, "What de hell is wit' you, eh?"

"I don't want that bitch you sold me."

Chardonnais shrugged. "Dat is your problem."

"Like hell," Bishop snapped. It was clear now that he was still at least a little bit drunk. "If I knew she wouldn't perform in the robes, I'd of never took her on."

Chardonnais laughed harshly. "If you can't make de lady happy," he said with an exaggerated shrug, "dat's your trouble." He smiled viciously. "Or maybe it is dat you want me to give you some pointers on how to do it, eh? Maybe you have no *couilles*, eh?"

"I don't know what the hell that means, but I expect it ain't a compliment," Bishop said angrily. He slid off his horse.

"No, it was no compliment, dat's for sure. I say maybe you have no balls, eh. Is dat your problem with de fair Snake madame?"

"You stinkin' piece of frog shit you," Bishop said, nearly boiling over.

Early and McFarland were leaning on their rifles. Early glanced over at McFarland. "You might want to call your boy off, Gilly. Lucien's about ready to pop."

McFarland shrugged. "Dale's a big boy. He can handle himself." He almost grinned. "If he can't, that's his problem."

Early nodded. "Just so we're clear on that."

"We are."

"Well, *puce*—you flea," Chardonnais said with a sneer, "what will you do, eh?"

"I'm gonna stomp your froggie ass into the god-damn dirt, you stupid little—"

Bishop did not have a chance to finish his statement, since Chardonnais had flung himself on him. The two tumbled to the ground. Chardonnais was wild, growling and snarling, sounding like a rabid wolf.

Bishop began to think he had overextended himself here, but he was a big man, strong and used to the harsh life of the wilderness. There was no way he was going to quit. Not now, not in front of all the others—particularly the woman.

Women, he thought as he bucked and jerked and tried to get the half-maniacal Chardonnais off him. *Damn 'em all! They're trouble, each and every goddamn one of 'em. Red or white or brown, they're trouble.*

He didn't understand why Running Deer would have nothing to do with him in the robes last night. It was not as if she were a virgin or something. She had been married to at least one white man—Casey Fitzsimmons—and had lived with Lucien Chardonnais. Bishop had no reason to believe that Running Deer had spurned the sexual advances of a man with Chardonnais's reputation. Plus she had two children. And because of all that, it was inconceivable to him that she would reject him, even if he had just bought her a couple of hours earlier.

He did not want to admit, even to himself, that with the amount of liquor he had consumed the night before, he would've been unable to function in the robes anyway. He knew damn well that whiskey could send a man's desire soaring while making his abilities plunge. He knew now that he should have eased off on that jug last night when everyone else had. *Damn!* he thought angrily. If he had quit when he should have, he wouldn't be rolling around now in the snow, fighting off a panther that uttered a continuous stream of curses in French, English, and probably Spanish, too.

Chardonnais let no such thoughts interfere with the business at hand. He was like that—when he was rage crazy, as he was now, his whole mind and body focused on his anger. When he had leaped at Bishop, he had done so with no plan in mind. He simply fought with animal instinct and fury.

Bishop was losing badly, but he managed to get a few good licks in now and again. Chardonnais appeared not to feel them at all, other than to emit a soft grunt.

Bishop, on the other hand, felt every punch or kick that the wild little French-Canadian landed. With the lack of sleep, the anger at Running Deer, and the whiskey still coursing through his veins, he was in deep trouble. And he knew it.

Bishop's good friend Kurt Schmidt shifted his weight and set his rifle down on the ground. He eased out his tomahawk. As he was about to step into the fray between Chardonnais and Bishop, Jed Boatwright sidled up to him.

"I'd keep my nose out of this here ruckus, friend," he warned.

"Eat shit, boy," Schmidt growled. He was a medium-tall man, but thick in the chest and middle and with powerful, thick legs. He had been in the mountains a good long time, had counted more than his share of coup, had bedded his share of women, and fought his share of Indians. He was not about to be cowed by a young pup like Boatwright. He glared at the young man a moment, fixing him with his hard, dark eyes. Then he turned and took a step toward the fight.

Boatwright latched onto the back of Schmidt's

shirt with his left hand and jerked him backward. At the same time he thundered a punch into his kidney.

Schmidt gave little indication that he felt the punch. He simply whipped himself around, elbow up and out. It caught Boatwright only a glancing blow on the cheekbone, but it was enough to send him reeling.

"Mind your betters, boy," Schmidt snapped. "Keep away from me or I'll gut you." He turned once more and headed for where Chardonnais was pounding the bejesus out of Bishop.

"I'll have y'all know, Gilly," Rawlins said to McFarland and Cy Adler, "that I'm too old and too hung over to join in these doin's. I hope you two boys feel the same."

McFarland and Adler nodded. They saw no reason to join the fracas. Neither did Early, who stood there relaxed, watching.

Boatwright regained his footing and charged at Schmidt. He locked both fists together and swung them like a club, hitting Schmidt in the back of the neck.

Schmidt stumbled forward two steps and then sank to one knee. When he pushed himself up and turned, there was a mean, evil glint in his eyes. "That was a stupid thing to do, boy," he barked. He had almost no German accent, though his words seemed clipped off somehow. He raised the tomahawk.

Several feet away Rawlins and Early each pulled a pistol.

"Damn fool," McFarland muttered. He pulled his own pistol. "He's one of mine, Ez, Abe. I'll deal with him." But he had no reason to fire.

Even as McFarland was raising his flintlock pistol to shoot his own man, Boatwright slipped up close to Schmidt. He blocked the German's tomahawk with his left forearm, and at the same time he drove two hard punches into his abdomen.

Schmidt gasped as his breath burst out under the power of the two blows, and he dropped his tomahawk. He stood hovering, half-bent, trying to breathe.

As he did so, Boatwright calmly reached out, brushed Schmidt's fur cap off his head, and grabbed his long, grease-slick hair. He jerked Schmidt's head up a little and then plunged it downward while at the same time snapping up his right knee. The German's nose splattered with the impact, and though no one could see it, his eyes rolled up in his head.

Boatwright let Schmidt go and hopped around, clutching at his knee. "Goddamn, that hurt. Jesus. God-damn. Shit. Son-of-a-bitch bastard."

Schmidt fell onto one knee and hung there. Limping, Boatwright came up behind him, placed a foot against the back of his blanket coat, and shoved. Schmidt toppled forward onto his face.

"Tough young bastard, ain't he?" McFarland said to Early, pointing at Boatwright.

"He's got sand," Early responded.

The three men put their pistols away and looked back to the original fight.

Chardonnais had pummeled Bishop into a huddled ball. He was still swearing a blue streak, but he seemed to be running out of steam at least a little. Not that his rage had really lessened any. Indeed, moments after Schmidt was shoved to the ground, Chardonnais pulled out his butcher knife to put an end to Bishop.

"I reckon this's where me'n you ought to step in, Abe," Early said easily. The two mountain men dropped their rifles and moved forward. Each grabbed Chardonnais by an arm.

"That there's enough, *amigo,*" Rawlins said quietly. "Ye've done him enough damage for one day."

Chardonnais was like a wild animal. He jerked his arms and kicked Bishop a few more times. But Early's stolid calmness and Rawlins's reasoned words began to seep through to him. Chardonnais shook his head a few times, as if awakening. He looked at Rawlins on one side and then Early on the other. Then he looked down at Bishop, who was still huddled in a fetal ball.

Chardonnais kicked Bishop one last time. "*Caca d'oie,*" he spat. "Goose shit."

Rawlins and Early could feel the stocky little French-Canadian relax. "You all right, boy?" Rawlins asked.

"*Mais oui!* Let me go now, *mes amis.*"

"You ain't gonna thump Dale anymore?" Rawlins asked.

Chardonnais shook his head. "No. De hen-humping bastard is not wort' de trouble."

Rawlins and Early released his arms. Chardonnais turned and began brushing the snow off his blanket coat. He went and picked up his jaunty green wool cap and tugged it on. Then he walked up to Running Deer, who still sat on her horse, trying to look haughty. "Now you listen to me, madame. Dat," he said, pointing to Bishop, who had finally decided it was safe to uncoil, "is your new husband. You treat him good, eh. He fight for you like a man. You do what he says. You don' want to stay wit' him, dat is yours to decide. But you can't come wit' me. You don' like him, maybe later he can give you to somebody you like better. But for now, you go be his woman and act like it."

Chardonnais turned, walked over to Bishop, who was trying not to cower, and held out his hand. Bishop tentatively gripped it and allowed the trapper to pull him up.

"You fight good," Chardonnais said when Bishop was standing. "No hard feelings over dis, eh?"

Bishop looked at Early and Rawlins. "He always like this?"

"Like what?" Rawlins asked innocently.

"Crazy one minute, your friend the next."

"Mostly," Rawlins said.

"*Oui*," Chardonnais agreed. "Dat is me all right. Now, you go back to your lodge and have Running Deer take care of you, eh." He went to the fire, squatted, and poured himself some coffee.

McFarland's men looked at him like he was crazy, which they supposed he was. Then, shaking their heads in wonder, they left, McFarland helping Bishop, and Adler helping Schmidt.

16

CHARDONNAIS WATCHED TWO DAYS later as McFarland and his three men rode out of the meadow under the soft sifting of snow. Chardonnais was no longer angry at Dale Bishop, but he was rather relieved that Running Deer and her two children were riding a little behind the man. So relieved was he that he waved a little and grinned hugely, showing a gap in his smile where two teeth once sat.

"You think you can keep your fat French ass out of woman trouble for a spell now?" Rawlins asked, stopping alongside Chardonnais.

"*Mais oui!*" Chardonnais said enthusiastically. Then he laughed and shrugged. "But who knows, eh? De mademoiselles can't keep their hands off me."

"It ain't the señoritas gettin' their hands on ye that ye got to worry about," Rawlins said with a strong laugh. "It's their fathers and brothers and, knowin' what a goddamn horny goat you are, husbands, you got to worry about."

"Ah, dat is one of de misfortunes of being irresistible to de mademoiselles," Chardonnais responded, still laughing.

"One of these days some rank son of a bitch whose wife or daughter ye soiled is gonna cut your nuts off," Rawlins said as he and Chardonnais stepped into Early's lodge. Boatwright followed them.

"He better bring an army den," Chardonnais said stubbornly, but with a smile nonetheless. He sat and poured himself coffee. "Besides, *mon ami*, it won't be de first time, would it?"

"That little señorita . . . what the hell was her name, Abe?" Early asked, picking up the thread of the conversation right off.

"Inez, weren't it?" Rawlins splashed a little whiskey into his coffee.

"*Mais oui!*" Chardonnais said with a laugh. "She was some fine-looking t'ing, no?"

"Damn, she was that, certain," Rawlins agreed with an accompanying nod.

"I don' feel like talking about dat," Chardonnais said diffidently.

"Like hell ye don't, froggie," Rawlins said. "Tell it."

In some ways, Chardonnais really didn't want to discuss it. It brought on too much hurt on occasion. But his irrepressible ebullience usually overcame that quick enough. "Well, let me see now. Dat was in twenty-eight, I t'ink. Maybe twenty-nine."

The three men had ridden hard into Taos, full of piss and vinegar and looking for women who smelled and dressed differently than Indian women. Not that any of the three had anything against their Ute women; they just needed a change every so often. Especially Chardonnais.

Early and Rawlins had gone off somewhere— Chardonnais figured a saloon, though he had been asleep when his two friends left and was uncertain. He was looking for them near the plaza when he came across a splendid-looking young woman who was being harassed by strutting peacocks who thought their fathers' wealth gave them leave to do as they pleased. It was apparent to Chardonnais right off that the young woman did not share their opinion.

She was a little taller than Chardonnais, with a young woman's lithe grace. Though she was slim, she seemed firm, and she stretched the fabric of her dress at bust and hips. Her dress of finespun cotton was a soft blue color and left her neck and most of her shoulders bare. It had short sleeves, revealing most of her arms, and reached only as far down as midcalf, so a fairly generous portion of leg was visible. She wore plain, simple slippers on her feet. Her long black hair hung in waves almost halfway down her back. She wore no hat, but she carried a folded fan in one hand. The skin of her shoulders and arms was smooth and a deep rich brown. "*Ma chère!*" Chardonnais said loudly, as if suddenly discovering his long-lost love right there in front of him. "Dere you are! I 'ave been looking for you all over. Come, we must hurry." He stopped alongside her and smiled at her once before turning his coal-dark eyes, smoldering in anger, at the two young *hacendados*.

"Who the hell are you?" one asked in Spanish.

"*No comprendez,*" Chardonnais said innocently. He understood far more Spanish than he was willing to admit, though he could speak it only a little.

The two Mexican men looked at each other and shared a smug smile. "Let's kick this fool's ass," one said to the other in Spanish.

Chardonnais understood, and fought back the smile that rose to his lips.

"Excusa, por favor," one said obsequiously. He and his friend separated just a little. "Excuse us, please. We meant no harm to the señorita."

Chardonnais ducked the punch the one man threw and came up fast and hard with a powerful, driving punch that broke at least two of the Mexican's ribs on the right side, low down.

"Help your friend home, asshole," he said in English. "And bot' of you should learn to treat de señoritas better." He looked at the woman and smiled. "I am Lucien Chardonnais," he said simply. He held out his left arm. "Mademoiselle." He waved his right hand with a flourish.

Señorita Inez Mejia tentatively slipped her hand through the crook of Chardonnais's arm. She was a little frightened, but she tried not to let it show. After all, this was an American, or close enough to one. Like all the rest of them, especially the trappers, he walked with a swagger in his step and in his eyes. He was garishly dressed in decorated, fringed buckskin pants, bright red calico shirt, and green wool cap, with the top flopped over. A silver medal of some kind added to his myriad colors and brightness.

But another side of her was attracted to him. He had, after all, saved her from Mariano Torres and Pablo Estrada. She almost shivered when she thought of them. They, too, were swaggering young men, like this funny-sounding American. But where Estrada and Torres had nothing to back up their arrogance except perhaps their fathers' money, her short, bowlegged escort seemed to exude manliness.

"And where shall we go, señorita?" Chardonnais asked when they were a little away from the two men who had accosted her.

"Home," she responded in English. Her voice was soft and sweet, almost breathless. It excited him.

"You must show the way."

They walked in silence, across the plaza to a side street, where there were a few houses with tall adobe walls and imposing gates. "This is it, señor," she said, stopping at one of the wood gates, painted a bright red.

Chardonnais nodded. "Will I see you again, mademoiselle?" he asked politely.

"Perhaps," she answered coyly. "There's a *baile* tonight. Perhaps you will see me there."

"I'll look for you," Chardonnais said gallantly. He bent and kissed the back of her right hand. Looking at her, he smiled and asked, "Would you tell me your name, señorita?"

"Inez."

"Just Inez?"

"That's enough for you to know now." Then she spun and disappeared behind the gate.

Chardonnais stood there for some moments, thinking that perhaps he had had no more than a vision, that the lovely Inez had been manufactured by a tired brain. Then he smiled. Her perfume hung in the air, and he knew she was real. He turned and headed off, his step even more jaunty than usual.

He spotted her that evening at the *baile* and headed straight for her. She was dressed this time in a dress of dark red silk, again exposing a fair amount of skin. The color suited her well, Chardonnais thought. With an exaggerated flourish, he asked her to dance. Her father looked annoyed but gave his consent.

While he was dancing with Inez, Chardonnais spotted the two young men. They were dressed in tight pants and short wool jackets. Silver conchos ran down the outer seams of their trousers. Their faces were shaded by their large sombreros, but Chardonnais still thought one was holding himself very carefully and was in pain from his cracked ribs. Chardonnais felt not the least bit guilty about it.

Two dances later, he and Inez slipped away under the cover of the shadowy night. Within minutes, they were in his room, where some of his gallantry slithered away along with his and Inez's clothing. Inez did not seem to mind this time. Or the second. Or the third, either.

Chardonnais couldn't get enough of Inez. Her soft, dusky skin, her firm, dark-tipped breasts, the swell of her belly slipping smoothly down to her hidden treasures—all excited him no end.

For her part, Inez was fascinated by Chardonnais. She wondered where he had gotten the large, nasty-looking scar on his chest. Such thoughts fled, though, when his hard, callused hands moved over her body, touching and stroking her in ways she had never encountered. She was not innocent of men, not by a long shot, but no man had ever made her feel like this short, insatiable little French-Canadian had.

As much as she was enjoying herself, though, she knew he had to go sooner or later. With regret, she told him so.

"Ah, but de night is still young, yes?" He smiled at her.

"I wish it were so," Inez said with a sigh. "But it's not."

"Well, dere is time for another liaison," he said with certainty.

"I don't think so. My father is . . ." Her arguments wilted as he caressed her with strong, sure hands, insistently touching her womanhood, touching, teasing. She melted. "*Sí*, there is time," she said, giving in to the pleasures. *No,* she thought dreamily, *no man has ever been like this.*

Sometime—Inez wasn't sure how long—later, she and Chardonnais finally rose from the bed and dressed with more than a little reluctance. Then Chardonnais escorted her back to the party. Just before arriving at Don Esteban's house, where the *baile* was being held, Inez stopped and kissed the trapper lightly. "Will I see you again?" she asked, smiling. How recently he had asked her the same thing. Despite her smile, she was worried. Chardonnais might be a man to take his pleasure where he found it and then move on.

"*Mais oui!*" he said.

Inez's father gave Chardonnais a harsh glare when he escorted the young woman to a chair. While Chardonnais strolled off to find Rawlins and Early, if they were there, he noticed Don Esteban Mejia talking with the two men who had accosted Inez earlier in the day. He shrugged it off as of no consequence to him.

Chardonnais could not find either of his friends, so he headed back toward his room, yawning. It had been a long—but ever so delightful—day. Suddenly four shapes loomed in front of him. The flickering of the torches lining the street showed that two of the men were the ones who had accosted Inez. They moved into a semicircle in front of Chardonnais, backing him up against an adobe wall.

One of them flashed a large knife. "I am Mariano Torres. I and my friends will make certain, *Americano* pig," he spat in English, "that you don't molest any more of our fine young ladies."

Chardonnais laughed. "*Merde,*" he offered, "you wouldn't know what to do wit' a real woman even if you could find one stupid enough to lay wit' you."

Torres swept in on Chardonnais, knife raised. Chardonnais grabbed the knife arm and shoved it up and away. At the same time he kneed Torres in the stomach. Torres dropped the knife and Chardonnais kneed him in the face before flinging him away—in the direction of another of the young men. That Mexican danced away from his friend.

At the same time Pablo Estrada—he of the fractured ribs—moved gingerly toward Chardonnais, as did the fourth man.

"You want some more broken bones, eh?" Chardonnais said to Estrada.

Estrada hesitated. "Don't listen to that fool, Pablo," Inez's brother Fernando said. "He can't hurt you."

"Like hell." Chardonnais jumped forward and slammed three quick, hard punches into Estrada's stomach and ribs. Estrada screeched and fell, clutching his midriff.

Mejia and the fourth man, his and Inez's brother Luis, charged in on Chardonnais from opposite sides. Chardonnais swung to face Fernando Mejia, and when he did, Luis Mejia jumped on his back, trying to lock an arm around his throat.

"Hold him," Fernando Mejia shouted. "Hold him."

Luis tried, but Chardonnais backpedaled until he slammed the Mexican's back against the adobe wall. Fernando Mejia charged in, just in time to have Chardonnais head-butt him. He staggered backward.

Chardonnais looked around. Torres had gotten back up, with his knife in hand. His eyes gleamed hatefully eerie in the torchlight. "I'll get you now, you son of a bitch," he snarled in Spanish.

Ezra Early stepped up behind Torres and slammed the butt of a flintlock pistol against the back of his head. Torres fell.

About the same time, Rawlins had grabbed Fernando Mejia by the back of the head and slammed his face into the adobe wall twice. Mejia sank like a stone.

Chardonnais looked around. All four men were down—not unconscious maybe, but out of the fight nonetheless. He wiped his hands. "I t'ink maybe dat takes care of dem, eh," he said with a grin.

For the next three days Chardonnais looked for Inez Mejia, but could not find her. Then a sympathetic Mexican friend pulled him aside in a saloon one day. "Give up your search, Señor Chardonnais."

"Why?" Chardonnais asked, angry and surprised. "She been hurt or somet'ing?" he demanded. "I will kill whoever does dat to her."

"She's not hurt." Arturo Gómez licked his lips nervously. "She's been sent to Mexico City. To a convent."

Chardonnais stood dumbfounded, angry and sad all at once. But he knew there was nothing he could do. He tried to put her out of his mind over the years, but he never completely forgot her.

17

THE REAL WORK OF SETTING up the winter camp began for the four men . . . and their wives. Their lodging was taken care of with their tipis, though Early's needed a few new lodgepoles and Boatwright's needed some patching.

That still left enough things to do, and those took plenty of doing. Enough wood for the winter had to be gathered, chopped, split, and stored. Fodder had to be gathered for the horses and mules. The animals would be left to fend for themselves as much as possible, but in the harshest months, they would have to rely on what had been gathered for them. The men had already made a lot of meat in the form of jerky and pemmican, but with ten mouths to feed they would need more. That meant hunting, butchering, and tending fires for smoking meat. There was still trapping to be done, too. The plews they pulled in now were prime ones, thick and lush.

The women, too, had their tasks to perform. They played a large part in the making of meat. They had to tend to the children and the lodges. Clothing—warm

buffalo-wool moccasins, coats, gloves, mittens—had to
be repaired or made. The women also gathered firewood and tended the fires. They had to cook, tan buffalo robes, elk skins, and any other furs and put the
finishing touches on beaver plews.

Such work kept all but the children busy.

The men still managed to find time for visiting with
the Utes camping not far off. Chardonnais and his two
longtime friends felt quite at home in the Ute village.
They had been dealing with Strong Bear and his band
of Uncompahgres for years now and were both
accepted and welcome.

Boatwright, on the other hand, was rather uncomfortable about it all. He had been in Indian villages
before, but always with a larger group. Now, however,
he was with only three other men, and men who were
as at home here as they were in Taos or some other
city. Having a Ute wife helped, but Boatwright still felt
he didn't fit in.

Still, the Utes treated him courteously and with the
respect due to a great friend of the Utes' three great
friends—Lucien Chardonnais, Ezra Early, and Abe
Rawlins. Sitting in Strong Bear's lodge one night,
Boatwright began to feel a bit more at home. He wasn't
sure why. Perhaps it was the warmth of the fire as the
wind whipped and howled outside. Perhaps it was the
closeness of the men sitting around the fire. Perhaps it
was the sated feeling from the buffalo meat he had
eaten, or the coffee he had consumed. Whatever had
spurred it, he relaxed some.

It was at times like these that he really had a
chance to study the Utes. The warriors, generally of
medium height or a little smaller, were stocky as a
rule, with strong chests and broad shoulders. Their
long hair was generally worn braided and wrapped in

fur. They were darker than many of the Indians Boatwright had encountered, but that didn't surprise him much, mainly because he had been living with Blue Rattle for a couple of months now. They were all full of life and humor—much of it crude, which suited Boatwright just fine.

They were unlike other Indians, though, he was surprised to learn, in that they did not live for war. It seemed every other tribe Boatwright had run across was far more bloodthirsty than the Utes. Not that the Utes were cowards, if Chardonnais and his two friends were to be believed. Even when laughing, they looked strong of arm and strong of character.

Strong Bear, of course, had the seat of honor, facing the door, and it was to him that everyone looked to guide the conversation.

When a lull in the talk arrived, Boatwright gathered up his courage some and said, "Lucien's told me there's an interestin' story about this place, Strong Bear. That true?"

Strong Bear's big, round head bobbed up and down, but he said nothing.

"Well, for Christ's sake, ye dumb Injun, tell it," Rawlins said with a snort.

Several of the warriors chuckled, but Strong Bear just gazed haughtily at Rawlins for a few moments. Then he grinned. "I will do this," he said in Ute. "For my great friend—Jed Boatwright." He laughed.

"Sorry ol' fart," Rawlins growled, not meaning it.

"One day many winters ago," Strong Bear said in his strong, rich baritone, "there was a chief of the People. Strong Bear was his name, too, I am told." He smiled a little.

"Strong Bear, my ass," Rawlins said in an obvious whisper.

Boatwright listened intently as Strong Bear spoke in Ute. Chardonnais, who was sitting on Boatwright's right, translated for him.

"This old chief," Strong Bear went on, pretending that he had not heard Rawlins, "used to come to this place and use the waters. The warmth was good for his old bones, and eased his tired and aching body. But then one day a band of young warriors came here while the wise old chief was soothing himself in the waters."

Strong Bear paused for another bite of meat, sliced off a rib bone braced over the fire. "The young ones were not content to sit and use the waters as was the old chief. No, they wanted to move on, to see new things. 'Tell us, old man,' they said, 'how to get across the mountains to the east. There are many horses there for us to steal. We will become big men in our band.'

"But the old chief was wise, and he told them, 'The tribe to the east is a mighty one. They have many warriors, and will kill you all.' "

"But they went anyway, didn't they?" Boatwright asked. He would have gone, and he figured any young warriors worth their salt would have, too.

Strong Bear nodded. "Of course. They did ask the old chief to lead them. But the chief—wise old Strong Bear—knew better," he added with a small smile. "And he refused."

Strong Bear stopped speaking and sat staring into the fire for a few moments, as if he could see the tale unfolding in the flickering flames. Then, suddenly, he spoke again.

"The young men were very angry and called the old chief many names. They accused him of cowardice, of being a woman. But he remained resolute. Finally the young men elected a new leader from among themselves, one that had a strong heart and knew no fear. Or so they thought.

"As the young men left they made more fun of the old chief, who took their insults calmly, and then he said, 'I will wait for you here, at this spot, until you return.' Until they returned, that was the old chief's vow."

Once more Strong Bear grew silent, listening to the snap and pop of the logs in the fire. Then he smiled wryly. "They never did come back. Never did. And yet the chief waits—will wait for all eternity—as he sits by his campfire. The old chief's fire is what keeps these waters hot for all to use."

Then there was silence. Into the breach rose Rawlins's soft, deep voice. "Well, now, Strong Bear, that was some tale ye told there. Goddamn if it weren't. But I've knowed better. Damn true I have. Lucien, why don't ye tell these here boys about the time me, you, and Ezra was up in the Teton land."

"De time when we had dat run-in with de buffalo?"

"Yeah, that's the time," Rawlins said with a nod. He fired up his old pipe and then leaned back, relaxed.

Chardonnais nodded and rubbed his hands together a little. "Well, we was up dere by *les Grande Tetons*—de Big Tit mountains—in de wintair. De snow, it was high almost to de top of de lodges. It was a cold time, too, and we were facing starvin' times. *Mais oui!* We were about ready to eat our moccasins when we see dis buffalo. '*Mon Dieu*,' I say to myself, 'but dat is de biggest buffalo I ever see.' It was maybe ten feet tall at de hump and weighed maybe twice dat of a regular buffalo. '*Sacré bleu*,' I say to myself, 'but dis will make meat to last us de whole rest of de wintair!'"

Chardonnais stopped for a sip of coffee. Seeing Rawlins's pipe reminded him of his own, and he took his time in filling and lighting it. The others waited with outward signs of patience, but all of them—save Rawlins and Early—badly wanted to hear the rest of the story.

"Now," Chardonnais said once he had gotten his pipe going, "where was I? Ah, *oui*, de buffalo. My friends dere, dey knew dis buffalo would end our starving times, even if it was poor bull. And me, I know dis, too. But de trouble is, dis buffalo, he won't just fall over and die."

"Why didn't you just shoot it?" Boatwright asked. The answer was so simple.

"Didn't I tell you?" Chardonnais said in complete innocence. "Dere was so much snow dat all our powder was wet and no good. About de best we could do wit' dem rifles was to club de buffalo wit' dem. And dat, I t'ink, would only make de buffalo mad."

"You didn't have no dry powder at all?" Boatwright asked.

"*Mais non!* Didn't I tell you, we 'ad lost all our powder in de river."

"But you said . . ."

"Well," Chardonnais said in something of a huff, "if you don' want me to tell dis story, den I'll shut up and let someone else talk for a while." He crossed his arms firmly across his chest.

Boatwright looked around at the Utes. It did not matter a whit to them that the whole thing was fabricated. Their interest was in the *telling* of the story, not the story itself. "I'm sorry," he said innocently, "I hadn't heard you say that. That'll teach me to pay more attention." He paused just a moment. "Please, go on."

"Not at de risk of more interrupting," Chardonnais said haughtily.

"I ain't gonna interrupt you no goddamn more,"

Boatwright said with some exasperation. "Just get on with the tellin' of it, for Christ's sake."

"Well, we decide dat while I will distract de ol' bull, my two *amis* dere, dey would attack de bull wit' knives and tomahawks. So I start creeping up on de buffalo, since I don't want to scare him too soon." He stopped to puff on his pipe a little.

"De trouble wit' dat is de buffalo, he sees me de whole time. And he don't look too happy about it neither. He starts pawing de ground, and shaking his great shaggy head. His horns suddenly look to me to be ten feet across. I say to myself, 'Monsieur Chardonnais, you got damp powder here and no fire to dry it.' Den Abe dere, brave hoss dat he is, he say to me, 'Well, Frenchie, you're supposed to be distracting him. Don' just stand dere. Do somet'ing.' So I square my shoulders and I walk straight up to dat buffalo."

Chardonnais paused to knock the ashes out of his pipe. For some reason, it did not taste right to him just now, and so he could see no real reason to continue smoking it. He set it carefully down next to him, wishing he was in his own lodge. Then he'd have a jug handy to cut his thirst. He sighed. He was not in his own lodge and so would have to do without.

"De buffalo, he looks at me even meaner dan before. But I just rap on his forehead. I say, 'Monsieur Bison, me and my friends are some hungry. *Mais oui!* And you might be one stringy ol' critter, but we need to make meat of you.' I don' t'ink he like dat very much either. So I look around, looking for my friends. Dey were supposed to be helping out with dis, but I don' see dem nowhere."

"We was too busy laughin' to be much of a help," Rawlins said.

"Damn right," Early added. "We figured you were gonna talk that damn ol' critter to death."

"Dat's because you 'ave no courage," Chardonnais retorted. He sighed with great exaggeration. "I start den to ret'ink t'ings, seeing as how de buffalo was looking meaner and meaner every second. Den I turn and run like hell, hoping I can make de hill before de bull hooks me in de ass."

Rawlins was laughing now, his voice low and raspy, caught in the fire smoke. "That was some goddamn sight, the likes of which this ol' niggur ain't seed in many a day."

"Bah!" Chardonnais growled in mock anger.

"I ain't ever seen ol' Lucien there move so fast. Not before, not since," Early added with a chuckle.

"Well," Boatwright demanded, "how the hell'd you kill that damn critter?"

Rawlins laughed all the more. "First I got to tell ye, that as much as we were in starvin' times, we had us one good meal of Mexican spicy beans just that day."

"So?" Boatwright asked, baffled. "What's that got to do with anything?"

"Well, dose two frightened bastards wasn't being no help to me, and—"

"Hell, Frenchie, me'n Ez was layin' there laughin' our asses off as that gigantic buffler charged after your ass."

"It still don't make no sense."

"Ain't you ever ate Mexican food before, boy?" Early asked.

"Yeah. It's so spicy that it . . ."

Rawlins, Early, and Chardonnais were roaring with laughter now. "That's right," Rawlins managed to squawk. "Ol' froggie there let a fart go that stopped that buffler dead in his tracks."

"Hell, killed half the goddamn trees in that valley, too," Early said in a voice strangled by laughter.

"But the worst part of it all," Rawlins wheezed, "was that it spoilt all that goddamn meat!"

Everyone was rocking with laughter, and it took more than a few minutes for it to die down. When it did, Chardonnais wiped his eyes and stood. "Well, *mes amis,*" he said, "it's time for dis ol' hoss to be in de robes."

18

THE SUDDEN DIN OF THE dozens of Ute dogs yowling in concert made Chardonnais and his three friends stop their work and look up, alarmed.

"What the hell's that?" Rawlins asked, his breath forming a cloud in front of his long face.

"*Merde!*" Chardonnais said. "De village, it is being attacked."

"Who the hell'd be crazy enough to attack a Ute village?" Rawlins wondered aloud. "In the winter yet?"

"Only ones crazy enough for such doin's is the goddamn Blackfeet," Early said. "Or the goddamn Crows."

"We gonna go and help?" Rawlins wondered.

"Not me," Chardonnais said flatly. "We go over dere, and dose red devils'll be over here stealing our horses, plews, and women. Strong Bear's people can stand up for demselves."

"This chil' feels the same," Early said.

"Reckon I'm with ye, then," Rawlins added.

"I'm happier'n a pig in shit dat dey hit de village first," Chardonnais said quietly. "We had twenty Crows

144

or Blackfeet ride in here on us and we would've been made wolf bait of in a real quick hurry."

"Well, we'd best make some plans," Rawlins said. "Them red devils're still likely to be comin' down on us anyway. Unless the Utes send 'em packin'."

"We can always hope for that," Early responded. "But we best get ready just in case." He thought for an instant, then nodded. "Jed, get the animals back into the trees and stay with 'em. Lucien, you get the women and young'ns back in there, too. Come on, Abe, we'll show them niggurs somethin', they choose to come by here."

The men all moved off, acting with swift certainty. It was snowing again, though not very heavily. The snow muffled sounds some, which Early saw as a slight disadvantage. Still, it would partially hide them as well as the enemy, which would be a help.

Early moved off into the trees to the left of the tipis, just enough to have some protection while allowing a clear shot. Rawlins did the same to the right. Even while they were moving into position, checking their weapons and supplies of powder and ball, Chardonnais was shooing the women and children into the safety of the aspen grove. Boatwright was busy moving the horses and mules into the trees, too, working quietly but hastily.

Then they hunkered down to wait. Despite his heavy blanket coat, Chardonnais could feel the cold seeping into him, so he stood and walked around a little, speaking a few words to the children and some to the women. All were used to such things, and did not see it as out of the ordinary.

The group could still hear the Ute dogs raising a racket, and there were frequent war cries but few gunshots. It was eerie sitting a couple hundred yards from the battle but unable to see it or hear it very well. It seemed to the group that the battle was somehow not a part of this earth, happening in another time and place.

It did not stay that way for long. Suddenly a half-dozen warriors on painted horses materialized through the snow. Early and Rawlins fired their rifles, and two of the warriors went down.

The other four pulled up in a flurry of snow and confusion. They were Crows. By the time they regained their equilibrium—having been surprised that anyone was in this area—Early and Rawlins had dropped two more.

The last two whirled and headed back into the sifting snowfall.

"You all right up dere?" Chardonnais shouted.

"What the hell do *you* think, you dumb frog bastard," Rawlins snapped without much vehemence.

"Knowing how bad you shoot, I'm not sure, you chicken fart."

"Eat sh—" Rawlins paused. "They're comin' again! Looks like a heap of 'em, too. You best watch them women and kids, Frenchie."

"Dose red devils ain't going to get . . ." He threw his rifle up to his shoulder and fired. A Crow bounced off his horse ten yards out from the trees. Chardonnais swiftly reloaded, but then dropped the rifle. Crows were on foot now, and moving into the trees.

Early saw one head into his lodge. "Son of a bitch," he muttered. He stood and headed for the tipi as another Crow ducked into the lodge. Early slid out his tomahawk and had a bloody greeting for the first Crow, who stepped outside the lodge with Early's extra rifle in his hand. He never knew what hit him as Early's tomahawk cleaved his forehead.

Early slid silently into his lodge. The second Crow

was bending over a parfleche box, pawing through the contents. He was unaware of Early until the mountain man whistled a single note. The Crow's head spun halfway around, and then he, too, had his head split.

Rawlins was dimly aware of Early's actions, but he was too busy on his own. He fired his rifle again and then dropped it. A moment later Rawlins began to rise as a Crow jumped at him. The Crow hit him halfway up, driving him back a little.

Rawlins bounced when he hit, but so did the Crow, and neither could get a firm grip on the other. Hampered by their heavy coats and mittens, they struggled up, still trying to gain a handhold.

The Crow head-butted Rawlins, who slumped, stunned. The warrior ripped out a knife and raised it, poised to plunge the blade into Rawlins's heart.

Chardonnais had shot one Crow at close range with one of his pistols, and a moment later a second leapt upon him. His short, bulky body absorbed the shock of the fall, and then he shoved the Indian off him. He jumped up and kicked the Crow in the face before the warrior could get up. He was about to move in and finish the man off when Looks Again shouted.

Chardonnais jerked his head around and saw the other Crow just about to kill Rawlins. He ripped out his second pistol and fired. The Crow jerked from the impact of the lead ball, but Chardonnais was not sure if he had killed him. He swung back and hatcheted the Crow at his feet, then swung around, ready to charge to Rawlins's rescue, if needed.

Rawlins had gained his feet and stomped the chest of the Crow Chardonnais had wounded. Then he drew his tomahawk and finished the Indian off.

Rawlins fired his pistol at another charging Crow. The Indian was so close that his momentum carried him forward until he crashed into Rawlins, who fell, the dead Crow on top of him.

"Damn," Rawlins muttered as he shoved the body off. He just managed to get his head out of the way of still another warrior's tomahawk, which chunked into the snowy earth mere inches from his left ear. Rawlins jerked his left arm up, crooked at the elbow, and snapped it forward. His elbow hit the Crow between the eyes. He had little leverage, but it was enough to freeze the Indian for a second—just long enough for him to jab a thumb into the warrior's right eye.

The Crow recoiled, back arched. Rawlins grabbed his throat and squeezed hard. At the same time he shoved up and over. Once he got atop the Crow, he quickly strangled the life out of him. Just then he was clubbed on the back of the head. He fell forward, groaning, his face slapping into the dead Crow's.

Chardonnais was overwhelmed by three warriors. All four men went down in a squirming, kicking pile of arms, legs, and torsos. Chardonnais lashed out with fists and feet, connecting on a fair number of blows, but he received at least as many as he gave.

Somehow—he wasn't sure how—the trapper got to his feet. As he did so, he caught one of the Crows' forearms in both hands, barely stopping the plummeting knife inches from his chest. Another warrior punched him hard in a kidney. "*Merde,*" Chardonnais gasped, sagging a little but not releasing the other Crow's arm.

Chardonnais jerked that Crow forward and around. The warrior who had punched him was just fixing to stab him. Instead, the blade sank deep into his own comrade's back.

Chardonnais let go of the warrior's arm, and the

Crow fell. The little trapper jumped over the body and latched his hands around the throat of the Indian with the bloody knife. The Crow responded by kicking him in the knee.

"*Merde*," Chardonnais cursed again as he lost his grip on the Crow.

The third warrior who had attacked him now pounced on his back, knocking him forward. He landed hard on his chest, and his face smacked the snow-covered ground. Chardonnais thrust upward with arms and legs, lifting the Crow, who quickly clamped a forearm around his throat. Chardonnais still managed to get to his feet, and he grabbed the forearm and strained to break its grip.

The second warrior charged, knife blade leading the way. Still trying to get loose from the insistent arm on his throat, Chardonnais braced himself to be stabbed, tightening his stomach muscles, knowing all the while that it would not keep him alive.

Suddenly Looks Again materialized between her husband and the Crow. The warrior pulled up in surprise, and Looks Again slickly plunged her favorite butchering knife up under his ribs. The Crow's eyes widened in shock. Looks Again pulled the blade free and then plunged it home again and again. The warrior finally toppled, managing to get an arm on his killer and knock her down.

While Looks Again struggled to get out from under the weight of the dead Crow, her husband tried with renewed fury to get the other Crow's arm off his neck. His air was choked off, and dark spots danced before his eyes. In desperation, he used one hand to pat frantically around on his chest, until his fingers found the small patch knife dangling from the thong around his neck. He jerked it over his right shoulder.

The Crow screeched as the two-and-a-half-inch-long blade sliced into his right eye. His arm left Chardonnais's throat as he instinctively clutched at his eye with both hands.

Gasping for air, Chardonnais spun as quickly as he could. He kicked the Crow in the groin. "Ass-licking maggot," he wheezed in French. Then he pulled his tomahawk and split the top of the warrior's head. He turned to face whatever else might be coming at him.

Early stepped out of his lodge and almost got a dose of his own tomahawk medicine. He managed to dodge the war club a Crow had swiped at him with. His left arm snaked out and grabbed the Indian's arm, the Crow's hand almost in his armpit, his own hand clamped just above the back of the warrior's elbow. Early jerked the arm upward a little, making the Indian rise to his toes. Early chopped at him three times, taking chunks of flesh and ribs out with each blow. He contemptuously threw the body away from him.

"Waugh!" he grunted. "Come and get me, you bloody-ass savages," he added, upper lip curled in a sneer. He howled in defiance as he saw more Crows heading into the camp, snaking through the trees.

Two broke off and took him up on his challenge. They did not understand the words, but they knew full well what this tall, rangy white man meant.

Early pulled his tomahawk up over his right shoulder and then flung it forward. The blade of the weapon thudded into one Crow's chest. The warrior stumbled on a few more steps and then collapsed.

Early jerked out his second pistol and fired at the second Crow. The ball punched a bloody gouge in the Indian's neck, tearing open the carotid artery. Blood sprayed out in a thick red fount. The warrior stopped and grabbed his throat, almost strangling himself in an effort to stem the torrent of blood.

Early glanced at Rawlins, who seemed to be in a little trouble. He was about to go help his old friend when he heard shouting coming from Boatwright's position back in the trees. Ripping his tomahawk out of the Crow's body, he ran like hell for the small herd of animals, leaping over logs and boulders as he did so.

Four Crows were swarming over Boatwright, who was fighting like a wild man, cursing up a blue streak. He had a bridle in one hand and a knife in the other. Both were doing some damage to the Crows, but Early knew his new friend could not keep up such a fight much longer. He waded in, ow-ow-owing like a Ute warrior.

He almost severed one warrior's head with his tomahawk. He grabbed another by his waist-length hair and jerked him backward. The warrior fell, landing hard on his rump. Before he could get to his feet, Early had whirled and hacked him to death. He turned to help Boatwright again, but saw that the young man needed no help—or at least none killing Crows.

With Early's sudden appearance, Boatwright found an ounce more fury inside him. Still clutching his knife, he grabbed the bridle with both hands and began flailing away. One Crow's face began to disappear, replaced by torn strips of bloody flesh.

The fourth Crow spun and ran.

"Take him, Jed!" Early shouted. His blood was running hot with the lust to kill. "I'll see to the horses."

Boatwright wheeled and raced off, catching the Crow in a few strides. He jumped on the Indian's back, bringing him down in a heap. In seconds his knife had completed the bloody job.

Boatwright had tied all the horses and mules to trees, and while they were skittish and nervous, they were not going anywhere. Early looked back to see if he could help anyone else. "Jesus goddamn Christ, no," he hissed, feeling as if his chest had been torn out. Abe Rawlins was prostrate, and if he wasn't dead already, he would be in a moment as a Crow, heavy war club raised high, loomed over him.

Early was too far away to be of any help. And both his pistols were empty. He glimpsed Chardonnais out of the corner of his eye. The French-Canadian was also too far away to help Rawlins, and it appeared as if his pistols, too, were empty.

Early could not believe his eyes when he saw the Crow suddenly fall atop Rawlins, three arrows sticking out of his back.

Then Utes were flooding into the trees, hunting down whatever Crows were left. Those Crows still living were fleeing, leaving behind their dead and dying.

19

THE CROW WARRIOR SAT AT the fire, his
demeanor stamped with defiance. He was a handsome
man, with a clear, broad face and regal-looking nose.
His features were finely formed and his carriage was
straight. His crowning glory, though, was his hair. The
glossy black mane hung loose and full to about halfway
down his buttocks. Half a dozen eagle feathers were
tied to the back of his head.

Chardonnais and his three friends were sitting
around the fire in Strong Bear's lodge. Most of the
other Ute warriors were crammed inside.

"Speak and you will die a warrior's death," Strong
Bear said to the Crow in sign language.

The Crow spit into the fire.

"What's your name?" Chardonnais asked in hesi-
tant, heavily accented Crow.

"Black Blood," the Crow responded.

"Did you and your friends come here on purpose?"

Black Blood shrugged. He wished he had died
with the others, or had fled with the others. Anything
rather than having to sit in this stinking Ute lodge and

153

listen to the grumblings of the fat Utes and their white-skinned friends. Black Blood really had nothing against whites; indeed, he called many of them friends. But not ones who would consort so openly with Utes.

"The hell with him," Rawlins drawled. "The dumb bastard ain't got the balls to answer us, we'll just get to hackin' him into pieces. Kind of like that ol' niggur you took care of today, Ez."

Early nodded. "My 'hawk's been bloodied near enough for one day, but I reckon one more Crow won't make no difference."

Both were quite certain the Crow understood enough English to know what was being said.

"But dat leaves us wit' all de bodies to take care of," Chardonnais protested mildly.

"The goddamn wolves and buzzards can have 'em," Rawlins said.

"Dat is all right wit' me, too, but we'll have to get dem away from our camp, I t'ink. I don't want to be humping my woman while de wolves and de coyotes're snarling and howling over the stringy remains of some fool Crows."

"You got another idea, Frenchie?" Rawlins asked.

"Well, if dis stupid *fils de garce*," Chardonnais answered, pointing at Black Blood, "talks to us, maybe we can send him home—wit' what's left of his friends."

"I got no problem with that," Rawlins said flatly. "But I ain't aimin' to set here all the goddamn day whilst numb nuts there tries to make up his mind." He was in a foul humor, as he always was when he was almost killed. His head pounded from being nearly brained by that one Crow, and that did nothing to boost his spirits.

"What about it, Black Blood?" Chardonnais asked in his poor version of Crow.

"What do you want to know?" Black Blood asked diffidently.

"You attack the Utes on purpose?"

"Maybe." He shrugged. "We were looking for horses and maybe a little bit of war before heading home again to stay until the winter passes."

"And you just stumbled on Strong Bear's village here?"

Black Blood nodded again.

"There's somethin' I want to know, Lucien," Early said. "Why didn't they attack our little camp? Hell, they had done that we'd all be laying out there as scavenger food instead of those Crows."

Chardonnais asked the question in Crow as best he could.

"We didn't know it was there," Black Blood said honestly. "If we had, we would've overrun you easily."

"You just stumbled on us?"

"Yes," Black Blood said, his annoyance growing. If only he and his men had scouted a little more instead of attacking straight off, they would have found the camp of the mountain men. It would have been mere moments before all four white men were dead, scalped, and hacked up. Then Black Blood and his men would've had the four women to play with, plus all the horses and mules.

Black Blood shook his head at his ill fortune. "Split Face was among the first who found your camp. He rode quickly back here and told us. We left here to go there."

"Buffler shit," Rawlins snapped. He understood enough Crow to know what the warrior had said. "You came chargin' over to our camp, you pus-suckin' little fart, 'cause Strong Bear's men were whippin' the shit out of you. All you boys was doing was tryin' to save your asses."

Everyone could tell by the momentary flash of anger on Black Blood's face that Rawlins had hit the mark plumb center.

"You numb-nut bastards probably thought the Utes wouldn't follow you boys, didn't you, you dog-eatin' peckerwood? Or maybe you was just hopin' they wouldn't."

Black Blood snarled, but said nothing.

There were some moments of silence, and then Chardonnais asked, "Well, what do we do wit' him?"

"You want to send him back—along with what's left of his friends out there?" Rawlins asked.

Chardonnais shrugged.

"Jesus goddamn Christ Almighty, you frog-fartin' little bastard," Rawlins snapped. "You was the one brought it up in the first place."

"You don't mind?"

"I don't give a shit, Frenchie. But I'll tell you one thing, boy—this ol' niggur ain't fixin' to help ye none. Ye want it done, ol' hoss, you'll have to do it. Maybe you can get a few of Strong Bear's kids to help you."

"Hah!" Chardonnais snapped. "When did I ever need help from de likes of you, eh? You tell me dat."

"Maybe ye never did," Rawlins said reasonably. "But if that's so, ye best hope and pray that ye never do need it, 'cause ye ain't gonna get it."

"I—"

"That's enough, goddammit," Early snapped. He sighed, suddenly annoyed by everything. There was still too much work to be done and full winter would be on them much too soon. He did not feel like sitting here debating the future of a bunch of Crow corpses.

"Well, what do you t'ink, Ezra?" Chardonnais asked.

Early shrugged. "I don't give a shit what happens to 'em. You want to send 'em back to Absaroka, go on ahead. But I ain't gonna help you neither. And if you are gonna do it, best get to it."

Chardonnais's face colored with anger. Early had spoken to him as if he were an errant boy. He did not like that. But he also knew that Early and Rawlins were right. He looked at Strong Bear. "You will let Black Blood go?" he asked.

Strong Bear searched the lodge for a few moments, his eyes encountering everyone else's on their circuit of the tipi. He saw some resistance in a few pairs of eyes, but not much. He nodded.

"Will any of your men help me?"

Striking Hawk, a young warrior who was as fearless and as homely a man as Chardonnais had ever seen said, "I will help."

Two others—Moving Thunder and Walking in the Sky—said they, too, would help. Boatwright also volunteered.

The five men left the lodge, leaving Black Blood to sit there while the bodies were tossed onto Crow horses. It did not take long and soon they were back. "Time for you to go, asslicker," Chardonnais announced to Black Blood.

The Crow stood, showing little effect from the arrow wound in his side. He moved around the fire toward the flap in the tipi, but before he could bend to move out the hole, Chardonnais stopped him.

"A moment, monsieur," the trapper said with quiet force. "Just to make sure you don't t'ink you have bested us because I am a fool with a soft heart, I will give you a few t'ings to t'ink about."

Chardonnais drew his knife in his right hand. With his left, he stroked the thick beard he had allowed to grow of late. Then he grabbed a fistful of the Crow's buckskin shirt and plunged the knife into the cloth and sawed it open. When it was cut, he pointed the knife. Striking Hawk jerked and tugged the shirt off.

Chardonnais then slit the buckskin thongs holding up Black Blood's leggings, followed by the buckskin thong that held up Black Blood's breechclout. He did the same with the bear-claw necklace and tossed it to Striking Hawk.

"Your moccasins, monsieur," Chardonnais ordered.

Keeping his face blank, Black Blood kicked off his moccasins, and then stood there completely naked.

"Just one more t'ing, monsieur," Chardonnais said quietly. The only sound in the lodge was the popping of the fire and the men's regular breathing. Chardonnais walked around to Black Blood's right, lightly tapping the warrior's shoulder with the knife blade. When he got behind him, Chardonnais slid the blade lightly in the crack between Black Blood's buttocks cheeks. He drew the knife upward ever so gently, straight up the Crow's spine. Then, suddenly, he grabbed Black Blood's long mane in his left hand and whipped the blade across it, severing it a couple inches above the neck.

Carrying the Crow's hair in his hand, Chardonnais came around to face Black Blood again. The Crow's face was still blank, but Chardonnais could see the hate in his eyes. He was not concerned about it. "I don't like it when you try to kill me, eh?" he said quietly, harshly. "And I don't like it when you try to kill my woman and my friends." He lightly pressed the tip of his knife on the underside of Black Blood's jaw. "I give you your life dis time, monsieur. But if I ever see you again, I will make wolf bait of you. And don' you t'ink I won't."

Chardonnais moved the knife and picked up a thin blanket he had brought back with him. He handed it to Black Blood. "I don't want you to t'ink I'm a heartless man, eh. So you have dis blanket to keep you warm on your ride back to Absaroka. Now, *ras-y*. Outside." He shoved Black Blood.

The Crow whirled, coming around with his elbow heading toward Chardonnais's face.

Chardonnais ducked and then butted Black Blood in the chest with his head. Black Blood stumbled backward out the flap and into the freezing snow. A number of Utes, mostly women, pointed and laughed at the Crow.

Chardonnais stepped outside, sliding his knife away. "You mess wit' dis ol' chil' again, you will join your friends dere." He pointed at the string of ponies burdened with dead Crows. "Now get your ass out of here." He stood and watched as Black Blood pulled the blanket around him, leaped on a pony, and rode off, trailing his grisly burden behind him. When he was out of sight, Chardonnais turned and reentered Strong Bear's lodge.

"That was a hell of a show, Frenchie," Rawlins said, his spirits raised a bit. "Goddamn if it weren't."

Chardonnais grinned as he took his seat. "Somebody had to show dem Crows a t'ing or two. You certainly weren't going to." He chuckled. "You mind tellin' dis ol' hoss just what de hell you was doing by taking a nap in de middle of de battle?"

"I was bored," Rawlins said without missing a beat. "I wasn't of a mood to have to come savin' your fat ass again, so I took a rest."

"Hell, it wasn't for Striking Hawk dere, you would be laying over dere by your lodge chopped into pieces."

"Well, now, I'll allow that I might've needed just a touch of help there," Rawlins drawled. "But, see, I knew Strikin' Hawk was comin' to help. If I'd of had to wait for ye, frog shit, I'd of been in real trouble."

"Well," Chardonnais countered, "if you weren't takin' a nap dere, you wouldn't of needed any help. And me and Ez wouldn't have needed to fight off a couple dozen of dem red devils. But we had to take on our own share, plus yours, too." He crossed his arms over his chest, smug in his statement.

"Well, if you hadn't of been hidin' back in the trees with the women and kids, you might've been more help there at the beginning," Rawlins countered. "But no, it's just like you to hide behind a woman's skirts like ye do every goddamn time we get into hard times. Jesus, Frenchie, have a little respect for yourself."

"They always like this?" Boatwright asked Early, who was sitting next to him.

Early grinned. "More often than not. Yep. It keeps 'em out of trouble at times." He let the banter continue for a while, not wanting to stop the act, which the Utes found quite humorous. Finally, though, he interjected himself into the chatter. "Shit, both you boys was about useless. Me'n Jed here killed us maybe fifteen, twenty of them red niggurs, and all the while watchin' over the horses. Meanwhile, Abe, you was takin' a nap, and Lucien, Christ, he was over there playin' hump the frog with a couple of them Crows. . . ."

Rawlins and Chardonnais hooted at him. When the noise had died down, Chardonnais asked seriously, "Did Jed handle his end of t'ings?"

Early nodded. "Ol' hoss here was whalin' the shit out of four Crows with a bridle and a knife when I come along. That ol' chil' shined. Goddamned if he didn't. Plumb shined."

Boatwright's grin almost lit up the lodge. He was proud of himself, and suddenly felt as if he had really become a part of the small fraternity he had joined a few months ago.

20

"WE BEST GET ON BACK to our own camp now, Strong Bear," Early said. It was well into the afternoon, and much had to be done yet.

Strong Bear nodded, then said, "You come back tonight. We'll have a Scalp Dance."

Chardonnais grinned. "It's about time we had us a spree, dammit," he said almost gleefully. The morning's battle and the subsequent humiliation of Black Blood had almost faded from his memory, or so it might have seemed to the others.

They left and rode back to their camp with their women, leaving the children behind with relatives. The children would enjoy the change, and it would keep them out from underfoot as the adults cleaned up the wreckage of the fight.

As the men dismounted and began unsaddling the horses, Early said, "I reckon we ought to move our camp a little closer to Strong Bear's."

"You figure them Crows'll be back?" Rawlins asked. He sounded disinterested.

"Not so much that I figure they'll do so," Early said

162

with a shrug. "But if they do, they'll be comin' straight for us. And I expect they won't be full of cheer for us."

"Now you see, froggie, goddammit," Rawlins said in mock irritation, "if you hadn't of gone and shamed that stupid shit of a Crow, we wouldn't have to be worryin' about such things."

Chardonnais dropped his saddle on the ground. "When did you turn into a chickenshit, eh?" he said, turning to look at his friend.

"I never said nothin' about bein' afraid of them red shits. I just said we wouldn't have to go and move our camp."

"Dis camp was getting no good anyway. De grass is gone, and all your shitting has made de place foul."

"Don't ye go makin' no statements about my shit stinkin', ye peckerless little bastard. You with farts big enough to bring down that there big buffler ye was tellin' of the other day."

"Well," Chardonnais said, nonplussed, "some of us have talents, and some of you don't."

Early laughed. "Let's see you top that one, Abe," he said.

"Suck eggs," Rawlins said. But he grinned.

"Where're we going to move, Ezra?" Chardonnais asked.

"That spot down along the creek there, near where it empties into the little pond."

Chardonnais nodded. That was as good as any other spot, he figured, and better than most.

The move went without trouble, though it took a lot of work. The women packed up their goods and then helped each other strike the lodges. While they were doing this, the men had hooked up travois to a few of the mules. They loaded as much of their firewood supply on the travois as they could, and then walked the animals to the new campsite.

The men found suitable spots for their lodges among the trees, and each marked his own spot. Then they unloaded their wood and went back for more. It took a fair number of trips—Chardonnais lost count of how many—to get the wood over to the new campsite. Then they had to begin moving the plews they had caught in the fall hunting season.

By the time the men had finished with the wood, the women had all four lodges up in their new location. And by the time all the plews were in the new site, the women had moved all their household belongings.

While the women made fires and unpacked, the men herded the horses and mules over. It was just about dark when they finished. As they sat down to a hasty meal of pemmican and biscuits in his lodge, Chardonnais said, "I think we'd best cache de plews tomorrow. Or soon anyway."

"Should've done it already," Rawlins said nonchalantly.

"I didn't hear you mention it. Nor the offer of diggin' the hole."

"Shit, if I wanted to dig holes, I would've stayed back in Tennessee and made my livin' as a grave digger."

"We keep killing Crows like we did today, and you might have dat as your job anyway," Chardonnais said with a chuckle.

"Not if you keep sendin' 'em home."

"Maybe you got somethin' there, Frenchie," Early said, laughing. "Tell you what—every time we have a run-in with some red devils, you make sure one of 'em's left alive to take all his partners' bodies home."

"Not unless I get some plews in return. Dat was too much work today. I t'ink I go back to de old ways."

"The old ways?" Rawlins said with a laugh. "You mean like yesterday's ways?"

"Well, no. It goes back to what . . . last season? I t'ink I let de wolves and de other scavengers have dem."

"I figure we ought to try'n mess with red critters as little as possible so we don't run into such problems," Early said.

"Except for Blackfeet," Rawlins appended.

Early nodded. "Except for Blackfeet."

"And Comanches," Chardonnais added.

"And Comanches," Early agreed.

"And Apaches," Rawlins tossed in.

"And Apaches," Early allowed. "No others?" he asked after a moment.

"Well," Rawlins said, "Frenchie don't like Pawnees much."

"That's true."

"And," Chardonnais added, "long face over dere, he don' much like de Arapahos."

Early laughed. "You boys know what I think?" he said more than asked. "I think we ought to just not worry about killin' any Injuns, except maybe the Utes. All them others, they're just gonna have to take their goddamn chances if they paint their faces black against us."

When the murmurs of jovial agreement wound down, Chardonnais said, "Well, boys, this ol' chil' figures it's about time we got ready to fandango."

The others nodded, rose, and walked outside. "What do you mean, get ready to fandango, Lucien?" Boatwright asked.

"De Scalp Dance," Chardonnais answered, surprised.

"I know what for. But what do we need to do to get ready?"

"*Sacré bleu!*" Chardonnais exclaimed. "Don't you know to get fancified up?"

"Fancified?" Boatwright asked, heart dropping. "I got nothin' to get fancied up in. All I got's what I'm wearin' and an extra cloth shirt."

"Dat'll never do," Chardonnais said thoughtfully. "You have anyt'ing dis hoss can wear, Abe?"

"I expect I can dredge up a pair of pants that'll fit him. Of course, he's lucky in that. If he had to rely on you, you stump-legged little shit, he'd be in a world of trouble."

"Maybe it's true I'm short," Chardonnais allowed. "But I'm big where it counts, eh." He grabbed his crotch and laughed.

"You best keep your distance from froggie there, Jed," Rawlins warned. "He'll fill your mind with poisonous thoughts, boy."

"You just wish you was more like me dere," Chardonnais chuckled.

"Like hell. I don't want no pecker that's two inches long and six around." He was laughing.

Boatwright shook his head, amazed yet again at these men's easy camaraderie, at the insults that fell so easily off their tongues, and the return fire of crude wit. And yet they were as tight as ticks.

"Come on in my lodge here, Jed," Rawlins said. "I'll see what I can dig up for ye."

Rawlins managed to dig up a soft pair of elkskin pants. They were fringed and even decorated a little. "The Utes ain't much for fancywork with beads and porcupine quills and such," he said. "But these're a hell of a lot fancier'n that shit you're wearin'."

"Gee, thanks," Boatwright said a little sarcastically.

He figured now was as good a time as any to test what he felt was his newfound camaraderie with his three new friends.

"Bah, you're gettin' to be as bad as froggie," Rawlins growled.

Boatwright breathed an inward sigh of relief. He took the pants and flung them over his shoulder.

"You said you had a fancy shirt?" Rawlins asked.

"Fancier than this I'm wearin', though it ain't no real great shakes."

"It'll have to do, ol' hoss. I ain't got nothing but two workin' shirts and my fancified war shirt."

"I'll make do, then."

Half an hour later it was fully dark, and the four mountain men were sitting outside in the cold night with Strong Bear, Striking Hawk, Moving Thunder, and a number of other warriors. All four men were, like the Utes, dressed in their finest—fringed, decorated buckskin pants; war shirts for Early and Rawlins, patterned calico ones for Chardonnais and Boatwright, all of them covered by blanket coats; warm though plain moccasins; fur hats, Early's a wolf's head, Rawlins's a badger head, Chardonnais's his familiar knit cap with the peaked top flopped over and pinned in place by a silver cross, and Boatwright's made of bear fur with a hard leather brim.

Several fires were burning, and next to the one in front of the medicine man's lodge was a pole laden with scalps. When Chardonnais's group arrived, they sat with many of the other warriors in a large circle around the medicine man's fire. Other warriors, who had not taken too large a part in the battle early that day, sat in another circle behind Strong Bear's.

The drums began, first one played by the medicine man and then by a few others. Then the women—including Looks Again, Scatters the Clouds, Falling Leaf, and Blue Rattle—also dressed in their best finery, began dancing around the pole, keeping time to the persistent drumming and their own rattle playing.

"Don't the men dance, Ezra?" Boatwright asked.

"Not in the Ute Scalp Dance."

"That's odd, ain't it?"

"I suppose. The men have their own dances, like the Dog Dance."

The women started chanting, first low, then loud, then low again. Several of them, their faces painted black, lamented the death of the two Ute warriors. Then they danced to and around the pole, their chants changing in intensity. Finally they began singing the praises of the men who had fought so bravely today. First and foremost was the name of Strong Bear.

"He really that special, Lucien?" Boatwright asked, pointing to Strong Bear.

Chardonnais nodded. "*Mais oui!*"

"Why?"

"De bear is a special animal to de Utes. De bear, he is big medicine with de Utes. De Utes, dey t'ink de bear is de second bravest animal of dem all."

"And what's the first?"

"Mountain lion. But even dose big cats don't have all de power of de bear. In de spring, de Utes, dey have de Bear Dance. Dat, too, is big medicine to dem. You'll see."

"But what's all this got to do with Chief Strong Bear there?"

"De Utes, like all de other Indians I know, take names dat have special meaning to dem. Somet'ing important to their lives. Now wit' what I tell you about de bear and what dat animal means to de Utes, and what Strong Bear's name is, do you t'ink he's very important to dese people?"

"A whole heap, I expect."

"It helps by what he has done, too. He has earned dat name."

"How?"

"De Utes, dey aren't like many of de other tribes. Dey don' live for fighting."

"You already told me that."

"*Oui.*" Chardonnais paused to watch the dancers for a few moments. "When dey do fight, dey are fierce warriors—like today. One time, a long time ago, de Arapahos t'ought dey would come across de mountains and hunt in de lands of de Utes. And dey t'ought dey would use de hot springs where we met Abe and Ezra. De Utes, dey don' like neither of dem t'ings, and so dey tell de Arapahos to go away. But de Arapahos, dey don' listen to reason, and so de fight starts."

Chardonnais stretched out his legs. They had grown stiff and cold in the frosty air. Ten years of wading in freezing beaver streams had left him—as well as every other mountain man he knew—with a dose of rheumatism and a sensitivity to cold at times.

"Dere was much fighting and many men died on both sides. Finally a truce is called and dey have some talks. Dey decide dat one man from each tribe will fight. De Utes, dey send Strong Bear. But de Arapahos, dey send out t'ree men. De Utes were some upset about dat, but Strong Bear says he is not afraid, and dat he will face de t'ree men."

"Since Strong Bear's sittin' right over yonder, I expect he whipped the three Arapahos."

"*Mais oui!* And so de Strong Bear becomes a big man wit' his people, and dey look to him for strong medicine."

21

WINTER HAD LAID ITS cold, unforgiving hand upon the land and seemed extremely reluctant to ease its grip. Snow made a thick covering over the meadow outside the cover of the spindly, bare, sometimes wind-twisted aspens. Within the partial protection of the forest, the lodges were comfortable havens. Inside, the four mountain men and their women and children were safe and secure, well fed and warm. But they were bored and restless.

As winter dragged on, the restlessness increased, and with it the tension. Tempers flared on occasion, but were usually soothed over quickly. Having the Ute village so nearby helped, since it allowed visiting, which acted as something of a safety valve, not only for the mountain men and their families but also for the Utes.

Still, there was only so much visiting that could be done, and it seemed almost inevitable that real trouble would crop up. And had anyone stopped to think about it, they would have known Lucien Chardonnais would be the one to explode.

A real monster of a storm had ripped into the valley, slapping it with a thick layer of snow that showed little sign of easing. The wind roared and growled, tearing at the trees and the lodges. The women and children were working in Early's lodge; the men gathered in Chardonnais's, where they cracked a jug to relieve the boredom and help them wait out the storm.

Even before he started on the whiskey, Chardonnais was deepening into one of his bouts of melancholy. After more than ten years together, Rawlins and Early were used to this and they ignored it as often as not. Boatwright, however, was new to the group, and had no idea of the depths Chardonnais could reach when he was in such a mood. Rawlins and Early figured the young mountain man would have to learn it for himself, so they said nothing while they quietly watched Boatwright's attempts to bring his partner out of his funk.

After a few hours of listening to Chardonnais mutter darkly to himself and of watching him frequently hog the jug, Boatwright said in only partially feigned exasperation, "Jesus, Lucien, get your paws off the jug. Me and the others want a snort once in a while, too, you know."

Chardonnais lifted his bloodshot, angry eyes and scowled at Boatwright. "Dis is my lodge," he said, words only a little slurred despite the copious amounts of whiskey he had consumed. "And if I want to keep dis jug"—he patted the earthen container that sat on his crossed legs—"I'll keep dis jug. You want to drink, you get your own Lightning."

Boatwright sat quietly for a few moments, stunned by the heated rebuff. Since the battle with the Crows, he had come to think of himself as a regular member of this small, exclusive club. The others had treated him as such, pretty much. He knew it would take plenty of time yet before he was accepted as a full and equal partner, but he was willing to wait. But at least they had let him in the door, so to speak. Now this. Boatwright didn't know what to say or think. Such treatment hurt him more deeply than he was wont to show.

"That *is* my Lightnin'," he finally allowed. He had brought it over when the jug from Rawlins's lodge ran out.

Chardonnais got a stubborn look on his face and took a long drink. Instead of swallowing, though, he spit the whiskey at the fire. The fine spray of alcohol flamed up a little. "Dat is what I t'ink of you, eh." He took another drink and swallowed this time.

"Ya know, Lucien," Boatwright said tightly, "I am plumb sick and tired of you and your horseshit."

Chardonnais sneered and shrugged. "I don't care what you t'ink." His voice suddenly sounded far away. It grew even more faint, until he was murmuring, his hands flapping in the air as they always did when he was talking.

Boatwright sat silently through it for some minutes before snarling, "If you got somethin' to say to me, you shit-faced little frog, have the balls to come out with it to my face."

Chardonnais's head jerked up and his eyes widened in rage as he glared at Boatwright. "You want I should tell you what I t'ink of you, eh? Is dat what you want?"

"Only if you'll do it before I die of old age," Boatwright snapped.

Chardonnais seemed not to have heard him. "Den I will tell you what I t'ink. *Mais oui!* I t'ink you are an agent of de Company."

Boatwright sat in stunned silence.

"I t'ink de Company send you out here to learn de best trapping places dat me and my two *amis* know. De Company knows we bring in de most plews and de finest plews. Dey would be willing to do anyt'ing to find out where we hunt de bevair."

Boatwright knew Rawlins and Early were looking at him, half smiling and waiting for his response. Trouble was, he was so flabbergasted at the accusation that he was having trouble coming up with anything to say. Finally all he could manage was. "You're out of your goddamn mind."

"Is dat all you can say?" Chardonnais asked with another sneer.

Boatwright's mind began working. "No, that ain't all I got to say, you loony French bastard. Where'd you ever get such a crazy notion?"

"It's not crazy," Chardonnais insisted, his voice harsh. "It's de trut'. Dis I know."

"You don't know shit, ya dumb bastard. How the hell was I supposed to be sent by the Company to follow you around and learn all your goddamn secret trappin' places? Answer that, you stupid shit."

"I just know," Chardonnais said smugly.

"Like shit. I was in Independence tryin' to figure out what to do. I didn't know you from Adam. And," he added pointedly, "you can bet your fat little ass the Company neither knows about you or gives a shit about you, you arrogant, egg-suckin' chickenshit."

Chardonnais boiled up and lurched forward, spilling the jug on the ground, where the contents began pouring out. He barreled into a surprised Boatwright, knocking him backward. The two rolled once and then stopped against a pile of furs along the buffalo-hide wall.

Boatwright caught a glimpse of Rawlins jumping up, and figured he was coming to pull the French-Canadian off him. He was rather disappointed when the only rescue Rawlins performed was on the jug. But he had no time to think about any of that. Lucien Chardonnais was a wild man. Short and stocky, he had a bear's strength and a badger's tenacity.

Chardonnais, partly squatting on Boatwright, aimed a punch at the young man's face. Boatwright managed to dodge out of its way and jerk an arm up to jab his attacker under the mouth with a thumb. That gave him an instant to shove Chardonnais off of him, which he did. He jumped up and immediately launched a foot at Chardonnais's head.

Chardonnais, who was rising, caught the foot in both hands and finished coming to his feet. Still holding the foot, he pushed Boatwright backward, figuring that the younger man would fall. Boatwright had managed to keep his balance, though, and hopped on his other foot, hoping for an opportunity to do something.

Chardonnais reached around and under the leg he held and punched the back of Boatwright's knee a couple of times. Boatwright could not reach the French-Canadian to stop the punishing blows, so he did what he could—he spit in Chardonnais's face.

Chardonnais let go of Boatwright's foot more in reaction than anything else, and then swiped at his face. He muttered imprecations in French and then charged.

Early and Rawlins winced as the little man plowed into Boatwright, driving both his opponent and himself out through the lodge's flap, which, having been secured because of the storm, was almost all the way ripped off.

Boatwright landed on his back, Chardonnais partly atop him, and they both slid a few feet down a short, very gentle little slope. Boatwright managed to grab Chardonnais's shirt and twisted, shoving him to the side.

Their brief slide stopped and Boatwright jumped up. He moved backward a few steps, trying to gain a few moments to get his breath back. But his moccasins slipped on the treacherous slope and he fell on his buttocks and then his back. He hastened to get up, figuring Chardonnais was coming for him. When he made it, though, he saw that the bowlegged French-Canadian was struggling a little through the two-foot-deep snow.

Boatwright jumped at the chance, tackling him around the middle. They both fell again, landing with a thud. For once, though, Boatwright was on top and he managed to get in two fairly good punches before Chardonnais was able to fling him off.

Boatwright rolled a couple of times and came to rest against the base of an aspen. He used the tree to pull himself up and then he leaned against it, breathing heavily. The wind was still roaring, battering the trees and lodges, and whipping the snow into an almost frothy cloud. "What the hell's got into you, Lucien?" he gasped.

"You know damn well what," Chardonnais spit.

Rawlins and Early peered out from the open lodge. "You boys know, don't ye, that it's a mite cold out there for such doin's?" Rawlins said.

"I goddamn know it," Boatwright said. "Trouble is, I ain't sure this crazy Frenchman knows it."

Chardonnais stood there, sucking in deep drafts of the frigid, snow-filled air. It was so cold that it hurt his lungs and made his nose feel as if it would freeze solid and then crack. He was glad—as he always was around this time of year—that he had such a thick growth of beard. It kept the bottom half of his face a little warm.

The cold had also cleared his head somewhat, and he wondered just what he was doing fighting outside in this weather with a man who was supposed to be his friend. And as quickly as his dark mood had appeared, it fled, leaving him regretful of his actions. Not that he was one to be too apologetic. After all, if a man was to call Lucien Chardonnais a friend, he had to accept certain things. Each man had his own ways, and the others were expected to understand it and be forgiving.

"Come, *mon ami*," he said with a small smile. "It's too cold out here for anyt'ing. Let's go back in de lodge and have another drink. I will bring de jug dis time."

Boatwright hesitated, looking at the trapper warily, suspecting a ruse to get him in Chardonnais's clutches again.

"Hell, boy," Rawlins said with a chuckle, "if you got any balls at all—which I suspect ye do—you're gonna loose 'em to the cold. Come on inside now."

"I ain't sure I can trust this loony bastard."

Rawlins's face hardened a bit. "Frenchie says it's all over, then it's all over."

"Well, how the hell'm I supposed to know that? Jesus." Boatwright pushed away from the tree and took a few steps. He took Chardonnais's proffered hand and allowed the French-Canadian to help him up the tiny slope.

When they were all inside, Rawlins said, "You best do somethin' about the flap on the lodge here. Else I'm goin' back to my own lodge. I ain't about to set here with that goddamn wind howlin' up my ass."

"And I t'ought you were a man," Chardonnais said with a made-up sneer. "Maybe you should go set and drink some tea wit' de women and de little ones, eh."

"Eat shit, froggie," Rawlins said good-naturedly. "You're the one with wet 'skins."

"Dat is true." Chardonnais went and pulled the flap closed and managed to tie it shut with a rawhide thong pulled from his pants. When he turned, he saw that Boatwright was sitting almost atop the fire, shivering with cold. "Jed, *mon ami*," he said anxiously. "You are dat cold?"

Boatwright could only nod, his teeth chattering some.

"Come, den. Get dem wet clothes off. *Vite, vite!*" He rushed to the back of the lodge and found a four-point blanket.

Boatwright had stood and was working with icy fingers to get the wet buckskin pants and cloth shirt off his shuddering flesh. When he did so, Chardonnais wrapped him in the blanket and rubbed his arms and back vigorously.

"Here, Jed," Early said, holding out the jug. "This'll help warm you, too."

Boatwright took the jug and greedily poured a good dose down into his belly, splashing some on his blanket-covered chest. He stopped and handed the jug back to Early.

Meanwhile Rawlins had piled another couple of logs on the fire.

"Sit, sit, *mon ami*," Chardonnais said to Boatwright.

Boatwright did, and huddled in the blanket, hovering close to the fire again. Chardonnais and Rawlins hung his snow-wet clothes on willow backrests and set them near the fire to dry.

It was not very long before he had straightened up and loosened the blanket a little bit. Another couple of snorts of Taos Lightning, and he was back to his old self. Warily, he looked at Chardonnais, who was as cheerful now as he had been melancholy before. "What the hell got into you, Lucien?" he asked, wondering if he was about to provoke another fight.

Chardonnais shrugged. He was not embarrassed by his behavior, but he was not exactly pleased with it either.

"That's just froggie's way," Rawlins said. "He gets into these fits of gloom every now and again. I guess we all do. But Frenchie does it more'n most and it strikes him worse than most critters."

"That's right," Early added. "It ain't directed at you, boy. Nor anyone in particular. You see him gettin' that way again, you just leave him be. In due time he'll be the regular pain in the ass we all know—and can't stomach."

Boatwright looked from Early to Chardonnais. The French-Canadian grinned crookedly. "*Mais oui,*" he said with a shrug. "Dat's de way I am."

"Well, I reckon I can forgive you," Boatwright said with a sly chuckle. "If you get that jug you promised to bring out."

The others laughed. "He's got ye on that one, froggie," Rawlins said.

"*Mais oui,*" Chardonnais said with a sigh, as if being put upon by the world. But he rose and headed for his supplies for a jug.

22

THINGS WERE NOT ALL BAD, despite the cold and snow and often gloomy days. There was still visiting to be done, playing with the children in the snow, exercising the horses now and again, hunting when the weather permitted—and game was around.

Mostly, though, the men spent time yarning, drinking, gambling—among themselves as well as with the Utes—and fornicating. Chardonnais was an avid practitioner of the latter, much to Looks Again's annoyance. His demands and needs were nothing new to her, but there were times when she was tempted to throw his things out of the lodge, divorcing him, just so she could get some rest.

Still, about the time of year that her husband and his friends called Christmas, Looks Again accepted that she was about three months' pregnant. She had not been sure how she felt about it when she first realized it. She wanted a family, but she was not sure Chardonnais would be around long enough to see the child grow. As urgent as his needs often were, once he found out she was pregnant, she was afraid he might pack up and leave. She had, in some ways, invested too much of her life in this short, stubby French-Canadian to have him just up and leave her because she was with child.

On the other hand, she wondered what life with Chardonnais would be if he were a father. He loved children, that was plain for anyone to see. But she was not sure he would feel the same when the child was his own.

Looks Again knew she would have little trouble attracting a Ute husband, even if she did have a half-breed son or daughter. But, as little as she liked to admit it even to herself, she loved Lucien Chardonnais, and had loved him for some time now.

She also knew that she would have to tell him soon. His sexual demands had increased as the outside temperatures decreased, and she was afraid he would harm the new life growing within her. Trouble was, she was afraid that as soon as he found out, he might begin looking elsewhere for a wife. That would be risky for her, with the village so close.

Looks Again picked a day when Chardonnais was in one of his better humors. When he was in such a way, he was jolly, full of laughter, his face crinkled with smiles. She watched for a while as he went slipping and sliding in the snow with Rawlins's boy, Standing Eagle. Finally he stopped the play and headed to his lodge. Looks Again was standing just outside the lodge, blanket wrapped tightly around her. Her nose was running from the cold, but she didn't mind.

Chardonnais was puffing a little as he came up and kissed her on the cheek, then nipped playfully at the flesh. He threw his arms around her and pulled her close.

Looks Again knew it was now or never. Before he

could suggest retiring to the robes, Looks Again asked, "You like playing with the children, yes?"

"*Mais oui!*" Chardonnais agreed, his thick black mustache and beard parted by white teeth.

"Would you like to have a child of your own to play with?" Looks Again was more scared than she ever had been. More scared even than that time a Blackfoot war party had swung out of the northern lands and attacked her village.

"*Oui*," Chardonnais said seriously, nodding. Then the brilliant smile was flashed again. "And you know what I say, *ma chèrie*, eh? I say we should go in de lodge now and make us a good baby. A boy wit' his father's strong arm, brave heart, and big pizzle!" He laughed, slapping a thigh in amusement.

When Chardonnais calmed down some, Looks Again said quietly, "There's no reason to do that."

Chardonnais, who had turned and bent to enter the lodge, craned his neck around. "What's dat?" he asked, befuddled.

"I said there's no reason to do that." Once again the fear slithered up her spine like a frozen snake.

"And why is dat?" Chardonnais asked cautiously as he straightened and turned to face his wife.

Looks Again reached out tentatively and took one of his hands in her two. Despite the frigid temperature, her palms were damp with sweat. She tugged him toward her, until he was only inches away. She opened the blanket a little and placed his hand on her abdomen. "Your son is growing there now," she said, her mouth as dry as the desert out beyond the big salt lake far to the west.

"I don't feel notting," Chardonnais said stupidly.

"He's too small yet to feel," Looks Again whispered, still afraid of her volatile husband's reaction.

"And so how do you know it is my son?" Chardonnais asked in measured tones.

Looks Again shrugged. "I'm not sure, but a woman knows these things." She bit her lower lip to prevent herself from asking him how he felt about this.

Chardonnais pulled his hand free and then tugged Looks Again's blanket closed. He stood there glaring at her a moment, arms akimbo. Then he smiled, a great, gigantic smile that stretched his leathery face. He whirled.

"*Mes amis!*" he shouted. "*Mes amis.* Come. *Vite, vite!*"

Early and Boatwright tumbled out of their lodges, rifles in hand, trying to jerk on their coats. Both looked seriously worried. Rawlins, who had been playing down near the pond with his son, came charging up.

"What is it, Lucien?" Early demanded. He had neither seen nor heard anything out of the ordinary. He stopped close to Chardonnais. Boatwright, and, a moment later, Rawlins joined him.

"Well, froggie?" Rawlins snapped. "What the hell's got your balls in an uproar?"

"I am to be a papa!" Chardonnais shouted, his smile still as bright as the sunshine on the new snow.

"Jesus, Frenchie," Rawlins complained, "you caused all this ruckus just 'cause ye finally found enough man juice in ye to get her pregnant? Jesus." He turned and walked away muttering. Ten feet off he stopped, turned, and winked at his old friend.

"Well, I don't know what the hell you're crowin' about," Boatwright said in a false huff. "Hell, I got Blue Rattle with child before you done in her sister here. Jesus, you think you done somethin' special." He grinned and then headed off to his own lodge.

"See, Lucien," Early said as if he were weary, "I

told you and told you that if you didn't keep your pecker in your pants, you was gonna wind up in trouble. And sure as shit you are." He smiled. "Congratulations, my old friend."

"*Merci.*" Chardonnais was still beaming as Early left. Suddenly his expression grew very serious. "Does dis mean we can't hump no more till de baby comes?" he asked, a note of worry in his voice.

Looks Again shook her head. "No. But," she cautioned before he could get too overjoyed, "not so often."

Chardonnais nodded. He wondered what he would do when Looks Again began turning down his frequent advances. Then he shrugged inwardly. He would worry about that when the time arrived. "But you don't want to now, eh?" he asked disconsolately.

"I said we had no reason to do that now that I carry your child. But I didn't say I didn't *want* to do that."

Chardonnais suddenly grinned again. "Den let us proceed, *ma belle.*"

They hurried inside and did not even bother to undress except for what was necessary. In moments they were thrashing around in the robes, squealing and grunting out their passions.

Not long after they had finished, while they were still lying in each other's arms, Chardonnais began to worry again. He thought that maybe Looks Again would not want him coming around even after the baby was born. He feared that she would get used to not having him pester her so much that she would want to make it permanent.

Then he realized that was foolish. Looks Again was not like a delicate white woman back in the States. One like Marie Bouchard. He had not thought of Marie in some time, and it was so strange now to remember that he had come within minutes of marrying her. Granted, Marie was pretty, far prettier than Looks Again. But considering what she was, and where she was, her upbringing and church teachings, she would get no enjoyment from sex, he figured. He hadn't heard of too many white women who did.

In addition, Marie could do little of what a woman should be able to do. Chardonnais needed—and wanted—a woman who could cook on an outdoor fire, who could raise or break down her lodge quickly, who could tan a beaver plew or an elk hide or buffalo robe. A woman who would show no fear when enemies came against them. And maybe most of all, a woman who could meet his lusty earthiness in the robes. He had no desire for parties and teas and other social events that would be an important part of Marie's life in St. Charles. It would have driven him away from Marie pretty quickly. No, he was content with Looks Again.

That still left him the problem of doing something in the foreseeable future. He could not be put off every time he wanted a romp, and he was gentleman enough not to want to bother Looks Again more often than necessary. He began to worry that the rest of the winter was going to be very stressful.

"What're you thinking, Lucien?" Looks Again asked softly, running an index finger along the line of his thin lips.

"Notting."

"Don't lie to me, Lucien." There was no pleading in her voice. Just a statement of how she wanted to be treated.

Chardonnais drew in a long breath and then eased it out. "I am t'inking what I can do so I don't be too big a burden on you while you carry my child."

"Strong Bear's village is close."

"You want me to go over dere?"

"I didn't say that. I only said it was an option." She paused. "Do you want to go there?"

Chardonnais was torn. He cared for Looks Again more than he ever had cared for a woman before. It was one thing for him to have a number of flings when he was in Taos. That was to be expected, and they meant nothing. But to go a few hundred yards away and lie with another woman while your wife was left alone, that was an entirely different thing.

He tried to explain it to Looks Again, but did a poor job of it. She finally stopped him and said, "I understand." She licked her lips, unsure if she should proceed. She decided she should. "Do you love me, Lucien?" she asked very quietly.

"*Mais oui!*" Chardonnais said without hesitation. "More dan anyone. Evair."

Looks Again thought her heart would fly right out of her chest. "Then you may go to Strong Bear's village and see to your needs." Once again fear swept over her, dampening her joy. "As long as you come back to me."

"Every night," he promised.

Looks Again smiled and then squiggled atop him. She nipped the tip of his nose, and then rubbed her chin and cheeks gently on his beard. Usually such a thing irritated her skin, but there were times—rare, yes, but real nonetheless—when she liked the feel of his harsh whiskers on her skin.

"You want to know somet'ing, woman?" Chardonnais growled, voice thick with desire.

"What?" Looks Again slid the tip of her tongue along her husband's lips.

Chardonnais waited until she had finished that delicious little act. Then he said, "We have too much clothing on."

"Yes," Looks Again said solemnly. "You're right." Then she laughed, her throaty voice reaching down into Chardonnais's insides and exciting him. She pushed herself up onto all fours and then stood. In moments she had skinned off her garments. Then she knelt and peeled Chardonnais's clothes off for him. Finally she ended back atop him, her lithe figure pressed flat against his stocky one.

Chardonnais made sure a buffalo robe covered her back. It would not do well to have her getting sick. Not when she was carrying his child. He felt a flutter of excitement inside his chest at the thought. But for now, there were more urgent matters to think about.

Chardonnais's strong hands stroked Looks Again's back as far as he could reach. Looks Again squirmed upward on him a little, allowing his hands to touch her buttocks. She murmured and closed her eyes, enjoying the feel of his hard hands on her flesh.

"You going to stay dere like dat all day?" Chardonnais finally asked huskily.

Looks Again only nodded.

"We'll just see about dat, eh," Chardonnais said gruffly. He rolled, getting tangled some in the robes, but still landing on top of her. "Now what do you have to say for yourself?" he asked, eyes sparkling with joy.

She didn't feel she had to say anything. She simply smiled up at him, grasped his manhood, and helped him ease into her.

Chardonnais sucked in a breath at the exquisite pleasure he felt inside her. But he did not want to hurt her by lying on her too much, so he rolled again, holding her, until he was on his back once more and Looks Again hovered over him.

* * *

"You make me t'ink sometimes like I don' want another woman," Chardonnais said quietly when he had gotten his breath back.

"I like that idea," Looks Again responded. She was snuggled up as much as she could be, one of her legs resting across both of his, her head nestled in the crook of shoulder and chest.

"Maybe someday I'll control de beasts inside me," he said in a low, almost pained voice. "And den I can stay wit' you and no others."

"I like that idea, too," Looks Again said simply. "But I know how you are. And as long as I know you love me, I can be happy."

"I sometimes t'ink dat you are too good for dis ol' chil'."

"Oh, that's true enough," Looks Again said, raising her head to look into his eyes. Then she laughed, making her right breast jiggle against his hairy chest.

Chardonnais decided he liked that sensation, but he pulled her down close to him anyway. He kissed the top of her head. "You ever regret meetin' up with dis ol' hoss?" he asked softly.

"No!" Looks Again said firmly. She pushed herself up to the full extension of her arms. "Don't you ever say that."

"I didn't mean notting by it," he said defensively. "I just worry sometimes if you'd rather have another man. Most women would, considering how I act sometimes."

"You act like a man. All the good of a man, and some of the bad. And I am happy with you." She lay back down on him.

Chardonnais smiled up at the lodge's smoke hole, thinking himself perhaps the luckiest man in the world. Or at least in this part of it.

23

THE LONGER WINTER DRAGGED ON, the more restless the mountain men became. At the first tenuous sign of spring, Early announced that it was about time to move on.

"A mite early, ain't it?" Rawlins asked, stretching his long legs toward the fire.

"You want to sit here all spring?"

"Spring?" Chardonnais snorted. He was fidgety and wanted to be on the move, but he had no desire to run into a late-winter storm, or even an early-spring one.

"Sure, spring," Early said. "Hell, you boys saw that bear come out after hibernatin' just this mornin', didn't you?"

"Now you're gonna tell me bears don't get up of a winter day just 'cause he gets the notion?" Rawlins countered.

"There's other sign about," Early said testily. Though he did not look like it, he was even more eager than the others to push on. It happened to him every year about this time. He just burned with the desire to be on the move. It sometimes proved out to be dangerous, but that didn't change the fact that his inner self pushed him.

"Other sign, my ass," Rawlins snapped. He would just as soon leave now as later, but he could not pass up an opportunity to rib his friend. "Hell, the cricks and the ponds're still froze up. And the snow's still deeper'n a bull's hump."

"Goddamn gloomy bastard, ain't you?"

"Eat shit. When you want to pull out?"

"Day after tomorrow. That'll give us time for one last fandango over at the village," Early said.

"You t'ink you can get packed and loaded by den?" Chardonnais asked. "You've been moving mighty slow dese days." He shook his head and looked sadly at Rawlins. "Age is catching up to our friend," he intoned solemnly.

"It's a terrible thing to see with one's own eyes," Rawlins responded in kind.

"Christ, you two are really somethin'," Early retorted. "Couple of dried up old farts doin' nothin' but spoutin' wind."

"At least we got some wind to spout," Chardonnais said with a laugh.

"It's about all you got goin' for you, too, you tree-humpin' frog."

"You're just jealous."

"You two done spittin' at each other?" Rawlins asked drolly.

"And if we are?" Early asked.

"Then tell us where away."

"Up over Willow Creek Pass into North Park, I expect. We can trap the creeks south into Middle Park. Then maybe west along the Colorado. Once we get down around Canyon Creek, we can figure out where away from there."

"I still say we're gonna freeze our asses off leavin' this early," Rawlins said, just to be contrary.

"You don't want to go, sit here. Me, Lucien, and Jed'll go our own merry way."

"Jesus, you're just full of good cheer, ain't you?" Rawlins laughed.

The men were busy preparing throughout the day. It was so easy, they all knew from experience, to fall into a pattern of laziness over a winter. Supplies and equipment often lay for months, and within a day or two had to be repaired, cleaned, and packed. Yet no matter how often they had wintered up—and should have known better—bad habits returned without them really being conscious of it.

Chardonnais, being a temperamental man to begin with, began railing about his plight within an hour of getting to work. His loudness and intensity increased as the day lengthened, until he was almost shouting a continuous stream of French, English, and butchered Ute.

Rawlins, Early, and Boatwright kept a wary eye on him when he was outside, and cast amused looks at his lodge when he was not. Rawlins and Early were used to it, but Boatwright was still new enough to the group to know he had no place saying anything to the trapper about his behavior. He also figured that if Rawlins and Early could put up with him like this, well, then he surely could, too.

At long last, Chardonnais came out of his lodge and stood silently for some moments. Then, as he turned and headed toward the tipi again, an angry Looks Again suddenly appeared outside. "Go!" she said emphatically in English. She pointed off in the distance.

"But *ma chère*," he protested, arms wide in supplication.

"No. I won't listen to you anymore. Go."

"Where?" Chardonnais asked plaintively.

"I don't care. Just get out of my sight—and my hearing." Looks Again turned and went back inside.

Chardonnais stood there looking absolutely dejected for some moments.

"Christ, Lucien, go do somethin'," Rawlins shouted. "She ain't gonna let ye back in that goddamn lodge for a spell." He was a little surprised when he got no response.

"You keep standin' there like that," Early tossed out, "and you'll likely get stuck into one of Looks Again's parfleches and you'd be buried there till we figured out where you are. And I'll tell you what, boy, this ol' chil' ain't gonna go lookin' none too hard."

Chardonnais turned and with his head down shuffled through the snow toward the horses, among the trees. Early watched him. Rawlins sidled up to Early.

"You think there's somethin' wrong with him, *amigo?*" he asked.

Early shrugged. "Can't rightly say, though the ol' hoss sure does seem off his feed. More'n usual, even when he gets into one of his sulks."

"I reckon we ought to keep a close eye on him, at least for a little."

"Reckon so."

Rawlins headed back toward his lodge, but Early continued to stand there looking in the direction Chardonnais had gone. He was worried about his friend. He had seen Chardonnais in some black moods before, but this seemed somehow worse. The little French-Canadian appeared to have a haunted, wild look in his eyes. Early half turned and called softly,

"Falling Leaf." When his wife came out of the lodge, he said, "I'm goin' off for a bit."

"Is there trouble?" Falling Leaf asked when she saw the concerned look on her man's face.

"Don't know. Lucien's gone off on one of his melancholies, but this one looks worse, though I ain't sure why."

Falling Leaf nodded. She watched nervously as Early moved off with his long, ground-covering strides. Ezra Early was a big man and handled himself like one. Being from a short, squat race, Falling Leaf was proud of her husband's size. Because of it, he commanded attention no matter where he went.

Early glided through the trees almost silently. He made only a small whooshing noise in the snow. Even that stopped, though, when he wanted it to, which he did when he neared Chardonnais. The French-Canadian was sitting on a log, one of his flintlock pistols in his hand.

"That ain't no answer, ol' hoss," Early said as he slipped up almost alongside Chardonnais. He hadn't spoken until he was within at least diving reach of his old partner.

"Dis is none of your concern," Chardonnais said stiffly.

"Buffler shit." Early plunked himself down on a large rock opposite Chardonnais's log.

"Go back to de others," Chardonnais said quietly.

"What the hell's got into you, Lucien?" Early asked. "You've had the sulks and the gloomies and all such shit before. But I ain't ever found you with pistol in hand trying to get up the balls to blow your brains out—if you got any. Such a thing ain't likely considerin' the way you're actin'."

"What de hell do you know about anyt'ing?" The little trapper's voice was harsh and flat.

"I know you're actin' like a goddamn fool, and you got no reason for it. What the hell's been so bad of late? Can you answer me that?"

"Well, dere's—"

"There ain't shit. We had us a good fall trappin' season, and the likelihood of a good spring one. We've wintered up safe and sound. We've got a new man in Jed, one who's provin' out to be a good hand. We've had a good winter bein' near Strong Bear's. Hell, it ain't every year that ol' hoss brings his people this far north and east. And you're gonna be a father. Shit, more'n once you've said you wanted that. So what's put the bug up your ass this time?"

Chardonnais really didn't know, which was what was so angering and frustrating. He had no idea of why these black moods possessed him at times, coming—and going—with no rhyme or reason. "Dese t'ings," he croaked in embarrassment, "dey just come and dey just go."

"No harm in that, I suppose," Early said, stretching out his long legs. He cut a chaw of tobacco and shoved it in his mouth. "Don't mean you have to go shootin' yourself."

Chardonnais nodded, dark eyes looking pained.

"Look, Lucien," Early said quietly, "we been *amigos* a good long time now. I care more about you and Abe than I ever did about my own damn family. So I ain't fixin' to let you blow your brains out. And if I have to knock you on your short little froggie ass and take away your gun to prevent it, I sure will." He let a suggestion of a smile tug at his lips.

"Won't bother me any to make wolf bait out of you before doing de same to me."

"Waugh! That's the biggest pile of shit I've ever heard." He stood. "But if makin' wolf bait out of yourself is where your stick floats, then, by Christ, I ain't about to stand in your way." He took two steps and then came back. "Just remember, though, you self-servin' sack of shit, that there's others countin' on you. Me'n Abe. Jed. But we'll get by if you was gone under."

Chardonnais looked up at his friend, something dark and mysterious in his eyes.

"But Looks Again ain't gonna have so easy a time of it. I don't know why, but that goddamn woman loves you. Christ, how she can do that when you're pawin' at her every five minutes is beyond my ken, ol' hoss. But it's a fact." Early paused and sighed. "But there's one other's countin' on you for certain."

Chardonnais's bushy black eyebrows raised in question.

"That little one growin' in your woman's belly," Early said flatly. "The little bugger'll need a father. I figure you ain't gonna be much of a pa to it, but you're better'n none at all, I reckon."

Chardonnais nodded solemnly. "I need to be alone now, eh," he said softly.

Early shrugged and walked off. Near his lodge he spotted Looks Again tentatively heading in his direction. He stepped in front of her. "Leave him be for now, Looks Again," he said quietly.

"But I—"

"He needs to be alone. You know he gets like this of a time. He'll be all right," Early added with a lot more assurance than he felt. "Go on back to your chores."

Looks Again beseeched Early with her soulful, almost black eyes. But she saw in his stern visage that he would not relent. Silently, she turned and shuffled off, more worried about her husband than she ever had been.

Everyone went to back to work, but they did so in silence. It was as if they were in a cemetery and they were trying to keep from disturbing the ghosts that haunted the place. Once in a while one of them would stop what he or she was doing and stare blankly into the trees, as if expecting someone or something to materialize.

An hour after Early had returned, Boatwright walked up to him. The older man quit what he was doing and waited to hear what he had to say.

"You think I oughta go after Lucien and see that he's all right?" Boatwright asked, his worry evident.

Early shook his head. "We all get this way at times. And every damn one of us wants everybody else to butt the hell out when we do. Lucien'll come through this just fine." He had always thought that before, but he had never seen Chardonnais this bad. It was a worrisome thing.

Another hour passed, and Early began to relax a little. Chardonnais had done nothing in all this time, and he figured the French-Canadian would come strolling out of the trees soon, a grin splitting his black beard and mustache, and he would be himself again.

A single gunshot almost made Early jump. He was kneeling in the snow, tying a bale of beaver plews. He stopped his work and rose, while turning to face the deeper woods.

At the sound of the shot Rawlins and Boatwright boiled out of their lodges, looking worried. Early waved them away when they looked ready to charge after where Chardonnais had gone. Early stood there, gazing into the trees, a chill knifing its way into his stomach. A tear rolled unchecked down his marred cheek. He did nothing to wipe it away.

A moment later Looks Again came out of her

lodge. Her face was drawn and stricken-looking. She let out a wail that hurt the ears and pierced the heart with its pain. No bird chirped, the horses quieted, rolling their eyes nervously; even the wind seemed to stop momentarily.

24

CHARDONNAIS STROLLED OUT of the woods into the little clearing, his face brightly smiling. "Hey, look at dis!" he said, holding up a large turkey. "One shot and—" He stopped and looked from one face to the other, stunned at the looks he saw there.

"You puke-suckin', peetrified, snake-humpin', stump-high sack of dead buzzard shit," Early exploded. "I'm of a goddamn mind to rip your goddamn ass off and pull it down over your head, goddammit."

"And after that, goddammit," Rawlins added angrily, "me'n Jed're gonna get real goddamn nasty, you festeratin', maggot-infested bag of raven innards."

"But what is wrong, eh?" Chardonnais asked, stupefied.

"What's wrong?" Early bellowed. "Jesus, goddamn, you . . . son of a . . . why . . . goddamn . . ." He stopped, unable to continue. He had never been at a loss for words, but there were just not enough words to express his rage. "Peckerless bastard," he finally managed. He bent, scooped up a good-size handful of snow, patted it swiftly into a ball, and threw it at Chardonnais.

197

The French-Canadian ducked, still looking mystified at his closest friends' anger. He had little time to ponder it, though, as snowballs were flying at him with some regularity now, thrown by Early, Rawlins, and Boatwright.

"Hell," Rawlins finally roared, "this ain't near good enough." He charged toward Chardonnais. Early and Boatwright were only a moment behind. Rawlins plowed into Chardonnais, knocking him down and sending the dead turkey flying. Moments later Early and Boatwright joined the pile.

"Get de hell off me, you stupid bastards!" Chardonnais roared.

"Eat shit," Rawlins muttered.

Early, Rawlins, and Boatwright were pummeling Chardonnais. Not enough to do real damage, but certainly hard enough to let him know their displeasure. They finally gave up the fight and stood. A suspicious Chardonnais warily took Early's hand and allowed himself to be hauled up.

Once he was on his feet, he asked, sounding offended, "What de hell was dat all about?"

"We thought you shot yourself, you stupid, goddamn idiot fool," Early snapped.

"But why?" Chardonnais's eyes widened. "Yes," he said, nodding, "I can see how you would t'ink dat. *Oui*." He sighed. "But I didn't, as you can see. I'm all right now."

"We can change that right goddamn quick," Rawlins threatened.

"You keep away from me, you goat humper," Chardonnais said crossly.

"Why, I—"

"Let him be, Abe," Early said. "He ain't worth the effort." He turned hot eyes on Chardonnais. "But I'm warnin' you, Lucien, you pile of goose shit, don't you never pull no doin's like this again, goddammit, or I'll finish it for you."

Rawlins, Early, and Boatwright strolled off, heading back to their work. Shrugging, Chardonnais picked up his turkey and, with a jaunty swing in his step, headed for his own lodge. He was met by a decidedly frosty Looks Again, who waited outside the lodge, her face stamped with anger.

"You, too?" Chardonnais demanded, some of his ebullience disappearing.

"What's wrong with you, husband?"

"Dere is notting wrong with dis ol' chil'," Chardonnais said proudly, jabbing his puffed-out chest with a thumb.

"Child is a good word for you." Looks Again's anger had not cooled so much as a degree.

"I'll show you who's a child," Chardonnais boasted.

"With that little thing?" Her voice was withering. "You aren't so special there."

In his head, Chardonnais knew she was lying, trying to insult him for giving her such a scare. But in his heart, he was wounded by her harsh words and her even harsher look. "You always like it before," he said quietly.

"Maybe I do sometimes. Maybe I don't."

"But I'm—"

"I'll tell you what you are, you worm. You are— how do your friends say it?—yes, a goddamn son of a bitch. You're a goddamn son of a bitch." She crossed her arms on her chest and glowered.

"You're trying my patience, woman," Chardonnais said, his anger beginning to rise.

"You don't like it living with me anymore, you can take your things out of the lodge. I won't hold you."

"Is dat what you want?"

"I didn't say that. I said you can do it if that's what *you* want."

"Can we talk this over inside de lodge?" Chardonnais asked. He hefted the turkey. "Maybe over dis roasted-up turkey?" he added with a hopeful note.

"That turkey's not roasted."

"It will be soon."

"So," Looks Again said with her nose in the air, "not only do you scare me half to death, you come back and want me to lay down for you and then pluck, clean, and cook your turkey? Why should I be so foolish?"

"Den I will pluck and clean and cook de turkey by myself," Chardonnais said, trying to control his temper. "And den I will eat de whole t'ing by myself, too."

"Ah, I see you're not only mean-spirited, but selfish, too."

Chardonnais tossed the turkey into the slushy snow. He was exasperated, and his gloom was beginning to manifest itself once again. He was about ready to go back off into the woods by himself.

Looks Again could see it in his eyes, and hoped she had not gone too far. She had been frightened out of her wits when she had heard that gunshot, and she was sure her husband had killed himself. Silently, she turned and went into the lodge, giving Chardonnais no encouragement to follow, but at the same time not sending out a signal that he would be unwelcome if he did so.

Chardonnais stood there looking at the open flap of the lodge. He was torn between his desire to go in after Looks Again and his urge to flee. He sighed and went inside the tipi. He took his normal seat at the fire and then busied himself filling and lighting his pipe. The coils of smoke he drew into his lungs settled him a little.

Looks Again moved around, doing nothing in particular, but not sitting idle either. Mainly she was still trying to adjust to the fact that Chardonnais really was not dead. She knew that if she didn't love him so much, she wouldn't be in such a fit.

After some minutes Looks Again went outside, closing the flap behind her. Nervous, Chardonnais poured a cup of coffee and sipped at it, waiting, trying to convince himself that he was not really staring at the flap waiting for Looks Again to return.

When she finally did, she had in her hand a cleaned, plucked turkey. She knotted a rope that was hanging from one of the lodgepoles around the turkey's legs, so it hung over the fire, high up where the fragrant smoke would work at it over time. Then she sliced off a few chunks of meat, skewered them, and hung them from an iron rod a foot over the fire.

That done, she sat near the fire, a few feet to Chardonnais's right. She took a mug of coffee.

"You still mad at me?" the trapper asked quietly.

Looks Again nodded. "I can't help it."

He nodded glumly. "I never t'ought I—"

"Yes, you didn't think!" Looks Again hissed. "Not about anyone but yourself. If you had thought at all—considered how we all would feel—you wouldn't have done such a foolish thing."

"*Je le regrette*," Chardonnais said honestly. "It is de way I am," he added with a shrug. "I can't change de way I am any more dan a skunk can change his stripe or his smell."

Looks Again was not mollified, though she acknowledged to herself that he was probably right. The trouble now, though, was that she was not sure she could handle another such day, at least not while she was pregnant.

Neither said anything for some time, since neither had anything to say. They just sat and listened to the flames crackle and the sizzle of fat dripping from the turkey.

Finally Chardonnais reached out and pulled one of the iron skewers off the fire. He blew on the meat a bit and then held the tip of the rod toward Looks Again. She tentatively plucked off a piece of meat and bit into it. Chardonnais took a piece for himself.

"I wish I could change de way I am," he said softly. "I am too many times in de melancholy, as Ezra calls it. And I am too demanding of you in de robes. But I can't change dose t'ings. I would if I could. *Mais oui!*"

Looks Again believed him. Now all she had to do was decide if she could live with him that way. The frequent—and usually exciting—intercourse she had no problem with, but the black moods that often swept over him was another thing altogether.

Looks Again began to think that perhaps her husband was touched by the spirits. Or maybe just touched by the spirits at some times. Even if both thoughts were not right, something surely caught Chardonnais up at times. Whether it was big medicine or black medicine she did not know.

She sighed. There was really no choice, she thought. She loved Chardonnais, she was fairly sure that he loved her, and she was carrying his child. She would have no trouble getting another husband, she knew, but it would not be the same as being married to this short, feisty French-Canadian. Once she thought about it, she realized she kind of enjoyed his moodiness—at least at times. He also made life interesting. He was known suddenly to burst into song, or, like the Utes, he might just begin dancing because he felt like it. He was good with the children around him, and she expected him to be that way when their child was born. He was a hard worker, strong and vital. And there was no doubt at all that he was a man.

Looks Again realized that Chardonnais's good points far outweighed the bad. But she would have to make him see that he could not frighten her the way he had today.

Without saying anything, she picked up another skewer, moved a little closer to him, and then offered him the first choice of the meat.

Chardonnais stared at her a moment, trying to decipher her look. He believed he was being forgiven, but he could also sense that Looks Again was still simmering in anger and fear. He vowed silently to make a grand effort to keep the melancholy from disturbing their lives too much. He was not sure he would succeed, but he figured that Looks Again deserved as much effort as he could give.

Chardonnais finished his chunk of turkey and then wiped his hands on his cloth shirt. He grinned lopsidedly at Looks Again. *"Veux-tu coucher avec moi?"* he asked quietly.

Looks Again, who spoke English and French almost as well as she did Ute—and far, far better than Chardonnais could speak Ute—smiled and said, *"Mais oui!"*

The two rose and headed toward their bed. Looks Again wondered for a few moments if she wasn't wrong in this, but then she decided she was not. Sacrifices always had to be made, and she was comfortable with the ones she was being called on to make. She thought of what she got in return—Chardonnais's love, protection, company; his strength, pride . . . and his child.

Still, just a small bit of anger and fear lingered in the back of her mind. But even that fled some minutes later when Chardonnais was inside her and they were riding each other's passion.

"There's still much to be done," Looks Again said later.

"*Oui*," Chardonnais said with a sigh. He was content to lie here with his wife in his arms for now. He did know, though, that there was too much to do if they were to leave the morning after next. With some annoyance, he roused himself and straightened his clothing. Whistling a song he remembered from childhood, he headed outside. Just before passing through the lodge's flap, he paused momentarily, wondering what his three friends would have to say to him. He was quite relieved when he saw none of them outside. He hoped that with the cold temperatures, their anger would have cooled, since he felt bad for having put such a scare into them.

25

THE DAWN WAS A BITTER COLD but sunny one as Ezra Early led his group out of the tree-ringed meadow. They headed north, in the same formation as when they had left the hot springs far to the southwest back in the late summer.

For a while yesterday Chardonnais had thought they would never have everything done and be ready to pull out. But by late afternoon, everything appeared to be done, and they still had enough time to get themselves all fancied up and go have a dance with Strong Bear's band of Utes.

The Utes would miss their white friends, and their women, but they would see each other before long. Strong Bear planned to head east for the plains within a couple of weeks. There the Utes would have their big spring hunt—and maybe time to teach the Arapahos, Crows, and Cheyennes a few lessons in warfare.

Then they would swing south and travel along the front range of the Rockies before taking the ages-old Ute trail back toward their lands in the Uncompahgre country. If all worked out, the Utes and Chardonnais's group would meet there. After some dancing and feasting, the white men would make their annual trip down to Taos.

Early had roused them all well before the dawn. After hasty meals, the women began striking their lodges while the men began loading the mules and travois.

Finally they had mounted up. Just before leading the way out of the camp, Early rode back and stopped his horse next to Chardonnais's. "I'd be obliged," he said dryly, "if you was to tell us if you're set to go loony again."

Chardonnais glared at him a moment, not sure if Early was sincere. Then he shrugged. "Are you going to sit here all de day? Or are you going to lead dis goddamn fandango out of here?"

Early grinned. "Reckon I'm of a mind to move out."

They moved slowly, the way they had on the way out last year, trapping a day here, a couple of days a little farther on. A week after leaving their winter camp, they sat out a two-day blizzard in a camp along Beaver Creek.

Despite the blizzard's fury, they all knew it was winter's last gasp. The nights still had temperatures well below freezing, and they still occasionally had to crack a thin rime of ice on a creek for water and for trapping, but they could feel spring's soft approach.

As the weather warmed a little the beaver became more active, and the men pushed harder and faster, working against time. The beavers' fur was pure prime now, but it would not last long, and they wanted to trap as many beaver as possible as quickly as they could. It meant sometimes long days of traveling to reach the next likely spot for trapping. Even in camp, it meant long days and plenty of hard work for everyone.

The results were worth it, though. The plews they took were all prime—sleek, soft, and thickly luxurious. The only drawback was that they were not bringing in nearly as many plews as they had a few years back.

"What do you make of dis, *mes amis?*" Chardonnais tossed out as they sat at his fire one night. He cracked an elk-leg bone with his hatchet and scooped out the marrow.

"This what?" Rawlins asked. He was tired and irritable. He cut a chaw of tobacco and worked on it more to keep busy than for pleasure.

"Dis poor season for de bevair."

"It ain't all that bad," Early said.

"It don't shine worth shit," Rawlins snapped.

"Well, hell," Early retorted, "it wasn't all that goddamn shinin' last year."

"You know what I t'ink?" Chardonnais asked. Not waiting for a response, he said, "Dis area's been trapped heavy for years. We all knew dat. We only come back here since it was close to Taos and de Utes. De same as last year. Den it was because of Ezra's friend Bart. Dis year I am de one making us late getting going. But next year we will go far to de nort', eh."

"All you're gonna get up there is a Blackfoot lance up your ass," Rawlins said grouchily.

"You turned into a coward over de wintair when we weren't looking?"

"Don't press your goddamn luck with me, froggie. I ain't of a mind for such doin's."

"Now I am frighten," Chardonnais said sarcastically. He snapped his wrist, sending a glob of marrow flying at Rawlins. It landed on his sleeve.

"Ye damn well oughter be, ye pissant little bag of

wind," Rawlins snapped, flicking the marrow off his filthy shirt.

"Christ, Abe, what the hell's got stuck in your goddamn craw?" Early asked.

Rawlins shrugged. "Ah, hell, Ez, I don't know. I'm just of a mind to be contrary is all, and for no reason."

Early nodded, accepting it. He sighed, annoyed at Rawlins, and at himself, the latter because it had been mostly his doing that had caught them up late last year. While he was at it he figured he would be annoyed at Chardonnais, too, for bringing them such a poor season this year.

Early spit into the fire. "I think you're right, though, Lucien," he said. "Next year we got to go someplace else. Two poor years down in these parts don't shine with this ol' hoss."

"Well, maybe if you and froggie here hadn't spent so goddamn much time with doin's that don't have nothin' to do with trappin', we wouldn't have had two poor seasons." Rawlins was disgusted with himself for acting this way with his friends.

"You want to be a pain in the ass, ol' hoss," Early said flatly, "that's your own affair. But don't dump that shit on me, less'n you're fixin' for a fandango with me."

Rawlins scowled at his partner but said nothing.

Early sighed. "Well, none of this's gonna make a goddamn bit of difference to us now. We just got to hunt as best we can, cut our losses, and drag our asses down to Taos soon's we can and have us a spree."

"Sounds like you t'ink we're going to be made wolf bait of by dem Blackfeets next season, eh?" Chardonnais said with a small laugh. "Like you plan to have one last spree before you go under, eh?"

Early laughed. It was always possible to be killed by Indians out here. If a body was to worry about such a thing, he would be better off not even coming to these lands. The knowledge that one could die in any number of ways was just another part of life, as natural as the need to defecate and the need to fornicate. It was just something a man thought about as little as possible. "What the hell, if we're gonna go under," he said, "we might's well have us one hell of a doin's before we go."

Chardonnais and Boatwright laughed. Even Rawlins cracked a smile.

They pushed on the next day, now heading south. A week later they swung westward, following the Colorado River. As usual, they trapped wherever they could find beaver sign until they had trapped the region out; then they would move as swiftly as possible to the next likely spot. When they came to a stream flowing into the Colorado, they would move up it, trapping. Near its source they would cross it and then move across land to the next stream and trap that stream until they got back to the Colorado, and follow that to the next stream.

They finally crossed the Colorado, and then pushed quickly through Glenwood Canyon. Soon after, they headed southeast, along the Roaring Fork, still trapping wherever the opportunity presented itself. Their travels brought them ever higher into the mountains, where the air was still freezing and could make a man feel funny if he wasn't used to it.

They found plenty of beaver sign near Woody Creek, and they settled in, figuring on a week's stay. They also needed to take some time to hastily press and pack their new plews and to make some meat. This pleasant little meadow looked like an ideal place to stay. There was plenty of wood, forage for the horses, and game.

The four Ute women liked it when they could stay at a place for more than one day. Since it was still far too cold for sleeping in the open, they had to use their lodges. It was a lot of trouble to put them up in late afternoon and then take them down again before dawn the next day, so staying in one place even two or three days helped.

Even so, the women had plenty of work to do. They had to gather firewood, build the fires, and cook. Falling Leaf and Scatters the Clouds also had to take care of their children. The four women had to cure the beaver plews and butcher the meat the men brought in. Clothes still needed to be repaired and water bucketed up from stream or pond. Hides needed tanning, and meat had to be dried.

Not that the men had it easy. They had to saddle and unsaddle the horses and tend them. They had to load and unload the mules and take care of them, too, making sure the animals were not being rubbed raw by their packs. Horses and mules had to be checked regularly to make sure their shoes were holding up. If not, the men would break out their meager pack of blacksmithing tools—including the small anvil—and fix any problems they found. On top of it all, they had to keep track of their trap lines, and they had to hunt.

One of the most difficult tasks for the men was protecting their families and the camp. Not that they were under constant attack—or any attack. It was more a matter of being on the alert every minute of every day. It was wearing on them, but it had to be done. Though they were deep in the heart of Ute country, the Arapaho, Shoshone, and Crow made regular forays down here, bent on counting coup and stealing women and horses. Blackfeet also journeyed this far south looking for trade, war, and adventure. Even the Jicarilla

Apaches, who were close friends with most of the seven major bands of Utes, would not hesitate to attack a camp of white men. Chardonnais and his two long-time friends knew almost none of the Jicarillas, and the three would be dead long before the Apaches could determine that the white men were great friends with the Utes.

Even with their unflagging vigilance, the four men could not see everything. And the longer they stayed in one spot with no trouble, the more comfortable they became.

After four days at Woody Creek, the small group began to enjoy life a little, with the prospects for the season looking better than they had in a spell. The cottonwoods, willows, and pines were covered with dangling beaver plews stretched on willow hoops. Three small meat racks were set up as the women made some pemmican and jerky in case times got lean again. Such a thing was all too possible, and all knew it far too well for comfort.

The men and women fell into a smooth routine, enjoying the slightly warmer days and the somewhat better trapping they had here. It made them a little lazy, lulled as they were by the comfortable life they had found—and would lose again all too soon. They had had no trouble, and had seen no reason to expect any.

Then the three Shoshones showed up.

26

THE FIRST HINT OF TROUBLE was a hoarse shout
followed by a whistle. Then the cavvy of horses and
mules, all of which had been hobbled, was moving,
pressed on by three whooping, shouting Shoshones.

"Mon Dieu!" Chardonnais shouted as he grabbed
his rifle. He and Boatwright were in the camp with the
women and children, who quickly ran into Rawlins's
lodge, since it was the closest. Early and Rawlins were
away seeing to the trap lines. Chardonnais fired, and
then cursed again when he hit nothing but a tree.

Boatwright fired, too, but also hit nothing. "Shit,"
he mumbled angrily. He and Chardonnais dropped
their rifles and ran, pulling out pistols as they did.

Chardonnais hoped—and even prayed—that no
more Shoshones were lurking about. If there were,
everyone in the camp would be dead within moments.

Both men fired a pistol, but it was too late—the
Shoshones and every one of the mountain men's
horses and mules were gone.

Rawlins and Early ran into camp a few moments
later. They were on foot, having seen no reason to saddle

212

horses for the quarter mile or so trip upriver through thickets and brush.

"What'n hell's all the goddamn shootin'—" Early started to say, but stopped, jaw tightening in anger. "The whole goddamn cavvy's gone?" he asked, his anger tempered by astonishment.

"Yes, de whole goddamn cavvy is gone," Chardonnais retorted. "What you t'ink—de animals are hiding in de trees?"

"How many of 'em was there?"

"T'ree. Snakes."

"You let three goddamn pus-suckin' Snakes walk in here and ride off with all our stock?" Early's temper was rising fast.

"*Oui*," Chardonnais snapped. "Me and Jed just sit here and tell dem Snakes, 'Please, Messieurs Snakes, please take all our horses and mules. We have no use for dem anymore, so you take dem away. Dat way when de great Monsieur Early—de chil' who never was counted coup on—comes back, he can make stupid accusations to me.' *Oui*, dat is what we did."

"Ah, shit, Lucien," Early said with a grimace, "you know I wasn't really accusin' you of nothin'." He sucked in a breath and let it out in a long-drawn-out stream. "You get any of them red devils?"

"Not a damn one."

"You have any warnin'?" Rawlins asked. He was leaning on his rifle, eyes flicking about, trying to find if there were any other Shoshones about.

"*Oui*," Chardonnais said flatly. "De sound of de animals running away."

"Anybody hurt?" Rawlins refused to see if his wife and child were all right, but he wanted to know, badly.

Chardonnais shook his head. "Dey run into your

lodge at de first sign of trouble. But de Snakes, dey didn't do notting but grab de animals and run."

"Well, that's somethin', then," Rawlins said dryly.

"Let's get out of this goddamn cold whilst we figure out what to do," Early said, heading toward his lodge.

"Don' you want to check de rest of de traps?" Chardonnais asked.

Early stopped and turned. "No," he said sharply. "If there's beaver in 'em, they'll keep in this cold. If there ain't, it ain't gonna make no difference. But more pertinent is the fact that without the horses and mules we ain't got no way to get the plews to Taos. Till we solve that little problem, I don't care a Crow's ass for the traps." He swung back and headed into his lodge.

Moments later the four men were gathered around the fire. Falling Leaf and Scatters the Clouds moved around, handing out horn bowls of stew and making sure some fresh meat was spitted over the fire. Looks Again and her sister, Blue Rattle, took the two children into another lodge.

"Well, this here's shit-poor doin's, and this ol' chil' don't mind sayin' so neither," Rawlins said.

"That's helpful," Early said sarcastically. "You assholes got any idea of what we should do?"

"Go get 'em," Boatwright said boldly.

"Dat's a stupid goddamn idea," Chardonnais snapped. "Dey're all mounted and riding hard. We'd be on foot, in de mountains. We couldn't catch dem if we had two years to do it."

"You got a better suggestion?" Boatwright asked defensively.

"*Oui.* Since I am to blame for all dese troubles, I'll go get some more horses and mules."

"Where're you gonna do that, you dumb-shit frog?" Rawlins asked.

"From de Utes."

"There ain't no goddamn Utes around here. Besides, most of 'em ain't about to just up and give us a couple dozen animals."

"Strong Bear will," Chardonnais said evenly.

"But he's—"

"I know where de hell he is, goddammit. And I know where de hell he's going. And I know he's got enough animals wit' him to give us a whole new cavvy without hurting himself any."

"But he's miles—"

"Enough, Abe," Early snapped. "I think Lucien's got an idea there. The worst part would be gettin' through Hunter's Pass. Once he's done that, the rest ought to be easy."

"*Oui*. I can do it in a mont'. Maybe a mont' and a half."

"That's a heap of time, Lucien," Rawlins said quietly.

Chardonnais shrugged. "*Oui*. But what other choice do we have? We can carry de packs of plews on our backs, but I don' t'ink dat'd work so good, eh."

"There ain't nothin' else to be done, Abe," Early said. "The only thing is to get some more animals. We've got some choice there, but not much. One of us can try'n find another band of the Uncompahgres out west and try'n talk 'em into givin' us some animals and tell 'em we'll pay 'em soon's we trade in our plews. Someone could head south for Taos and see if he can find someone who'll put up horses and mules against our take for the season."

"Ain't too many of them bean-fartin' bastards'll be willin' to go that way."

"Sure as hell ain't." Early lit his pipe. "About the only one who'd have that much stock and the where-

withal to let us have 'em on credit is Charlie Bent or
Ceran Saint Vrain."

"There's no guarantee they can manage it
though," Rawlins said. "I figure most of their animals're
on the trail."

"I know."

"Might be one other thing we can try," Rawlins
offered. "Cache the plews and walk south. We can hole
up along the Ute trail till Strong Bear and his people
come by. We can get animals from him then, ride back
here, and get the plews."

"No," Chardonnais said harshly.

"What's the matter, froggie?" Rawlins sneered. "Afraid
you can't make it on them stumpy-ass legs of yours?"

"I can outwalk you, *mon ami*," Chardonnais said,
his voice hard and flat. "And I can outdo you in anyt'ing
else." He paused. "Except maybe in making an ass of
myself."

"No," Early said, "you could outdo him in that for
sure."

Chardonnais nodded. "Yes, I could do dat." He
looked at Rawlins. "De reason dat won't work is dat de
women'd have trouble walking dat far. And de children, dey maybe would die."

"Hadn't thought of that," Rawlins said sourly.

"I didn't t'ink so," Chardonnais said sarcastically.
"I—"

"That's enough of the horseshit, Lucien. Abe, you,
too. This here's goddamn damp powder and no fire to
dry it. We ain't got time for playin' the fool with each
other." Early cracked his knuckles and then stretched.
"When're you leavin', Lucien?" he asked.

"Soon's I can get a pack ready." He paused and
smiled in embarrassment. "And as soon as I dampen
my pizzle, eh."

Early sighed. The extra five minutes—or an hour—wouldn't make much difference at this point, he knew. Still, it irritated him.

"I'm goin' with him," Boatwright announced.

"No, you stay here," Chardonnais said.

"No, goddammit, I'm goin'. I'm as much at fault here as you are that those goddamn Snakes stole our cavvy. And, by Christ, I aim to help make it right."

Chardonnais stared at him for a few moments, then looked from Early to Rawlins. "Either of you object to dat?" he asked.

Both men shook their heads.

"Den it's settle." Chardonnais looked at Boatwright and smiled tightly. "Get some jerky and maybe a little pemmican. Make sure you got powder and ball, and your bullet mold, eh. Take a good, heavy blanket and your best, fur-lined moccasins. And you better make de beast with two backs with Blue Rattle. It might be de last time."

"I aim to get back here," Boatwright said flatly. "I might do it alone, but I'll be with Blue Rattle again."

Chardonnais smiled a little and nodded. He pushed up. "Well, *excusez-moi,* messieurs," he said as he turned and walked out.

Just over three quarters of an hour later Chardonnais and Boatwright walked out of camp. Each wore thick heavy moccasins. On the outside they were covered by a good coating of beeswax and bear tallow; inside they were stuffed with warm fur. Each wore pants of fringed buckskin that were almost black from grease and smoke. The bottoms to just above the knees had been cut off and replaced by pieces of good blanket. They had heavy blanket coats—Chardonnais's

down to his knees, Boatwright's just past the hips.
Chardonnais wore his perennial green wool cap.
Boatwright had his bear fur hat with leather brim. Both
coats also had hoods. Fur mittens covered their hands.
Each also had a wide leather belt around his middle,
over his coat. Their pistols, knives, and tomahawks
were stuck into the belt in various places, where they
would be easy to get to.

Each carried his supplies in a hastily fashioned
buckskin haversack. They had a few pounds of pemmican, wrapped in small packages of buckskin. They also
carried a fair amount of jerky. Chardonnais carried
some coffee and a small brick of tea, plus a sack of
cornmeal and half the precious little sugar the men had
left. Boatwright carried a coffeepot and a single iron
skillet. They had tobacco and some small-size trade
goods. Each carried an extra tin of powder in the
haversack and a thin bar of lead. As a matter of course,
each had a fire-making kit with flint, steel, burning
glass, and tinder.

With rifles resting in the crook of their left arms,
they moved out side by side, setting a good, strong
pace as they headed southeast, toward Hunter's Pass.
"Don' look back dere, boy," Chardonnais said quietly.

"Why?" Boatwright asked, surprised.

"It's easier dat way. Believe me."

Boatwright nodded and forced himself to keep his
eyes straight ahead, though he wanted more than anything to take a last look at Blue Rattle to etch her face
into his mind. The feeling faded as he and Chardonnais
rounded a few curves, putting the camp out of sight
anyway.

"You love Looks Again, Lucien?" Boatwright asked
as they walked.

"*Oui*. Why do you ask?"

"I love Blue Rattle," Boatwright answered, a little embarrassed. "And I thought maybe I was the only one of us that actually loved his woman. Some of the boys I saw with the Company, well, those old niggurs didn't give a shit about their women. All they wanted 'em for was a camp keeper, cook, pack animal, and bed partner."

"Dere's many a man in dese mountains who feels dat way," Chardonnais agreed. "But me and my *amis,* we ain't like dat. No. We have good women dere."

"Is Looks Again your first Ute woman?"

"*Mais non!*" Chardonnais answered with a small laugh. "No, dere have been many. De first was Yellow Feather. She was a good woman, but she couldn't . . . accommodate me."

"Accommodate?" Boatwright's face reddened. "Ah, yes, I see."

"Dat was de trouble wit' most of dem I had. But Looks Again, she is different. She don' mind dat I have to fornicate so often. She takes pleasure in it."

"What was your first woman, Lucien?"

"You're a nosy young bastard, eh?" He smiled. "But I tell you anyway." He paused, allowing the years to fade away. "She was one of my people—one of de French-Canadians come to live in St. Charles. I was almost fifteen; she was old." He laughed a little. "At de time she was old to me. I ain't sure how much, but I t'ink she was almost t'irty."

"On death's door," Boatwright said flatly.

Chardonnais laughed. "To a fourteen-year-old boy it seemed dat way."

Theresa Dubois did seem old to the young Chardonnais, but she also was the only woman, young or old, who seemed to understand his needs. She was the butt of all the jokes by the children of the area, including Chardonnais, until she managed to entice him into her cramped, ill-smelling room.

Even now, almost two decades later, he could smell that room, the old food, the sweat, and things he could not fathom on the filthy straw mattress. He could see the crinkles radiating from the corner of her eyes and lips, could feel the rough skin of her face, but the smooth glossiness of her lips.

He could remember the way she had pulled her old, thin cotton dress off and dropped it on the floor and stood there brazenly without a stitch of clothes on. Chardonnais's mouth went dry, but he could feel a stirring in his groin.

"Come," Theresa said, arms outstretched. Then she lay on her back on the bed.

Chardonnais moved forward, slowly, his legs weak. As he placed a knee on the bed Theresa startled him by saying, "Your clothes."

"What?" he asked.

"Your clothes. Take them off."

"Oh," Chardonnais said dumbly. He stood and stripped, embarrassed at his state of readiness. Then he crawled onto the bed and lost himself in the feel, smell, taste, and perfectness of her. It did not matter then that her breasts sagged, or that her face was lined from a hard and dissipated life, or that she smelled of yesterday's onions. Nothing mattered but the sensation that ripped and tore through him, making him spasm with its power.

It was over in all too brief a time, but Chardonnais found out that he was ready again soon after. That time took a little longer. The third time even longer. But then Theresa had kissed him and told him to leave.

He went back to see her two more times, but then she told him not to come back anymore. Devastated, he asked why.

"You are a man now, Lucien," she said in her husky, life-besotted voice. "You must go and find others to have your pleasure with." She smiled. "I am too old for you."

Feeling a strange sense of loss and hurt, he had left. He worried about it for several days, but then he met a young woman, one with the promise of life bright in her, and he almost forgot Theresa Dubois.

27

CHARDONNAIS AND BOATWRIGHT wheezed and gasped as they struggled slowly up into Hunter's Pass. Though it was only twenty miles or so from their camp, it took Chardonnais and Boatwright almost a week to get halfway up to the pass's 12,095-foot summit. Then they stopped, winded and quaking.

"I can't go no more, Lucien," Boatwright gasped.

"Me neither." He was bent over, forearms on his legs just above the knees while he cradled his rifle in both hands. He looked up toward the summit of the pass so far away. The steepness of the trail was nothing compared with the ten or fifteen feet of snow that clogged their way. Chardonnais and Boatwright had struggled though snow that was almost knee-deep, then over knee-deep. Where they had stopped, parts of it were waist-deep. They had managed to flatten out a spot by the simple expedient of flopping down over and over.

"What now?"

"Next pass south. I ain't sure of de name. It's a couple days south of here."

"Christ, Lucien, I don't know if I'll make it."

"Don' look to me for help. You can't make it, you're going to die here. Or dere."

"Go to hell."

"I expect I will." He straightened. "But not just yet. *Allons-y.*"

They headed back down, struggling through the snow again. Then Boatwright slipped and fell on his rump. His momentum made him slide perhaps a dozen feet.

"*Merde!*" Chardonnais announced with a grin. "Dat's de way to go!" He ran a few steps and then threw himself down, legs out, onto his rump. The slide carried him a little ways down the slope.

It became something of a fun way to get down the hill, and they employed it when they could. But the novelty soon wore off and they went back to trudging doggedly on.

Three days later they were heading up another pass, this one nearly as steep and with almost as much snow. The two men were better prepared this time. They had taken a day just to rest up and fill their bellies with fat-rich pemmican—and to make themselves snowshoes. The latter helped considerably, but their trek was still awesome. And the snowshoes didn't do a thing to help them clamber up and over cliffs.

"Jesus goddamn Christ," Boatwright said when they collapsed after reaching the summit.

"*Oui.* I don' want to ever do dat again."

"Shit, me neither." Boatwright rolled out his blanket, fell into it, and was asleep almost instantly.

Chardonnais grinned and within minutes had followed suit.

They were stiff and sore the next day, their legs

aching. But Chardonnais forced himself to move, heading eastward on the faint trail down from the pass.

"Where the hell're you goin', you crazy goddamn Frenchman?"

"Down de hill a ways."

"What for?"

"To find a better place to stay. Somewhere wit' some wood. I want some tea or some coffee."

"Damn," Boatwright groaned as he rose. He felt like every muscle he had was screaming in outrage at being asked to move after having been treated so poorly in the past two weeks. But he finally made his feet and lurched onward.

Chardonnais wasn't sure how far they went, but it took more than six hours. He finally found a spot he deemed suitable. Walking like wooden men, they picked up some firewood and made a fire. While Boatwright scraped snow into the pot, Chardonnais pounded a chunk of the brick tea in a piece of cloth with his tomahawk. They heated some pemmican in their one pan and then ate hungrily until their hands and faces were dripping with grease.

They holed up there for two days to regain their strength, then pushed on. Boatwright figured—hoped was more like it, though he wasn't about to admit it— that the worst was over. With such thoughts in his head, he felt like sitting down and crying when Chardonnais brought them to the foot of another massive pass several days later.

"Jesus, Lucien," he said, looking up toward the wind-battered summit.

"What's de matter wit' you now?" Chardonnais asked. He was in pain from head to foot, he was hungry, and he missed Looks Again something awful. He was still angry at having lost the horses and mules, necessitating this whole damned trek. He was about ready to explode, and he didn't need Boatwright complaining to him about the difficulty of the journey.

"You didn't tell me there was another one of these goddamn things to get over."

"And what good would it have done if I told you, eh?"

Boatwright grinned crookedly. "Guess I wouldn't have gotten my hopes up that the rest of these doin's was gonna be easy."

"You can't be dat stupid."

Boatwright looked as if he had been slapped. "Instead of standin' here passin' wind at me, maybe you best turn your ass around and head up the goddamn hill."

"You t'ink you can keep up wit' me, boy?"

"Anywhere you care to lead, gramps."

Chardonnais almost grinned. "*Allons-y,*" he said, turning and marching off.

Cottonwood Pass was every bit as muscle killing and heart wrenching as the previous one had been, and it took them five days to get across the summit and head far enough down the eastern slope to make a halfway decent camp to rest up.

"I hope to hell there ain't another one of these goddamn passes waitin' for us up ahead."

"No," Chardonnais grunted. He had never been through such a torturous several weeks. Not in all the time he had been in the mountains, and he had been through some incredibly rough times in some thoroughly nasty territory.

"Good. I ain't sure I could make it through another."

"I know," Chardonnais said quietly. His temper had been kicked out by the brutal trek he had undertaken. He had been beaten into submission, at least for now.

They ate the last of their pemmican and washed it down with the last of the coffee. All they had left for supplies was a handful of jerky strips and a small slab of the brick tea.

"We're going to be in piss-poor shape soon if we don't take some meat, *mon ami*," Chardonnais said as they prepared to move off again.

"We'll take meat, old man. Don't you fret."

"*Merde*," Chardonnais muttered.

Three days later they made it into a long, narrow wooded valley. Most of the snow had melted here, and grass was growing. Chardonnais and Boatwright found a few buffalo and shot one big cow. While Chardonnais began butchering the cow, Boatwright quickly gathered firewood and built a fire only a few feet from the buffalo carcass.

For the rest of the day and throughout the next, the two men sat at their fire and ate almost nonstop. Chardonnais could feel his body filling and growing back to its normal size and shape. He hadn't realized how much he had gaunted down in the weeks he and Boatwright had been on the trail. He would down several pounds of meat and then rest a bit before hacking off another slab and gnawing it down.

With renewed spirits and energy, the two moved off the following morning. From there it was a relatively easy journey, mostly level across huge flats, and downward a little as they began to near the plains to the east. The few passes they had to take were much gentler, and crossed without difficulty. Now that they were at lower altitudes, the temperatures were a little warmer as real spring edged into the high country.

Game was plentiful enough here that they didn't have to worry about meat, but Chardonnais was becoming concerned about time. As best as he could figure it, he and Boatwright had been gone almost a month and a half. The Utes might already be on the trail west through the mountains.

They finally reached the plains and stopped to rest a little before the last push and to repair their moccasins, which were full of holes. They shot a buffalo cow and built a fire of buffalo chips nearby. They stayed a day and a half, eating frequently, letting their bodies rest. They patched their moccasins with pieces of fresh buffalo hide hurriedly scraped and smoked.

As they packed their meager supplies the next morning, Boatwright asked, "Which way?"

"South."

"Why south?"

"If dey are past here and heading home already, us going nort' won't help us any. If dey aren't on de trail west yet, dey will catch us as we walk."

"So might a passel of Cheyennes or Arapahos," Boatwright said dryly. He sighed. "Well, let's get movin'."

They trudged onward, moving slowly. Their legs seemed to be constantly on fire, their backs were sore, their feet bruised. It all served to slow them.

Sometime in the afternoon three days later, Chardonnais suddenly dropped to the ground. "Get down!" he hissed.

Boatwright was startled, having lost himself in some reverie or another, but he wasted no time in flopping facedown on the dusting of remaining snow on the new grass. "What is it?" he asked, after slithering up beside Chardonnais.

"Arapahos. T'ree of dem."

"We gonna take 'em down?"

"*Oui.* Just as soon as we can."

"I just hope those goddamn ponies don't go runnin' off."

"Well, if dey do, we have lost notting, have we?"

"Reckon not."

They eased up their rifles, made sure they were loaded and primed. Then they waited. It was an odd experience for them. The sun on their backs was warm, yet underneath them the ground was still cold. It did little for their comfort.

The three warriors were riding slowly, in no hurry, laughing as they talked. They were hunting, not out to make war.

When they were less than fifty yards away, Chardonnais fired. One of the warriors tumbled off his horse. A second later Boatwright fired and another warrior went down. The third wheeled his horse and raced off.

Chardonnais hurriedly reloaded, his movements swift and sure from years of practice. He came up to one knee and set himself. Then he fired.

The third Arapaho was two hundred yards or so away, and it took a second for Chardonnais to know for sure that he had hit him. Then the warrior fell while his horse continued to race away.

"Good shootin', ol' hoss," Boatwright said with a grin.

Chardonnais shrugged as he and Boatwright stood. The trapper reloaded his rifle. "Now," he said, "let's see if we can catch dese goddamn ponies before dey go running off."

They walked slowly and steadily, not wanting to frighten the horses. Ten yards from where two of the ponies stood pawing the ground, Chardonnais and

Boatwright eased themselves onto their bellies and began creeping forward, stopping each time a horse snuffled nervously. The two men moved apart, each slinking toward one of the ponies.

Finally Chardonnais reached out and gently grasped the simple rope rein to one horse. Making sure he had a good grip on the horsehair rope, he stood and leaped onto the pony's back. The horse bolted, and Chardonnais almost dropped his rifle. But he managed to keep himself on and within a few hundred feet brought the animal under control. Once he did, he dashed back toward Boatwright, who was standing forlornly.

Boatwright had been just ready to grab his horse's reins when Chardonnais had jumped onto the other horse. Boatwright's horse whinnied and raced off. He made a desperate dive for the rope but to no avail. Then he had stood and watched, almost laughing, as Chardonnais tried to bring his new mount under control.

Now the French-Canadian veered off, toward the other pony. That horse didn't mind that the stranger rode right up to it and reached out to grab the rein. Five minutes later Chardonnais and Boatwright were loping toward the south, feeling better than they had since before their own horses had been stolen.

They shot another buffalo late in the afternoon and made camp right there. They made sure they hobbled the horses well.

It was with much better spirits that they rode out the next day. At midmorning, Chardonnais called a halt. He dismounted and handed his pony's rein to Boatwright. He scouted around, looking at sign. Then he grinned and remounted the horse.

"What did you find?" Boatwright asked.

"Strong Bear's band camped here. Three, maybe four days back."

"You sure?" Boatwright asked skeptically.

"*Oui*. De sign is unmistakable."

"Think we can catch 'em?"

Chardonnais nodded. "Tomorrow. Maybe de day after."

"That soon?"

"Yes. Dey are moving slowly with all de women and children and the old ones. They have no reason to hurry."

"But we do, old man," Boatwright cracked. "Let's move."

28

CHARDONNAIS KNEW THEY WERE closing in on Strong Bear's people well before they saw them. There were telltale signs that the band had made camp for the night, though it was not too late in the afternoon. The circling of buzzards and vultures was one clear sign. With all the refuse of a fair-sized Indian band, the scavengers were never far away.

Strong Bear came out of his lodge to greet the two white men, surprised but not showing it. "Welcome, my friends," he said magnanimously. "Come, we will sit and talk as men should."

Chardonnais nodded. He and Boatwright slid off the horses and let the animals be led away by a boy. The two followed Strong Bear into the lodge, as did several other warriors. They ate and then had a small ceremonial smoke. Finally Strong Bear asked, "What brings you here to our camp?"

"Some goddamned Snakes run off all our cavvy."

"All?" Strong Bear asked, eyes raised.

"Every goddamn one," Chardonnais said with a sad shake of his head.

"When was this?"

"Almost two moons ago. Me and Jed left dere right after it happened and worked over the passes to the plains and den came down dis way looking for you."

"Where'd you get those two ponies?"

"Caught a few Arapahos out on de plains. We shot dem dead and took der ponies."

"Well, that's something," Strong Bear said with a laugh, in which the others joined. All had been through similar things, and could understand and appreciate it.

"*Oui.*" Chardonnais reached over and grabbed a piece of meat from the fire and popped it in his mouth.

"Now that you've found us, what can I do to help?"

"We need horses and mules," Chardonnais said flatly. He did not like having to beg for help. "Enough to replace all our own."

"Why would I let you have all those?" Strong Bear asked, a hint of anger in his voice.

"So we can get our plews down to Taos and sell dem for enough supplies for de next season, and to buy some goddamn foofaraw for you and your people." The trapper's tones matched Strong Bear's.

"I have no reason to worry about such things." Strong Bear smiled inwardly, enjoying teasing his son-in-law.

"In a pig's ass," Chardonnais snapped.

Strong Bear looked as if he had been slapped. "I thought you knew better than to speak to me that way," he said, more surprised and hurt than angry.

"And I t'ought you knew better dan to treat me like an enemy," Chardonnais retorted.

"What have you done for me—or the People—to think I'd be so generous?" Strong Bear asked haughtily. He didn't hate Chardonnais, but he was mighty angry at him. Their banter had gone from teasing to insult. Strong Bear was too important a man to his people to suffer such treatment.

"You have to ask dat?" Chardonnais countered, voice biting. He could not understand what had gotten into Strong Bear. They had always enjoyed an easy camaraderie. Suddenly it seemed to him as if the Ute leader didn't know him. It was baffling.

The two men stared at each other, eyes and wills locked, waiting for the other to relent.

Then Boatwright sneezed, loudly and forcefully. "Ah, shit," he cursed as he wiped snot off the lower half of his face.

Chardonnais was the first to crack, with an almost imperceptible smile that rapidly grew until he was chuckling. Strong Bear could not contain himself either, and within moments he, too, was laughing.

With the tension broken, Chardonnais finally asked, "Well, Strong Bear, can you help out a few piss-poor, starving bevairs?"

Strong Bear nodded firmly. "Of course. When do you want the animals?"

"Morning?"

Strong Bear nodded again. "It will be done." He paused. "But I think you should take a few of the men with you."

"I don't want to put you out any more dan I have already. And I don't want to impose on your young men."

"Some of them'll be glad to go."

Chardonnais nodded. "If any want to volunteer, I won't mind having dem along."

"Then it's settled."

Once more the ceremonial pipe made its way around the circle of men. When that was done, the men relaxed some. Chardonnais, though, was still smarting a little from his altercation with Strong Bear. It was so unlike the old chief. Finally he just had to ask: "Why did you give me a hard time before, Strong Bear?"

"I didn't mean to. I wanted to have a little fun with my old friend. Then you began to insult me."

"Well, shit, Strong Bear, I didn't know you were having fun. Me and Jed, we've been on de trail almost two mont'. We have faced starvin' times, almost died in de mountains wit' blizzards and snow up to de ass of a man standing on a horse. We plumb wore ourselves out." He grinned ruefully. "I wasn't of a mood to make jokes, especially when I didn't know dat's what you were doing."

Strong Bear nodded in understanding. "One of the many problems men who don't speak the same language and who are of different peoples have is trying to make the other understand when he isn't serious about what he's saying."

"An unfortunate problem," Chardonnais agreed.

"And one I'm glad we've overcome, at least for this time."

The next morning Chardonnais and Boatwright rode out with a herd of twelve horses and sixteen mules. Riding with the two mountain men were six Ute warriors — Striking Hawk, Walking in the Sky, Moving Thunder, Runs Back, Red Stone, and Spotted Bull.

They moved swiftly west and into the gigantic San Luis Valley, where they turned north, riding up the flat, seemingly empty valley on the western side of the Sangre de Cristo Mountains. Some days later Poncha Pass slowed them, but only a little.

Two more days' ride north, they turned west, heading up into Hunter's Pass. Cottonwood Pass, which

Chardonnais and Boatwright had taken on the way out, was a little easier generally, but only a little. And Hunter's Pass cut some miles off the journey. It was almost summer now, and much of the snow would be melted. But Boatwright still felt a tightening of the groin and a nervous buzzing in his stomach as they approached it.

It took them three days, but they made it without the loss of life or livestock. They rested a day on the western side of the high, forbidding Sawatch Range, before pushing deeper into the mountains.

Then, two months and twenty-five days after Chardonnais and Boatwright had left, they rode back into their camp.

"Well, I'll be damned," Rawlins said laconically, "if it ain't the wanderin' buffler shits."

"Don' you dare come over here and give me a kiss, you ass wipe," Chardonnais retorted. He slid off his horse, walked swiftly to Looks Again, grabbed her arm, and hauled her into his lodge. He didn't much care that she was now very pregnant, or that he hadn't said so much as a word to her. He had had a woman in Strong Bear's village the one night he and Boatwright had stayed there, but that had been a few weeks ago, and that was the only time since he left. He hadn't gone three months at a stretch without a woman since he was sixteen.

Looks Again knew what to expect if he returned. As soon as she heard the shouts of greeting, she had swiftly made sure the robes were ready, and then she had gone outside to wait for him. She felt an almost girlish delight in seeing her man come riding into the camp. It didn't matter a whit to her that he was filthy and that his clothes were torn and tattered. She realized that not only did she know what to expect from him, she also looked forward to it.

As always when he first returned from time away from her, Chardonnais had eased her down onto the robes—on her hands and knees, in deference to her bulging pregnancy—and within seconds was churning away inside her. Then came release, and he collapsed onto her back for a few moments. Then he lay down, bringing her around and down with him.

"Damn, woman, I missed you somet'ing fierce," he said when he had his breath back. He rubbed small circles on Looks Again's buckskin-covered belly. "Even if you are so big." He grinned at her to let her know he was just teasing.

"If my belly displeases you," she said, trying to hide a small smile, "just remember it was you who made me this way."

"*Mais oui!*" Chardonnais said with a laugh. "*Le grand homme* Monsieur Lucien Chardonnais."

"I missed you, too," Looks Again said quietly, stroking his thick-furred jawline. "The others thought you were never coming back. Ezra was planning what to do. He said he would give you till the end of this moon and then have to decide. But I told him you'd be back."

"You have a lot of faith in me, woman," Chardonnais said quietly.

"With good reason."

"You might give me a swelled head with such talk."

"That's not what I want to get swelled right now." Looks Again was not a woman to let some false propriety stand in the way of what she desired.

"Well, den," Chardonnais said with a smile, rolling onto his side to face her, "let's just see what we can do about dat, eh."

*   *   *

Boatwright wasn't nearly as blunt and direct at hauling Blue Rattle into the lodge, but he wasn't much longer getting to it either. He watched Chardonnais's performance with a grin and then nervously headed toward Blue Rattle. He stopped in front of her, unsure of himself. His desire was plain in his eyes and on his face. Blue Rattle's answer was in hers.

With a smile, Boatwright scooped his woman up into his arms and headed with her to the lodge. He could not wait for many of the niceties, and when he was done, he felt ashamed because he had no control over his urges, and because Blue Rattle was unfulfilled.

"I'm sorry," he said quietly, face red.

"There's nothing to be sorry about."

"But you . . . Well, you know, you didn't . . ."

"That doesn't matter right now. It makes me happy to see you have so much pleasure. And there will be other times." She giggled. "Soon."

"No," Boatwright said, skin burning with shame and self-anger. "I ain't up to it." He realized what he had said and wanted to cut his own throat.

"You underestimate yourself, Jed." The word still felt odd to her tongue. Its harsh, biting consonants were foreign to her mellifluous language.

"No, I don't," he insisted. "I ain't like Lucien, you know." He had never envied Chardonnais in that area. While it might be fun at times to be so randy, it would also be troublesome, he had seen. However, right now, he would trade just about anything he owned for his partner's abilities and stamina for this one night.

"I don't want Lucien," Blue Rattle said, rolling awkwardly over so she could push herself up a little until she was sitting. "I want you."

"But I can't—"

"Is it because of this?" Blue Rattle asked, patting her stomach. She felt sick at the thought of him not wanting her because she was pregnant.

"No!" Boatwright said, startled out of his own self-disgust. "Don't you ever say that again. I love you, Blue Rattle. I don't love you any more—or any less, nei-ther—when you're pregnant than when you're not."

"Even though I'm as fat as a buffalo cow? And I have trouble sitting down and getting up?"

"Even though." He moved into a sitting position and reached out to pull her close and kiss her.

As their lips parted, Blue Rattle gently pushed Boatwright back.

"This ain't gonna work, Blue Rattle," he protested.

"Quiet," she commanded softly. "You'll be ready again soon." When he was lying on his back, she stood and shimmied out of her dress.

"Damn, you are somethin', woman," Boatwright breathed.

She smiled and sat on her lower legs, trying not to be angry at herself for her awkwardness. She pulled Boatwright's pants completely off and then bent over him.

Boatwright was rather surprised—pleasantly so—as he felt himself growing hard again under her quiet, insistent ministrations.

"See," Blue Rattle said breathlessly as she lowered herself gently onto him sometime later, "I told you."

All Boatwright could do was nod and give himself over to the feelings.

The men convened in Early's lodge just after dark. They all ate—out of hunger and want as opposed to routine. When they were mostly sated, Early said, "Well, tell it, Lucien."

Chardonnais did. It didn't take long. Early and the others did not need to hear about the heart-stopping effort over Cottonwood Pass or the hunger that stretched their bellies. Nor did they need to know of the long, endless days of walking, when a man's legs felt like someone was beating on them with hickory wiping sticks, when his feet were cut and bruised, feeling every rock or cactus. Nor the feelings of helplessness and hopelessness when they were afraid they would never make it out of the mountains alive. No, all these men—red and white alike—had been through similar experiences.

When Chardonnais was done, everyone else nodded. Then Early asked, "Where away from here, boys?"

"We got to make Taos in a real hurry we want to have a spree and then get back to the mountains," Rawlins said.

"What about rendezvous?" Boatwright asked.

"We'd never make it," Early answered. "Not on time. As best I can figure it, them doin's ought to be startin' in a week, maybe less. And since Blue Rattle and Looks Again're near about ready to drop their young'ns, we'd be movin' a little slower than we might otherwise." There was no accusation in his voice. It was a simple fact, as it had been the time Falling Leaf had been pregnant. That time, though, Falling Leaf had gone to Strong Bear's village and Early was on his way to Taos for his spree.

"You boys anxious to get back to your village?" Rawlins asked the Utes. When they all shook their heads, he said, "How's about this, then? We stay here—or maybe move to another camp not too far away. Game's almost gone from here, and we've fouled the place pretty well. Soon's Blue Rattle and Looks Again drop the kids, we send all the women and young'ns back to Strong Bear's in the company of our friends here." He waved a hand at the Utes. "Then the four of us can ride like hell for Taos. We might not have much of a spree, but we can get some time in, plus still get our supplies and get back up here."

The others thought about that for a bit. Then Chardonnais asked, "What about next season? Dese last two have been poor. We were figuring to go to Blackfeets country."

Rawlins shrugged. "We'll just have to ride like hell back this way, too. And not take time for visitin' and all that buffler shit with Strong Bear. We get to the village, we grab the women and kids and then move. We might not make Blackfoot country, but we can get to some halfway decent trapping grounds up in the Uintas or somewhere."

"You mind taking our families back to Strong Bear's, Striking Hawk?" Early asked.

"No."

"Then it's settled. We'll move the camp day after tomorrow." He grinned without much humor. "And then ask the Great Spirit to bring on them babies afore too much time goes by."

29

CHARDONNAIS WAS SITTING ON A LOG braiding a rawhide rope when he suddenly stopped and sat very still. Everything seemed normal, but something had reached into his brain and tapped him to alertness. Carefully, he scanned the camp. Looks Again and Blue Rattle were scraping the hair off a buffalo hide, jerking the heavy skin back and forth on a rough log braced up against a tree. Early and Rawlins were checking over the horses and mules. Boatwright was splitting wood, and Falling Leaf and Scatters the Clouds were picking berries, their children with them. The six Utes were sitting together, playing a game of hand. Birds still offered their songs to the skies, and the wind ruffled the trees.

Suddenly two arrows appeared in Moving Thunder's back. The Ute lurched up, took two steps, and fell. By then, though, the five other Utes had headed for cover, grabbing bows, arrows, and war clubs before they did so.

Chardonnais shoved to his feet, his rifle in hand, and set loose a sharp, high-pitched whistle. Then he headed for Looks Again and Blue Rattle, shouting.

The two women needed no encouragement. At the sound of Chardonnais's whistle, they dropped the buffalo hide and waddled as fast as they could for the nearest lodge, Early's.

Seeing them do that, Chardonnais shouted at Boatwright and pointed to the lodge. Boatwright nodded and ran. Chardonnais broke to the side and dashed into the woods. Early and Rawlins would have their hands full trying to keep the horses and mules from being taken again, so Chardonnais took it upon himself to try to find his two friends' wives and get them to safety. He wondered where the Utes were, though.

Suddenly a large, mean-visaged Crow appeared in front of him, tomahawk raised. "*Merde*," Chardonnais gasped as he slid to a halt. He managed to get his rifle up, crossways in both hands. The Crow's tomahawk thudded on it and fell. Chardonnais jerked the butt stock of his rifle and smashed one of the Crow's cheekbones. As the Crow staggered backward, Chardonnais swung his rifle down in his left hand and grabbed his knife with the right. In a second he had plunged the blade into the Crow's chest twice. Then he ran on.

Early had looked up as he heard his partner's whistle of warning, and in an instant saw Moving Thunder, with two arrows in him, dying.

"Ye see what they are?" Rawlins asked. As usual in such situations, he sounded calm.

"I can't see anything but one dead Ute. But whoever's out here ain't friendly." Without missing a beat, he added, "You take that side." He pointed. "I'll take the other. I ain't about to let no goddamn red devils get these horses and mules. Not after that last time."

Rawlins nodded and sprinted. He stopped and leaned against a large pine, back toward the camp. He didn't figure whoever was out here would be stupid enough to go running out into the open camp. Not with all this forest to sneak through.

The world seemed strangely quiet, which was worrisome. Rawlins would have much preferred facing a bunch of enemy warriors in the open somewhere. But he stayed where he was, eyes sweeping in regular arcs, looking for anything out of the ordinary.

He wasn't quite sure what caught his attention, but something had. With his focus on the spot, he missed the other Crow, who crept up on him. He ducked and barely got his head out of the way of the Crow's stone war club. He reacted instantly, jerking his rifle out away from the Crow and then butt first back into the Crow's side, staving in several ribs.

The Crow still had a heap of fight left in him, though, and he grabbed Rawlins, trying to wrestle him down. He half succeeded, and that was enough to make the arrow fired by a Crow in the bushes miss him. It thumped into the tree.

"Shit," Rawlins growled as the tenacious Crow kept clinging to him and dragging him down. He managed to latch a hand onto one of the Crow's ears. He made sure he had a good grip, digging his fingernails in. Then he jerked it with all the strength and leverage he could manage. The Crow howled when his ear ripped away from his head, and his grip on Rawlins lessened.

Rawlins pulled his knife and stabbed the Crow half a dozen times, then shoved the warrior off his legs. He grabbed his rifle and leapfrogged the body, just missing getting hit with another arrow. He flopped down onto his belly and fired his rifle. A muffled grunt followed by a crash made him think he had hit his target. Still, he was not about to test his luck by blindly walking that way.

Rawlins rolled several times, until he was near some brush. He got behind the bushes and reloaded his rifle. Carrying the weapon in his left hand, he pulled a pistol with his right. Warily he began making his way toward where the Crow was—or had been. He moved slowly, alert to the possibility that there might be one hell of a lot of Crows out here. He finally found his quarry, dead.

With a sigh of relief, he headed back toward his post. Two Crows jumped out of the brush and hit him, knocking him down. Both firearms skidded away across the dirt and pine needles. He snapped a hand backward, the back of his fist hitting one Crow in the face. He kicked the other, never really connecting well but with enough force to get the Indian to let him go. He scrabbled away, pulling his other pistol. As he rolled over onto his back and snapped the hammer back, both warriors fell, one with an arrow running from the back of his neck through his throat, the other with an arrow in his upper torso.

Striking Hawk popped up from behind a bush, shot a grim smile at Rawlins, and then disappeared.

Rawlins picked himself up and gathered his weapons. Once more leaning against a tree, breathing heavily, he brushed some of the dust off his shirt. "Ezra?" he called. "Ez, you all right over there?"

Early was too busy to answer, since three Crows had come at him hard just after he had set himself, kneeling at a tree to make a smaller target of himself. The Crows had appeared out of the dark forest, two with war clubs, one with a knife.

Early snapped his rifle up and fired from the hip. The ball hit one Crow in the leg, breaking the bone and sending him to the ground, skittering forward on his face and chest. Early dropped his rifle and charged, pushing up with his long, strong legs.

He slammed into a second Crow's midsection, driving him back. The warrior managed to regain his equilibrium and thumped Early a hard shot on the back with his war club.

"Ah, shit," Early groaned. He lost his grip and fell to hands and knees. The Crow kicked him in the ribs, flipping him over. Early crashed onto his back. He wanted to move, to be able to stop the looming warrior from killing him. But he couldn't, at least not with any speed or effectiveness.

A moment later the Crow's head was jerked backward, and a blade swiftly slid across the vulnerable throat. Early was so fascinated by the sight that he did not see the third Crow slide up alongside him. He sensed the attack and began turning his head, and then felt the slice of cold steel in his innards, and then again into his chest, where it clacked on a rib.

Then Walking in the Sky smashed the Crow's head with a war club, splattering his brain over Early's face and chest. The Crow fell on Early, who barely noticed. He was too busy attending to the excruciating, almost exquisitely burning pain in his guts.

Walking in the Sky grabbed the back of the dead Crow's shirt and hauled him off his friend. Then he knelt next to Early. "You all right, my friend?" he asked in Ute.

"Just fine," Early gasped.

Walking in the Sky nodded. It seemed certain that Early would die, but if he could answer with a little levity, he just might make it. The Ute warrior wasn't sure, but he would stay here and defend his wounded friend.

"Falling Leaf?" Early suddenly asked, voice faint and raspy.

"I don't know. Lucien went for her and Scatters the Clouds."

Early nodded and closed his eyes.

Chardonnais had found the two women and two children fairly quickly. He never did find out how the four had been missed by the Crows, but he didn't give it any thought when he got to them. He held a finger to his lips when they spotted him. He ran up and stopped. "Crows, dey attack de camp. *Allez. Venez. Vite, vite.*"

The women dropped their baskets and grabbed the children. Chardonnais shooed them back toward the camp. He stopped them at the edge of the trees and surveyed the camp. "Jed!" he shouted. "Jed."

"What?" Boatwright's voice had come through the lodge's skin wall.

"I am sending in de women and de children. Falling Leaf will come first, wit' Straight Calf. When she is safe, I send Scatters de Clouds and Standing Eagle."

"Do it."

"Go, Falling Leaf," Chardonnais said. "Straight to Ezra's lodge and inside. *Vite.*" He gave her a soft push on the back. Holding her child tightly, Falling Leaf scooted out of the trees and around to the front of the lodge. Then she was inside with Looks Again and Blue Rattle—and Jed Boatwright.

"Send the others!" Boatwright shouted.

Chardonnais nodded at Scatters the Clouds. Her son was somewhat bigger than Falling Leaf's daughter, but she seemed to have no trouble running with the boy in her arms. Then she, too, was in the haven.

"You comin' in, Lucien?" Boatwright asked.

He was about to answer in the affirmative when he

aw Early across the camp in the trees with the horses.
hree Crows were heading for him. *"Merde,"* he spat.
No, I'm going to help Ezra."

"Want my help?"

"No, you stay wit' de women and kids." Taking a
eep breath, he ran out into the open. Suddenly a Crow
aced out in front of him, almost dead center in front of
he lodge. They collided and fell. Chardonnais landed
ard on one of his pistols on a hip and with his leg
artly under him. He could feel the knee wrench and
e winced at the sudden sharp pain.

He knew, though, that he had to either get up, and
ast, or get a pistol out. If he didn't, he'd be dead in
noments. However, the task was easier said than
one. He pushed up as best he could, seeing that the
Crow was already up and moving toward him, toma-
awk in hand. Then there was a blur.

Boatwright heard the collision outside the lodge,
nd he shoved the flap aside, knife in hand, ready to
ill whoever was out there. He had given his rifle to
Blue Rattle, and pistols to Falling Leaf and Looks
again, figuring them to be their own last line of
efense. He saw the Crow strutting arrogantly for
Chardonnais, his tomahawk raised.

Boatwright burst out of the lodge and dove even as
he warrior was swinging the glittering tomahawk. He
anded on Chardonnais, and the tomahawk thudded
nto the back of his neck. He never felt it.

"You son of a bitch, bastard, shit-eating goddamn
ed goddamn son of a bitching devil!" Chardonnais
creamed in French.

While the Crow was bent over trying to free his
omahawk from Boatwright's neck, Chardonnais man-
ged to shove his friend's body off him. He jerked out a
pistol and jammed it under the Indian's chin. Then he

pulled the trigger, blowing out the top of the warrior head.

Chardonnais got up, favoring the wrenched knee. He grabbed a handful of the Crow's brain-splattered hair and pulled him off Boatwright. One glance to him that his young partner had been killed instantly his head almost severed.

A loud, piercing screech shook him and he turned to see Blue Rattle coming out of the lodge, screaming in her grief.

"Get back in dere," Chardonnais ordered harshly. He pushed her back. "We'll see to him later." He looked at his wife. "You make sure she don't go hurting herself, eh?"

Looks Again nodded and Chardonnais went back outside. When his eyes saw Boatwright again, the rage flamed in them. He furiously charged off into the forest, seeking out Crows. He found two and butchered them, chopping them into bits with his tomahawk and knife.

Then he found a third. The warrior managed to knock Chardonnais's tomahawk loose. That did not slow the maniacal French-Canadian, who grabbed his pistol and began clubbing the Crow with it, battering his face into a bloody mush. The Indian fell, but Chardonnais continued to mash him with the pistol butt.

He came to his senses—and then just barely—only when Runs Back grabbed his arm. "That's enough, my friend," the Ute said quietly. "He is no more."

"Den I want more Crows to kill," Chardonnais snarled, spittle flying.

"They're all gone."

"You sure?"

Runs Back nodded. "Now there are more important things to do."

"Yes," Chardonnais said. "Jed."

"And Ezra needs our help."

"He's hurt?"

"Bad."

In French, Chardonnais cursed every saint he had ever heard of, and the God who would allow good men like Jed Boatwright and Ezra Early to go under or almost for no good reason that any thinking man could see. Finally, he wound down. He wiped his nose, which had started running when the tears had come. Then he nodded. *"Oui,"* he said firmly, "dere is much to be done."

30

CHARDONNAIS AND RUNS BACK hurried back to the camp. Rawlins, Striking Hawk, and Walking in the Sky were carting Early's inert form across the clearing toward the lodges.

"Shit," Rawlins snapped when he saw Boatwright's body in front of Early's lodge. "Damn." Jed Boatwright wasn't Rawlins's best friend by a long shot, but the young man had proven to be a steady hand, a willing worker, and a man with an abundance of wit and humor. Rawlins would miss him.

"Where're Spotted Bull and Walking in de Sky, Abe?" Chardonnais asked as Rawlins and the two Utes carried Early into his lodge.

"Out in the bushes makin' sure there ain't none of them pus-suckin' Crows left about."

The three men placed Early on the robes, and the two Utes stood. "We'll go help Spotted Bull and Walking in the Sky make sure we're safe," Striking Hawk said in Ute.

Rawlins nodded absentmindedly, not bothering to look up. The two Utes went outside, where Runs Back joined them. Rawlins and Chardonnais didn't notice, or care. They didn't really notice either that the women and children had come into the lodge and were sitting as far away from Early as they could. Blue Rattle was in shock, her eyes glazed as she blubbered quietly in her grief.

Rawlins and Chardonnais knelt on each side of their wounded partner. Without a word, Rawlins pulled his knife and cut through Early's tough buckskin shirt and then flapped the two ends open. "Jesus goddamn Christ," he breathed.

"*Oui*," Chardonnais said dully. He ripped off his shirt, wadded it up, and pressed it to the bigger of the two wounds to try to stanch the flow of blood. "He is gone under for sure."

"Over my dead ass," Rawlins hissed. "I aim to fix ol' hoss here."

"How?" Chardonnais asked, sick at the thought of his friend dying, and doing so in agony.

"Fuck if I know," Rawlins said. "But he ain't goin' under long as this chil's got any say-so in it."

Falling Leaf edged up tentatively and knelt next to Rawlins. Her face was coated with tears, but she was in control of herself.

Rawlins looked at her. "It looks bad, Falling Leaf," he said flatly.

She nodded.

Rawlins sat for a moment, thinking. Then he nodded. "Chardonnais, get our medicine kit. Falling Leaf, get some poultice medicine made up."

"What're you going to do?" Chardonnais asked.

"Try'n sew him up. It's about all we can do for him. That and poultices."

Chardonnais nodded sadly. "You've never done such stitching up." Early had been the closest the three men had to a doctor. He had done some surgery on both his companions. Now it was their turn to help him, but neither had any experience.

"I know. You don't either, but you're welcome to give it a try if ye think ye can do better'n me." Rawlins sounded a little testy.

"I wasn't criticizing, *mon ami*. Just sayin' de trut'."

"It's a truth I'm powerful aware of, Lucien." He sighed. "But it's got to be one of us, I expect."

"I can do it," Looks Again said quietly. She had walked up to stand just behind Falling Leaf.

"You done such before?" Rawlins asked.

Looks Again nodded.

"Can you do it in your condition, *ma chère?*" Chardonnais asked.

"*Oui,*" Looks Again said. She spoke French well, though she seldom used it.

Rawlins and Chardonnais looked at each other. Placing Early's life in the hands of someone they had known far less time than they had known Early was not an easy thing to decide.

Chardonnais nodded first. Looks Again was his woman, and he knew her better than Rawlins did. He also trusted her.

"You sure?" Rawlins asked.

"*Oui.*"

"All right, let's get it done."

Chardonnais hurried off to get the small kit of doctoring gear. It was precious little. Falling Leaf went to her supplies, and then she and Scatters the Clouds went outside, leaving the grief-stricken Blue Rattle with the two children.

Chardonnais returned with the small buckskin box and a bottle of whiskey. He gave the box to Looks Again, who opened it and swiftly picked out a piece of sinew and a long, curved needle. When Rawlins shifted to give her room, she moved into the spot he vacated. She threaded the needle and then held it out.

Chardonnais poured whiskey over it, and over Looks Again's hands.

Looks Again shook off the excess and then bent over Early. She decided even before she touched needle to flesh that she could not work that way. She was just too big. "I can't," she said plaintively, close to tears.

"What do you need to get it done?" Chardonnais asked.

"He must be raised where I can work on him."

Rawlins and Chardonnais thought for some moments. Rawlins was about to take the needle and sinew from Looks Again and do the job himself when Chardonnais snapped his fingers. "I'll be right back," he said, jumping up and running. He returned several minutes later, carrying two thin logs, about the width of lodgepoles. Red Stone followed him in, carrying a buffalo robe and a coil of rawhide rope. The rest of the Utes entered, too.

"What the hell're you fixin' to do?" Rawlins asked suspiciously.

"Just you watch." Chardonnais set the poles down about three feet apart. Red Stone placed the buffalo robe over the poles and set the rope down. The two swiftly began jabbing some holes in the robe and then cutting off short lengths of rope, which they used to tie the robe to the poles. They were done in less than five minutes.

They brought the device to Early's side. Rawlins, understanding, helped Chardonnais gently move Early onto the makeshift stretcher.

"Let de Utes help me hold Ezra up," Chardonnais commanded quietly.

"Suck shit," Rawlins snapped. "Ol' Ez's my best friend. Even more'n you, you stump-ass little frog."

"I know dat. But you are half a foot, maybe more, taller dan I am. De Utes are all close to me in size, eh. We can hold Ezra level dat way."

"I hate you when you make sense, you little bastard," Rawlins said, conceding his spot.

"Besides," Chardonnais added, "Looks Again will need your help."

Rawlins nodded, feeling useless. Chardonnais, Striking Hawk, Red Stone, and Runs Back knelt, hoisted the stretcher, and set the end of a pole on a shoulder each.

Relieved, Looks Again knelt, her back straight, and pulled Chardonnais's shirt out of the wound. Then she began stitching the soft inner flesh of Early's abdomen. But the stretcher was swaying and she found it hard to do.

"Hold on there, Looks Again," Rawlins said. He had found a way to help, and that made him feel a tad better. He lay under the stretcher and then came up on hands and knees, back forming a flat surface that bore much of Early's weight and made it easier for Looks Again to work.

Looks Again returned to her task, first closing the inner wound and then sewing the gaping edges together. She took a few minutes to stitch up the other, smaller wound, too. Then she took the concoction Falling Leaf and Scatters the Clouds had made up and applied a generous coating to both wounds.

"Let him down now," she said softly.

Rawlins clambered out from underneath, and then Chardonnais and the three Utes lowered the stretcher gently.

"Lift him off the travois," Looks Again commanded as she turned to take the long strips of thin blanket

Scatters the Clouds had handed her. When the men complied, she swiftly wrapped the bigger wound, punctured four holes in the blanket, and inserted wood pegs into the holes to hold the bandage tight. She swiftly did the other. "Put him down again," she said wearily.

The men did, and Chardonnais turned to look at his wife, his face beaming with pride, and was shocked. "*Mon Dieu!*" he breathed. "Looks Again, what's wrong?"

Looks Again had rocked back so her buttocks were on her calves. Her face was coated with sweat and she was grimacing. "The baby," she gasped.

"It's coming?" Chardonnais asked, stunned and suddenly frightened.

Looks Again nodded, clamping her lips to prevent the scream she felt working its way up her windpipe.

"Christ," Chardonnais blurted out. He looked at Rawlins, panic-stricken. "What do I do, Abe?"

"Help her over to Jed's lodge. She can use that as the birthin' lodge."

"What about Blue Rattle?"

"She can stay in here for the next few days. Or she can stay in my lodge, if you'd rather."

"I'll worry about dat later. Come, help me get her dere. *Vite!*"

The two men lifted Looks Again under the arms and hoisted her up. Then they practically carried her to Boatwright's lodge and set her down. Falling Leaf had stayed behind with her wounded husband and Rawlins's son, Standing Eagle, but Scatters the Clouds, Blue Rattle, and Early's daughter, Straight Calf, had come along. Blue Rattle was still in shock, but was making an effort to come to her senses. As soon as Looks Again was lying down, the two other women shooed Chardonnais and Rawlins out of the lodge.

"Come on, ol' hoss," Rawlins said to Chardonnais. "We got us work to do."

"But . . ." Chardonnais mumbled, looking back toward the lodge where his wife lay.

"It's best ye leave these things to the women."

"I am. . . ."

"And it's best you find somethin' to occupy yourself with. It'll keep your mind off what's goin' on in there."

"Dere's no work dat important."

"We've got to see to Jed."

"*Oui*," Chardonnais said, hanging his head. He had forgotten about his friend in all the rush. Now that he had thought of Boatwright again, he was filled with rage and a feeling of loss.

They walked to the body, and saw Moving Thunder's body. It did not surprise them. The Utes, like many Indians, did not like death, and usually bodies were buried as soon as possible. The two whites figured that their Ute friends didn't really know what to do with Moving Thunder here.

The Utes were still inside Early's lodge. Rawlins bent, stuck his head through the entrance, and called them out. "You want us to bury Moving Thunder white-man style, alongside ol' Jed?" he asked when the Utes were standing outside.

The five warriors talked quietly among themselves for a few minutes. Then Striking Hawk—the oldest and most experienced—nodded.

Chardonnais went to get shovels while Rawlins scouted for a decent place to bury their two friends. Each taking a shovel, they began digging. Chardonnais found he liked the physicality of the task. It was hard and hot work, and it did indeed keep his mind off the death—and life—surrounding him.

When the side-by-side holes were deep enough, they got two blankets, spreading one in each hole. Then they carried Boatwright's body carefully to the hole and lowered him into it. They did the same with Moving Thunder's corpse.

"We need some things to help these two across to the spirit world," Rawlins said.

"I know. I have some ideas on dat." Chardonnais called the other Ute warriors over and told them, "I want you to get de scalps from all de Crows we kill today, and bring dem here."

The Utes were puzzled, but they ran off to do what had been requested. Meanwhile Chardonnais went to Early's lodge. "I need you to do somet'ing for me, Falling Leaf," he said quietly. "I'll watch over my great friend."

"What do you want me to do?" Falling Leaf asked dully.

"Get Jed's rifle, a handful of jerky, dat badger-claw necklace he favored sometimes, and his hat."

Falling Leaf nodded, stood, and left. Chardonnais sat there watching Early's chest as it feebly rose and fell. He didn't know what he would do if his great friend died.

Falling Leaf returned in minutes with the requested items. She handed them to Chardonnais and then sat back down at her husband's side.

Chardonnais headed back to the graves. The Utes were back, holding eleven fresh scalps and some other items. Chardonnais knelt and placed Boatwright's rifle, necklace, and hat on his chest. Striking Hawk placed Moving Thunder's shield, tomahawk, and pipe on his corpse.

Chardonnais stood. "Put five scalps into each grave, *mes amis*," he said, voice constricted. "De other one'll be for Ezra's lodgepole."

It was swiftly done, and then they all muttered a few quick prayers. The Utes left as Rawlins and Chardonnais began filling in the graves. When they were done, they went to Rawlins's lodge and broke out a jug.

"I reckon this'll take away a little of the hurt," Rawlins said, patting the jug. "But I also figure we shouldn't overdo it. We got us some decisions to make."

Chardonnais nodded. They had a few swigs of whiskey and then put the jug away. They ate silently, each living with his own thoughts. Before long the Ute warriors entered the lodge and sat, dipping into the kettle of elk stew over the fire.

An hour later they heard a baby's first squall, and Chardonnais relaxed a little. Some minutes after that, Scatters the Clouds came into the lodge and said, "You have a son. Looks Again will call him He-Who-Comes-During-The-Big-Fight-With-The-Crows. He is a big, strong boy, and Looks Again is fine."

Chardonnais nodded, greatly relieved.

"Sorry the young'n had to come now," Rawlins said. "A birth ought to be a time for celebratin', but to tell you true, *amigo*, this ol' chil' ain't got it in him for a spree."

"Me either," Chardonnais admitted. He was proud to be a father now, but he wished his son had been born at a less dismal time. The birth would, however, serve to remind him of his loss this day as well as his gain.

31

"WELL, OL' HOSS," RAWLINS said, "we're in deep shit here and with no help in sight."

"*Oui.* Dis is evident to anyone."

"Reckon that's so. Question is, what're we gonna do about it?"

Chardonnais shook his head sadly. He had known the question was out there, and he had tried to keep from thinking about it. "Dere's notting we can do. Not right now. Not wit' Ezra so bad off, and Looks Again wit' our new child, and Blue Rattle nearly ready to have hers."

"It does limit our options, don't it?" Rawlins mused. "We could do some things."

"Like what?"

"I can leave you here with the women and Ez and ride on down to Taos, trade in our plews, and get our supplies."

"And have yourself a spree while Ezra is maybe dying?" Chardonnais asked harshly.

"You know better'n to say somethin' that goddamn stupid to me, you bastard," Rawlins said, voice rasping.

Chardonnais nodded. He did not voice an apology, but one was evident to Rawlins nonetheless. "Any other choices?"

"I could stay here and you could take the plews to Taos. But it ain't my woman just had a child."

"And den I could have a spree, eh?" Chardonnais said in an attempt at humor that fell very flat.

Rawlins ignored it. "We could maybe see if the Utes'd ride to that old Bent-Saint Vrain place down on the Arkansas. They'd not be unwelcome there, I figure, which they sure as shit would be in Taos."

"Dat might work," Chardonnais said less than enthusiastically.

"Only other thing I can think of is for all of us to ride on down to Taos."

"Dat'd kill Ezra for certain." Chardonnais paused. "Dere is another choice." When Rawlins raised his eyebrows at him, he said, "We can do notting. For a time."

"You best explain that goddamn notion a heap more, boy," Rawlins said irritably.

Chardonnais nodded. "We need to wait to see if Ezra gets better. We should know in a few days—a week at most—if he's going to live." He almost choked on the words. "If he goes under first, dat will answer all de questions." He paused briefly. "We also should wait till Blue Rattle has her child. By den, maybe Ezra'll be able to travel some, even if in a travois. Or maybe by den he'll be gone under."

"We ain't got much time for waitin', hoss," Rawlins warned.

Chardonnais nodded.

Rawlins puffed on his pipe a few moments, then asked, "What happens if Ez goes under?"

"I don' know about you, *mon ami*, but as soon as

Ezra is consigned to de Great Spirit's embrace, I'll cache de plews and go after de Crows."

Rawlins nodded and smiled grimly. "What I was hopin' to hear, *amigo*." He puffed awhile, then said, "I reckon your idea's the best, but not for long."

"Two weeks," Chardonnais said, deciding. "Dat'll be long enough."

"Agreed." Rawlins paused. "What about you men?" he asked, looking from one Ute to another.

"We're in no hurry to go anywhere," Striking Hawk said blandly.

Rawlins couldn't be sure, of course, but he thought he detected a faint touch of fear in Striking Hawk's eyes—just enough to make the Ute warrior not want to get back on the trail so soon after a passel of Crows had raided the camp. Rawlins nodded. "If that's where your sticks float." He didn't mind having them stay. If the Crows, or anyone else, thought to attack the camp, it would be good to have five hardened Ute warriors on one's side. Besides, the Utes were someone else to talk to, since with Early unconscious, there was only Chardonnais. And the women, but they wouldn't be interested in men's talk.

Blue Rattle went into labor five days later, and she was tended by Scatters the Clouds and Looks Again, who had left the birthing lodge two days before. Scatters the Clouds and Looks Again also watched over Straight Calf so the girl's mother could stay with her husband.

Blue Rattle also gave birth to a son, whom she named Little Rider.

Scatters the Clouds stayed with Blue Rattle that night while Looks Again went home to be with her husband. Their new son slept in a cradleboard nearby.

"I don' want you to take dis de wrong way, Looks Again," Chardonnais said quietly, "but I t'ink we should bring Blue Rattle into de lodge wit' us."

Looks Again stiffened. "Now that I'm a new mother, you don't want me anymore?" she asked, knowing all the while how stupid a question it was. But she was hurt by his statement.

"Yes, I want you. I don' mean she will come to be my wife wit' you. But she can't stay in dat lodge by herself. She needs people around." He smiled up at the smoke hole. "And she's your sister."

"It'd be nice having my sister here with us," Looks Again said thoughtfully. Then she hesitated. "But I'm afraid."

"Afraid of what?"

"That you'll want her instead of me. She's younger and prettier."

"Younger, *oui*. Prettier, *mais non!*"

Looks Again squeezed Chardonnais's arm. "People will think she is your wife, too," she said warily.

"Who de hell cares what de others t'ink? If dey want to t'ink she is mine, too, let dem. We will know dat she is here for our help and protection, eh. She needs someone to help her wit' de new child. She needs someone to hunt for her."

"What happens when we get back to the village?"

"Dat'll be up to her. If she wants to stay wit' us, she can stay wit' us—if you t'ink dat's all right. If she wants to find another husband, den she'll be free to do so."

Looks Again nodded and rolled over to kiss him. She had missed Chardonnais while she had been in the birthing lodge, and seemed unable now to get enough of him. He did not mind. He just accepted her enthusiasm and lust and reciprocated.

Looks Again told Blue Rattle about the plan the next day. Blue Rattle was quite relieved. She had worried what she was going to do now. Even with the other women in her lodge—which she now thought of almost strictly as the birthing lodge—she was uncomfortable. She certainly did not want to stay in there alone. Her husband's spirit was still present and saddened her. But she knew she could not just walk up and ask Looks Again to move into her lodge.

Scatters the Clouds and Looks Again continued to watch over Blue Rattle and the children—including Falling Leaf's daughter. All the while, Falling Leaf remained in her lodge, sitting beside her husband's barely breathing form. She left the tipi only to relieve herself or to get water or wood. She might leave Early's side for a few minutes to make herself some food or a new pot of coffee.

Falling Leaf changed Early's poultices several times a day and bathed his face gently with water periodically. He had gotten fever and moved in and out of delirium. When the delirium came over him, Early thrashed around, and it was all Falling Leaf could do to keep him from hurting himself.

She slept next to Early, too, though her sleep was restless. She was acutely aware of every move he made, and she woke up each time to settle him and then try to resettle herself. After a week she felt drained. Her eyes were filled with grit and her hair was stringy from sweat and smoke. She had not eaten properly and had ignored her personal grooming.

Once Blue Rattle was out of the birthing lodge and settled in Chardonnais's lodge, she, Scatters the Clouds, and Looks Again set out to help Falling Leaf. They took turns watching over Early, taking charge of the children, and forcing Falling Leaf to care for herself.

Chardonnais and Rawlins also took turns watching Early, but otherwise spent their time hunting—and worrying.

Through it all, Early's condition did not change much. He still experienced periods of delirium, but he never woke. Then, eleven days after being wounded, he regained consciousness.

Falling Leaf heard a weak groan, and when she looked down, Early's eyes were open. Her heart pounded and she screamed. Moments later Chardonnais and Rawlins charged into the lodge.

"*Mon Dieu,*" Chardonnais said in an awed whisper as he knelt next to Early.

"Jumpin' goddamn Jesus," Rawlins contributed as he squatted beside Chardonnais.

"How's doin's, ol' hoss?" Rawlins asked.

"Fine," Early squawked, his voice dry, sounding like crinkled paper.

"It's about time you come back to us, *mon ami,*" Chardonnais said with a smile. "You've be lazing about long enough."

Early tried to speak, but couldn't work up enough spittle to make his tongue work.

"Falling Leaf, some water. *Vite!*" Chardonnais said. He looked back down at Early. "Don't try to say anyt'ing, *mon ami.* It'll be all right now."

Chardonnais and Rawlins lifted the upper half of Early's torso so that Falling Leaf could pour a little water into his mouth. The liquid seemed to make his eyes brighten and he indicated he wanted some more. After a few more mouthfuls he whispered, "Better. Down."

His two friends eased him back onto the robes. "I ain't no medicine man, ol' hoss," Rawlins said, "but I think maybe you're gonna shine again one day."

"How long I been out?" Early managed to squawk.

"Eleven days," Rawlins answered.

"You boys make them Crow bastards come, did ye?"

"*Mais oui!*" Chardonnais said, but there was no real heart in it. "I don' know how many got away, but we made wolf bait out of eleven of dem red devils."

"Anyone else hurt?" Early's voice was still far away, faint, as if it had to fight its way up from the diaphragm.

"Jed went under," Chardonnais said with a hitch in his voice.

"Damn." The word was barely audible, and by the time it was fully aired, Early was out again.

Falling Leaf looked from Rawlins to Chardonnais. Her face was covered with tears. "He'll be all right?" she asked, voice quaking.

"*Oui,*" Chardonnais said with a firm nod. "De next time he awakes, he will be conscious a little longer. And each time after dat. Don' you worry. Now go get some sleep. Abe and I will stay with Ezra."

Falling Leaf nodded and left.

Early continued to improve over the next several days, though he was not awake much. He began taking in a little broth soon, and that seemed to strengthen him.

While they watched Early improving, Chardonnais and Rawlins delayed deciding what to do for a few more days, hoping he would recover enough to add his thoughts to the discussion of the near future. Things seemed to be improving, and Rawlins and Chardonnais began to think they would be able to move out soon, with Early in a travois, and get their new supplies.

Then, three days after Early woke for the first time, Striking Hawk whistled a warning. The two mountain men and the rest of the Utes stopped and

looked. Nothing could be seen yet, though some odd
sounds drifted faintly over them. Striking Hawk waved
a hand, and then he, Runs Back, and Red Stone melted
into the trees and disappeared. Red Stone was the first
to return, ten minutes later.

"White men coming," Red Stone said. "Many of
them."

Striking Hawk trotted up, followed a moment later
by Runs Back.

"How far?" Rawlins asked.

"Half a mile maybe," Red Stone answered.

Rawlins nodded. "You and your boys best keep out
of sight till we find out what's their intentions."

Red Stone agreed. Then he and his friends left,
heading into the trees southwest of the camp. The
newcomers were heading in from the northeast.

"Go tell Looks Again and Blue Rattle to keep out of
sight. I'll tell the others," Rawlins said.

Once that was done, Chardonnais and Rawlins sat
at one of the outside fires, sipping coffee and waiting.
Their weapons were close to hand. They weren't too
concerned, figuring it was some fur brigade moving
through the area, but one could never be sure.

The first one into the camp was a Delaware Indian,
who looked to be a scout. He stopped. When he realized that only two white men were in the camp, he
came on ahead.

"Coffee?" Rawlins asked, waving the Delaware to a
place by the fire.

"You two alone?"

"I asked if you wanted coffee, boy," Rawlins said
harshly. "I didn't ask for stupid goddamn questions
from a snake-humpin' peckerwood."

The Delaware glowered, and shifted the rifle in his
arms.

"You move that goddamn rifle toward me, you son of a bitch," Rawlins snapped, "and I'll shove it up your ass for ye. Now, either set and have some coffee or vamoose."

The Delaware grunted and squatted. He grabbed a loose cup and filled it with coffee.

A few minutes later the noise up the trail increased, and then several men came into view. Rawlins and Chardonnais stood and turned to watch the procession of men, horses, and mules. A tall, gaunt man with large ears rode a dull chestnut horse toward the fire as his men began moving a little ways off from Chardonnais's group's lodges. He stopped and dismounted.

"Name's Alastair MacDonald, booshway for this brigade of the American Fur Company," he said, holding out his hand.

Chardonnais and Rawlins shook the man's hand and introduced themselves. They did not reveal their displeasure with the American Fur Company.

"We're on our way toward the Uintas, and then north from there," MacDonald said as he poured himself some coffee. "You mind was we to stay the night here?"

Rawlins shook his head. "Nope, long as your boys keep away from our lodges and our animals."

MacDonald nodded. "Fair enough. I—"

Everyone looked up when someone shouted, "Hey, Lucien, *mon ami!*"

32

CHARDONNAIS'S EYES WIDENED and he hurried toward a man who had stopped with the brigade. Rawlins, watching from a distance, grinned and shook his head as the two men embraced briefly.

Chardonnais had approached Michel LeBeau cautiously. The last time he had seen his longtime friend, he had stolen Marie from him. Chardonnais was not sure how he would react to that, though he certainly seemed happy to see Chardonnais.

"*Bonjour, mon ami!*" LeBeau said with a great smile on his face.

"*Bonjour,*" Chardonnais responded, relaxing. They hugged a moment. Then the little trapper asked, "What're you doing out here?"

"Well, dat's a long story, *mon ami.*"

"You can tell me later. Come, meet my friends."

They walked over and stopped at the fire. "Michel, dis is my great friend, Abe Rawlins. Abe, an old friend, Michel LeBeau."

"Is dis one of your partners?" LeBeau asked.

"*Oui.*"

"I t'ought you said you had two partners."

"*Oui*. De other was hurt bad in a fight wit' de Crows a couple of weeks ago. He's in de lodge."

"You're not alone here, are you?" LeBeau asked.

"What do you mean?" Chardonnais asked warily.

"You have no women? De great fornicating Lucien Chardonnais is out here wit' no women?"

Chardonnais grinned. "My woman is here. She just had my child two weeks ago," he said proudly.

"Well, let me see . . .him?"

"*Oui*. A son. Dere is time for dat later. Come, sit. We'll talk some."

As they sat at the fire MacDonald rose. "Well, gentlemen, thank ye for your hospitality. I'd better see to my camp." He looked at the chunky Delaware. "Badger, back to our people."

Badger showed no emotion. He simply rose in a movement that was quite smooth despite his squat, powerful body. He trotted off.

"Before you leave, Mr. MacDonald," Rawlins said, "we have several Ute friends with us here. They're out in the woods now, but I expect they'll be back soon. It wouldn't shine with this ol' chil' if your men were to fire on 'em."

"You have my word, Mr. Rawlins." MacDonald mounted his horse and rode away.

"Well," Rawlins said, rising, "if you two boys're gonna set here jawin' over old times, I reckon I'll go see how Ezra's doin'."

Chardonnais poured a mug of coffee and handed it to LeBeau. Then he poured one for himself. Once he got his pipe going, he said, "Tell me how you came to be out here. I t'ought you'd be married to Marie now."

LeBeau scowled at these words. "She wouldn't

have me no more after you ran out on her. Damn, dat made me angry at you for some time."

"I was a little surprised you didn't show any anger when we met a few minutes ago."

"Well, it's been a while, and I've had some time to get over it."

"Was it bad?"

LeBeau nodded. He pulled out a cigar and lit it with a flaming twig from the fire. "Bad enough. Or so I t'ought at de time. But I can tell you, Marie was very put out on you running." He scowled again. "What made me so mad at de time was dat she told me she wouldn't have anyt'ing to do wit' me. I t'ink she t'ought I had somet'ing to do with your running off like dat, and so she was determined not to go back to me."

"Dat must've hurt, *mon ami,*" Chardonnais said sympathetically.

"Very much." He paused and looked around, taking in the serenity of this high mountain meadow. "I don' know if anyone told you, but I've done work for de Company from time to time. Mostly clerking duties back in St. Charles or St. Louis, though I've been on de Yellowstone twice. Stayed with de Crows both times."

"Don' talk to me about Crows," Chardonnais said curtly. "Not now."

"But why—?" LeBeau nodded. "Ah, yes, your friend. Sorry." He sighed. "Anyway, I decided right after you left, when I realized dat I had no chance to rekindle Marie's love for me, to head west with one of de Company's brigades. I was fortunate to catch a steamboat up de Missouri to Fort Union, where I caught on with a few of Mr. MacDonald's crew, who were at de fort for some supplies dat hadn't made it to de rendezvous. Or so dey said."

LeBeau paused to puff on his cigar. He pulled off his knit cap and dropped it next to him. He scratched his sweaty, greasy hair, and then angrily flicked something away. "Goddamn lice," he said in irritation.

"Didn't MacDonald's men tell you what to do about lice?" Chardonnais asked.

"Dere's a solution?" LeBeau asked, surprised.

"*Oui*. Find yourself a handy anthill. Strip down and lay your clothes over de anthill. De ants'll take care of dem damn lice. And while you're waiting for dem ants to finish dere work, you can get most of de ones on your skin and in your hair."

"Dat really works?" LeBeau asked skeptically.

"*Oui*."

"I'll have to try dat." LeBeau tossed out the remains of his coffee. "I t'ought maybe I'd see you dis summer."

"Where?" Chardonnais asked.

"Rendezvous."

"Ah," Chardonnais said with a nod. "Dat's de problem. Me and my two friends, we always go to Taos."

"Why?" LeBeau asked, surprised. Through the years he had worked for the Company, he had often heard the men speak of the rendezvous with something approaching awe. He had looked forward to seeing Chardonnais at the annual two-week debauch. Once he had seen it himself, he could not believe that anyone would willingly go elsewhere.

"Several reasons," Chardonnais said with a shrug. He shifted his rump and settled back a little more comfortably against a log. His ears perked up when he heard a hawk's whistle. "It's all right, Striking Hawk," he said. "Come on in."

The five Utes materialized out of the forest. With a look of disgust at LeBeau, they headed toward their fire. With Chardonnais's—and Blue Rattle's—permission, they had moved into Boatwright's old lodge.

"Friends of yours, eh?" LeBeau asked, pointing his cigar toward the Indians.

"*Oui*. De Utes're good people."

"You got a Ute woman?"

"Yes."

"You have her when you were back in St. Charles dis last time?"

Chardonnais nodded. "It was one of de t'ings dat brought me back here," he said quietly, not really ashamed of saying it, but not happy about it either.

"How could you t'row over Marie for a goddamn savage?"

"Looks Again is no savage," Chardonnais said harshly. "She's a damn good woman, and de type I need." He managed a small grin.

LeBeau stared blankly at him for some seconds, then laughed. "Ah, yes, your legendary appetite for de women." He nodded. "I can see where you might have a problem in dat area wit' Marie."

"*Mais oui!*" Chardonnais let the laughter dwindle. "Marie is somet'ing special, and not de sort dis ol' hoss meets often. I t'ink I would've ruined her life as well as my own had I stayed dere and married her." His voice was touched with pain. "I suppose," he said with a sigh, "dat I am saying to you I apologize for taking Marie away from you."

"It's all right, *mon ami*," LeBeau said with apparent sincerity. "Really, it is. Like I said, I was hurt and angry at first, but a year out here in de mountains has done wonders to remake my spirit."

Chardonnais nodded.

"You never did explain why you go to dis . . . what'd you call dat place? Toes?"

"Taos," Chardonnais said with a laugh. "It's a village down in de Mexican lands. De people are friendly, de food good, and de mademoiselles—dey are called señoritas down dere—dey are somet'ing special. *Mais oui.* Dey are dark and mysterious, and free wit' their favors."

"*Mon Dieu,* Lucien," LeBeau said, apparently offended. "First you refuse a fine French girl, one who would make a fine wife and mother. Den you have a child wit' a savage and you consort wit' Mexicans."

"Dere is somet'ing wrong wit' dat?" Chardonnais asked sharply.

"Of course dere is," LeBeau insisted. "It's . . . it's just not right, *mon ami.* No, no, no, no, no. Not right."

"You haven't lain wit' an Indian woman?" Chardonnais asked.

"Of course I have. But what—"

"Did you like it?"

"*Oui.*"

"How many of our women have you fornicated wit', eh?"

"A couple. Women along the docks. You know the type."

"*Oui.* I know dem very well. But you have never lain wit' someone like Marie, eh?"

"No. Good women don't do such t'ings."

"Good *white* women don' do such t'ings. Good Ute women and good Nez Percé women and good Mexican women do. Dey make a man feel wanted, not like someone dey want to get in and out to get dere piece of gold and go on to de next."

"It still doesn't seem right, Lucien."

"Well, it's right to dis ol' chil'."

"Maybe you're right, Lucien," LeBeau conceded with a sigh. "Perhaps one day I'll visit dis Taos place and see for myself."

"It's a good place. Doesn't look like much. All de buildings are made of mud. And de food." He laughed a little. "So hot it'll make your shit come out in flames. De people mostly are friendly, and dey will have a ball at de drop of a hat. Somet'ing going on nearly all de time."

LeBeau was still laughing a little. "Now you have me intrigued, *mon ami*. Visiting dis place is now high on my list of t'ings to do before I die."

"I'd wager you won't regret visiting dere."

"I expect so." LeBeau set down his cup and pushed himself up. "Well, I had better get back over with my companions before MacDonald sends dat fat Delaware over here to drag me back."

"We wouldn't want dat to happen," Chardonnais said dryly.

"Hell, no."

"Come on back here when you finish. We'll sup together."

Moments after LeBeau left, Rawlins strolled up and sat. "Friend of yours?" he asked sarcastically. "Or are ye plannin' to marry him as soon as ye can get shed of Looks Again?"

"Ah, I see I have made you jealous," Chardonnais countered.

"I'd rather hump a dead, festerin' snake." He grinned. "You know him long?"

Chardonnais nodded. "He and I grew up together."

"He the one you took the woman from?"

"*Oui,*" Chardonnais said dully.

"He don't look none too put out by it."

Chardonnais shrugged. "He said he was some hurt at first, but a year can cover a lot of hurt. Speaking of which, how is Ezra?"

"Same, pretty much. Seemed a little more alert a

few minutes ago. Damn, that's some nasty wound he's got there."

Chardonnais nodded. He and Rawlins wandered off to do chores, and the rest of the afternoon began slipping away. Chardonnais finally realized it was getting dark, and he put aside his ball-making gear and stood. He could see LeBeau heading toward him in the thickening dusk. Chardonnais led his friend into Early's lodge and introduced him to Early, who seemed to be quite alert.

Chardonnais, Rawlins, and LeBeau ate fresh elk while Falling Leaf fed Early some broth with small bits of elk meat in it. After eating, Early suddenly said, "You boys made up your minds on what to do?"

Chardonnais almost jumped out of his skin as he swung around on his buttocks. "No," he finally said. "We've been waiting till you either got a little better— or went under," he added dryly. "I t'ink dat as soon as you're able to move, we'll head to Taos."

"I ain't gonna be able to move—not real good anyway—anytime soon. You best leave me here and do what you need to."

"I t'ink he's in delirium again, Abe," Chardonnais cracked.

"I reckon you're right, Frenchie."

"What's de problem?" LeBeau asked. "If you don't mind telling an outsider."

Chardonnais explained it in a few terse sentences, then went back to discussing the options with Early and Rawlins.

LeBeau sat cross-legged, his brain working furiously over the problem. He knew there was a way to reach his own long-sought goal tied up with this suddenly discovered problem. He could not let such an opportunity pass. If only he could get a solution to coalesce.

It did, or at least it began to. He smiled inwardly as the pieces began to fall into place.

"*Excusez-moi*, messieurs," he finally said quietly. "Maybe I can help."

33

CHARDONNAIS AND RAWLINS TURNED to face LeBeau. Early lay where he was, but he was attentive. "How?" Chardonnais asked warily. Something didn't seem right here, but he couldn't lay a finger on it.

"Well," LeBeau said, rubbing his hands together slowly in front of his face, "I t'ink I can talk Monsieur MacDonald into freeing me from my contract. At least for a while."

"What de hell does dat mean?" Chardonnais asked irritably. LeBeau was his friend from childhood, but Early and Rawlins were his real friends now. They had saved him many times, and he them. He did not want them to be subjected to some lunatic ramblings because of an old, long-ago-foundered friendship.

"Hear me out, Lucien. If I could get someone else from de Company to go wit' me—or if you want to go, Lucien—I could take your plews to Taos, sell dem to whoever you direct me to sell dem to, get your supplies, and den ride back here. Perhaps den, your friend dere will be in better shape, and you can escort me back to de brigade." He ended with a hopeful note in his voice.

Chardonnais sat in thought, knowing that Rawlins's eyes were on him. He did not want to make this decision himself, but he did not feel right discussing it in front of LeBeau. Finally he said, "Dat sounds like it might work, Michel," he said guardedly. "But my friends and I will have to discuss it."

"I understand." LeBeau rose. "I'll let you talk. In de meanwhile I'll go back to my camp and talk it over with Monsieur MacDonald to see if he has any objections. However, *mon ami*, I'd not wait too long to make your decision. De brigade is leaving in de morning."

When LeBeau left, Rawlins and Chardonnais went to sit next to Early. "What you t'ink, *mon ami?*" the French-Canadian asked Early.

"I think it makes sense," Early said weakly. "If some conditions're met."

"Like what?"

"First off, I got to know if we can trust him." He cast a dim eye on his diminutive partner.

"I t'ink so," Chardonnais said hesitantly. Then he nodded. "*Oui.* I can trust him. He was my friend when we were children. When I stole his woman away, and now we meet dis time, he didn't try to raise my hair. I t'ink all will be fine."

"What do you think, Abe?"

Rawlins shrugged. "I got no idea. I ain't met him but for just this little bit here. He seems a shifty little niggur to me, but then again, I think all frogs're shifty little niggurs."

Chardonnais bit back a retort.

"With that settled, we need to figure out who goes with him."

"I ain't goin'," Rawlins said flatly. "It's bad enough I got to deal with this damn old froggie here. I ain't 'bout to set my traps with another one."

"Afraid you might learn somet'ing?" Chardonnais retorted.

"Like?"

"Enough!" Early said, voice a little stronger. "I can't stay awake long enough to have you two assholes smart-assin' each other." He paused. "You want to go with him, Lucien?"

Chardonnais shrugged. "I'd rather stay. I don't like de idea of leaving Looks Again."

It was Rawlins's turn to bite back a retort, heeding Early's earlier admonishment.

"Or leaving de baby. Not when he's so young. But 'll do it if dere is no other choice."

"Wait," Rawlins said suddenly. "How about the Utes?"

"What about dem?" Chardonnais asked, surprised.

"Why don't we ask them boys to ride down there with the other frog?"

"Dat's crazy," Chardonnais said with a snort.

"Is it?" Early asked. "I wonder."

"De Utes'll never get into Taos."

"Hell, I know that. But it might work anyway. The Utes can wait a couple miles outside Taos. They can watch over the plews while Michel goes to Bent-Saint Vrain's to do the business. When Ceran sends a crew to get the plews, Michel can bring our supplies. He meets up with the Utes, and they can escort him back here." Early leaned back, sweat coating his forehead.

Falling Leaf, sitting on the opposite side of her husband from Chardonnais and Rawlins, started flapping her hands. "That's enough!" she hissed. "Leave him. Go now."

Both mountain men knew better than to argue with a Ute woman who was protecting her husband. At least this Ute woman protecting this husband. They stood. As they headed for outside Chardonnais said "Don' you worry, *mon ami*. Abe and I will figure it all out."

"That's what I'm afraid of," Early groaned.

Outside, Rawlins said, "We might's well go ask Striking Hawk and his boys right now. They say no and we'll have to come up with somethin' else."

They entered Boatwright's old lodge when granted permission, and then they sat. Red Stone dragged out the ceremonial pipe, but Rawlins held up his hand. "What we got to talk about's important business," he acknowledged, "but I ain't of a mind to play games with the pipe. Let us say what we got to say. We can decide later whether it has to be sanctified with a pipe."

Striking Hawk put the pipe down. He did not look particularly offended.

Rawlins outlined the plan swiftly. There really wasn't much to tell. He ended by saying, "And if you boys go, there's a new rifle in it for each of ye, with all the fixin's."

The Utes talked quietly among themselves for some time while Chardonnais and Rawlins tried to keep from fidgeting. Finally Striking Hawk nodded. "We will go. Except for Runs Back."

"He afraid?" Rawlins asked sarcastically.

Runs Back cast a black look at Rawlins.

"Of course he's not afraid. He just misses his family and wants to see them again."

Rawlins nodded. "That might work out best any way. How about if you go with the others, Runs Back until you cut the Ute trail? You can head west there and catch up with Strong Bear. When ye do, ye can tell

Strong Bear what's happened here and what we're doin' about it. He might be worried about Looks Again and Blue Rattle, and wonderin' where his daughters are."

"You won't leave your women in the village this time like usual?" Striking Hawk asked.

"No. There's no time. We're gonna be hard-pressed to get our supplies back here and hit some decent trappin' country before winter sets in again."

"Will you do dat, Runs Back?" Chardonnais asked.

The pudgy Ute nodded solemnly. He was quite happy, despite the somber expression. Not only would he get back to his wife and children soon, he was also entrusted with an important task.

"Then it's done," Striking Hawk said. "When do we leave?"

"If this thing works out, first thing in the mornin'. We should find out ourselves directly. Once we do, we'll let you know for sure."

"The rifles?" Striking Hawk prodded.

"I'll have the frog see to buyin' each of you one down in Taos. You can have 'em for the trip home."

Striking Hawk nodded and picked up his pipe. This was indeed a deal that needed to be sanctified by sacred smoke.

After the pipe had made the rounds, Chardonnais and Rawlins left and walked to the Company's camp. MacDonald spotted them and waved them to his fire, where they were given coffee after they took seats on a log.

"One of my employees says he wishes to get out of his contract," MacDonald said bluntly. "The idea is to help you and your friend. Is that correct?"

"*Oui.*" Chardonnais did not like MacDonald's attitude.

"And why should I do such a thing? The Company values its employees and is loath to discharge them for no reason."

"It's like dis—" Chardonnais started.

"No, *amigo*, let me," Rawlins interrupted, placing a hand briefly on Chardonnais's arm. He glared at MacDonald. He was not pleased with the booshway's attitude either. "It's like this, you penny-pinchin' little fart," he said harshly.

Other men of the Company's brigade edged closer. A few readied rifles or pistols, but the majority would make no move against anyone who stood up to the booshway of an American Fur Company brigade.

"Our old friend's lyin' in his lodge yonder with half his guts ripped open by some puke-suckin', pecker-bleedin' Crow. He can't be moved for a while yet, and if we don't find some way to get supplies for next season, we're gonna be six miles up a frozen creek with nothin' to push us along but our peckers. And such doin's'll piss this ol' niggur off somethin' fierce."

Rawlins paused for a breath and then drawled on. "Now, you got yourselves a whole passel of fellers here, and I can't see how you're gonna miss one pissant little frog for a couple of months. 'Course, this here is your brigade, and you can tell me to go hump a tree, but I'd advise against such a thing."

"Why?" MacDonald asked. His eyes were flaming with anger.

"Because the next booshway'll be a hell of a lot more reasonable, I suspect," Rawlins said flatly.

"The next . . ." The meaning suddenly became clear to him. "You'd not get two steps after killing me before my men would shoot you down."

"Dat right, asshole?" Chardonnais asked sarcastically. "If you t'ink dat, maybe you better look around at some of your men. Dere ain't t'ree of dem in de whole damned brigade'd cut a fart to help you, let alone shoot down two fellow mountaineers."

MacDonald sat there and stewed for a while, knowing that what Chardonnais had said was true. It was the lot of all men in his position, he figured. Still, he was not a hardheaded Scotsman for nothing. "LeBeau can go," he said. "But no one else."

"Fine," Rawlins answered.

"And he leaves here with nothing."

"He needs his rifle and fixin's."

"Nothing else."

Rawlins nodded. "We got a horse he can use. And blankets and such. We even got meat made, enough for him to travel."

"Done, then," MacDonald said, still barely reining in his anger. "I suggest you take the ungrateful wretch with you to your camp now."

"Michel!" Chardonnais yelled. "Come, *mon ami. Vite.*"

Rawlins stood and looked down at MacDonald. "Don't ever fuck with me again," he warned. He turned and began walking away. He dropped to the ground and rolled when he heard a thump behind him. When he stopped rolling, he looked up to see Chardonnais standing over the big Delaware.

"If you want to fight my friend over dere," Chardonnais said while straddling Badger's body and pointing a pistol at his head, "have de balls to do it face to face. Dis ol' chil' don' like chickenshits." He uncocked the pistol, stepped over Badger, and then walked toward Rawlins, not worrying for a moment that Badger would shoot them in the back. He was fairly certain someone would shoot the Delaware down before he could fire.

Rawlins picked up his hat, slapped it on, and stood. He and Chardonnais waited until LeBeau hurried over toward them.

"*Mon Dieu,* Lucien," LeBeau said. "No one's ever stood up to MacDonald like dat before. He's known t'roughout de mountains as a hard ass."

"He has a reputation as a bag of wind," Rawlins retorted. "He didn't have that pus-suckin' Delaware backin' him up all the time, somebody would've brained that dumb fart years ago."

At their camp, Rawlins went to his own lodge. Chardonnais brought LeBeau into his lodge. "Michel," he said, "my wife, Looks Again. And my sister-in-law, Blue Rattle. Mesdames, dis is Michel LeBeau."

"You got two wives?" LeBeau asked, seemingly impressed.

Looks Again nodded at Chardonnais, though LeBeau could not see it.

"*Mais oui!*" Chardonnais said with a hearty laugh. "A man wit' my appetites needs more dan one woman."

They sat at the fire and Chardonnais got a bottle of whiskey. Each man drank a little, and then LeBeau asked, "Well, are you going to this Taos with me, Lucien?"

"De Utes."

"What?" LeBeau exploded, spitting out a mouthful of whiskey.

"Just what I said. Dey will be de best protection for you."

"But . . . ?"

"You will be in fine hands wit' dem. Dey will wait for you a little outside Taos." Chardonnais finished explaining the plan.

LeBeau didn't like it, but he finally had to accept it. He had another long drink of whiskey. Then he sighed and asked, "Where do I sleep, *mon ami?*" He hoped Chardonnais would tell him to go sleep with the second wife—"sister-in-law," as Chardonnais had first called her. Blue Rattle was an attractive young woman, though she seemed scared of him. He wondered why.

"Back dere," Chardonnais said, pointing. As LeBeau moved in that direction the trapper warned, "Keep away from Blue Rattle."

"Why?" LeBeau asked, surprised and disappointed.

"Two weeks ago her husband was killed by de Crows. Den a few days later she gave birth. She's faced too many hardships in too short a time, *mon ami*. Get some sleep, you have a long journey ahead of you. *Bonsoir.*"

34

JULY TURNED INTO AUGUST, and August inched toward September, and the leaves of the aspens began changing to bright reds and vivid yellows. Early quickly progressed to recovery. By the time September arrived, he was able to walk around the camp and even do some small chores. The first time he managed to split a few pieces of wood for the fires, Rawlins and Chardonnais hooted at him.

"Well, lookee there, Frenchie. The lord of the manor actually got off his ass and is doin' somethin'."

"I am amaze," Chardonnais said with a shake of the head.

"Eat shit, the both of ye," Early snapped as he bent for another piece of wood. He was irritable, as he was every time he was sick or wounded. He had never been as badly hurt as this, though, and so his annoyance and self-anger were greater than ever before. He was a man who just couldn't take to being laid up. He hated feeling as weak as a newborn bear.

"Ooh, lordy, King Ezra speaks to the peons," Rawlins said, voice thickly sarcastic.

"Maybe we should go over dere and kiss his ass in t'anks for his good and true heart," Chardonnais suggested.

"You come anywhere near my ass, you tree-humpin' goddamn frog, and you ain't gonna be of any use to Looks Again—or anyone else," Early retorted. He split three more pieces of wood and then wobbled over to the fire, where Chardonnais and Rawlins were sitting. He plopped down heavily, face coated with sweat despite the cool temperatures. He looked as if he were in pain.

"You all right, *amigo?*" Rawlins asked, face reflecting his worry.

"No, I ain't all goddamn right," Early snapped, wincing as pain lanced into his guts. His hands were shaking a little, and he closed his eyes, sucking in air and blowing it out to try to settle himself.

"You want some laudanum?" a concerned Chardonnais asked.

Early shook his head.

"Whiskey?" Chardonnais asked, grinning.

Early's eyes popped open and he looked at Chardonnais. "As you might say, ol' hoss, *mais oui!*" he whispered, managing to work up a small smile.

Chardonnais nodded, rose, and left. He returned swiftly with a bottle that was only half-full. He handed it to Early. "Dis is all dat's left," he said flatly.

Early looked up at him, surprised, then nodded. It made sense, considering how long it had been since they had gotten supplies. "What else're we low on?" he asked, after taking a swig of whiskey.

"Everyt'ing but meat," Chardonnais answered as he sat.

"We out of anythin'?"

"Sugar, flour, cornmeal—and whiskey as soon's we

polish that off," Rawlins said, pointing to the bottle Early still held.

Early took that as a reminder, and he took another long swallow before handing the bottle to Chardonnais. "Why didn't you boys tell me about this?" he asked.

"We was just dyin' to," Rawlins said dryly.

Early nodded. "Guess I put my foot in it that time, didn't I?" He sighed. "We gonna be able to last?"

"*Oui,*" Chardonnais said with more assurance than he felt.

"If your goddamn friend gets back here in a reasonable time," Rawlins corrected.

"When do you expect him?"

"If he's been movin' as fast as he should, he ought to be back any day now."

"How long's he been gone?"

"Mont' and a half," Chardonnais said. "You remember meeting him?"

"I sorta remember, but I can't be sure. If you remember, I wasn't quite myself that day."

"We didn't notice," Rawlins said dryly.

"Up yours," Early snapped, angry at Rawlins, angry at himself, angry at the whole damn world. He got a handle on his anger.

"Whether you remember him or not, he left de next morning," Chardonnais said. "Just after de Company men pulled out."

"You did say you trusted him, eh, Lucien?"

"*Oui,*" Chardonnais said firmly. "Besides, Striking Hawk and his boys was wit' him. At least four of dem are wit' Michel. Runs Back was going to ride as far as de Ute trail and den head west. He wanted to see his family. So we told him to go ahead, and when he got dere, he could tell Strong Bear what's gone on."

Early nodded. "Well, till Mr. LeBeau does get back, we'd best cut back on whatever we can."

As the days passed Chardonnais and his two friends began to worry a little about Michel LeBeau. By mid-September, the three knew something was wrong. Chardonnais felt bad about it, as if he were responsible, and said so.

"Don't worry," Early said. "Just 'cause he ain't back yet don't mean he's gone bad. Hell, he could've been made wolf bait of by Cheyennes or Jicarillas. He could've got et up by a griz, or fallen off a cliff somewhere."

"Den where are de Utes?" Chardonnais countered.

Early shrugged. "Could've been the same thing that put your friend under."

"Well," Rawlins drawled, "it don't mean shit to me what happened to them boys. But if we don't get some supplies in a real big hurry, we're all gonna go under from starvin' or the cold. And such doin's don't shine with this ol' niggur at all."

"You have a suggestion?" Chardonnais asked, words hard. "Or are you just flapping your gums?"

"Yeah, I got a goddamn suggestion—somebody's got to go lookin' for that asshole." He glared at Chardonnais.

"And you t'ink dat someone is me?"

"He's your friend."

"There ain't no call to blame this on Lucien, Abe," Early said calmly.

"Bullshit, if it wasn't for the two goddamn frogs—"

Chardonnais struck Rawlins in the face with the back of a fist, then spun and jumped on Rawlins. The two wrestled and grappled in the dirt, throwing fists and elbows.

Early let it go on for a few minutes. Part of his

reluctance to interfere was in knowing that in his condition he didn't have the strength to separate them. Finally, though, he pulled a pistol and fired it at the log where Chardonnais and Rawlins had been sitting when the fight began.

Chardonnais froze half atop Rawlins, right fist cocked up near his head; his other hand was pressing Rawlins's chest down. Rawlins had his hands wrapped around Chardonnais's throat. He, too, froze and looked over at Early.

"Next one'll go through one of you two assholes," Early said easily. "I ain't sayin' which one."

Chardonnais looked down at Rawlins. "You had enough?" he asked.

"If you have."

Chardonnais shrugged and dropped his fist. Rawlins unwrapped his hands from Chardonnais's throat. They stood and then sat back on the log.

Early shook his head in irritation. "Damn, I wish you two'd stop actin' like children." He sighed. "What the hell's got into you anyway, Abe?" he asked. Rawlins was an easygoing man, usually one who did not go looking for a fight—at least not with his two partners.

"I'm just sick and tired of livin' with this little frog fart is all," Rawlins growled.

Chardonnais started to retort, but Early cut him off. "I don't know what bug's crawled up your ass, Abe," he said in withering tones, "but I've put up with about enough of your horseshit. You want out of this outfit, pack your shit and leave. You want to stay with us, you keep your fractiousness to yourself."

Rawlins glared at Early for some moments, hating his closest and best friend more than he ever hated anyone. Then he realized he was being an absolute ass.

He could not hate Early. Or Chardonnais. The two were closer to him than anyone—including his mother and father—had ever been. "Ah, shit, boys, sittin' here on my ass with nothin' to do don't shine with this ol' hoss. And sittin' here watching you damn near die wasn't no help."

"Well, I ain't goin' under now, dammit."

"I know, but I'm about half-froze to do somethin'—anythin'."

"How's about we all ride for Taos?" Early suggested. "That'd give you somethin' to do."

"It's better'n nothin'," Rawlins agreed.

"No," Chardonnais said. "No. I'll go."

"By yourself?" Rawlins asked. "You'll be put under."

"Dat can happen anytime."

"Why don't you want us along, Lucien?" Early asked.

"Couple reasons." He wriggled his jaw a little, trying to see if it was broken. Rawlins had caught him a good shot on the point of the jaw and it hurt. Chardonnais was glad for the thick beard, which probably had absorbed some of the punch's impact. "For one, despite his crude mouth and his lack of manners, Abe's right. Michel is my friend. Not yours or his. If he's hurt, us all going along wouldn't be a bad idea. But if he's gone bad somehow, I'll take care of it myself. It'll be my fault for getting you two to agree to de plan."

"Don't be so hard on yourself, *amigo*," Rawlins said in conciliatory tones.

"*Merci.* But it is de trut' nonetheless." He paused. "For another reason, if he got sidetracked somewhere and had to come back a different way, we'd all miss him on de trail. Dis way you'll both be here if he arrives."

"That makes some sense," Early allowed.

"And still another reason is de time. It's de middle of September already. Which means we don' have much time for getting to some better trapping grounds."

"So?"

"So, if we drag de women and de kids to Taos, or even close to Taos, it's going to take us a heap of time. On my own, I can be dere in maybe two weeks, and de same back."

Early and Rawlins looked at each other. "He's got us there, *amigo*," Rawlins said.

Early nodded. "Reckon so." He paused. "I got another reason, too. I'd slow you boys down even more'n the women and kids will in the shape I'm in."

"Hell, you're nearabout back to normal. Well, normal for you," Rawlins said.

"I'm doin' well. But I ain't full back yet, and I don't think sittin' a horse eighteen hours a day'd do me a world of good."

"You could do it," Chardonnais said.

"I expect I could, Lucien—if it was life and death."

"It is," Chardonnais said with a small laugh.

"Shit." Early sighed, feeling a sharp little pain in his side. He figured it would be a long, long time before all the pain left that spot. But he had seen plenty of others—including Chardonnais—who had been far worse wounded who had survived.

"I'll leave soon," Chardonnais said, rising. He headed for his lodge and explained the plan to Looks Again.

She nodded, worried but not letting him see that. She even managed a small smile as she dragged him to the robes.

Forty-five minutes later, he was riding southeast out of the camp. He carried no other supplies than a buffalo sleeping robe, a little pemmican and some jerky, the last portion of the partners' tea brick, a small coffeepot, and what they all hoped would be sufficient powder and ball.

He wasted no time, pushing his horse as hard as he could without wearing the animal down too much. He stopped only a few hours each night for sleep. He would awake before dawn, make one mug of tea, gobble down some jerky or, when he was fortunate, some fresh meat, and then hit the saddle again.

As he worked through the familiar pass he glanced east, remembering with a small shudder the hellacious trek he and Jed Boatwright had made through Cottonwood Pass. It was only a few months ago, he realized. It seemed like a lifetime.

A long day's ride from the pass, he cut more to the west, following a long, very narrow valley. He crossed Tomichi Creek and went almost due south, gradually working up again into the surrounding tall peaks. He swung southeast again, through North Pass, and another long day brought him to the flat spacious San Luis Valley. He had seen no one on the journey, which he figured was just as well.

Eleven and a half days after leaving the camp, he eased the horse from a trot down to a fast walk. He was within half a mile of the spot where the Utes planned to wait for LeBeau. It was a spot frequently used by the three partners. It was secluded, yet convenient to Taos.

Chardonnais heard nothing other than animals and birds as he began working through stunted cedars, on foot and towing his horse, toward the little clearing. That did not surprise him, since he really did not expect to find anyone there.

He stopped at the edge of the trees and scanned the clearing. He did not like what he saw. *"Merde,"* he spit out as a sick feeling suddenly bubbled in his belly.

35

CHARDONNAIS STEPPED INTO THE clearing and tied his horse to a tree near a dribbling brook snaking between trees and rocks. Then he went and checked what was left of the four Ute bodies.

They had been dead for some time. A month or so, he figured. Not only had they decomposed considerably, but scavengers had scattered their bones around the clearing. The only way he knew for sure that the bodies were those of Striking Hawk, Walking in the Sky, Spotted Bull, and Red Stone were by the personal items he found. He found two empty whiskey bottles, too, but attached no importance to them. Chardonnais and his partners weren't the only white men to use this as a campsite. He knelt and picked up one of the bottles and sniffed at the opening. It smelled a little odd, but considering what some people, especially those in Taos, used in making the poisonous liquor, that didn't necessarily mean much.

Chardonnais felt a chill growing in his guts as he began to prowl farther and farther in the clearing, looking for LeBeau's remains. He did not find them—or anything that would have indicated that he had been killed along with the Utes here.

Finally, he stopped and just stood, leaning on his rifle, trying to puzzle it out. The explanations of what had happened here were myriad. The Utes could've been killed while LeBeau was in Taos; LeBeau could have found the bodies and then gotten lost while trying to get back to Chardonnais and the others. The Utes could've been killed just after LeBeau had returned; LeBeau could have been carried off along with the supplies. LeBeau could have escaped as the Utes were being killed and was now wandering hurt and lost.

"*Merde,*" Chardonnais said, spitting. All this thinking was getting him nowhere. He could not know what happened unless he found someone who was here. And that most likely was impossible now.

He unsaddled his horse and then covered the entire area again, moving more slowly as he checked the ground, the trees surrounding the clearing, and anywhere else he could get to, looking for sign. When he finished, he went back to the circle of rocks where fires were made and he squatted there. He picked up an eagle-talon necklace that Striking Hawk used to wear and fiddled with it while he thought some more.

He had found mule tracks leading away from the campsite, heading northeast. The laden mules were the ones Chardonnais and his partners had gotten from Strong Bear. That meant nothing in and of itself. All the explanations he had thought of before still applied.

He rose, checking the sun in the sky. There were still a few hours of daylight left, and this was no time to delay. He had to get to Taos and see if anyone there had seen LeBeau.

He saddled his horse and moved on, arriving in Taos a little more than an hour later. He rode straight to Ceran Saint Vrain's store, pushed inside, and clumped up to the counter.

"Señor Chardonnais," the clerk said with a bright smile. "I deed not think I would see you this year."

"Ignacio," Chardonnais said. "Is Ceran around?"

"Sí. In the back."

"Get him."

Ignacio Sandoval stared at Chardonnais a moment. He had never seen the French-Canadian like this before, his face tight with exhaustion, anger, and worry, his words curt. The clerk shrugged and went into the back room. A moment later he came out again, walking behind Ceran Saint Vrain.

"*Bonjour, mon ami!*" Saint Vrain said jovially, hand outstretched. "*Comment-allez-vous?*" His humor fell. "What's wrong?"

"A man come in here a mont' or so ago and trade in our plews?"

"*Oui.* A Monsieur LeBeau."

"Did he get supplies?"

"*Oui.* Enough to load all your mules. He said one of your party was hurt. Yes?"

"Ezra."

"No! Bad?"

"It was, but he's near recovered now." Chardonnais paused to think. "Did anyt'ing seem strange about LeBeau?"

Saint Vrain shrugged. "Not zat I can think of. Other zan he came instead of you. We did t'ings ze same way as always. He said zere were four Utes watching ze plews at the usual place. Zat night me and my boys, we went out zere and loaded ze supplies on your mules, and ze plews on my mules. I calculated zat I owe you and your friends a little money. I tell zat to Monsieur LeBeau and say zat I will do as always and bank zat for you. He agreed. Zen we left."

"Did he get any unusual supplies?"

"I did t'ink it odd zat he asked for some extra fusees."

"He was supposed to give each of de Utes one."

"Zen why did he ask for a dozen?"

"He what?" Chardonnais exploded, shaking off some of his tiredness.

"He bought a dozen of zem. Just like I say. Is zere something wrong with zat?" Saint Vrain asked. He didn't see that this was a big deal.

"I'm not sure. Dis is a puzzle. You got some whiskey?" he asked.

"Of course." He turned. "Ignacio, *por favor*." He looked back at Chardonnais. "So, tell me, *mon ami,* what all zis is about."

"I'm not really sure." Chardonnais placed his rifle across the counter. He pulled his hat off and dropped it beside the rifle. "Michel came along wit' a brigade from de damn Company. He offered to bring our plews here and bring our supplies back."

"Didn't want to leave Ezra zere alone?" Saint Vrain asked as he uncorked a bottle and held it out.

"*Oui,*" Chardonnais said after a drawn-out swallow of whiskey. "We sent four Utes wit' him."

"When?"

"Soon after de rendezvous."

"You went to ze rendezvous?" Saint Vrain asked, surprised.

"*Mais non!*" Chardonnais said after another swallow. He put the bottle down. "De brigade was heading out from rendezvous. De booshway says dey were going to de Uintas, but I t'ink he's full of shit."

"So zis Monsieur LeBeau has been gone a long time," Saint Vrain said more than asked.

"*Oui*. He should've had plenty of time to get back to our camp."

"You suspect he ran off wit' your supplies?"

"I don' know what de hell I t'ink." Chardonnais grabbed the bottle again and slurped down another healthy dose. He put the bottle back. "I found de Utes in de place outside of town." He paused. "No, I found what was left of de Utes."

"Dead?"

"*Oui*. A long time. Dere wasn't much left but bones and dere weapons."

Before Saint Vrain could respond, Sandoval said, "The letter, Señor Saint Vrain."

"What letter?" Saint Vrain asked. Then his eyes widened. "*Mais oui!* Ze letter. You wait, Lucien. I'll be right back." He hurried into the back room and then returned. "Zis letter come for you just before last wintair. I was going to send it with one of ze boys, but everyone was gone by zen. So I kept it." He handed it to Chardonnais. "I forgot about it until Michel come here. I offered to give it to him, but he said he didn't want to carry it around with him. He seemed eager to see ze town, so such a thing wasn't strange. I meant to give it to him zat night when we went to get ze plews, but I was so busy, I forgot all about it and left it here."

Chardonnais tapped the letter on his left thumb, waiting for Saint Vrain to finish his spiel. As soon as he was sure Saint Vrain was done, he slit the letter open with his patch knife. It was written in French, and he read it silently.

Saint Vrain watched the emotions dance across Chardonnais's face. First interest, then rage mingled with hate, then loss, and once again hate. "What's it say?" Saint Vrain asked when he saw that the trapper was done.

Chardonnais said nothing for some time, just stood with glazed eyes. Then he straightened. "It is none of your concern," he said stiffly. "I mean no offense, *mon ami,* but dis is somet'ing better kept to myself." He tapped the letter again, then nodded. "Can you let me have enough supplies for de wintair, Ceran?"

"On credit?"

"*Oui.* Unless I have enough money in your 'bank' to pay for dem."

"It doesn't matter, *mon ami.* You and Abe and Ezra have been good friends. We've helped each other many times. Zis is just another time."

Chardonnais nodded. "*Merci.*"

"When do you want zem?"

"In one hour. Time enough for me to get some food and have my horse seen to."

"You sure, *mon ami?* You look as if you never sleep."

"Dere will be time enough for sleep later."

Saint Vrain nodded. "You go eat, and maybe clean yourself up some. I'll see zat your horse is fed and watered. We'll have mules loaded out back by zen."

"*Merci, mon ami.* I am in your debt."

Saint Vrain shrugged, unconcerned.

Chardonnais shoved the letter into his possible sack and stomped out.

Sixty-five minutes later the trapper trotted out of town, trailing nine heavily laden mules behind him. He did not stop at the place where Striking Hawk, Walking in the Sky, Spotted Bull, and Red Stone had died. And he rode until well past dark, covering a fair stretch of the San Luis Valley.

He finally pulled to a stop and made himself a quick meal of slab bacon and tea, then rolled in his blankets without bothering to unsaddle the horse or unload the mules. He was back on the trail before dawn.

It took thirteen punishing days to make it back to the camp, slowed as he was by the mules. He was weak and shaken when he arrived, but that didn't matter to him. He tumbled off of his horse into Looks Again's arms, and she helped steady him.

"Michel is not here, eh?"

"No. Didn't you find him?"

Chardonnais shook his head.

"Mornin's soon enough to tell it," Early said. "Take him to the lodge, Looks Again."

"Little bastard'll like that," Rawlins commented.

Chardonnais looked up at Rawlins with exhaustion-blurred eyes. He tried to grin but couldn't quite manage it. "You're wrong dis time, *mon ami*," he mumbled.

"Go on, Looks Again," Early said. "We'll take care of the supplies."

Looks Again nodded.

"You need help with him?"

Looks Again shook her head. With Chardonnais leaning much of his weight on her, she led him toward their lodge.

Early, still feeling some of the effects of his wound, left most of the heavy work in unloading the mules to Rawlins, who grumbled throughout it all. Once he began hearing the muttered complaints, Early began issuing orders, directing where things should be put. He finally quit that when Rawlins began casting seriously grim looks at him.

Chardonnais slept through the afternoon and night. When he awoke just after dawn, he was no longer tired, but he was no less enraged. He ate a considerable amount, more because he knew he needed the strength the food would give him than because he was hungry.

Looks Again was stunned when her husband rebuffed her advances and went outside. He tromped over to Early's lodge and entered. Early and Rawlins were sitting at the fire. "About time you woke up," Early said.

Chardonnais didn't bother to answer. He sat cross-legged at the fire and poured himself a cup of coffee.

"Tell it, old friend," Early said quietly.

Chardonnais thought it over for some moments, then said, "Michel made it to Taos and traded in de plews. He got supplies and den disappeared."

"What about Striking Hawk and the others?" Rawlins asked.

"All dead at de meeting site."

"Dead?" Early said, surprised. "What killed 'em?"

"I don't know. Dere was notting left of dem except bones, and dey were scattered all around."

"You sure it was them?" Rawlins asked.

"*Oui.* Dere foofaraw was dere."

"No sign of LeBeau?"

"No. I went down to Taos and talked with Ceran. He said Michel got de supplies when he gave Ceran's crew de plews. Dat was de last time dey saw him."

"Well, shit, Lucien," Rawlins said. "Michel's probably gotten his ass put under and all them supplies stole."

"Dat's what I t'ought at first. Den Ceran gave me dis." He pulled the letter out of his possible bag and held it up.

Early and Rawlins could see that it was in French.

"Well, read it, Frenchie, goddammit," Rawlins snapped.

36

CHARDONNAIS SAT SILENTLY FOR some moments, absentmindedly tapping a foot while staring blankly at the paper in his hand. Finally he shook himself out of his stupor.

"It's from my brother Jacques. It was written less dan two weeks after I left St. Charles. Jacques says dat when I left, Michel tried to court Marie again. But she turned him down." Chardonnais grinned weakly. "Jacques says Marie told him she told Michel she didn't want notting to do wit' him, dat she still loved me."

Chardonnais stopped, having to fight with his emotions. "After a week of trying to have his way wit' Marie and not getting anywhere, Michel killed her."

"Jesus," Rawlins breathed, "that's one chickenshit niggur. Killin' a woman—hell, not much more'n a girl—just 'cause she didn't like where his stick floats."

Chardonnais nodded.

"They sure LeBeau was the one killed her?" Early asked.

"*Oui,*" Chardonnais said flatly. "Jacques saw it.

Before anyone could catch LeBeau, he run off. I t'ink LeBeau was telling de trut' when he said how and when he hooked up wit' de Company."

"So you think he killed the Utes and run off with our supplies?" Early asked.

"*Oui.*"

"But where'd you get them supplies you brought in yesterday?" Rawlins asked.

"Ceran let me have dem on credit."

Early nodded.

"What puzzles me, Lucien, is how a pus-suckin' little puke like LeBeau was able to kill four Ute warriors," Rawlins said.

"I t'ink Michel poisoned dem. I found two empty whiskey bottles, and so I t'ink he put somet'ing in dem and dey died after drinking it."

"That'd explain it," Rawlins said flatly. "He might be your friend, Lucien, but to me he's a peckerless bastard."

"He's not my goddamn friend anymore," Chardonnais said in cold, bitter tones.

"How'd you just come into gettin' the letter?" Early asked.

"Ceran said it came dat fall I got back here. All de traders and such were gone, so he held it to give it to me dis year. But of course dis year we don' go to Taos. He said he told Michel about it, but he said to give it to him when dey changed de plews for supplies. Ceran told me he forgot about it."

"Damn lucky thing, too, hoss," Rawlins commented. "LeBeau had gotten his goddamn paws on that letter, you'd never have known what that pissant little prick done."

"*Oui,*" Chardonnais said sadly.

"Looks Again know about this?" Early asked.

Chardonnais shook his head. "I had told her about Marie not too long after I come back here. She understands dat. But I don' t'ink she needs to know about dis." He paused. "Besides," he added carefully, as if measuring his words, "I'm not sure his killing of Marie is de reason I want to kill him. Oh, dat is important. *Mais oui!* But it's more dat I feel like a fool to have trusted him wit' all our plews. Damn! A whole season's take gone—poof!"

"Hell, boy, you couldn't've known," Rawlins said.

Chardonnais shrugged. To him it really didn't matter. He felt he was responsible for everything—Marie's death, the loss of all their plews and supplies, being left in debt to Saint Vrain, the deaths of the four Utes.

The men fell quiet, each lost in his own thoughts. Rawlins finally broke the silence. "Well, where away now, ol' hoss?" he asked.

"I go looking for Michel. It was my doin's dat cost us all our plews and supplies. And he was my friend. So now I go to settle t'ings with dat ass-licking *fils de garce.*"

"No," Early said quietly. "We'll all go after him, ol' hoss."

"Dis is my doin's," Chardonnais insisted.

"Don't matter none," Early responded. "It was all our plews he took, all our supplies he stole, and our friends he killed. We're partners, us three. Have been for more'n eleven years now. And will be until one of us goes under."

"You ain't cuttin' us out of these doin's, Frenchie," Rawlins added. "Not while this ol' hoss has got blood and balls."

Chardonnais looked from one to the other, almost overcome by emotion. Then he nodded. "I'll be glad to have my old friends around. But remember dis," he added pointedly, "if we catch Michel, he is mine. For killing Marie. And for making me de fool."

"Not if, *amigo*," Rawlins said quietly but forcefully. "*When* we find that shit-suckin' son of a bitch."

Chardonnais nodded, then asked, "Are you well enough to do dis, Ezra?"

"You ain't leavin' me out of these doin's, even if I got to go along in a travois. Or crawlin'. This ol' chil's in, boy, and don't ye think different."

"*Très bien,*" Chardonnais said. "Let's go."

"Tomorrow's soon enough, boy," Early said. "There's a heap of work to be done yet. We'll take care of that and pull out in the mornin'."

"Where away we headin', boy?" Rawlins asked.

Chardonnais shrugged. He hadn't given it much thought.

"You ain't plannin' to head to the Uintas, are ye?" Rawlins asked.

"No."

"Good thing. I figure MacDonald was lyin' through his teeth when he gave us that shit."

"You think he'll go back to the Company, Lucien?" Early asked.

"*Oui.* He has worked for de Company off and on for some years. I can't know what kind of deal he made wit' MacDonald, but I—" He stopped, thinking hard.

"What is it, Frenchie?" Rawlins asked, mystified.

"I just t'ought of somet'ing." He took a few more minutes to allow the idea to coalesce. "I t'ink dat Michel come out here to kill me. I am certain of dat. He told me he had figured to see me at rendezvous and was surprised when I told him we go to Taos."

"Sounds reasonable to think that," Early said. "So?"

"So . . . Well, I don' know if dis will help us in looking for him, but I t'ink dat when he saw me here, he t'ought to kill me den and dere, but he couldn't wit' all dose other men here. So he put on de face of my friend and talked to me to lull me. I t'ink once he heard of our problem wit' de plews, he concocted de plot to steal de plews and supplies, right den and dere."

"He did seem a mite eager to help us out," Rawlins said, thinking back on it.

Early nodded and added, "And he looked plumb taken aback when we told him the Utes'd be goin' with him. I reckon he had plenty of time on the trail to solve that riddle."

"That still don't help us none," Rawlins said. "Whether it's true or not."

"But wait. I t'ink dere is more to dis. Now dat I t'ink about it, it seems strange dat MacDonald would let him out of his contract—heading out to trap. If dey had been heading to rendezvous, MacDonald would've paid him off and let him go."

"Goddamn, that's right," Rawlins said. "That's one sneaky niggur."

"*Oui*. I also t'ink—or suspect—dat he made a deal wit' MacDonald to bring him de supplies."

"He's the kind of skunk-humpin' bastard that'd do such a thing," Rawlins agreed.

"That still doesn't help us find him," Early said.

"Maybe. Maybe not. If my t'inking is right, den we only have to look for MacDonald's brigade, not just one man in all dese mountains."

"You have any ideas of where to look?" Early asked.

"De only t'ing I can t'ink of is up in Absaroka. Michel said to me dat he had been out here a couple times and dat dey usually dealt wit' de Crows."

"Then why come through here?" Rawlins wondered. "That don't make sense."

"It might," Early said. "Just because they planned to winter with the Crows—if they did—they could've been on their way to the Uintas to trap and work their way back up to Absaroka to winter. MacDonald did say they'd be goin' north from the Uintas."

Chardonnais grinned grimly. "Den we head for Absaroka ourselves, eh?"

The two others nodded.

Dawn was just cracking the sky when they rode out of their camp the next morning, a morose and forbidding-looking group. By noon, the clouds had moved in and snow began falling. It was a light snowfall, but a harbinger of what they would face.

They moved northwest, up the long narrow valley, heading toward the Colorado River, which they reached late on the day after they had left. They swung northeast the next morning, following the river through Glenwood Canyon. The day after, they followed the river a little way on the south bank and then crossed the river. The water was bitter cold already and Early decided that they should make camp and stay there through the next day and night. He was still feeling the effects of his wound, and the women and children as well as the animals needed some rest.

It was snowing again as they began loading the mules just after dawn two mornings later. They were almost done loading the mules when Rawlins stopped, thinking he heard something. Suddenly an arrow appeared in the neck of the mule he was loading. "Cache!" he bellowed, then ducked into the brush along the river.

The others did not stop to see what was wrong; the

men just grabbed their rifles, and the women grabbed the children, and they all headed for cover.

Rawlins was nearest the women and children, who were huddled in a tight little shelter of pines and rocks, so he charged over there and squatted nearby. He set his pistols on a stump next to him and chunked his tomahawk into the wood. "Ye all all right back there?" he asked.

There was a chorus of affirmatives, and Rawlins settled in to wait.

As Early slipped into the woods, moving swiftly, cautiously, he wished he had some of the Utes along with him this time as they had last time. He was good in the forests, but he was not a Ute.

Suddenly an Indian leaped on his back, arm snaking around his throat. Early dropped his rifle and clamped two strong hands on the Indian's arm. He twirled wildly, trying to throw the Indian off his back, but to no avail. He stopped and then charged backward as hard as he could. His vision was blurring, and he was barely able to keep the Indian from squeezing the life out of him.

Early slammed the Indian's back against a tree trunk, staggered two steps forward, and then did it again. The Indian grunted and loosened his grip on Early's neck fractionally. It was enough for Early to jerk the Indian's arm free. He snapped his head backward, mashing the Indian's nose.

Early lurched forward a few steps, gasping and choking. The Indian slammed into his back, knocking him down, but falling to the side in so doing. Early rolled onto his back. Seeing the Indian—a Crow—trying to get up, he pulled his knees back toward his chest and then shot his feet straight out. Only one foot connected, but it managed at least to partially hit the Crow's already broken nose.

Early yanked out his knife as he crawled toward the Crow, and then he sank his blade into the Indian's chest. He wiped the blade on the Crow's blanket coat and rose. Then he grabbed his rifle and headed off, gliding through the trees.

A gunshot from where he figured the women would be sent him in that direction. He wasn't sure if Rawlins or Chardonnais were with the women, but whoever it was might need some help. He moved cautiously but swiftly, threading around the trees and rocks, fallen trees and clumps of brush. The sound of the river so nearby masked most other sounds, but that worked to the Crows' disadvantage as much as to the mountain men's.

Early neared the site and he slowed, creeping forward. He spotted Rawlins grappling with a Crow. He was about to rush forward to help his friend when he saw two other Crows heading for the fight. He brought his rifle up and set himself. He had only one target, since the third Crow was behind Rawlins and the warrior he was fighting. He fired and the warrior went down. Then he ran.

Early barreled into another Crow, a man about Early's own height of six foot, but outweighing Early's one eighty-five by at least a hundred pounds. Early thought he had run into the side of a mountain, and he went down.

The monstrous-sized Crow grinned, his face an eerie mask of red-and-black paint, and lifted his lance. Suddenly Falling Leaf leaped on the Crow's back, her butcher knife darting in and out, slashing and hacking at any piece of flesh she could find.

The Crow bellowed and reached back to grab Falling Leaf's hair. He flung her to the ground and then spun back to finish off Early.

But Falling Leaf's action had given Early enoug
time to get up. He fired both pistols point-blank at th
huge Crow. The balls slapped into the warrior's blu
ber and sent globules of flesh and blood flying out th
back. The Crow grunted and stood there, not dead, bu
seriously hurt.

"Die, you fat, stinkin' son of a bitch!" Early said a
he tomahawked the Indian three, four, then five time
hacking out huge chunks of flesh.

Finally the Crow fell, crashing down like a ligh
ning-struck tree. Early whirled to see Rawlins slittin
another Crow's throat. He spun back and knelt besid
Falling Leaf. "You all right, woman?" he asked, wo
ried.

She nodded, though she looked a little daze
Early helped her up and escorted her back to the oth
ers.

"You seen Lucien?" Rawlins asked.

"Not since we all cached. I did hear a couple gu
shots from way over yonder, though."

"Damn. I'm gonna go check on him—and see
there's any more of them goddamn Crows out there."

Chardonnais had run into three Crows almost th
moment he had run into the trees. One was standin
behind a tree and had reached out to grab his hair. Sti
running, he was jerked backward and onto the ground

The Crow suddenly loomed over him, war clu
raised. Chardonnais desperately jerked his rifle up an
jammed the muzzle into the Indian's stomach and fire
it. The blast ripped out a sizable portion of the wa
rior's back and spine, and knocked him backward.

Chardonnais got up and was immediately slamme
into a tree and then down onto the ground facedown,

row spraddling him. He jerked an elbow backward
nd hit the Crow in the testicles. The shot didn't have
uch power, but it was enough to make the Indian
iss and partially rise. Chardonnais shot his back up
ke a wild horse, throwing the man off him. He got up.
hough he was unsteady, he managed to kick the
row in the face, then shoot him with a pistol.

Breathing heavily, he bent to retrieve his rifle and
as barely missed by an arrow that stuck into the tree.
e rolled behind the tree and swiftly reloaded his rifle.
e peered around the trunk, but could not see any-
ing but foliage. He waited, wondering how many
ther Crows were lurking around.

The time dragged on, and he grew impatient. He
ipped backward on his stomach until he was behind
nother tree next to a small thicket. He got behind the
rush and stood. Then he trotted off, figuring to make
 small circle and come up where the Crow who had
hot at him might be hiding.

He didn't have to go that far. He and the Crow
topped at the same time, spotting each other ten feet
way. The Indian went to bring his bow up and found it
ntangled in a bush. Without delay, he dropped the
ow, howled his war cry, and charged with a toma-
awk in his hand. Chardonnais brought up his rifle and
ulled the trigger.

"*Merde!*" he snapped as the rifle misfired. With the
row almost on top of him, he simply swung the rifle
ke a club, staving in several of the ribs in the warrior's
eft side. The Crow went down in a heap.

In an instant, Chardonnais was kneeling on his
ack and was pulling his head up, ready to slit his
hroat. Then, for no reason that the trapper could
athom, he decided not to kill the Crow—yet. He
ropped the knife and ripped off one of the fringes on

his pants. In a moment the thong was tied around on of the Indian's wrists.

The Crow was bucking and jerking, trying to ge free, so Chardonnais hammered him in the wounde side with a fist. In the brief time the man needed fo the pain to subside, the French-Canadian got the thong tied around his other wrist.

Chardonnais rose, grabbing the back of the Crow' shirt and hauling him up. The warrior tried to kick him, so he swiftly moved his grip from the Indian' shirt to the back of his neck and then slammed his fac into a tree.

"Don' give me no more shit," he warned as he pulled the Indian around. He got his first good look a the warrior. "I'll be goddamn," he said in surprise. He shoved the warrior. "Walk."

37

"SHIT, GODDAMN, SON OF A BITCH, bastard!" Rawlins raged.

"What the hell is it?" Early asked, puffing from having just run up.

"Six of the goddamn mules're gone—with all their damn packs."

"Shit," Early breathed. "We've sure had us a goddamn run of poor luck with horses and plunder of late, ain't we?" He was angry, but couldn't be too angry. It would have been almost humorous if it wasn't so serious.

Chardonnais came wandering up, pushing an Indian ahead of him. "De mules're gone?" he asked, face regaining its flush of anger.

Early and Rawlins nodded.

"We're going to look for dem, no?"

"Reckon we should," Early said with a sigh. "I just hope we can find 'em without takin' all day at it."

Rawlins and Early looked at the captive for the first time.

"Hey, Lucien, ain't that the red devil that led the

attack on our winter camp?" Rawlins asked, pointing to Chardonnais's prisoner.

"*Oui*. He's Black Blood, de one I sent away without his clothes—and without his hair."

"What's he doin' here?" Rawlins asked.

Chardonnais shrugged. "Dat's why I didn't cut his t'roat."

"How many men was with you, boy?" Early asked, stepping up in front of Black Blood. His side hurt like hellfire from all the activity, and he was not in the best of humors.

Black Blood spit at Early, the glob landing on the front of his shirt.

Early's eyes narrowed angrily. He drew back, ready to slug the Crow.

"Just wait now, Ezra," Chardonnais said almost cheerfully. "If you want to hit him, I say to do it right here." He grazed Black Blood's wounded side with a forefinger.

Early nodded and did as he was urged. Black Blood groaned and sagged, only being held up by Chardonnais's strength.

"I'd answer him, Black Blood," the trapper said curtly. "He's nasty when he's in a foul mood."

"Seven," Black Blood answered, voice surly.

"I got two, plus that one Falling Leaf helped me with," Early said.

"I got two," Rawlins added.

"And I got two, which is seven," Chardonnais concluded.

Early nodded. "Set him down somewhere so he can't run. I'd like to talk to that chil' some more—after we go lookin' for the mules." He went off to have the women rekindle the fire they had let go out in preparation for their leaving. The men would want coffee when they returned, and for while they questioned the prisoner.

Rawlins got some rope and tied one end around Black Blood's neck and the other to a good, stout log. He and Chardonnais rebound Black Blood's hands, once again behind his back, with a longer, heavier piece of buckskin and did the same to his feet.

"Falling Leaf had to help Ezra?" Chardonnais asked quietly as he and Rawlins were tying up Black Blood. He was a little worried. "Maybe he's still too hurt."

Rawlins chuckled. "Nah, he's fine. You should've seen this red devil. Fat bastard must dress out about three hundred pounds. Ez run into him and fell right on his ass. That goddamn Crow didn't even blink. He was about to pin ol' Ez's ass to the ground permanent with his lance when Falling Leaf jumped on him, knife in hand."

"No!" Chardonnais was amused.

"Hell yes. She didn't do him too much damage, but it gave Ez enough time to get up and blast that pus-suckin' son of a bitch." He laughed a little. "It was some, I tell ye."

Chardonnais laughed, too.

Early was already saddling his horse, and the other two were at it moments later. As they worked, Rawlins asked, "What're we gonna do about the women, Ez?"

"Leave them and the young'ns here. I gave Falling Leaf one of the rifles I took from a Crow. Did the same with Looks Again. I told 'em to shoot the red niggur if he managed to get loose. I told 'em to try not to kill him, if possible, but not to risk their lives over it."

"What if there're other Crows lurkin' about?"

"Then we're in deeper shit than we realize. We've got to go after the mules, and it'll go a heap faster if we all do it."

"I just hope you're right, *amigo,*" Rawlins said as he pulled himself into the saddle.

As Rawlins began riding off Chardonnais called, "Give it two hours. No more. That means be back here in two hours."

Rawlins waved over his shoulder, not looking back.

Early and Chardonnais rode off, in different directions.

Chardonnais was the first back into camp, but only by minutes. Rawlins was the only one to come back with a mule. The animal had lost much of the contents of his pack, but Rawlins had salvaged some of it.

Discouraged, the three sat at the fire and poured themselves coffee. The women, relieved to have their men back, were sitting to the side, working and watching the children play in the snow. They had reported that there was no trouble while the men were gone.

"Jesus, I didn't see hide nor goddamn hair of any of the goddamn mules," Early snapped. The renewed pain in his side did not help his anger over the lost mules. "Hell, I didn't even see much in the way of supplies. I reckon we might want to not pack them mules so well."

"I didn't see any mules or supplies either," Chardonnais added.

"I saw two more besides the one I come back with." Rawlins grimaced. "Both of 'em at the bottom of a goddamn canyon, deader'n hell."

The men sipped coffee for a few minutes, sitting silently. Then Early refilled his cup and rose. "Reckon it's about time we went to talk to ol' hoss over there."

Rawlins and Chardonnais also freshened their coffee, then walked over and squatted in front of Black Blood.

"Was this your idea? Or'd somebody put you up to it?" Early asked.

Black Blood was silent, just sat there with his face revealing nothing but hate for the white men.

"Look here, boy," Early said, still calmly. "You're gonna die. You know that. Thing is, not answering us isn't gonna make the goin' any easier on you. But if you were to answer us, I give you my word I'll kill ye quick and leave your hair so you can go to the spirit world whole."

"We'll face each other again then," Black Blood said in passable English. "And that time I'll win."

"Mayhap. But I'll worry about that when the time comes." He paused for a sip of coffee. "Now I can't believe you come all the way down here, so late in the year, just to avenge whatever honor you might've lost when we sent you packin' bare-assed."

"You should've killed me then," Black Blood hissed. "So I could be with my brothers."

"I reckon you havin' to cart home all your dead *compañeros* might put you in bad humors," Early agreed. "Still, we could've butchered them and raised their hair before sendin' you home. But we didn't."

"The shame of losing all my men was great."

"I can understand that." He sipped coffee again. "But that still doesn't explain whose idea this was. And the more I think about it, the more I figure somebody put you up to it. You had no idea where we'd be unless someone told you. And you ain't stupid enough to take seven men on the warpath at this time of year just for the hell of it. So, who's behind these doin's?"

Black Blood looked at Early, eyes widening involuntarily, but he said nothing.

"My great friend Ezra Early has much patience," Chardonnais said. "But I am not blessed wit' such a t'ing. So, you answer our questions now, or I will do some very nasty t'ings to you."

"Best listen to him, asshole," Rawlins offered. "He's one crazy son of a bitch. Hell, you remember what he done to you that last time."

Black Blood believed him, and he sighed. There could be no harm in telling. And if it might buy him a better entrance into the spirit world, that had to be considered. He looked from one set of hostile eyes to another, and knew that these men would have absolutely no hesitation in killing him in as painful a fashion as they could devise. He nodded. "Coffee?" he asked.

"After you start talking," Chardonnais said flatly.

Black Blood shrugged. "A white man came to me. A white man like him." He nudged his chin in Chardonnais's direction. "He say I should take men to kill a little bastard name Lucien Chardonnais. He describe you to me, and I say, I know this man, he's caused me great shame, and I'll be happy to hunt him down. I picked seven men, and the white man—Michel LeBeau—gave us each a fine rifle. And many supplies."

"That festerin', skunk-humpin' puke," Rawlins snapped. "Jesus, Frenchie. He pays your goddamn assassins with your goddamn plunder."

The thought had already crossed Chardonnais's

mind, and he was fighting his rage. His hands were
white-knuckled and he thought he might break his
teeth from clenching them so hard.

Black Blood smiled a little, appreciating the irony
of it all. "He say that when we get back, he give us
whiskey."

"Serve you right, you pus-suckin' bastard," Rawlins
said.

Black Blood's eyebrows raised in question.

"We sent four Utes to escort him down to Taos to
get us some supplies—the ones he used to pay you,"
Early responded. "We found all four of 'em dead."

"So?"

"So, we think he gave them poisoned whiskey."
Early grinned grimly. "This way you can go to the
spirit world as a warrior, not poisoned like a dog."

"What you t'ink of de irony now, *caca d'oie*—goose
shit—eh?"

"Let me go, and I'll kill him," Black Blood said honestly.

Chardonnais laughed, but it was a humorless
sound. "You're a goddamn fool."

Black Blood shrugged.

"You were just supposed to ride in here and kill
Lucien?" Rawlins asked.

Black Blood shrugged again. "LeBeau figured you
two bastards'd be along. We figured to kill you, too,
though he didn't pay us for that." He smirked.

"Didn't do too damn good a job at it, did ye, asshole?" Rawlins retorted.

"No." The word was surly.

"Were you plannin' to do anything else?" Early
asked.

Black Blood smiled viciously. "Kill the little bastards and take the women with us. Except one." He

grinned that nasty grin again and said, "Yours." He pointed at Chardonnais. "LeBeau said he wanted us to abuse her the worst we knew how and then kill her."

Early, sitting on one side of Chardonnais, and Rawlins, sitting on the other, each grabbed one of Chardonnais's arms, figuring he would go crazy. They could feel the rage in his arms, but he did not move.

"I've answered you," Black Blood said. "Now kill me, dammit."

"In due time," Rawlins said reflectively.

"I don't know anything more."

"Mayhap you do," Early said. "Like where's LeBeau winterin'?"

"I got no idea."

"My great friend Lucien Chardonnais told you I have patience, and I reckon that's true, boy. Except when it comes to liars. I can't abide folks who don't tell me the goddamn truth. Now, I ain't gonna ask you this but this one more time. Where's LeBeau winterin'?"

"He said MacDonald's brigade was gonna winter in a meadow valley in the Big Horns, along the Tongue River."

Early nodded. "*Gracias.*" He looked at Rawlins. "You got anything more to ask ol' hoss here?"

"Reckon not."

Early turned and asked Chardonnais the same question.

Chardonnais shook his head.

"You want to kill him, Lucien?" Early asked.

"*Mais oui,*" the French-Canadian said bluntly. "Would one of you get me some of dat bear grease we have? And a big rope?" he asked.

Rawlins and Early exchanged startled glances. Then Rawlins shrugged. "Sure," he said, and left.

When he returned and handed Chardonnais the coil of buckskin rope and the tin of grease, the trapper said, "Cut him loose from de log. And untie the t'ongs on his feet, but keep dem handy. I'll want dem again."

Early did so, then started tugging him along at his partner's command. Chardonnais stopped at a tree that had a large branch hanging well out from the trunk. He set down the tin and then threw the rope over the branch.

"Ye fixin' to hang this red devil?" Rawlins asked, surprised.

"No," Chardonnais said flatly. He handed Rawlins one end of the rope and then retied Black Blood's feet. Then he cut the Crow's clothes off.

"You gettin' to like such doin's, froggie?" Rawlins asked.

Chardonnais did not answer. He took the other end of the rope and began wrapping it around the Indian's torso and arms. He finally tied it off. "Pull de ropes so he is on his toes, Abe," he commanded.

When Rawlins had done so, Chardonnais got the tin of grease. He knelt and began smearing it over Black Blood's feet and worked upward, until Black Blood was coated from head to toe. Then he stepped back and took the end of the rope from Rawlins. He began hauling Black Blood up toward the tall branch. He stopped when Black Blood's feet were five or six feet off the ground. He tied the free end of the rope around the tree trunk.

"*Allons-y*," Chardonnais said. "We have much traveling to do."

"Goddamn, Frenchie," Rawlins said with admiration, "you're really some. That was a hell of an idee you had there."

"It don't suit this chil'," Early said a little peevishly.

"I promised him we'd kill him quick and clean."

"*Mais non, mon ami*," Chardonnais said, wagging a finger at his friend. "You said *you* would kill him quick and clean. I never made dat promise."

"I wonder how long it'll take some griz or a pack o wolves to come along and make meat out of him? Rawlins mused as they headed for their horses.

38

T TOOK THEM A MONTH TO find MacDonald's American Fur Company winter camp on the Tongue River in the Big Horn Mountains. It had been a tough month, too, constantly cold and with snow as often as not. While they needed a great deal of food to help their bodies fight off the weather, they were constantly short of supplies. The men had a fair amount of success in hunting, so they rarely wanted for at least some meat. But other things were not so easy to come by. They ran out of sugar about two weeks in, flour four days later, coffee the day after that. It seemed they were constantly facing starvin' times, but they persevered and pushed on as hard and long as they could every day.

They followed the same trail north that they had taken south after wintering with the Utes the year before. The wind and cold and snow in the mountains were disheartening, and there were days when they made only a few miles. But the traveling got a little easier when they reached the high, wide, arid valley where they had wintered, and north of that. Mostly it

was high plains, with short rugged hills here and there
which allowed them to make good time—unless a
storm brewed up on them. Out here in the open, there
was no place to hide from the howling demon of a
wind, no trees to cut some of the wind and snow, no
sheltered valleys. Twice they had to sit and ride out a
hellish blizzard.

They veered a little northeasterly to make their
way across the small saddle of land between the south-
ernmost tip of the Big Horn Mountains on the east and
a stubby peak to the west. They swung a little northwest then, until they hit the Big Horn River. A week
and a half of following it brought them to where the
Tongue River joined it.

They slowed their progress then, not wanting to
walk into MacDonald's camp by accident. It was easy
to spot once they got near it, though. With thirty men,
perhaps fifteen women, and a number of children, plus
horses and mules, the place was rather noisy, and the
stench could be smelled half a mile off if the wind blew
in one direction.

Early called a stop when they first suspected it was
the camp. "One of us best scout up there and make
sure it's the right place," he said.

"Ain't we just gonna walk in there and make wolf
bait out of that asshole LeBeau?" Rawlins demanded.

"No," Early said flatly. "We've got no love for Mac-
Donald nor anyone else hooked up with the Company
and I suspect MacDonald's feelin's for us're about the
same. I don't think he's gonna hand LeBeau over to us."

"You got a plan?" Rawlins asked.

"Not much of a plan. Just some thoughts on tryin'
to keep us from gettin' put under."

"Well, are you gonna tell us, or are we gonna have
to sit here and guess at it?" Rawlins asked.

"If that's the camp, I think we ought to go find us a nice cave, one where we can defend ourselves. We get the women and kids settled in there and then the three of us can mosey on down toward MacDonald's camp. Lucien, you go in alone."

"*Merci*," Chardonnais said sarcastically.

"If MacDonald's gonna give you LeBeau, you're comin' in alone might make him feel a little more comfortable. If he ain't gonna give you LeBeau, he might not be as frumptious as he'd be if the three of us ride in there."

"Besides," Rawlins tacked on, "it'll be easier to explain your presence here. Tell them boys you found out what you found out, and left us wintered up somewhere while you hunted down LeBeau."

Chardonnais nodded. "Dat might work," he said skeptically. He wasn't afraid of going into MacDonald's camp. He was just worried that he'd be prevented from gaining his vengeance.

"Well, if he turns you down, just come on out of the camp. They still won't know me'n Abe're hereabout. We can make some mischief for them bastards." He grinned a little.

"*Mais oui!*" Chardonnais said, his enthusiasm rising. "I will go look now and see if it is de right camp."

As Chardonnais moved off, Early called, "Don't you go doin' nothin' stupid, boy. We ain't come this far to have you put under by bein' a dumb ass."

It didn't take long for Chardonnais to return. "It's dem all right," he said. His voice betrayed his eagerness to kill LeBeau.

Early nodded. "You've done your part for now, Lucien," he said. "You stay here with the women. Me'n Abe'll see if we can find us a place to hole up."

It took them considerably longer to return, and

Chardonnais was beginning to worry a little, when they finally came back.

"You find a place?" he asked.

Early nodded. "A real big cave—big enough for the horses and mules—up about three quarters of a mile on the other side of MacDonald's camp. That's what took us so long. We had to circle the camp by a fair piece."

"Dis side of de river?" Chardonnais asked.

Early nodded.

"Is it defensible?"

"Yep," Rawlins said, slipping off his horse. "Trail's only wide enough for one rider at a time. There's a shelf that juts out at the bottom, so they won't be able to see us up in there, and they can't just go shootin' in there hopin' to hit something."

"Only problem might be wood," Early said. "There's some small trees on the shelf, along with some brush, but I think we'll have to cart up most of our firewood."

"Well, if MacDonald has any sense, we won't have to worry much about dat," Chardonnais said.

"If MacDonald had any sense, he wouldn't be the asshole he is," Rawlins noted.

They moved off again, as quietly as they could. They went two miles or so to the south to keep away from MacDonald's camp. They weren't worried about the camp in itself so much as about being caught by hunters. But they made it to the foot of the cliff below the cave.

Rawlins led the way along the thin trail that crawled up the cliff; Early brought up the rear. Once there, the men began unloading the mules while the women set up housekeeping. As soon as two mules were unloaded, Early and Falling Leaf took them down the hill. They gathered enough firewood to last a couple of days and then went back.

They spent the rest of the day finishing up their camp, eating and resting. The next morning the three men rode down the cliff, leaving the women and children in the cave. Falling Leaf and Looks Again still had the fusils Early had taken from the Crows. None of them really figured there'd be much trouble.

Early and Rawlins took up positions in the trees outside the meadow where MacDonald's men were camped. Between the overcast, the snow, and the thick pines, the two felt fairly sure they would not be seen. Early watched the camp; Rawlins kept an eye on the woods behind them.

Chardonnais rode brazenly into the camp. No one really seemed to notice at first, thinking he was just one of their companions. There weren't all that many men outside anyway, considering the weather, and those that were outside were bundled in capotes, blanket coats, buffalo robes, or blanket ponchos.

He stopped in front of the largest tent, figuring it to be MacDonald's. He left his horse untied and walked into the tent. MacDonald looked up, surprised and angry at the intrusion. The big Delaware, Badger, was standing alongside MacDonald's traveling desk, leaning on his rifle.

"What the hell're you doing here, Chardonnais?" MacDonald asked.

"Looking for someone."

"Who? Your friend LeBeau?"

"*Oui.*"

"What for?"

"I have some t'ings to settle wit' him."

"What kind of things?"

"Several t'ings. None of which're your business."

MacDonald glowered at him. "Well, I'm not about to just hand over one of my employees so you can kill him. But I'm a fair man. Go get LeBeau, Badger." When the Delaware had left, MacDonald said, "I'll give LeBeau a chance to answer your accusations before I throw you the hell out of my camp."

Chardonnais's temper flared, but he managed to control it. He moved to the side of the tent, into the shadows.

A few minutes later LeBeau and Badger entered the tent. "You wanted to see me, Monsieur MacDonald?"

"Someone here to see you." MacDonald pointed.

Chardonnais stepped out of the shadows. "Michel," he said coldly.

LeBeau's face drained of blood. Then he forced a smile and said cheerily, "Lucien! *Bonjour!* I t'ought you were dead."

"Black Blood and his boys're dead. But not before dey told me some t'ings."

"I have no idea what you're talking about, Lucien," LeBeau said defensively.

"Jesus goddamn Christ, Michel!" Chardonnais snapped. "Have some balls for a change."

"What're you doing here?" LeBeau asked, sidestepping Chardonnais's statement.

"I come to kill you."

"For what?" His voice quavered.

"Stealing a year's take of plews from me and my two friends. Stealing our supplies. Using most of de supplies to pay some goddamn stinking Crows to come kill me and my woman. And for killing de four Utes." His eyes bored into LeBeau's, until LeBeau looked down. "But maybe de biggest reason is dat you killed Marie. Jesus, Michel, why?"

LeBeau finally found a little backbone. "Why? You

'ave de nerve to ask me why? Because of you, you son of a bitch. Marie was terribly hurt when you didn't come to de church dat day, and she wouldn't have anyt'ing more to do with me. When you didn't show up at de wedding, Marie was distraught, and she accused me of doing somet'ing to hurt you. She refused to marry me or even let me court her anymore. 'Even if you did nothing to hurt him—if Lucien had run off—I still wouldn't marry you,' she told me. 'Lucien has taken my heart, and now no one else shall have it.' "

LeBeau stopped for a moment, eyes wet. "I went crazy when Marie said dose t'ings to me. And den, *mon Dieu*, I killed her."

"Did you come out here just to get away from de constable?" Chardonnais asked icily. "Or were you planning to kill me, too?"

"Bot'. Like I told you before, I t'ought I would see you at de rendezvous. When I didn't, I didn't know what to t'ink. But I couldn't go back to St. Charles, so I decided to stay out here awhile longer. Den, *voilà!* I find you."

"Den you concocted your plot?"

"*Oui.* Everyt'ing worked to perfection. Till now. I traded in de plews and den killed de Utes."

"Wit' poisoned whiskey?"

"How'd you know?" LeBeau asked, shocked.

Chardonnais shrugged. "Den you met some Crows and paid dem most of my plunder, plus de extra fusils you got to kill me and my friends. And to kill my woman."

"But how . . ."

"It don' matter how, you *fils de garce*," Chardonnais snarled. "You have killed too many good people and caused much harm. And it's time to pay for dose t'ings."

"Whoa there, ol' hoss," MacDonald said. "I don't much give a damn whether any of this is true. I'm not going to hand over one of my men to you. I told you that before."

"But he must pay for de t'ings he has done," Chardonnais said, fighting the raging of his temper.

MacDonald shrugged. "Mr. LeBeau was hired by the American Fur Company, and as an employee, he is immune from your accusations while under contract to the Company, and while he is in these western lands where there is no law."

Chardonnais stood stock-still. Every fiber in him told him to kill LeBeau here and now, and then do the same to MacDonald, if necessary. But he knew he would never make it out of the camp alive.

"Badger," MacDonald said arrogantly, "please escort Mr. Chardonnais out of the camp." He looked at the trapper. "If you know what's good for you, boy, you'll go find yourself a winter camp many miles from here. I catch you in or around this camp again, I'll have Badger carve you up. Understood?"

"You send numb nuts dere," Chardonnais said, pointing to Badger, "dere won't be enough left of him to bury in a parfleche."

"Badger, take him away."

The Delaware grinned and waved a hand toward the outside. Chardonnais lifted his rifle and headed out. Badger helped him with a substantial shove on the back. Chardonnais reacted by snapping his rifle back with both hands. The butt hit Badger a few inches below the navel. The Delaware doubled over.

Chardonnais turned and pulled one of Badger's pistols. "*Au revoir, espèce de cochon*—good-bye, you big pig," he said, just before clubbing Badger on the head with his own pistol.

As Chardonnais threw the pistol down, he looked at MacDonald. "Keep that asshole away from me, monsieur." He turned his hard, cold gaze onto LeBeau. "Your day will come, Michel. And soon." He spun and walked out, mounted his horse, and rode slowly out of the camp.

39

AN ENRAGED CHARDONNAIS STOMPED back into the cave, muttering great imprecations in French. Finally Early got him to calm down some. "Set your ass down, hoss, and tell me'n Abe what's got your balls all in an uproar."

"Dat bastard MacDonald sat and listened to LeBeau explain everyt'ing, and den he says to me, too bad, but he's a Company man and you can't have him."

"Goddamn fool idiot," Rawlins snapped.

"What do you want to do now?" Early asked.

"I want to go on down dere right here and now and take on de Company's brigade."

"Don't be a fool," Early said. "We'd be outnumbered and outgunned by a considerable lot."

"Do you have a better idea?"

"I just might."

For the rest of the day and all of the next, they gathered firewood and made sure their cave camp was as comfortable as they could make it. The following day the three headed on foot down from the cave and melted into the pine forest. They prowled around the periphery of MacDonald's camp like restless spirits. Twice they caught one of MacDonald's hunters who was not expecting trouble. The first time it was Rawlins who pulled the hunter off his horse and slammed him facedown on the ground. After he pounded the man on the back of the head with a rifle butt, the three partners rifled his possibles bag and took the elk meat he had. Then Early and Rawlins threw the man's inert form across his horse and smacked the animal on the rump.

"Should've just killed de bastard," Chardonnais grumbled.

"Jesus, you're gettin' to be a bloodthirsty stump of a feller, ain't you?" Rawlins said.

Chardonnais didn't see that such a thing needed a response.

The second instance went about the same as the first, only it was Early who did the honors of flattening the man.

The three went back to the cave for a spell to get out of the cold, to eat, and to bring their booty back.

Over the next couple of weeks they continued their phantom raiding, assaulting Company hunters and taking the meat. They also began running off horses. They didn't keep the horses, just drove them a few miles away and let them go. Some returned on their own to the camp; others were picked up by roving Crows.

Since they had lost most of their supplies during the Crow raid, the three took to raiding Company stores whenever they could, but taking only small amounts each time. It wasn't as if they were trying to be kind in their thievery. It was more a matter of not being able to carry too much up to the cave. Early also figured it would drive MacDonald's men crazy, accusing each other of taking more than their fair share of this or that.

Then one day Chardonnais found a note stuffed into the crook of a tree. He called the others over and read the note. It was short and to the point:

> *Mr. Chardonnais:*
> *I know you're behind the trouble of late. It's time these things stopped. I will send a "peace" messenger tomorrow to the meadow along the river a mile upriver from our camp. If you want to meet him, be there at noon.*
>
> *Alastair MacDonald*

"You gonna meet him?" Rawlins asked.

"*Oui*. Maybe de bastard's coming to his senses."

Rawlins and Early were out at the spot early the next day and checked the area. All three men figured MacDonald might be setting up a trap. Then they stayed up in the rocks that led up to the meadow while Chardonnais waited in the meadow.

A man Chardonnais did not know rode up and stopped close to him. "My name's—"

"I don' give a shit what your name is," Chardonnais snapped. "Just state your business."

The man glowered a moment, then shrugged. "Mr. MacDonald wants to know what you want."

"Tell him I want LeBeau. A fair fight, one-on-one, just me and him. No guns. Knives or tomahawks, yes, if LeBeau finds de balls to come against me dat way. If I win, I get enough supplies to last me and my partners and families de wintair, plus half de plews in your camp, since LeBeau stole all ours from last year and we really haven't been able to catch any on our own."

"And if you lose?"

"It's evident what de result will be if I lose," Chardonnais said flatly. If he did lose, Early and Rawlins would be on their own and nearly empty-handed.

"I'll tell Mr. MacDonald."

"You do dat. If he agrees, I will face LeBeau at noon tomorrow. Oh, and tell dat old bastard dat if he tries to have some of his boys kill me, dere will be hell to pay."

"How do you figure that, you stupid little frog?" the man asked with a sneer.

"De Utes know what I'm doing," Chardonnais lied easily. "If I don't show up dere soon, dey will find Mac-Donald and all de others."

The man didn't look so cocky anymore. "How do I get you an answer?"

"One hour. Here. You come alone. Or MacDonald can come himself—alone."

"Mr. MacDonald agrees," the man said. "Noon tomorrow. At the camp."

"He agreed to all de conditions?"

The man nodded. "He said to tell you he gives his word that no one else'll interfere."

"LeBeau have anyt'hing to say?"

"He was not at all happy about the decision," the man said dryly.

Chardonnais strolled confidently into MacDonald's camp. The men of the brigade were lounging around in the bitter cold and the swirling snowfall, waiting. He stopped in the middle of the camp. "Michel LeBeau!" he shouted. "Come out and meet your Maker!"

Badger strolled arrogantly out of MacDonald's

tent. "Mr. LeBeau sends his regrets that he can't come out and face you now. He sends me."

A moment later Badger lay dead, his blood staining the snow. And a moment after that came the report of the rifle.

"MacDonald!" Rawlins roared from out in the trees somewhere. "Get LeBeau out there or you'll be the next to get a lead pill!"

LeBeau came out of MacDonald's tent, having been shoved. MacDonald followed him, and shoved him again.

Chardonnais pulled off his blanket coat and dropped it on the snow. He let the thought of LeBeau's crimes percolate inside, building up the rage and the anger. It would help him.

LeBeau hesitantly walked toward him. There were some jeers from the other men of the brigade, and LeBeau straightened his shoulders. He also pulled off his coat and dropped it.

"You have much to pay for, you snake-humping *fils de garce*," Chardonnais said.

"You won't be de one to make me pay," LeBeau said with some bravado.

Chardonnais grinned, and it sent a chill up LeBeau's spine. "Let's get to it, ol' hoss," he said. Then he charged.

LeBeau was unprepared, and when Chardonnais barreled into him, he went down like a half-empty sack of flour. He did manage to dodge the kick his opponent aimed at his head. Chardonnais slid on the snow and fell.

LeBeau seized the opportunity and jumped onto Chardonnais, scrabbling to get his knife out at the same time. But he found himself grappling with a wild man, who quickly pitched him off.

"You'll have to do better dan dat, *mon ami*," the trapper said as he rose. He could have easily killed LeBeau when he tried to get up, but he wanted to prolong things a little.

LeBeau got up, breathing heavily. He pulled his knife and crouched, moving slowly forward, blade dancing in the air before him. "I'm going to make wolf bait out of you, just like I did to Marie," he said with a sneer. He was a good man with a knife, and knew it. His confidence was rising fast. "I carved her up in several ways. Just like I'm going to do to you."

Chardonnais saw red at the image of Marie being butchered. But he stayed put, letting LeBeau come to him. LeBeau's blade came ever closer, until it was brushing his shirt. Suddenly Chardonnais's left hand darted out and latched onto LeBeau's wrist. Chardonnais shoved the knife hand up and at the same time kicked LeBeau in the stomach.

LeBeau grunted and sagged. Chardonnais twisted the wrist he held as he punched LeBeau in the face. He twisted the wrist some more, forcing LeBeau down to the ground with his shoulder off the snow, and the elbow on it. He suddenly stomped down on LeBeau's upper arm, where it was not touching the ground. The bone snapped and LeBeau screamed.

Chardonnais let LeBeau's wrist go, and the knife fell. He pulled his own knife and knelt next to LeBeau. "Dere are many t'ings—horrible t'ings—I could do to you now, *mon ami*," he said in chilling tones. "But I t'ink dat Marie would not like dem t'ings."

"Don't kill me," LeBeau pleaded, his voice full of pain.

"You never lived like a man," Chardonnais said coldly. "At least you should die like a man."

LeBeau was weeping, but it had no effect on the trapper.

Chardonnais took his knife and slowly slid the blade into LeBeau's abdomen just above the pubic area. LeBeau's eyes widened at the sharp pain. Chardonnais then began working the knife upward until it was stopped by the bottom of the sternum.

Chardonnais pulled the knife out and wiped the blade on LeBeau's shirt before sliding it away.

"It hurts," LeBeau whined.

"*Oui*. And I hope you suffer such pains for all eternity. But even if you do, it will not be enough." He stood. "MacDonald!" he roared. "Bring out de plunder and de supplies you promised. *Vite.*"

Suddenly Rawlins yelled, "Watch LeBeau, Lucien!"

Chardonnais looked down and saw that LeBeau was trying to cock his pistol, even as he whimpered while his blood flowed out of his guts.

"We cannot allow such a t'ing," the trapper said. He stomped the broken arm again. LeBeau screamed and dropped the pistol. Chardonnais kicked it away. He looked back at MacDonald. "I said to hurry."

"Suppose I don't give you any plunder?"

"You remember Badger?" Chardonnais asked, pointing to the body. "One of my great friends will give you a lead pill without a second t'ought."

MacDonald nodded and began issuing orders.

Early led the way west along the Tongue River two days later. While the cave had been comfortable, it was impractical, and they did not want to have to worry about MacDonald sending over his men one night when he found out where they were.

Strung out behind Early were Falling Leaf, Straight

Calf, Blue Rattle with her child in a cradleboard, Looks Again with her son also in a cradleboard, Chardonnais, leading sixteen mules—ten with supplies, the other six loaded with plews—Scatters the Clouds, Standing Eagle, and Rawlins.

Not far from the cave, on a promontory that overlooked a vast area, Chardonnais gave the rope to the mules to Looks Again. He pulled out and rode a little way back and stopped, looking to the east. Back there was where the trouble had started, but there were warm memories besides: a childhood spent playing with Michel LeBeau, a caring brother, and Marie Bouchard.

"You will see her again in the spirit world, my husband," Looks Again said quietly.

Chardonnais was surprised, not having heard her ride up beside him. He looked back and saw that Blue Rattle was now holding the rope to the mules. "*Oui,*" he said sadly. Then a grin broke out, sparkling in the morning sun. "But I have you, and dat is enough for dis chil'."

Together they turned and trotted to catch up to the others.

ohn Legg is a full-time writer and newspaper editor
who lives in Arizona with his family. This is his eighth
book for HarperPaperbacks.

Saddle-up to thes

THE REGULATOR *by Dale Colter*
Sam Slater, blood brother of the Apache and a cunning bounty-hunter, is out to collect the big price on the heads of the murderous Pauley gang. He'll give them a single choice: surrender and live, or go for your sixgun.

THE REGULATOR—Diablo At Daybre
by Dale Colter
The Governor wants the blood of the Apache murderers who ravaged his daughter. He gives Sam Slater a choic work for him, or face a noose. Now Slater must hunt down the deadly ren gade Chacon…Slater's Apache brothe

THE JUDGE *by Hank Edwards*
Federal Judge Clay Torn is more than a judge—sometimes he has to be the jury *and* the executioner. Torn pits himself against the most violent and ruthless man in Kansas, a battle whose final verdict will judge one man right…and one man dead.

THE JUDGE—War Clouds
by Hank Edwards
Judge Clay Torn rides into Dakota whe the Cheyenne are painting for war and the army is shining steel and loading lead. If war breaks out, someone is going to make a pile of money on a riv of blood.

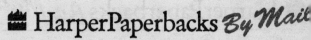